THE NOVEMBER PLOT
A NOVEL BY TOM ULICNY

A MYSTERY UNFOLDS OFF THE FROZEN SHORES OF LAKE SUPERIOR

Tom Ulicny

Copyright © 2024 Tom Ulicny
All rights reserved.

No part of this book may be reproduced in any form or by any electronic or mechanical means including information storage and retrieval systems, without permission in writing from the author. The only allowed exception is to an acknowledged reviewer who may quote short excerpts in a review of this work.

This book is a work of fiction. Fictional names, characters, places and incidents are entirely the work of the author's imagination. Any resemblance to actual persons, living or dead, or to actual events is entirely coincidental.

ISBN-9798335628617

ACKNOWLEDGEMENTS

Thanks go out to my family and to my local writing group for their continuing encouragement that helped bring this book over the finish line. I especially appreciate friend and fellow author Elizabeth Nowicki for her thoughtful read of my early manuscript. Her countless comments, opinions and suggestions helped breathe life into this book and into its characters.

Thanks also to my beta readers who pointed out the remaining rough edges and helped polish this work into its final form.

Cover Graphics: Computer generated from a word-image composed by the author. Title, caption and all literary art contained here-in are entirely the work of the author.

OTHER BOOKS BY TOM ULICNY

The Lost Revolution

The Caruso Collection

The Scientist's Accomplice

Dr. Thornhill's Last Patient

The Dawson Expedition

For Sarah

Tom Ulicny

THE NOVEMBER PLOT

Tom Ulicny

CHAPTER 1

Gull Harbor, Michigan

Sheriff Jackson Holiday woke as always, ten minutes before his five o'clock alarm sounded. He reached over, flicked it off then rolled back and blinked his eyes clear. Through the window, beyond the snow topped roofs of the buildings across the street, the stars still twinkled. When he was a kid he'd known the names of some of them.

His childhood memory of getting a telescope for Christmas popped into his head, forced out just as quickly by the familiar sound of Carla Manning's Dodge pickup rattling along the street below. This was followed soon after by the piercing squeak of her worn out brakes a block down at her donut shop. In an hour she'd be open for business and, likely as not, he'd be her first customer. The thought of hot coffee with a splash of cream along with a couple of still warm glazed donuts made his stomach rumble.

He gave Beth a light kiss on the cheek. When she didn't respond, he nuzzled her neck at which she gave a bothered sigh and defensively gathered the blankets around her. He showered, then dressed in yesterday's mostly clean and moderately wrinkled uniform. Tightening his belt, he backed it off a notch and gave his stomach a pat. Yep, got to do something about that.

"Bye, Jack," said Beth sleepily, making room for him as he sat on her side of the bed and put on his shoes. Her eyes were still closed. "Have a good day. Come back safe."

He kissed her cheek again as his phone buzzed. "Always do."

He got up, hustled out of the bedroom closing the door quietly. He pulled his phone: *Caller Unknown. Potential Spam.* "Holiday here," he said with a shrug, starting down the stairs.

"*Sheriff* Holiday?" The voice was disguised, a man's voice deep and wavering, buried in static, almost a whisper.

Jack stopped his descent. "Yes, who is this?"

"A crime is being committed, out on The Point. You need to get out there right away."

A crank call? Maybe, maybe not. "What crime?" The last thing he wanted to do right now was to go out along the Lake Superior shore facing the bitter October wind.

"Bring your gun but do not intervene. Watch, and listen, then call Agent Cooper at the FBI office in Duluth. Tell her what you saw."

"Why would I—" The phone clicked dead. Jack reached the bottom of the stairs. He stared at his phone trying to remember how to do a call back. Star something or other? He tried a few combinations unsuccessfully then pocketed his phone. Hell of a way to start the day.

He walked through the darkened center aisle of Beth's still closed pharmacy. The old wooden floor creaked with each step. At the front door he put on his coat, hat, gloves and boots then wrapped a scarf around his neck. It was the scarf Beth had made for him. What he wouldn't give to be back up in his warm bed with her. Still, Carla's coffee and donuts sounded almost as good right now. Almost. He pulled the hood over his head and stepped out.

The cold wind outside hit him like a bull moose. His hood flew back. His nasal fluids froze. In the wash of the security lights his breath streamed out in a sideways cloud as he hurried around *Holiday Drugs* to his police cruiser.

It was starting to snow. He started the engine, shifted the heater to defrost then let out a vaporous sigh, thinking of the call.

He couldn't delegate the follow up to Ron or Bob. His deputies were part time and were still in bed. No, this was his to do...or not to do. He pulled out.

One block down, at his rap on her front window Carla unlocked her door and fixed him up with coffee and a carryout bag. He hurried out.

Wipers slapping, he drove north, drank half his coffee and wolfed down both donuts. Still chewing, pulled up to the barricade where the road ended. Lights off, he kept the car running. He sat there, watching the snow streak left to right. The heater was only now starting to warm. He notched it up. *The Point*, as everyone around here called it, was really more of a small bay. Shielded from the pounding waves it was known by some of the more foolhardy locals to be a good ice fishing spot. Staring out in that direction, Jack saw only darkness.

Had the call been somebody's dumb idea of a joke? Maybe some kid trying out one of those voice disguising speakers he'd gotten for his birthday. Yeah, there was probably nothing at all out there. Still, he had to be sure. But he remembered the caller's warning. And what did the FBI have to do with this? Who the hell was Agent Cooper?

But, even though disguised, there was urgency in the guy's voice.

Shit! Better get out there.

Jack ran his gloved fingers over his mouth and chin to clear away any donut debris. He checked his gun, holstered it. He killed the engine. He pulled his hat down tight, tied his hood and got out. Yeah, great morning for a walk on the pitch dark beach. The moon had set hours earlier.

He flicked on his flashlight and started out. The biting wind fought him, coming in gusts, draining his energy. Halfway, he stopped to rest. The donuts rested heavy in his stomach. The snow remained steady but light. The horizon was just starting to brighten.

Jack now had a clear but distant view of The Point up ahead where the Keweenaw shoreline curled northeast out into Lake Superior. The chimes of the buoys carried with the wind as they rocked with the waves. Being careful, he shut off his flashlight. There was no sign of any activity at the point or anywhere else. Yeah, crank call. But he had to be sure.

After another 500 yards he saw it. He'd been so focused on the shore and his footing he'd been oblivious to the dark vessel looming out in the open waters just beyond the ice shelf. It was a freighter, her bow pointed west. She was a small ship compared to the increasingly common thousand footers. Totally dark she drifted slowly with the wind.

Jack's heartbeat rose a notch. The ship was way out of her shipping lane. Her captain must be nuts bringing her so close to shore. And no running lights? Was the ship in trouble? Had she lost power?

Jack was about to radio Sharon, his station manager when a sharp metal on metal sound came from further up the shore. He peered ahead. Flashlight beams waved chaotically. Three men, dressed in black, were struggling with something heavy. They were having a tough time, stumbling, sliding then trying to lift it. This had to be what the call was about. Shit. Probably some kind of smuggling operation. More drugs coming into the country. Or maybe guns. The guy had told him not to intervene. But hell, he should at least find out what they were up to.

Jack ducked behind a boulder, fingered his radio.

"Hey, boss. What's up?"

Relieved to hear Sharon's voice, he filled her in.

"You're out there now? What the hell?" The rattle of her keys told Jack she was in the process of unlocking the front door of the station. "You need backup. If that ship's in trouble we should call the Coast Guard, right?"

"Hold off on that. There's no trouble yet. Look, just try to raise Ron or Bob. Have them get back to me ASAP."

"Will do. What do you think's happening out there?"

"Smugglers probably. Don't know right now."

"You should wait for…"

"I'll be fine, don't worry." He killed the radio. He raised his head above the icy edge of the boulder squinting through the snow. It was coming down harder. Icy flakes stung his face. The men out there were still at work. Wait, they weren't bringing something ashore, they were moving something, a stack of boxes maybe, sliding it out over the ice to the darkened freighter. Man, there were plenty of easier ways to smuggle stuff. Why use a freighter? He wondered again about the caller. The guy had sounded serious. And something *was* really happening out here exactly where he said it would.

He took another look at the freighter. He could almost read the white markings on the freighter's bow, but not quite. He saw no flag. Hell with it. He unsnapped the safety strap on his holster stood and edged closer.

The men wore wet suits. They were moving quickly now. He could hear them talking but was unable to make out what they were saying.

Heart pounding, he took a knee. His radio crackled noisily.

Shit!

The men stopped. They turned in his direction. Jack held his breath. *Do not intervene*, the caller had said. He moved his hand down to his gun.

One of the men pointed directly at him. Another shouted something. Suddenly, a brilliant yellow light shot out from the bow of the freighter. It lit the shore. Jack winced in the glare.

Two of the three men were running toward him. The third had a rifle. He was taking aim but hadn't fired. They hadn't seen him yet.

Hell with it! Jack pulled his gun. He took off running for the trees that lined the shore twenty yards away. Once there he'd have some cover and could call for backup. He forced his frozen legs to move faster. Ten yards now. Then five.

Something moved in the trees. A man stepped out, his handgun pointed directly at him.

Jack leaped to the side, twisting. A shot cracked the icy air. He felt the bullet slam into his back. He fell forward hitting the trunk of a tree. Blazing pain knifed through his spine. Face down, Jack couldn't move. Hell, shot in the back only a step from the trees that might have saved him. And...where was his gun?

The sound of footsteps told him the gunman was coming closer. He'd take one more shot to finish him off. Could he somehow lift himself up and crawl into the woods? Or should he play dead? Yeah, that was easier. He had no strength.

Jack closed his eyes. He tried to control his shivering. Shit! If he didn't die from the bullet in his back, if the gunman didn't finish him off, he would likely freeze to death. Not a great choice of options. And the choice wasn't his to make.

Jack held his breath. He lay still. He braced himself. He thought of Beth, just opening her pharmacy right about now. Then he thought about the caller. *Do not intervene*, the man had said.

He should have listened to him.

CHAPTER 2

From the moment that fool Carter lit up the shore with the bow mounted floodlight, Captain Harlan B. Lattimore knew something had gone seriously wrong. Through his binoculars he spotted someone running for the woods. Then, at the gunshot, he fell "Shit! What the hell's going on out there?"

"We're still drifting captain," said Executive Officer, Joe Sullivan, next to him at the helm. "We'll be aground if we—"

"Hold on," shouted Lattimore. He grabbed his radio then hurried to the hatch that led off the bridge. He forced it open against the wind and stepped out into the cold. From the rail, he could see his men, three black forms frantically shoving their load across the ice. They were still a hundred yards out. Wait, was there a fourth man out there? Yes, there were two men pulling at the front of the load and two men pushing from the rear. The guy who'd driven the cargo out to the shore must be helping. Well, good for him. They could use all the help they could get.

Lattimore's eyes shot down the length of the hull. Even though the holds of *Endeavor* were empty and her ballast minimized, Sullivan had good reason to worry. The waters here were well charted but the depths varied from season to season. If he didn't engage the engines soon, they'd be scraping bottom. As it was, the hull was up against the jagged edge of the ice shelf now, pressing hard. The ice warped and groaned. Already a few cracks radiated shoreward where the ice grew thicker.

The men struggled with their load. Three wore insulated wetsuits but that forth man did not. Even so, none of them would last long if they fell into these frigid waters. Lattimore knew it and his men knew it.

At the bow, Carter redirected the light down on them like a spotlight following on stage performers. Fifty yards out. Damn! This was going to be tight.

Lattimore radioed back to Sullivan. "Engage the bow thrusters. Align us forty degrees out from shore. Prepare for quarter speed at the mains. We have to give them more time."

"Aye, that," said Sullivan.

Turning back to the rail, Lattimore felt the ship vibrate with the thrusters and turn ever so slightly, pivoting on her stern. He heard the stern cargo door rattle up. He leaned farther out. The cargo ramp was being slid out onto the ice. A net and winch were being readied to get the cargo aboard. The men were close now, pulling, pushing their load, negotiating the cracks in the ice.

Latimore felt the ship list slightly to starboard. A soft scraping of steel on hard sand added to the thunder of the buckling ice. Quickly it grew to a shrill scream of metal on hard rock, shaking the very bones of the ship.

The men were almost to the ramp when a chunk of ice ten yards across broke free. The men scrambled. The ice tilted. One of the men fell into the dark water. No! Had the man been pushed? What the hell was going on out there?

Lattimore was stunned. As the remaining three men secured the net around the load then jumped for the ramp he stared into the black water where he'd seen the fourth man vanish. He saw nothing. He was gone, surely drowned by this time, and the other three men, his men, had made no attempt to save him.

What the hell? First the shooting, now this.

But there was no time for regrets or questions. Lattimore keyed his radio. "Engage the mains," he shouted. "Take us out of here, Mr. Sullivan, quarter speed dead ahead."

"Quarter speed, aye."

Latimore ran back onto the bridge. He closed the hatch then braced himself against the bulkhead. The hull screamed, then went silent. The ship rocked back, settling level. They weren't out of danger yet. If the ship's prop hit bottom, or if a block of ice was sucked into it, they'd be in real trouble. At its powerful, rhythmic slosh the ship shook violently.

Come on *Endeavor*, Move! Move, you son of a bitch!

As if heeding his command, the ship picked up speed. Lattimore breathed again. Through the window, in the beam of the floodlight, the shoreline slowly faded behind the curtain of windblown snow. Then finally, Carter had the good sense to shut off the damn light.

Laying aside the end goal of this dubious mission, Lattimore lost himself in a brief moment of pride for his ship and crew. He'd captained *Endeavor* for five years now. Strange how attached you get to a giant hulk of floating steel. He heard the cargo hatch closing at the stern. He exchanged a glance with Sullivan. His XO seemed pleased and relieved. He had no idea that two men had died and Lattimore wasn't about to tell him. Not yet anyway.

An hour later, *Endeavor* resumed her course for Duluth, her engines drumming, everything back to normal. But Lattimore didn't feel anything close to normal. He took the cargo elevator three decks down to the galley where the shore party would be waiting. They were classified and paid as able bodied deck hands but, on occasion, these men had other duties which doubled or even tripled their pay. For today's work Lattimore knew they would want more. And more they would get despite the fuck up with the shooting and drowning.

They sat at a table, disheveled, exhausted, nursing coffees. The conversation they'd been carrying on ended as if by a switch when Lattimore walked in. "A man was shot on the shore. Who was he?" asked Lattimore

"We don't know," said Foster, a swarthy, bearded man. A towel was draped over his neck. Sweat and seawater still beaded his forehead. "He had a radio. That's what gave him away."

"A radio? Not a phone?"

"Could have been a phone, I guess. We thought he was a cop."

Lattimore shook his head. "Not likely at that hour. Was he dead?"

"The driver guy got him right between the shoulder blades. We didn't have time to check, but yeah, I'd lay odds on him being dead."

"Laying odds isn't good enough. You should have made sure." He leaned closer, a fist on the tabletop. "What about the driver?"

Foster stroked his beard. "Yeah, too bad about him."

"I saw him slide off the ice into the water. Was he pushed?"

Morris's eyes flared. "We were lucky. He wasn't. We barely made it back alive. Maybe you would have liked to be out there with us."

"You took too long with the cargo."

Morris shared a glance with Foster. Lattimore waited. This couldn't be good.

"We had trouble with the crates," said Morris. "The wood was rotten. Splintered. One crate had a crack up the side and fell as we were lifting it out of the truck. We picked up what was inside and managed as best we could. Then that guy showed up. I swear, captain, it looked to me like a good clean shot, straight to the vitals. The guy's gotta be dead. And even if he isn't, he didn't see much of anything."

"Oh? You don't think he saw our ship? And you don't think someone won't spot the truck?"

"We wiped down the truck good," said Foster. "And that took more time."

Lattimore stiffened and drew back. "You *knew* the truck would be left there. You knew the driver was never supposed to make it back to the ship. He was supposed to slip off the ice and drown. Is that right?"

"Yeah," said Foster, head down. "We had orders. We did what we were told to do. But things turned out okay. Right?"

"Except for that guy on the beach."

"He's dead."

Morris shook his head. "We did the best we could."

Lattimore had heard enough. Behind a practiced stoic expression, he hid his distaste for the possible loose end. Why the hell was that man out there at that hour in the bitter cold? A drunk who'd lost his way home? And what if he did have a radio? A cop? Well, if he's dead it doesn't matter. The body will be covered with snow in a few hours. Hell, it may not be discovered until the spring thaw. Too bad for him. But, the truck. That's bound to get some attention. Lattimore scanned the three faces. "Anything to add?"

"It was a close call out there," said Babcock, the strongman of the group and a former marine.

"And your point is?"

"Just saying..." Babcock shook his head, his voice trailing off.

"You men are involved in dangerous business. High risks, high rewards."

Morris stared down at his coffee, Babcock took a sip from his, Foster, drummed his fingers eyes downcast. These were capable men, each an ex-con, but none, so far as Lattimore knew, had ever been involved in murder—until now.

Lattimore turned, considered a to go cup of coffee for himself then decided against it. "All right, we're done here. Get some food. Get some rest."

He left the galley and headed up to his quarters where he sank exhausted into his leather chair. He fingered a mole on the left side of his chin then closed his eyes.

Except for taking the ship in so close to shore, today's action should have been routine. But it wasn't. Who was the guy on shore? What if someone came looking for him? They'd find his body. They'd find the truck. But they wouldn't find much else. Nothing to worry about.

With an effort, he pulled himself up from his chair. Beside his desk a framed photograph was attached to the bulkhead. It was a photograph he once treasured. He slid it aside on its double runners to reveal a small, black wall safe. He worked the combination, opened it and pulled out a specially programmed cell phone. He keyed the single letter *G*, standing for green he supposed, meaning all was good. He pressed send, waited for the

Delivered prompt, then put the phone back in the safe beside a wad of cash and a Browning automatic. He closed the safe, and spun the dial.

Sliding the photograph back in place he gave it a closer look then turned quickly away. He should have burned that photograph long ago, but knew he never would.

Lattimore sat on the edge of his cot. He shook off thoughts of the distant past then wondered about the secret cargo that had just been loaded and hidden somewhere aboard his ship. He knew it was something important. He knew it was something dangerous. And that was all he wanted to know.

He set his alarm to go off in two hours, then stretched out and closed his eyes.

CHAPTER 3

Flat on his stomach, Jack opened his eyes to a darkened room. Dots of light blinked and floated, some red some yellow, one green. The green one that stayed on and stayed put, grabbed what little attention he could manage. Some electrical thing was beeping, low and slow. He knew he was in a hospital bed. Each breath came with an effort but, apparently, he wasn't dead!

How the hell could that be?

He remembered being out at The Point. He was running for the woods. He took the bullet in the back. He was freezing cold. Then...nothing.

He tried to swallow but winced at even that small movement. His back hurt like hell. Could he even move? He decided not to try. He closed his eyes and fell back asleep.

"The bullet grazed your spine doing no damage then passed right on through," Doctor Sandy Ambrose explained when he was awake and well enough to sit up.

He'd learned from Beth, beside him now, that Sharon had gotten hold of Bob and Ron. They'd found him quickly then called in a chopper to fly him to the hospital in Houghton. Jack found Beth's hand and squeezed it gently while the doctor pressed on with a rambling list of particulars from his medical chart.

"You're a lucky man, sheriff," Doctor Ambrose said. She stood in the classic doctor pose, white lab coat, stethoscope draped at the ready over her neck, eyes—blue eyes, fixed on the clipboard she held. She returned the clipboard to its spot at the foot of his bed then met his gaze. Yes, her eyes were a startling blue. "How're you feeling?" she asked.

"Better."

The doctor glanced at the untouched bowl of mush on the tray in front of him. "You need to eat. You need to get up out of bed and you need to walk. We'll start getting you up and around tomorrow. So...eat."

"I will." Jack looked down at the mush.

"He will," affirmed Beth, folding her arms as if relishing her role as the enforcer.

Jack scooped up a spoonful. The doctor held her stare. He shoveled it into his mouth.

"All right then," said the doc, leaving.

Beth gave a tired sigh and turned to him. "You ready to talk about it?"

"I was stupid. I got a call as I was leaving for the station. A guy with a disguised voice. You know, electronically disguised. Something's going on out at The Point, he said." Jack paused, giving it more thought. "No, that's not right. He said a crime was taking place. He told me not to intervene."

"But you did."

"Yeah. It was just plain stupidity. I saw a freighter, close in to shore, skirting the ice. I saw men moving something out from the woods toward the ship. I moved in closer, too close. They spotted me. I pulled my gun. I ran for the woods. I dove for cover, too late." Jack shook his head.

"Bob and Ron were lucky to find you. After you were flown here to the hospital they went back out to The Point with Chief Brewster. "He wants to talk to you."

Yeah, I bet he does, thought Jack, picturing the Station Chief in Houghton salivating at the chance to get involved in a real crime. "Did Bob and Ron find anything?"

"If they did, they didn't tell me. It's an 'ongoing investigation'. You know the drill and you know Brewster. Everybody's tight lipped about it. And they're upset. Sharon too. I was frantic. We all thought...well, you didn't look so good,

Jack." She gave him a kiss on the top of his head that made him feel like a sick child. She drew in a shaky breath.

"I'm fine, Beth. You heard the doc. I'll be up and around tomorrow. Home before you know it. Right now, I'm just godawful tired. You look tired too. You should go home and get some rest." He gave her hand another squeeze. "I'm staying until you finish the rest of whatever the hell that stuff is." Jack sighed, and did as he was told.

That afternoon, Chief Brewster appeared in the doorway. In full uniform, gun at the hip, he gave the open door a single knock and strode in. He was a large man, overweight with a clean-shaven playdough face and wire rimmed glasses. He adopted a solemn expression. "Hi Jack."

"Chief."

"You look like hell."

"Thanks." Jack raised the head of his bed.

Brewster sat. "The docs say you'll be good to go soon."

"So I'm told."

Brewster got the obligatory we-were-really-worried stuff, out of the way then pulled his phone. "Mind if I record this conversation? I'm not good with taking notes."

"Sure, why not." Jack had worked with Brewster on a few cases over the past few years. While the two of them had a good working relationship, the man never missed an opportunity to make it clear, who was the sheriff and who was the chief. For the most part, Jack was okay with that but, on occasion it got under his skin.

With his phone set up in record mode, the chief rattled off the date, time, location and other particulars. Then, he slipped into interrogator mode. "All right sheriff, take me through the events that occurred on the morning in question."

The chief cued him with a nod. Jack told his story.

Brewster waited then asked: "Anything else you can remember about the ship or about the men and what they were doing?"

"No."

"What about the caller? You got his number?"

"Might be on my phone but there was...something." Yes, Jack remembered it clearly now. "The guy told me to call someone in Duluth about whatever was going on out there."

"Call who?"

Jack thought for a moment. "A guy named...Cooper. Yeah, it was *Agent* Cooper. He wanted me to tell him what I saw."

"*Agent* Cooper? You mean like a real estate agent?"

"FBI."

Brewster rubbed his jaw, reminding Jack of Mr. Potato Head. "That's all we need, getting the damn feds involved in this." Brewster took his phone off record mode. "You're sure about this? The guy said to call the FBI in Duluth?"

"I'm sure."

"I'll try calling. I can give the particulars but this Agent Cooper may want to talk to you directly. You up for that?"

"Oh, you mean now? Sure, why not." He rubbed his eyes and took a sip of ice water. "You know anyone there?"

"Nope," said Brewster, busy with his phone. "Never been to Duluth. Ah, here's the number." He put the phone to his ear, waited, then rolled his eyes. "I've got their auto attendant. 'Thank you for calling...press one for...' Wonder if they'll have music on hold."

In the end he left a message. He stowed the phone then stood. "Damn feds."

"Beth told me you went out to The Point looking for evidence. Did you find anything?"

"We saw some cracks in the ice."

"Caused by that freighter I saw."

"We also found a nice new off-road Silverado sitting in the woods. The truck had dealer plates. Turns out it was stolen off a lot in Munising a few weeks back. No prints. Somebody wiped it clean. There wasn't so much as a stale French fry under the seat." He shook his head. "My guys are still going over it. As for the rest of the area, there's a fresh layer of snow covering everything so we haven't been able to find much else. Anything specific you can remember about the freighter?"

"Reddish hull, I think. But it was dark, hard to tell. There should be a record of the shipping traffic out there at that time."

"Yep, we're on that. We're putting together a list of all the ships in the area that morning." Brewster paused. "Look, Jack, I need to gain access to your phone. The hospital has it with the rest of your stuff. I'll need your okay for them to hand it over. There's a form you need to sign." He pulled out a folded over document and handed it to Jack along with a pen. "I'll also need your phone code."

Jack signed the form then wrote his code on the back.

"Don't worry, I won't look at any of your private stuff."

"Better not," said Jack, handing it back.

The chief stood, hefting his belt up an inch or two. "I'll call you when anything new comes up or if I hear back from the FBI. Give me a call if you...well, I guess you can't if I've got your phone."

"I've got a room phone."

"Look Jack, you get yourself feeling better. That's the main thing. We'll talk more." He took on that solemn look again, then left.

Jack relaxed, glad to be alone again. He let his head sink back into the pillow, and slept.

Two days later, dressed in clothes Beth brought from home, Jack was wheeled out of MTU Patrons Hospital. Bright sun, blue sky, brisk air and Beth's smiling face greeted him at her car. He turned down any help getting inside and winced only a little at a stab of pain at the base of his spine as he settled into his seat. Yeah, not bad for having been shot in the back less than a week ago. Beth helped with his seatbelt.

"You still planning to go into the station today?" she asked, pulling out of the parking lot then onto the highway.

"I won't stay long. Just want to check in and say hi to the guys."

"And to thank them for saving your life."

"Yes, that too," said Jack, bothered as he always was by Beth driving too slowly.

"Sharon's been a mess, worrying about you. I think she took it personal, not insisting that you wait for backup before blundering out there in the dark."

"I didn't blunder. I got that tip and I had to check it out. That's my job, remember?"

"How can I forget? But you don't need to take risks like that. There are *other* things in life."

"Like running a pharmacy, you mean?"

"There's nothing risky about running a pharmacy. But yeah, I guess I get wrapped up in that too. Sometimes I think it's the pharmacy that runs me."

"Well, the money's good. It's a lot more than I make."

"But you like what you do, right? I mean, maybe not now, not after getting shot, but…"

"Yeah, I like it…most days."

They put on a few miles in silence, then: "Jack, we should have a baby. You almost died out there. When I found out you'd been shot, that was all I could think about. I drove like crazy down to the hospital."

"What, you mean like five miles over the speed limit?"

"Don't make fun over this."

"I get shot and all you were thinking was that we should have a baby?"

"Of course not. I also checked your life insurance policy to make sure our payments were up to date." She reached over, placing her hand on his, softening her attempt at humor. "We're both in our thirties, Jack. We've waited long enough, don't you think?"

A baby? They'd talked about it before they were married and they'd both agreed to wait until they had some financial stability. Was that really ten years ago? Even now, with his meager pay, money was still a struggle. It was the money she made with the pharmacy that was keeping them afloat. He gave her hand a squeeze then let it go. "I think you'd better keep both hands on the wheel, ma'am," he said, taking up his traffic cop drawl. "And can you pick up the speed? You know, driving too slow can be just as dangerous as driving too fast." He gave her a glance, seeing her face, pretty as ever with her long hair tied back in a ponytail, a few more lines maybe, a hint of gray here and there, but yeah, pretty as ever. "I think we *have* waited long enough. Let's have a baby."

"I'm serious, you idiot."

"I'm serious too. Let's have a baby. Boy or girl?"

She returned his glance.

He thought better about giving her an eyes on the road ma'am, comment. Yeah, poignant moment like this, that would be a bad idea.

"One of each," she said with conviction, smiling, speeding up.

The Gull Harbor police station had once been a gas station and before that, a Thrifty Mart. It sat diagonally on the corner of Main and Third, two blocks north of *Holiday Drugs*, and two south of the Lodge each of which marked the extremities of the little town. Gull Harbor boasted a population of 350 permanent residents. Summer tourists combined with hunting season more than quadrupled that number right up until the December snows essentially shut the place down.

Beth pulled into the station parking lot and managed the doors as Jack hobbled in leaning heavily on his hospital issued, walker.

"Got some donuts for you, Sheriff. Carla sent 'em, fresh." said Sharon standing at her desk, face beaming.

"I'm not as bad as I look," said Jack, straightening. Beth helped him with his coat as he lowered himself into a chair. Sharon Jacobs, who'd hired on five years ago just out of high school was now an attractive young woman. Short haired, a born organizer, she gave him a loose hug and put a cup of coffee within reach. Bob, tall, lanky, clean shaven and always serious and Ron, the bearded, round-faced jokester of the station, both stepped up and shook his hand saying it was good to have him back. They were all at their spiffy best, each in freshly pressed uniforms. But Jack could see the awkward concern on their faces.

"I know I look like shit right now," he told them. "But I'll be back in the saddle soon enough. Hell, it's thanks to the three of you that I'm even alive. Thanks for all you did that day. You saved my life."

"You made the paper, Sheriff," said Sharon, handing him three 'special edition' copies of the single sheet, *Gull Harbor Guardian*. In big block letters they announced in turn:

Sheriff Shot
Sheriff Recovering and
Sheriff Back Today

"They're planning a welcome back celebration at the Lodge when you're up for it," added Bob.

"That's nice but I don't need any celebration." He took a sip of coffee that tasted way too strong, then took a bite of his glazed donut. As he chewed, he adjusted his back in the chair wincing at a spike of pain. He turned to Ron. "When you went out there looking for me, it must have been light by that time. What did you see?"

"We didn't see much of anything. The snow was coming down hard. It took us a while to find you, lying on the rocks at the edge of the woods. You were covered with snow and your face was blue. You were groaning some. That's how we found you."

"Did you see the freighter?"

"No," said Bob. "Sharon told us you saw one. By the time we got there the visibility was pretty poor."

"It was up against the ice shelf, so close to shore I thought it might've run aground. Chief Brewster said the ice looked fractured. He's checking the freighter traffic logs."

"We did see the pickup out in the woods," offered Ron. "A nice Silverado."

"Where's the truck now?"

"Impound lot, down in Houghton," said Sharon. "It was hauled out of the woods the next day."

Absently Jack took another sip of coffee then noticed Beth's let's get you home expression. Yeah, his body was still in hospital mode. He felt exhausted already. "Okay guys, thanks again for saving my life. I'd be dead if it weren't for the three of you. We'll go over things more when I come back, sometime...tomorrow."

"Or the next day," added Beth.

CHAPTER 4

With Beth beside him, Jack hobbled through the front door of *Holiday Drugs*, leaning heavily on his walker. Dave Bower, her long time, twenty something assistant, looked up from his spot at the checkout counter and ran over. "Here, sheriff, I can help."

"I don't need help," said Jack, shaking him off. He never liked the guy but Beth was always gushing about how she couldn't get along without him. With a square jaw, bright eyes and hair flowing down to his shoulders, he'd seen how Beth stared at him. Not now, but yeah, he'd seen it.

"It's all right, we can manage," Beth told him. "And could you..."

"No problem, I'll handle the store."

Yeah. Good old dependable, young and studly, Dave.

"Hey, sheriff. How're you doing," said Howard Duffy, looking up from the oral care aisle.

"Been better," Jack managed, straightening as he walked.

Once up the stairs and into a chair, Beth made him a plate of scrambled eggs. He was able to finish half. She checked the medication the hospital gave him. "Wow! This is the good stuff," she said. "Not opioids so no worries about that, but they'll fix you up for a long stay in dreamland. Best if you just take one. Sleep is what you need but you don't want to overdo it."

"My luck, marrying a pharmacist," said Jack, hitting the john then easing himself into bed. He slept through the remainder of the day and through the night. Back sore, he awoke the next day surprised to see it was already 7A.M., still dark. He rubbed the sleep from his eyes.

"Stay in bed," said Beth, dressed, watching him through the mirror as she brushed her hair in the bathroom. "How do you feel?"

"Good enough." He struggled to sit up. The room started spinning. He sank back, head plopping down on the pillow. He took a few breaths, shook off the covers and tried again, eventually managing to sit on the edge of the bed. He steadied himself with a hand on the bedpost then…stood.

Beth came over but knew better than to help as he made his way into the bathroom and shut the door. He avoided the mirror.

"My back hurts like hell," he said, done, coming back out.

"You should stay home."

"I need to go in."

"Stay home. Have some breakfast and we'll see how you feel."

"You talk like the doc at the hospital."

"The pretty one?" she teased.

He smiled. "Yeah, the pretty one." He thought again about Beth's occasional covert glances at Dave. Well, nothing wrong with incidental fantasies popping into your head every now and then, right? He realized he was suddenly curious as to what incidental fantasies Beth might have. He'd have to ask sometime.

"What?" asked Beth, returning his stare, walking beside him as he made it into the kitchen.

Jack cleared his throat. "Must be the drugs," he said, sitting at the table.

She gave him a kiss, her lips soft against his, her breasts brushing his shoulder. "Told you those drugs were good," she whispered.

Jack felt his blood pumping. "Yeah, guess they are." He took a few deep breaths then realized he was hungry.

"We've got the usual choice of cereals. What'll it be?"

"You choose," he said, watching her, realizing what a lucky man he was. He wondered what having a baby around might do to their daily routine. He'd heard nightmarish stories.

He finished a bowl of cereal and some orange juice but coffee still tasted bitter. He stared at the nearly full cup. His head went foggy. Yeah, still not quite back to normal. He jumped at the sound of Beth's phone going off.

"It's Sharon," said Beth, handing it to him.

"Sorry to bug you. Chief Brewster called. He'll be here at one. Says he needs to talk to you."

"Why didn't he just call *me*? Why didn't *you* just call me?"

"Chief Brewster has your phone. We have Beth's number here at the station, you know…for emergencies."

"Oh yeah, forgot, sorry." He caught Beth's caregiver eyes from across the table. "Yes, good, tell the chief I'll be there." He ended the call, and forced down the rest of his coffee.

"You're really going in, huh?"

"The chief's driving up. Yeah, I'm really going in. But I'll need a lift."

Beth drove him to the station, escorted him into his office. He sat down behind his desk. "Could you…"

She flicked on the space heater at his feet. "You okay."

"Just dandy."

"Call me when you want me to pick you up."

After she left, Jack looked around his office. Yes, it was time to start getting things back to normal.

He was startled by the slam of two car doors from out in the parking lot. He swiveled his chair and, through the window, watched a slim, red-haired woman in boots and black leather jacket stride toward the front door trailed by the chief. Who the hell is she?

Jack swiveled back around. He hated surprises, especially in front of Brewster. Unprompted, Sharon brought a second side chair into his office.

Jack watched the two visitors stomp the snow off their boots and wrestle out of their coats.

The red-haired woman caught his eye. "Sheriff Holiday, I assume?" she said, walking in, not waiting for Brewster. She extended her hand. "I'm Agent Cooper, FBI out of Duluth."

Jack tried to conceal his surprise, first at the mysterious Agent Cooper getting here so quickly, and second, at her being a woman. At his vague recollection of the tipster's call, had he referred to Agent Cooper as a *her*? They shook hands firmly. Her curly hair framed her reddened cheeks. Her brown eyes were all business.

"Those are my people you passed by," Jack told her. "Sharon Jacobs, my office manager, and my deputies, Ron Fiddler and Bob Packard. They saved my life."

Cooper turned to them. "Thanks for your quick, heroic work," she told them, giving a wave as she sat, plopping her leather satchel down on the floor beside her.

Brewster came in, closed the door, and sat.

"You're looking well, considering what you've been through," Cooper told Jack in a stern, mechanical voice.

It struck Jack that her mind was elsewhere. "Would you like coffee?"

"We should get started, sheriff," said Brewster. He reached into his shirt pocket. "Thought you might be needing your phone back," he said, sliding it across his desk. "We've got all the relevant data from it. There wasn't much."

Jack made no move to pick it up.

Cooper produced a notepad, pen clicked and poised. "I've listened to the call in you made to your station that morning, sheriff and I've got a summary of what you told the chief here. But, please, walk us through it again."

Jack retold his story, Cooper and Brewster interrupting with questions along the way, she taking notes.

"And the freighter, any distinguishing features?"

Jack shook his head. "It was a sterncastle type, Redish hull. Bow to the west. It was dark so I couldn't see much, just its silhouette against the clouds. I suppose, as freighters go, it was a smaller size but close up like it was, it seemed huge. I was trying to get closer when the guys on shore saw me. Then the floodlight came on. I was blinded. By that time, I had other things to worry about."

"And the men you saw were moving something out toward the freighter."

"Yes. And by this time, they were already out on the ice."

"You said they were moving boxes? What size roughly."

"Say a foot and a half wide by three feet long, maybe a foot high."

"And they looked heavy."

"Yes."

"Were they cardboard boxes?"

"I think so...I suppose they might have been wooden."

"Crates then?"

"Possibly."

"How many?"

"I saw three."

Cooper slipped her pen and notepad into her satchel. She folded her arms. "According to the navigational records and the satellite data for that morning, the closest freighter to was five miles off shore, heading west, making a steady nine knots."

Jack shook his head about to protest but Cooper lifted her hand. "You can check this out against the sat photos on line. There was a lot of cloud cover that morning. I believe that you saw a freighter, sheriff. And as you noted in your statement, it was close enough to shore to leave the fractures in the ice shelf as were seen the next day by the chief here."

"Bottom line, the vessel tracking system isn't perfect," said Brewster.

Cooper nodded. "And, it can be hacked. As you might know, the system depends on a transponder device present aboard every commercial vessel. It sends out a unique signal at regular intervals identifying the ship while giving position, speed, and direction info. This satellite system is backed up by land-based radar but there are blind spots. If a freighter captain had knowledge of these blind spots, it's theoretically possible to navigate through them, undetected."

Jack folded his hands. "So, if the transponder aboard the ship I saw had been disabled, it might not be trackable? What about real time satellite imagery?"

"As I said, there was a heavy cloud cover that morning." Cooper shrugged. "A disabled transponder is the best theory we have right now. The other theory, no offense sheriff, is that you were hallucinating and didn't see what you think you saw. We tend to believe that you did see a freighter close to shore. The tip of the Keweenaw Peninsula is about as secluded, yet accessible a place as we have in these United States. It provides shelter from prying eyes and, for any freighter captain ballsy enough to risk running aground, it provides an easy entry point for illegal goods."

"I know all that, Agent Cooper," said Jack, feeling as if she were treating him and the incident that nearly got him killed, way too lightly. "We've investigated criminal activity out there before, usually drug related. But, come on, you must have some idea about which ship was out there."

Cooper stood. "We're keeping our findings confidential. And, from this point forward, you will do nothing and say nothing related to this incident. I may be back in touch but until that happens, both you and Chief Brewster will consider this matter closed. Thank you for your time." She began picking up her things.

"You didn't ask about the guy who called me that morning."

"If we need anything more, I'll give you a call." Not bothering with a handshake, she walked out of the office. "Hope you feel better soon, sheriff," she said, putting on her coat.

Brewster stood, gave Jack a shrug and left with her.

Through the window, Jack watched them pull out of the parking lot.

"Short meeting," said Sharon from his doorway. "How'd it go?"

Jack shook his head. "I have no idea."

CHAPTER 5

Katerina Sokolov took another sip of sour mash whiskey. Savoring it, she computed in her head the exorbitant cost of each swallow. On this cold Duluth night, it warmed her insides in the most delightful way. She put the glass down. The ice cubes settled with a clickity-click. How could something so cold be so wonderfully warm? She stretched back in her recliner. Andrei would be pleased. His plan, or rather, her part of his plan, had finally been put in motion. What would he think of her now? What bargaining lever might this give her in the future? And what the hell was he planning?

Compartmentalization, he called it. Even the few members of his inner circle, of which Katerina considered herself a part, had been kept blind to his end goal. "Focus only on your part, and everything will fall into place," he'd told her. She was to have the cargo picked up then get it from point *A* to point *B*. That was all.

So far, things had gone perfectly. Well, almost perfectly. To use an American euphemism she'd grown fond of, there'd been only one minor hiccup of no consequence. The news so far was good but she knew that could change in a heartbeat. With such a long distance from point *A* to point *B* there was still a lot that could go wrong.

She once read of the many hours the American President Lincoln had waited at the telegraph office near what was then called the Executive Mansion. The anxiety he must have felt waiting for word from his generals about Bull Run, Gettysburg and all the rest must have wearied him to the bone. Or perhaps a better comparison was Joseph Stalin cooped up in the Kremlin as Hitler's armies fought their way to the very outskirts of

Moscow. Yes, those were critical times when the very existence of their nations hung in the balance.

She took another sip. She put down the glass, her eyes resting on her son dozing on the sofa across from her. Ilya would be twenty-two in just a few days, and there he lay sound asleep, snoring gently under a blanket. It was only eight o'clock.

It had been a long struggle raising the boy, now a man. The first blow had come on learning Ilya had been born with a severe mental handicap for which there was no cure. The next had come with the betrayal and desertion of her husband leaving the two of them alone and destitute. On that score there had been many warning signs. She'd simply chosen to ignore them.

With respect to her husband, she had had her sweet revenge long ago. But Ilya...yes, Ilya was a different matter. There he lay, asleep, looking perfectly normal. Even after all this time, she still expected him to wake up one day, normal in every way. She should accept reality and just assume Ilya would never speak, never laugh, never show basic human emotion, and never give her grandchildren. But somehow, she couldn't manage it.

She kept her eyes on him. Was he dreaming? Could he dream? He'd become a handsome young man, jet black hair, square chin, his appearance never betraying his condition.

Katerina reminded herself of the old joke about a boy, normal in every way but for the fact he didn't talk. The boy grew up in a normal family, mother, father, a couple of siblings all of whom failed in their best attempts to urge a word, a sound, any sound, out of the boy. Specialists were no help.

Then, a few days after the boy turned six, the family sat around the kitchen table. They started supper then, suddenly, the silent boy straightened in his chair and said: "Please pass the salt." The whole family was overjoyed. They stared at the boy in complete awe. "Son," said the mom, tears of joy falling, "You can talk! Why is it you haven't spoken a word until now?"

The boy cocked his head considering his answer, then said: "Well, so far, everything has been pretty much okay."

A sad joke, and not so funny. But oh, for a miracle like that for Ilya!

Katerina closed her eyes. In what seemed like an instant later, she woke with a start, her phone going off. It was past eleven, Ilya in bed by now. She picked up her phone, noting the caller then braced herself.

"He's been released from the hospital."

"Who? The man on the shore you mean? The man you thought was dead? I told you not to worry about him."

"He's a cop. According to the local newspaper, he's the sheriff of some town there."

Katerina brought her chair upright. Shit! This couldn't be happening. "What do you think he knows?"

"He saw us. He saw the freighter."

"And because he got shot, and because he's a cop, somebody will be investigating." She cursed under her breath. "What the hell was he doing out there—having an early morning jog in the snow? The idiot!" She relaxed the grip on her phone. She got to her feet and started to pace. "Where is this man now?"

"He's home recovering."

"Wife? Family?"

"I don't know."

"Your men should have made sure he was dead. Has he caused any trouble yet? Is anyone investigating?"

"We left no clues."

"That is not what I asked."

"Yes, they are investigating."

"Is the man, that sheriff himself, looking into things?"

"We've seen no signs of that. He's still recovering."

Katerina fingered her chin. "Keep your eyes on him. If he does nothing, then you do nothing. If he begins to stick his nose where it doesn't belong then you will make sure his luck runs out. Do you understand? Try to be subtle about it and let me know when it's done."

"Subtle?"

"A home break in, a car-jacking gone wrong, a gas leak that causes an explosion, a thief in the night. For God's sake, do I have to spell it out for you? Something that won't have people connecting his death with what he might have seen that morning. Do you understand?"

"Yes."

"Do not fuck this up!"

Katerina ended the call. She knocked back the last of her drink, watered down but still soothing. She poured herself another—neat, as fancy Brits might say.

CHAPTER 6

Jack lay in bed, eyes open. It was just light enough to pick out the largest of the cracks in the plaster ceiling. Three days had gone by since the meeting with Chief Brewster and Agent Cooper. Had the FBI made any progress? Would he ever learn what those men were up to that morning, or why he was shot? Yeah, he'd been told to stay out of it, but that didn't mean he had to like it.

He supposed he needed to get back to his normal routine—tracking down lost dogs, taking down a bear who'd wandered too close to town, breaking up a fight or two at the lodge. Nothing sinister, nothing dangerous, just the usual smalltown stuff a sheriff and two part time deputies could handle. After all, that was his job. And this was likely to be as far as his not so brilliant career in law enforcement would take him.

The pain in his back had become nothing more than a dull ache. Surprisingly, the drugs and the daily PT exercises Doc Ambrose insisted on seemed to be working. He used a cane now instead of the walker. Yeah, he was feeling better. He eased himself into a sitting position, then shifted his legs off the edge of the bed, careful not to disturb Beth.

She was skittish about him going back to full time work too soon. He knew he'd given her a scare. Hell, he'd given himself a scare, lying there alone, snow coming down, slowly bleeding out. And now she wants a baby. But, surprisingly, he did too. Yeah, it was about time they gave parenting a whirl. How tough could it be?

He showered, dressed then bent with an effort to give Beth a kiss. He made his way gingerly down the stairs and out the door.

The November Plot

He resumed his donut ritual at Carla's then got to the station at pretty close to his usual time. Once inside he turned up the thermostat. The furnace in the back room noisily kicked in. At his desk he turned on the space heater warming his feet. Yeah, this felt normal. He dug into his donuts and coffee. Coffee tasted good now. He went through the papers Sharon left from the previous day. There wasn't much.

He tapped the side of his near empty Styrofoam cup. He thought about the morning he was shot. He wondered what would have happened if he'd died out there.

Small funeral. Most in the town would come. Cremation maybe? Yeah, he supposed so. He wondered if Beth would stay up here running the store. Maybe she'd have Dave move in? No, she wouldn't do that.

Well, maybe she would.

And who would become sheriff? Bob and Ron would probably battle it out. But it was Sharon who, despite her relative youth, would get his vote.

She came in and hung up her coat. Through his open office door he felt her stare. "Yes, I'm here Sharon. And yes, I am doing fine."

"Is there anything I can..."

"No thanks, Sharon. I'm fine."

As the office warmed, Jack turned off the space heater. Sharon started clunking around making the first pot of coffee (not as good as Carla's). Bob came in, Ron soon after. Both said hi. Both stayed at their desks busy with overdue reports. Before long the full light of day was pouring in through the window behind Jack. The newest layer of snow sparkled off Main Street. The buzz of snowmobiles was in the air. He drummed his fingers. Yep, not much happening.

His mind wandered. He gave his phone a hard stare. Yeah, what harm could a phone call be? He picked it up.

"Sheriff Holiday, that you?" said a familiar voice a moment later.

"Yeah Sam, it's me. How're things in Thunder Bay?"

"Colder than a...well, pretty damn cold. Heard about you getting shot. You doing okay?"

"Much better, thanks." Jack had known Sam Harris, station chief for the RCMP up in Northern Ontario for more than ten years. Though they'd only met a few times they commiserated by phone so often that he considered him an old friend.

"Glad to hear it. I was worried but I knew you'd pull through. Probably should have called just to check in but...well, anyways, you called me on my bat-phone so I guess maybe there's a way I can try and make up for my lack of sensitivity."

"I need your satellite imagery of the Keweenaw for the morning of the shooting."

"You got a problem with your U.S. of A. pics?"

"Can't say right now."

"Ah, cloak and dagger stuff."

Jack could hear his smile. "Can you get them or not?"

"Sure, I guess so. What're you looking for?"

"Freighter traffic. You guys are on a different system than ours so..."

"Something wrong with your spy in the sky?"

"Just send what you've got okay?"

"Guess I'm asking a few too many questions, this being on the QT and all, hey?" He paused to clear his throat. "Anyhoo, yep, sure thing sheriff. I'll get you what I've got. Always glad to help out."

"Great. And send it via fax."

"Fax? Thought you fellas would have thrown out your old tech hardware. I'll see if I can remember how to use mine."

After a minute or two of small talk, Jack ended the call. He got up and made sure his own fax machine was plugged in and had paper. He got more coffee then went back to the important business of drumming his fingers on his desktop. He thought about Agent Cooper, then about the Silverado that was found in the woods. He rubbed his jaw. He looked up another number.

His call was answered after two rings: "Sergeant Adams."

"Hey Cody, how's it going?" asked Jack.

"That you Jack? Man, I heard what happened. Meant to stop by the hospital to see you but…"

"No problem. I'm doing just fine now." How many times was he going to have to say that today?

"Glad to hear it. Man, that was really messed up. You're lucky to be alive."

"Yes, I am. I'm calling about the truck you've got, the one that was found in the woods up here the morning I got shot. Anything new on that?"

"Yeah, spanking new Silverado. It was stolen off a lot. It looked like the thing had been wiped clean, no prints and no other kinds of evidence. But one of our guys got lucky and came up with a partial thumb print on the heater control switch. Your timing was pretty good calling about it. We got a match on a guy down in Cadillac. He's got priors. He was busted for GTA. Looks like he's at it again. These guys never learn, do they. I can send you his rap sheet."

"That'd be great. And do you have an odometer reading from the truck?"

"Sure, I'll send that too."

"And Cody, can you not tell Brewster we talked?"

A momentary silence at the other end. "You aren't pulling an end run on us are you, Jack?"

"No. I'd just prefer he didn't know. If he presses you on it, then sure, tell him. Otherwise, don't."

"Okay, will do. And if I pick up on anything related, I'll give you a shout."

"Great, thanks. I owe you one."

"Yeah, you do."

Jack ended the call. A few minutes later the email from Cody came in. Jack scanned it quickly. The guy's name was Michael Fuller, born 1995, present address unknown. Jack stared at the photo. Dark eyes, drawn face, long stringy hair, thin lips stretched out in a smirk above a pointy chin with a prominent cleft. He did ninety days in Alger County Jail in Munising for…yes, grand theft auto. He was released on a technicality in 2020, no record before or since.

It was the 'released on a technicality' thing that caught Jack's eye. That usually meant the guy had a decent lawyer. There weren't many decent lawyers in Munising. Jack placed another call, this time to the Munising Public Defender's Office. He didn't know anyone there but, because of the news of him getting shot, he was counting on them knowing him.

"Yes, of course, be glad to help, sheriff," said paralegal Maxine somebody. "I remember the case. Fuller was represented by an out-of-town lawyer, a Japanese fellow who I hadn't heard of before or since. He got the guy sprung with a reduced sentence which raised some eyebrows even here in the PD's office. That's why I remember the case. Sure as hell someone was paid off." She paused. "You figure him being involved in whatever it was that got you shot?"

"I'm just following a possible lead. Can you check the court records for the lawyer's name."

"Yes, I can do that. I'll get it to you this afternoon."

"Thanks very much. You're a big help."

Jack ended the call. He leaned back in his chair and closed his eyes. The damn meds were making him sleepy. It was the throbbing of his wound that snapped him back awake. He thought about another cup of coffee but decided against it. He stared at Fuller's photo again. Prominent chin, the thin lips, closely spaced eyes. Could this be one of the men he'd seen at the point that morning? There was no way of knowing. And all they had on the guy was a print on the heater knob of a high end Silverado. But had he seen that face here in Gull Harbor? He couldn't be sure. He could show the photo around the office, but that would start rumors flying. Then, he had a better idea.

He checked the time, folded up the rap sheet and stuck it in his shirt pocket. With an effort, he got up and put on his coat.

"I'll be at the Lodge," he told Sharon as he passed her desk.

Her eyebrows lifted in a disapproving way. "You know, it's not good mixing alcohol with pain killers."

"Thanks doc, I'll keep that in mind."

The November Plot

Jack walked into the place to a round of applause from the late lunch crowd. Embarrassed, he held up a hand and tried to look pleased. Thankfully, the applause quickly died so he didn't have to turn and take a bow. He headed for the bar.

Full bearded Jason Spooner had bartended the Lodge for as long as Jack could remember. No matter the time of year, he always wore what looked to be the same checkered flannel shirt and the same ragged pair of baggy jeans held up over his barrel chest by a pair of red and green suspenders. For anyone who'd listen, he boasted that he was from Thunder Bay and was just down for an extended visit. The truth was unknown, but the man surely knew how to tend bar and he knew the citizenry of Gull Harbor better than anyone.

Jason filled a tall glass with foamy headed Labatt Blue and slid it in front of him. "'Bout time you get your ass in here, sheriff. You're the closest thing we've got to a celebrity. How're you feeling? You're lookin' a bit pale if you don't mind my saying."

"Feeling fine. Just need to get out in the sun a bit more." He eyed the beer.

"Don't worry, it's on the house."

"Thanks." He took a sip, then a swallow, surprised at how good it tasted. "I've got a question for you." He fished the rap sheet from his pocket and smoothed it out on a dry spot on the bar. "This guy look familiar?"

Jason picked it up. He held it up to the light and stroked his beard. "It's a rap sheet."

"Yes, I know."

"Fella looks a little like Aaron Rodgers, right?"

"He's not Aaron Rodgers. He's Mike Fuller. It says so right there."

"Yeah, AR's had better days but I guess he hasn't sunk to stealing cars yet, huh?"

"Have you seen him?"

Jason reached to give his beard another tug, then stopped. "You know, I think I have seen this guy in here. He was with some other fellas—hunters. Haven't seen any of them before or since."

"How many of them were there?"

Jason shrugged. "Three, no...could be four maybe"

"*Could be* four, maybe?"

"Could be, I guess." He handed the sheet back. "Hey, you think this guy had something to do with...you know..."

"When did you see him?"

"Just the one time. They stuck out like they weren't from around here. Dressed in top of the line hunting gear, camo stuff. Expensive, looked brand new. Stiff and starchy, if you know what I mean. That's why I noticed them. Can't say exactly when I saw them...two weeks ago maybe? But yeah, it was only the one time."

"Did they stay here at the Lodge?"

"No, I would have known if they had."

"Did they talk much? Did you see what they were driving?"

Jason shook his head. "You can talk to Doris. She might know more. She would have waited their table. She's off today though. Be back tomorrow."

Jason broke off to handle a customer at the other end of the bar. Jack pocketed the rap sheet. He finished half his beer then left. He thought about the four out of town hunters. He thought about Mike Fuller. Then he thought about Agent Cooper. She might want him off the case but, with every angry twitch of the bullet wound in his back, Jack knew there was no way he was staying on the sidelines.

CHAPTER 7

Doris folded a fresh stick of Juicy Fuit into her mouth and started working it. "Yeah, I remember that guy," she told Jack the next day, elbow on the bar. "He was with three other guys. Nice tip."

"Did they pay with a credit card?"

"Nope. Hard cash."

"What did they talk about?"

"Well, they didn't talk about committing a crime and shooting you." She stopped chewing. She lowered her voice. "Jason said you thought they might be the guys who, you know..."

"What did they talk about?"

"Like every other customer here, they talked about beer and they talked about food, they ate and they left. That was it. Look, sheriff, I'd like to help, really I would. But I serve a hundred meals a day here and a lot more rounds of beer and booze. Everything gets to be kind of like a blur if you know what I mean."

"Yes, I know the feeling," said Jack.

A few days passed. He ditched the cane and could walk now with only what he considered to be a slight limp. He hadn't heard from Brewster since he'd dropped by with Agent Cooper and he hadn't gotten any info yet from Sam or from Cody. October was almost gone. The lack of progress was driving him nuts. He decided to call Brewster.

"Have you heard anything from Cooper?" Jack said.

"No. Didn't expect to either. But it just so happens, I called her office yesterday. I got past their answering machine and got a real person to talk to. I asked for Cooper and was transferred to her boss. Turns out she's been suspended for the past two months."

Jack's ears perked up. "Why? What for?"

"It was something to do with a fracas out in Minnesota. He said it happened a while back. There's an investigation. Apparently, another agent was nearly killed in the incident, so it's pretty serious. I filled the station chief on what was going on here. He agreed with me that it's a local thing but asked me to let him know if things escalate." The chief paused. "So, we're back to handling it on our own."

"We've lost a lot of time. Who've you got on it?"

"I'm personally taking the lead on this."

"Anything new?"

"Well, we did get something from a print we managed to find in the Silverado. We've got an ID on it, a guy named Michael Fuller. He's got a record. We're following up now. I'll keep you in the loop."

Yeah, I bet you will. "Thanks, chief. I'll check into a few things on this end. I'll let you know what I find."

"I hate parallel investigations, Jack, you know that. But in this case, I know it's personal for you so I'll let it slide."

The call ended.

Cooper suspended! What the hell did that mean? Jack got more coffee. He closed his office door and, for the third time that day, checked his emails.

A new one gave a list of training videos available for law enforcement officials. Yeah, those were always fun. Most dealt with what to say and not to say while being interviewed by the press about a particular case or investigation. The fun part about those was seeing guys messing up, saying dumb things. Strange how it was always guys messing up while the examples showing a cop handling things *the right way* always seemed to feature police women. Then again, maybe that was just his imagination.

He clicked on one, got as far as the title: *WHAT NOT TO SAY. Part III*, when Sharon knocked lightly and walked in. He hit pause.

"Fax came in," she said. "Didn't think the machine was still plugged in. Scared the hell out of me when it started clacking." She handed him multiple sheets of paper.

"Thanks," said Jack. They were from Sam.

"Amazing it had enough ink," she added, leaving, closing the door behind her.

The first page was a spreadsheet listing all the vessels operating in Lake Superior on the morning of the shooting. Included were the names of each vessel, its line, flag, skipper and first officer. Also listed was info on cargo, net tonnage, port of departure, and destination. Sam had done a good job.

Jack leaned back in his chair. Cooper had to have access to this same information. Or maybe not, if she was suspended.

Next were satellite photographs of the tip of the Keweenaw. The images suffered from the reduced resolution of the fax machine but they were cloud covered anyway so that hardly mattered. They showed an outline of the coast with four transponder dots representing vessels sailing well off shore. The date and time stamp on the images correlated well with the time he would have been laying on the shore, bleeding out.

He went back to the spreadsheet.

Key crewmembers of any commercial vessel often found themselves looking for work. They kept their CV's up to date and easily accessible online. He looked up bios for each captain on the spreadsheet and obtained contact info. It was eleven by the time he picked up the phone and called the first name on the list.

A man answered in a gruff voice, "Bailey."

"David Bailey of the *Algoma Traveler*?"

"Yeah, you got him. Who is this?"

Jack introduced himself quickly. "I'm investigating an incident off the Keweenaw. It would have been five thirty in the morning." He gave him the date. "My records show that your ship was in the area. Do you remember seeing anything unusual about that time?"

"I don't recall anything," said Bailey. "My first mate had the watch round about then. Hold on. I'll check the log."

Jack waited, pen in hand. Over the phone he could hear the drumming of engines. Bailey's ship was probably making his last run of the season before laying up for the winter. He must be close to shore to have cell coverage.

Bailey came back on. "This have something to do with a cop getting shot out there? I heard about it on the news."

"Yes, it does." Jack wasn't above playing that up in trade for information: "I was the guy who got shot."

"Damn! I guess you're lucky to be alive. I'd like to help out. Always had a soft spot for you law enforcement guys. My dad was a cop in Grand Rapids a long time ago."

"Thanks captain. Was there anything in your logbook for that morning?"

"Nope. But that doesn't mean much. Sometimes a lot of shit happens that ain't worth an entry. I'll check with my first mate. He's sleeping after pulling the night watch. He wouldn't be too happy, me waking him up. Keeps his cabin locked anyway. Likes his privacy. I'll call if he knows anything."

Jack left his number. He made two more calls, leaving voicemails, had a quick lunch, then called Captain Steven Jacobs, skipper of the last of the four ships on Sam's list.

Jacobs explained that Jack had caught him at a bar in Duluth. There were a few shouts in the background but it was still early for the usual rowdiness of a dockside bar. The captain's words were only slightly slurred. He went on to explain that his ship, *Kingslip* had been far offshore that morning, heading west to Duluth. "We're taking on a load of ore in a few days," he explained, "then it's off to the steel mills south of Detroit. "Got to get my drinking in when I can." Jacobs said with a laugh. He remaining jovial until Jack got around to telling him who he was and why he was calling.

"No, nothing unusual that morning," the captain went on to say, his tone suddenly stiff and sober. "We were fighting an unusually strong current that was taking us closer to the south shore than I would have liked. Being west bound, that can be dangerous. You know, crossing into oncoming traffic. Lucky for us, there were only a few ships out. It drew an entry in the log but that was it."

The hairs on the back of Jack's neck were up. "Did you take on any cargo off the Keweenaw that morning, captain?"

"We're an ore carrier, sheriff. We load in Duluth, we off load at the mills. Been doing that for ten years. That is *all* we do."

"And you saw nothing out of the ordinary that morning?"

"I think I've already answered that question," he said testily.

Sensing the captain was about to hang up, Jack quickly left his number. "Call me if you think of anything else. Anything at all."

The connection went dead. On the spreadsheet, Jack circled Jacob's name. He tapped the pen on his desktop.

It was going on three weeks since the shooting and all they had were two leads. Michael Fuller, small time GTA guy who was MIA, and now Steven Jacobs, a freighter captain whose link to the incident was shaky at best. It wasn't much to go on.

Maybe it was time to try something different.

CHAPTER 8

"We should go to The Point together, you and me," Jack said to Beth over dinner. "We can take a video camera, record everything I would have seen that morning. Except we'll do it later in the day when the light's better. We'll view it frame by frame. Maybe we can figure out who was out there that morning and what the hell they were up to. Dave can manage the store."

Beth put her fork down. "Are you nuts? You're just getting your strength back and you want to go trapesing out in the fridged cold for a two mile walk along the shore? Jack, sometimes I…"

"We wouldn't be walking. Frank Packard's going to loan us his snowmobile."

"Well, that would make it doable, but why on earth do you want to do such a thing? What do you think we'll find after all this time?" She picked up her fork and stabbed a carrot.

"I think Brewster and the boys might have missed something. Yes, I know it's a long shot but I need to find out what happened out there, who called me and why I was shot."

"I thought the FBI was handling things."

"No, not anymore. And Brewster hasn't turned up much." Jack shook his head. "All I know is, it's bugging the hell out of me. I have to do *something*. I have to go out there, and I need you to come with me."

She met his eyes. She smiled as she chewed. "I heard about Frank's snowmobile. It's top of the line."

"All the comforts. Heated seats too."

"Glass of wine by the fireplace when we get back?"

"Cheese and crackers if you want."

She brought another carrot to her lips. "When are we going?"

The November Plot

Jack smiled. "Nine tomorrow morning. I've already got his snowmobile outside on a flatbed hitched up to my cruiser."

They dressed in cold weather gear, took the departmental video cam, and started out in the cruiser, Frank's trailer rattling behind. "You stopped at Carla's that morning, right?" she asked, camera on him as he drove.

"You don't have to record everything."

"I think we should record everything you did that morning. You never know what might be important. So do it, pull in here."

He sighed but complied. "This is nuts." He returned Carla's confused wave through the window.

"Anything out of the ordinary about her that morning?"

"Out of the ordinary? Like what? Come on, Beth, we're talking about Carla for God's sake."

"Okay, okay, I just wanted to get her in frame." She gave Carla a wave as he pulled out. "Maybe I am getting a little anal about this."

"You think?"

"Did you make any other stops?"

"No."

"See anyone walking the street?"

"No."

He drove to where he'd parked his car that morning. Two other cars he didn't recognize were already there, their owners likely kicking back with a brew or two among the shanties that dotted the ice shelf. Further out, white caps topped the blue waves of Lake Superior.

They zipped up their parkas and tied their hoods tight. They off loaded the snowmobile, and started out. From behind, Beth leaned into him, holding on. "It takes a while for the heated seats to kick in," he shouted over the buzz of the engine.

"What?"

He shook his head. His eyes were on the shoreline that curled into the distance. It was strange being out here again, reliving that morning.

From the corner of his eye, he saw Beth working the camera, panning and adjusting as they bounced along.

"You didn't see anything yet?" she asked shouting directly into his ear.

He shook his head, slowing then stopping. He extended his arm toward the shoreline ahead. "That's the spot out there. We're about halfway to it."

"You couldn't see the freighter from here?"

The wind bit the skin of his face like it had that morning. "It was dark. I could barely see my own feet."

"Your back's bothering you," she said.

Jack hadn't realized he'd been rubbing the base of his spine. "No, I'm good."

They started out again. Through his spine, he could feel every bump as they raced along. Maybe this hadn't been such a good idea. But he wasn't about to turn back.

He kept going for another few minutes then stopped. He started recognizing things. Beth had the camera on him. He pointed to the ice. "This is where I saw the freighter. It couldn't have been more than eighty yards out. Well, maybe a little more."

Beth panned the camera in that direction. "Any markings, flags, lights, anything unusual about it?"

"Just that it was in so close. I was surprised that there really *was* something going on here. I wondered how that guy who called me knew about it. I still wonder about that."

"And you can't remember anything specific about the freighter?"

"Reddish hull, sterncastle type. She was big but not like some. I already told Brewster that."

"And that's all you remember about it?"

"It was dark. And it was snowing."

"Did you hear anything? Its engines?"

"No, the wind was gusting, the freighter was dark and still. At least when I first saw it. I had the feeling it had been there a while. I was so surprised to see it, I just stared for a while. That's when I heard the commotion along the shore."

The November Plot

"What exactly did you hear?" She prompted, holding the camera steady, on him.

"There was a rattling. And a sharp, scraping sound." Jack took a moment to look around and get his bearings. "Yeah, the sounds were coming from out there." He pointed.

She aimed the camera in that direction. "And you walked closer."

"Yes, I walked closer. I went up to..." he spotted the boulder and walked to it. "I took cover here, trying to see what was going on."

"And..."

"Three men were struggling with something heavy. I couldn't see what it was. I thought they were trying to get something ashore, you know, like you'd expect if they were smugglers. But then I saw they were trying to get it out to the freighter. They were sliding it along, over the rough ice, having a tough time of it."

"You said they were boxes."

"Yeah, heavy boxes."

"Did the men say anything? Were they talking?"

Jack shook his head, immersed in that moment. He could almost see them, pulling, pushing their load. Desperate. "They were in a hurry. That's when I radioed Sharon."

"And you asked for backup."

"Not yet." Jack ignored her disapproving grimace. "I told Sharon what was going closer and that I'd get back to her if I needed help. I signed off. The wind wasn't as bad that morning as it is now but it was colder and the snow was coming down pretty good."

Beth kept the camera on him as he retraced the path he'd taken. He walked past the boulder, further along the shore to where the tree line jutted out. He talked to the camera over his shoulder as he went. "By this time, I had my gun drawn. I was trying to play it safe. I really was, Beth." He stopped near the trees where the snow drifted high. "Right here. This is where my radio went off. It had to be Sharon, checking up on me again. Anyway, the men on the ice stopped. They must have heard the

54

radio. Yeah, this is the spot. And this is where I saw another guy. He surprised me. He was only a few feet away. It was like he appeared out of nowhere."

"So, there were four men altogether."

"Right. And this guy had a gun ready, aimed directly at me. My gun hand was down. There was no time to raise it and fire."

"Did you say anything? Did he say anything?"

"No. I did the only thing I could. I turned and ran, trying to take cover in the woods. I almost made it. Over there is where I fell."

"Where was this fourth guy standing?"

Jack pointed.

Beth shifted the camera to that spot. "Was he dressed like the others?"

Jack thought about that. "No, he was dressed differently. Heavy parka, hood tight. I don't know what the others wore."

"Any distinguishing features? Would you recognize him if you saw him?"

"My eyes were on the gun he held. I remember him jumping back as if he was as surprised to see me as I was to see him. My only hope was to run right along here." For a moment, Jack forgot about the cold. He winced as the whole thing played out in his head: The blast of the gun, the piercing pain of the bullet, his body, as if it were someone else's, flying, hitting the snow hard. "This is where I fell."

Beth kept the camera on him.

Jack turned, looking along the shore from where they'd come. He took a step into the woods, then walked further.

"Where are you going? We should be getting back," shouted Beth.

"I know. But hold on. Let me check something." He walked ten paces, stopped, then ten more, sidestepping stumps and snowdrifts. He could make out the clearing where the two track was. "That must be where Bob and Ron found the truck," he shouted back. Hands on hips, he turned toward Beth. The trees hid her from view. It was as if he were alone. The wind whistled.

Tree limbs fifty feet up swayed and rustled, shedding snow and ice in the gusts.

The snow drifted feet deep in some spots while, in others, the frozen ground lay completely bare. He started back to Beth, taking a different route, eyes on the patches of bare earth. He was nearly to her when he spotted something.

"Come on, Jack," said Beth, taking a few steps toward him. "I think we've been out here long enough."

"Hold on." He took a knee. He pulled aside some frozen brush under which driftwood lay scattered among the trees. Most were rough branches but, some...were not.

Beth tromped out, camera on him as he worked. "Did you find something?"

"Don't know," he said, pulling out a few splintered lengths of wood.

"Kindling from a campfire."

He shook his head. "Maybe. But out here by the trees, well, it's a funny place for a campfire."

"I can't feel my toes, Jack. And Frank's heated seats are for shit. Let's get going."

With his gloved fingers numb from the cold, Jack picked up the larger pieces of wood. Though grayed with age, they came up easily as if they hadn't been there long. He carried them in the crook of his arm and hurried to catch up with Beth who'd apparently lost interest in videography and was already back by the snowmobile.

CHAPTER 9

Three hours later, Jack awoke to the crackling of shifting logs in the fireplace. The shades were pulled against the afternoon sun and except for the flickering glow of the fire, their small living room was dark. He lay under a blanket, cushioned by a bed of lumpy pillows. Beside him Beth breathed softly, still asleep. But for the wool socks she always wore to bed she was naked, as was he, their bodies spent by the intensity of their lovemaking. The enormous release of tension had brought him the warmth and calm he remembered from the early days of their marriage. After so many years, their lovemaking had gotten routine, mundane even. He'd thought the long ago days of youthful thrills and sensations had been long lost. He'd been wrong.

Gently, he ran a hand over the curve of her hip, slowly up to the side of her face that lay partly covered by strands of hair. He stroked them aside and kissed her cheek. He felt her smile.

"It's almost worth freezing my butt off to be here now with you."

"Almost?"

"I'm pretty hard to please, you know."

He passed on the obvious counter quip and kissed her lips, softly at first then more aggressively, his renewed yearning for her surprised him, building inside. Could he really go again?

Hell yes!

It was six o'clock by the time they got off the floor. "We should eat," he said as they dressed.

"I should check the store. Dave's been alone all day."

"Poor fella," said Jack. "I'll make us a plate of eggs. If you're really worried about him you can take some down."

"He'll be fine. He pilfers Little Debbie's off the shelf all the time." She gave him a kiss. "How about some bacon? There's some in the fridge."

"As you wish, my sweet."

She smiled. "You haven't called me that in a long time." She started down the stairs as he pulled out a frying pan and found the spatula.

Soon the smells of breakfast filled the kitchen.

"It was a slow day for Dave," she explained as they ate. "Maxine Thompson's on the pill now."

With Beth's pharmacy being the only game in town, she knew everybody's secrets. And so did Dave. "You shouldn't be telling people things like that."

"I'm not telling people. I'm telling you."

"Do her parents know?"

"Probably not." She took a bite of toast. "Must be tough having daughters." She chewed thoughtfully. "I feel like we made one today."

"Made what? A daughter?"

"A baby, Jack. Our baby. Yes, I really feel like we did."

Jack put down his fork. "You can't really tell, can you?"

"No, not really. I won't know if I'm pregnant for a couple of weeks. It's just a feeling." She dabbed her lips with her napkin. "It was really great, Jack."

"Yeah, me too."

"Thanks for the perfect breakfast. How's about I do the dishes while you sort through that pile of wood you found. You can do it in the laundry room so you won't make a mess. Or you can use the wood to build up the fire."

"You think it's a waste of time."

She stood and gave him a light kiss on the cheek. "Maybe."

Beside the dryer, he set up a folding table and put down a towel. He gathered up the wood. In all, there were eight pieces. Each piece was darkened by mud and damp from the snow and ice melting off. Jack looked them over. The front and back faces were smooth, edges splintered.

With a dry rag and a coarse brush, he cleaned off the dirt. Some smeared, working its way deeper into the grain of the wood. On the smooth surfaces, darker areas appeared. Some of the pieces seemed as though they might fit together. That was interesting.

"I've got something that might help," said Beth, surprising him from behind. She left, returning with a can. She unscrewed the top. "You sprinkle this powder over the surface then, rub it off. The dirt will stick to the powder leaving the wood clean."

He tried some. "Seems to work," he said, not really encouraged. Beth left then returned later in her nightgown. "Anything interesting?" she said.

"I'm about to find out." He arranged the pieces, lining up two of them having a single smoothed edge parallel to each other. "It's like they were once part of something."

"Like part of one of the boxes those men were carrying? Is that what you're thinking?"

"Yeah. What would the odds of that be?"

"Slim to none."

Jack set up a floor lamp. Under the light he gently nudged the pieces of wood closer together where a dark splotch was. He shook his head. "There's no pattern that I can see."

"Maybe you're looking at the wrong side."

One by one, Jack turned the pieces over, then refit them. He stared at a blackened area centered where the two pieces fit together. He poured more of Beth's powder over it working it this time with a moist rag.

"It's got some lines to it," said Beth leaning over his shoulder, her warm breath on his ear. He kept rubbing then dropped the rag. He pulled her close. he pressed his lips hard against hers.

"Am I distracting you, sheriff?"

"Yes, you are."

"Just like the scene from *Ghost*...except with these pieces of splintered wood...and a little role reversal. You gotta love that movie."

"It's a sideways diamond with some letters in the middle. *M. F.* and *I*. I think it *is* a logo. Like a brand, burned into the wood."

Beth stared then pulled her phone. She adjusted the light and took a picture. "I know this website," she explained thumbing the phone. "Did you know there's a way to check out any business logo and get the company's backstory and...my God. Here it is."

"You are more of a nerd than even I knew," said Jack, impressed as she handed him the phone. He read the screen. "Mayfield Industries. It was a company based in Cadillac, Michigan. Out of business now. It says they did work for the OSS."

"What's the OSS?"

Jack shook his head. "I suppose we should look that up too." He scrolled down. "It says there was a fire that shut the doors back in '97. But that's it. Oh, here's a photograph taken back in 1954, I guess at the founding of the company. A few guys standing in front of a small industrial building."

"It's still a stretch to think this wood came from one of the crates you saw being loaded onto that freighter."

"Yeah, but if it is, this might be the best evidence we've got."

"Brewster and your guys should've found it."

"The spot was off into the woods. With the swirling wind, it could have been hidden by the snow when they looked, then unhidden by the wind when we looked. We just got lucky."

"So, what do we do about it?"

"I think I'll drive down to Houghton tomorrow. It's time the chief and I had a little face to face about this whole thing. I've been doing some other digging too so..."

"What other digging?"

"Mostly about the freighter and the truck that was out there. Haven't found anything solid yet but maybe we can piece things together with what Brewster knows. They also have a crime lab there." He printed out a copy of the photo then handed her phone back. "It's late now but I'll call the chief on the way.

"You can also drop off Frank's snowmobile. Tell him thanks but his heated seats don't work."

"I'll be sure to let him know."

CHAPTER 10

The next morning Jack tossed the pieces of wood from the shore into the trunk of his police cruiser. Without bothering to wake Frank, he dropped off the snowmobile and started for Houghton. He hadn't done much driving since the shooting. It felt good to be behind the wheel again, cold but the sun was shining. There was no snow in the forecast and no traffic to speak of.

After a few miles, he called Sharon and let her know what he was up to then glanced at his watch. He'd have time for breakfast in Houghton before meeting up with the chief. Sure, why not? He'd check in with Brewster from there. Waffles sounded good.

He tuned the radio to an oldies station and was about to turn up the volume when an engine revved from behind.

The grill of a black sedan filled his rearview. Where'd he come from? And what kind of dumbass would tailgate a cop?

The sedan swerved, straddling the centerline. Jack craned his neck to get a visual on the driver. He saw two men—and a rifle.

At a gunshot, Jack's rear window exploded in a storm of glass pellets. The sedan roared, trying to pass. Jack gripped the wheel and floored the accelerator. Heart pounding, he eyed the road ahead. A turn was coming up. He'd never hold the road at this speed. He shouted into his shoulder mic. "Officer under fire. Officer under fire."

Jack pulled his gun. He lowered his window. He fired wildly.

The black car raced alongside. Jack fired again, unsure if he hit anything. The attacking car swerved but kept pace.

The turn was coming up fast—too fast.

Jack cut the wheel. His tires screeched. At another shot, Jack's windshield blew out.

The cold wind hit him like a brick wall.

The sedan slammed sideways into Jack's car. The steering wheel jerked from his grip. The wooden guardrail whizzed by, his car careening toward it. Jack slammed on the breaks. His cruiser tilted up, doing a wild one eighty. As if shot from a cannon, it caught the guardrail and sailed through the air.

For a series of long, surreal seconds, Jack held onto the wheel, his car airborne. The sun circled his car once, then twice.

With a crunch, the two passenger side wheels hit the slope of an embankment. His spine took the brunt of the blow. Pain blazed. The car tumbled backward downhill, gaining speed.

Heart in his throat, Jack realized he was tumbling down the slope that bordered Lake Medora. Shit! He had no time. He fumbled with his seatbelt. He freed himself. He held tight to the wheel. Hurtling backwards, all he could see through what was once his windshield was a blur of branches and blue sky. He felt the rear of his car hitting the trees, but not slowing. He had to jump.

He pulled the doorhandle, held his breath and pushed the door open a crack. He shouldered it further. It caught on something. It flew open, yanking him with it like he'd been flung by a catapult.

He hit the snow hard. Shoulder over shoulder he rolled, as much sideways as downhill. He pulled his knees against his chest, tumbling, rolling. His breath left him. He squeezed his eyes shut. He shielded his face with his arms. The crack of a dozen saplings slowed him until finally, he stopped. Everything was quiet.

Jack opened his eyes. His car was nowhere in sight. He lay in deep snow, his back against a tree. Everything was quiet. He looked around for his gun and, amazingly, saw it lying in the snow only a few feet away.

He tried to move. Yeah, legs were okay. That was good. He tasted blood. Cracked rib, punctured lung? Yeah, bad but not life threatening, right?

He crawled over and grabbed his gun then maneuvered himself into a sitting position. He looked upslope. Whoever had forced him off the road would still be up there. Even now they might be on their way down to see if he was alive. But he had his gun, and he had the cover of the brush around him. Yeah, he would see them before they saw him.

Come on, you bastards. *Come on!*

No one came.

His shoulder radio was gone. He checked for his phone—gone.

Birds chirped over the sound of the wind in the trees. It was bitter cold and he had no gloves. He had to get moving.

Jack managed to get to his feet. Bent like an old man, he leaned against the trunk of a tree. He looked down toward the iced over lake, its edge no more than twenty feet away. He'd jumped just in time. Yeah, *Lucky Jack,* they'll be calling him at the Lodge—if he ever made it back.

He could see the path his car had blazed, sliding down the slope. But there was no sign of the car itself. Further down, beyond where he could see, it must have hit the ice and plunged through.

He looked upslope again. Snow, leaves, fallen branches and patches of withered brush covered the ground between the trees. The trees themselves were mostly saplings. He remembered there had been a fire in this area a few years back. Some fool campers had left a fire going down on the shore that had spread and taken down much of the older growth. Had his car plunged into those older trees he'd probably be lying dead, still behind the wheel of his car. Or maybe the airbag would have saved him. Or maybe...

He brought a hand to his eyes. He had to focus.

It would be easier to go down the slope to the lake where an ice fisherman might spot him. Or, he could go up and flag down the next driver that came along. Yeah, that was his best bet. But what if the gunmen were still up there?

Well, that's what the gun was for.

At another deep, painful breath, he started up.

The going was slow. He had no feeling in his feet or hands. He angled his path back and forth resting at the switch backs, leaning heavily against the saplings to keep from sliding back. At those times he looked up toward the road discouraged at how little progress he was making while at the same time relieved to not see anyone up there pointing a gun down at him.

Then, a little more than halfway up, he heard someone calling to him. A woman. Sharon? No. But the voice was familiar.

"Sheriff? Sheriff. Can you make it up? I don't have a rope but…"

She sounded like she was there to help. Or was she with the guys who'd forced him off the road? Did she want him to reveal himself so she could get a clear shot? He looked up through the trees. He could make her out. A black form leaning over the broken guardrail, looking down at him from the shoulder of the road. "Who are…"

"It's Cooper. Come on. You've got to climb up. We can't stay…Shit. Okay, I'm coming down."

Slipping and sliding, she kept her footing and made it down to him. "You look like hell," she said.

Jackson rubbed his eyes. He thought maybe he was dreaming. "What are you doing here?"

"I'll explain later. Come on we have to get moving." She grabbed onto his belt, pulling as they went, one step at a time. Jack hobbled along, bent, gasping all the way. His chest blazed with pain.

He staggered over the guardrail and fell onto the road. Cooper pulled him up. "Not a good place to rest, sheriff." With a grunt, she pulled him up.

Jack cried out as she helped him into the back seat of a car.

She slammed the door shut. Jack heard her get into the driver's seat. Felt her pull onto the road, then accelerate. He remained curled up on his side, resting. As long as he didn't move, the pain was blunted. He slowed his breathing. From the sound of it, she had her heater on full blast but he felt no warmth. He was cold, shivering.

"We're going back to town, right?" he asked after a few miles.

"I think you have a cracked rib, might just be a fracture or a bad bruise. I'm no medic. Oh, and you've been shot. I was going to take you to the hospital in Houghton, then I had this idea."

"I've been shot?"

"Just a flesh wound. Ha, always wanted to say that. Compared to what you've been through, trust me sheriff, it's nothing. And the cold is keeping the bleeding down."

"We're not going to the hospital?"

"I've got a first aid kit. I'll get you fixed up. Don't worry."

CHAPTER 11

Jack winced at the alcohol-soaked cotton ball being dabbed and dragged across the spot where a bullet had creased his shoulder.

"Another couple of inches either way and this might have been serious," said Cooper. She pulled his shirt further down his arm. "You should probably have stiches but, if you don't mind having a nice manly scar on your shoulder, I think some ointment and butterfly stickers will do fine."

Jack sat on the edge of an unmade bed, Cooper standing beside him. He grit his teeth as she worked, trying to focus on the painting of a farmhouse that hung on the pine paneled wall of Cooper's motel room. "Are you sure you know what you're doing?"

Cooper ignored the question. "Somebody wants you dead."

"Yeah, I figured that."

"They think you know something. What might that be?"

"I don't know." He kept his eyes on the farmhouse. On its porch an old woman sat, a dog at her feet. The warmth of Cooper's hands felt good on his skin as did the coolness of the cream she applied. He flinched as she pinched the wound closed.

"Sorry. I don't do this every day of the week you know. Almost done. Just getting these butterflies on, then a bandage over that and you'll be as good as new."

"Except for the broken rib you mean?"

"Let's hope that's just a fracture. I read somewhere that those kind of heal themselves."

"Coffee?" she asked him, once she'd finished.

Jack checked out her repair job in the mirror. "Thanks. Looks like you know what you're doing." Gingerly, he shifted his shirt back but left it hang open. "Yeah...coffee would be good."

She poured one for each of them, then sat in the stuffed chair just below the painting. She took a sip, eyes on Jack over the rim of her Styrofoam cup. "You've been investigating," she said.

Jack put his cup down. "I don't know what you're talking about."

"I'm not stupid."

"Neither am I. I know you've been suspended from the FBI."

This raised a dismissive smile. "That's a temporary thing. You've been looking into me and you've been looking into Michael Fuller."

"He was out on the shore that morning. He was the one who stole that Silverado."

"You also called a freighter captain named Jacobs."

"You've been listening in on my phone conversations."

"Come on, sheriff. You of all people should know there's no such thing as a private phone call."

Jack held his stare. "You should bring Jacobs in for questioning. He knows more than he's willing to say."

"Your call to Jacobs is what triggered that dust-up this morning."

"It was his ship, the *Kingslip* that I saw that morning."

"You're wrong about that. I'm pretty sure Jacobs doesn't have anything to do with what's going on, but he knows people who do. He must have told them about you poking around, asking questions." She walked to the window, pulled the curtain aside, glanced out, then turned to Jack. "The freighter you saw that morning was the *Endeavor*."

Jack stiffened. "That ship didn't show up on the sat pics."

"That's right, it didn't."

"What makes you so sure..."

"It was the *Endeavor*. That's all you need to know. The other day at your office, I was trying to protect you. The more you know the greater the danger you're in. Case in point, the little set-to you had this morning." She paused. "Where were you off to this morning?"

"I was going to meet with Chief Brewster."

"Does he know you were on your way to see him?"

"No but, with you being suspended and all, maybe I should be talking to your boss in Duluth."

This got a satisfying start out of Cooper. "Let me remind you, it was *me* who rescued you this morning. Trust me, you do not want my boss or anyone in the Duluth office involved in this. At least not now."

"Why is that?"

"Let's just say, I don't want them getting in the way." She retook her chair. It groaned softly as she leaned closer. "I'm on your side, sheriff and I just saved your life. I would think that'd give me a little credibility."

Jack took another sip of coffee. Warming his hands with it. "Okay. Thanks for saving my life, for patching me up, and for sharing at least some information." He put down the cup and began buttoning his shirt. "Now, I think it's time for me to head back home."

Cooper shook her head. "Sorry, that is one thing that is *not* happening. You just went to a lot of trouble staging your own death. Even if you'd planned it, you couldn't have given a more convincing performance."

"What are you getting at?"

"You just drowned in a frozen lake. Sure, your car is going to be pulled out and they're not going to find your body inside. But that'll take time."

"They'll see my tracks coming back up. Yours too."

"Your car tore the hell out of that embankment on its way down. The ground's frozen. No one's going to find any evidence that you made it back up or that you had help. Besides, any investigation into what really happened will be a long, dragged-out affair. That will give us the time we need."

"Time to do what?"

"Time for us to figure out who's behind all this and maybe, time enough to stop them from whatever the hell it is they're up to."

Jack shook his head. "That's not going to work."

"Why?"

"I can't have my wife thinking I'm dead. I *won't* have her thinking I'm dead. She's been through enough already."

Cooper went silent for a while. "Maybe we should…" She took another swallow of coffee. "We'll take her with us."

"What the hell are you talking about? I'm not going anywhere with you. And what do you mean, take her with us? My wife you mean? No. We are not doing that."

"We can't stay here. And you can't go home. If you do, they'll try to kill you again. They failed twice. They won't fail again. And, you know…taking her with us might be best anyway."

"I don't want her put in danger."

"She's already in danger. If they ever figure out you're still alive, their next step will be to abduct her to get to you. Anybody who knows anything about this thing is in danger. Now, did anyone besides your wife know you were going to Houghton?"

"Sharon knows. She's my—"

"I know who she is. Did she know you were going alone?"

"She probably assumed I was going alone but…oh shit! You want people to believe that my wife and I both drowned in that lake?"

"You're a little slow picking up on that, sheriff. But yeah, I'm really starting to warm up to this idea. It's tragic, I know, and all your friends will be sad but…oh well. Small price to pay if it keeps you both alive."

"The gunmen in the car will know that I was alone."

Cooper, rubbed her jaw. "Maybe not. Lots of confusion in a gunfight. Your wife would have ducked, you might have heroically shielded her."

"You're nuts."

Cooper smiled. "Yeah, I get that a lot." She checked the time then stood. She started putting on her coat. "It's still early. You're going to stay here. You're going to stay out of sight. You will not go out that door. If your phone rings, you are not going to answer it. You are dead! Got that?"

"I lost my phone. It's probably in the cruiser."

"Good. Now, I need something of yours so I can let her know she can trust me."

"How can I do that when I don't even trust you."

"Damn-it, we do not have time for this. Give me something. Write her a love note. I don't care. Anything!"

From his shirt pocket, Jack pulled out the Mayfield printout. He wrote a quick note on the back, folded it over twice and handed it to Cooper. "Give her this. She'll know it's from me."

She snatched it from him and left.

Alone in the motel room Jack tried to relax. He noted the letterhead on the desk stationary: *Pine Gap Motel*. He sat on the bed, watched TV and drank more coffee. He watched the clock and worried. Two hours went by before he heard a key working the lock on the door. He stood.

Cooper ushered Beth quicky inside, then locked the door. Through her open jacket he saw she still had her white lab coat on. Her eyes went wide when she saw him. "What the hell, Jack?"

He stepped closer. He placed a hand on her shoulder. "Sorry, Beth. It's best this way."

"What's best this way? What the hell is going on here?"

"Maybe you'd like some coffee?" suggested Cooper.

"Sorry, I drank the last of it," said Jack.

Beth glared, a volcano about to blow.

"All right. I'll explain," said Jack.

"He was shot then run off the road," said Cooper, clearly trying to move things along.

"My God, Jack, you almost died...again?"

"Yeah. It was another close one," he explained. "That's why we thought it was best that..."

"So now everybody will think we're both dead? That's the plan? You want it to look like we drowned in the lake. Hell! Are you crazy?"

"It was sort of your husband's idea to bring you here," said Cooper. "He didn't want you thinking he was dead."

Beth glared. "Thanks a lot for that, Jack."

"Would you really rather be back home, in danger, *and* thinking I was dead?"

"What? No, of course not. I'd much rather be here, in danger with you."

"You're not in danger," said Cooper. "Everyone's going to think you're dead—both of you."

"What about Sharon?" said Beth. "Does she think we're dead?"

71

"She will. You saw that police car we passed on the side of the road back at the lake. That was probably her."

"They're out there already?" said Jack, impressed.

Beth dropped her hands to her side. She shook her head. "My God. Half an hour ago I was getting ready to open the store. Now...this."

"Yes, and we need to get the hell out of here," said Cooper. "The farther we get from Gull Harbor, the better. We're in the middle of a high stakes gamble that could easily backfire on us."

"I think we have a pretty good idea how high the stakes are, wouldn't you say? It's been *me* they've been trying to kill."

"So, where do we go?" said Beth.

"South, for right now," said Cooper. "We need some time to work things out."

"South! Yeah, great idea. Wish I'd thought of that," said Beth.

"Look, being a cynic is not helping. We've got to get moving. We're all on board with this, right?"

Jack caught Beth's eyes. Neither said a word.

"I'll take that as a yes." Cooper led the way out to her car, a late model Ford SUV. "You get the backseat again sheriff. Keep your head down. We don't want anyone seeing either of you. You're dead. Don't forget that."

"You've been staying at this motel since our meeting with Brewster," said Jack as they piled in.

"Yeah. Glad to be leaving the flea bag place."

Cooper pulled out onto Route 41 heading south.

"We're stopping in Houghton," Beth told Cooper from the shotgun seat. "I need a toothbrush and...some other things. Shit, what a whacked-up way to start the day."

"Okay, we'll stop in Houghton, somewhere off the main drag. After that, we'll put on a few more miles. We can figure things out as we go."

CHAPTER 12

From his seat in the back, Jack watched Beth. She'd said nothing since leaving Houghton where they'd gassed up and bought toothbrushes, snacks and other necessities. She sat stiff and pale, her eyes fixed straight ahead. She hardly even blinked. Jack was glad she was with him and knew he would have been worried sick about her being alone back home thinking he was dead. He wondered what she was thinking now.

The pain in his shoulder started to throb. Then the pain in his chest chimed in. His legs ached from his climb back up to the road.

Driving, Cooper slowed to match the lineup of vehicles ahead. A light snow fell. Jack glanced at Cooper through the rearview. "I think it's time to tell us what you know, Agent Cooper," he said.

"You're going to be disappointed."

"Try us. You can start by telling us how and when you got involved in this whole thing. I'm betting it predates my getting shot...the first time, I mean."

She straightened in her seat. She caught his eyes in the mirror. "About six months ago I took a leave from FBI."

"You were suspended you mean."

"That was a cover story. I needed some time on my own."

"One of those mental health sabbaticals that seem so popular now? I wouldn't have thought the FBI would go for that."

"Don't make fun, Jack," said Beth. "My own mental health isn't so great right now."

"According to Chief Brewster, you got someone killed."

"That's partially true," said Cooper.

"You got someone partially killed?"

"It's complicated. And look, I'm tired. I could do without your smart-ass quips. Do you want to know what's going on or not?"

Beth sighed. "It's his way of dealing with excessive estrogen in a confined space. He'll settle down once you stop setting him up for those not so funny one liners of his."

"Yeah, well neither one of you are very funny right now. It was my partner who died. We were close and...I let her down."

Jack saw her cold expression soften. "I'm sorry. That must have been tough."

"It has nothing to do with what's happening now. But, while I was dealing with that and even considering career moves, I was contacted by someone I knew. He was a guy who'd done some undercover work for us. I once had a relationship with him. He said something big was in the works and he found himself on the inside of it. He had no proof but I took him seriously. He's not the type to make shit up."

"Why tell you? Why didn't he just go to the FBI directly?"

"Like I said, he had no proof. He was afraid for his life. And with a couple of priors on his record, his credibility would have been an issue. He didn't want to be implicated in whatever was going on. He felt he had to tell someone. He trusted me so I'm the one he told. And I believed him."

"So, what did he tell you?" asked Beth.

"Not much. Just that something big was going on and he would be in touch when, and if, things started happening."

"This inside guy," said Jack, "he wouldn't be Captain Jacobs, would he?"

"No."

"Jacobs sounded like he knew something more than he was willing to talk about."

"Yeah, you told me that. And maybe he does know more than I think. Freighter captains belong to a pretty exclusive club. They talk to each other and when they drink, they talk more. Some get careless."

"Who is this undercover guy?" said Beth.

"It's best you don't know. Not right now anyway. Besides, I haven't heard from him in a while."

"You think something happened to him?"

"Yeah. I'm beginning to think so."

"So far you're not doing a very good job of laying your cards out on the table," said Jack. "We're out here with you running for our lives. We deserve to know everything."

Cooper shook her head. "I'm sorry. I should never have gotten you involved in this."

"What do you mean?" said Jack straightening, suddenly stunned. "Wait a minute. That was you who…"

"Yes, I'm the one who called you that morning. I'm the one who got you shot. All of it, all of *this*, is happening to you because of me. My guy on the inside tipped me off that, at that very moment, things were starting to happen on the Keweenaw. He gave me the exact location. I was stuck in Duluth. You were the only law in the area. I needed eyes out there. You were my only option."

"Why did you disguise your voice?"

"I didn't want to reveal my connection with my informant. If you'd just stayed back and watched what was going on like I told you, none of this would be happening."

"You've been playing dumb this whole time. You even tried to get me to believe I'd imagined the whole freighter thing."

"That was for your own good."

The three of them were silent until Beth asked: "Does Mayfield Industries have anything to do with this?"

"Never heard of them."

"It's probably nothing then," said Jack.

"Why'd you ask?"

"Beth and I went out to the Point yesterday to have a look around. You know, to see if we could find anything new. We thought it might jog my memory about what happened. We found some splintered wood with the Mayfield logo on it."

"Wait, that was on the back of the note you had me give your wife."

"It was handy so…"

"That was sweet, Jack," said Beth, turning to him. "Your note, I mean."

"Yes, Jack. It was sweet. Sorry, I peeked. Can't be too careful you know."

"So, you don't know anything about Mayfield?"

"No. But we've got time. Tell me about them."

"It was a business down in the lower peninsula near Cadillac. The place had a fire and was closed down a couple of decades ago. That printout I gave you, the one with my note, had some info on them. Did you read it?"

"I gave it a glance, that's all. Do you still have it?"

Beth pulled it from her pocket and handed it to her as traffic started to move again.

"No, you keep it," Cooper told her. "Read it out loud."

Beth began reading. She'd gotten nearly to the end of the article when Cooper stopped her.

"Hold on. Did you say they did work for the OSS?"

"Is that important?"

"Read that part again."

"...As a research and engineering company, Mayfield Industries started out in the late 1940's doing work for the OSS. From there they..."

"Okay, stop." Cooper pulled her phone. She handed it to Beth. "Take a picture of that page. Flatten it out and get some light on it. Do it right now. We're not far out of Houghton so we should still have some cell coverage out here. I'll pull over first chance. We need to get someone on this right away."

With a hand on the seatback, Jack pulled himself closer. "What's the OSS."

"It's the Office of Strategic Services," said Cooper. "It was a government group back in the forties. They were the CIA before there was a CIA."

CHAPTER 13

Captain Lattimore woke early, showered and dressed. From his fifth-floor hotel room, he looked down at the city, dull, gray and seeming to shiver under the coating of new snow that had fallen through the night.

Duluth in November. Not much to do but eat, drink and sleep and after two days he was tired of all three. He had made a few woman friends over the years here and he'd thought about looking one of them up. Then he thought better of it. He wasn't in the mood. His sex drive wasn't what it used to be. Yes, that was another depressing thought.

Endeavor had been queued up waiting to take on her load of taconite. Today they would finally start loading, and he'd be back aboard. He made a mental note to check the latest weather and ice conditions. It'd be a risky run this late in the season. But he'd done it before; one time as late as early January. This would be his last run, not just for the year, but his last run *ever*. He'd miss working the lakes but right now he just wanted to get on with it. Maybe he'd retire someplace warm.

He elevatored down to the nearly empty breakfast room off the hotel lobby. It was the same buffet food as yesterday and the day before. He was tired of dry scrambled eggs and limp, underdone bacon. This morning, he went with oatmeal, toast and coffee. He sat, sprinkled a little brown sugar onto the oatmeal and dug in.

Up on the flatscreen, CNN delivered the news. Well, they delivered their opinion of the news, then delivered more like minded opinions of it from their panel of so called experts. Some new political scandal, then some revolt or rioting going on in South America. FOX and all the others did the same. All breaking news all the fucking time.

Finished with his oatmeal, Lattimore got a refill of coffee, bit into his toast and looked around the room. By this time the breakfast crowd had swelled to fill maybe half of it. A few of the men he'd seen before. There were a couple of suit and tie types but most, like him, wore flannels, jeans, and work boots.

A woman walked in. She would have been good looking had it not been for her tired eyes and obvious exhaustion at dealing with the two hyperactive kids she had in tow. Lattimore wondered where the dad might be. Alive? Dead? Was she divorced? He guessed the woman to be in her mid-thirties. He watched her fill her kid's plate then get her own food. She'd no sooner sat and managed a sip of coffee when one of the kids spilled his orange juice.

Without batting an eye, the mom got up, wiped up the mess, got the kid another OJ then sat. Yes, everyday grace under pressure. He admired that. Still, he couldn't help also admiring the woman's figure, wondering if she was good in bed. He brought his napkin to his lips. Funny what a decent breakfast can do to your libido.

"Mind if I join you, captain?"

He looked up, startled to see an attractive woman in a business suit, well made up and appearing just in time as if offering a more attractive option to the woman with the kids. But Lattimore knew *this* woman. He knew she was here for a very different reason. Too bad.

He said nothing. He took another sip of coffee.

She put her to go coffee down on the table, tossed her coat onto an empty chair, and sat. He kept his eyes on the mom and kids. Things were relatively peaceful now, the kids occupied with their brightly colored cold cereal.

"You ever have children, captain?" said the woman on the chair beside him.

"No."

"Come now, you should expect by now I know everything about you."

"Then why ask the question?"

"Because I think you're protecting someone."

Lattimore locked eyes with her. Katerina Sokolov, pretty as ever. "I don't know what you're talking about."

She shrugged, "All right, have it your way."

"Why are you here?"

"Just making sure things go smoothly."

"Say what you need to say then leave. You don't need to be here. Everything's in order. Nothing will go wrong."

"But if something does go wrong...Or what is more likely, if you *make* something go wrong, what then?"

"Why would I do that?" Even as he fought to contain his anger, he had to admit, Katerina was the same beautiful, seductive woman he'd once thought he loved. Even now, he felt the urge to get her into his bed, tear off her clothes, and fuck her senseless. Yeah, maybe his sex drive was having itself a little renaissance. Had it really been five years since that first time with her? Back then, at least on his part, it had been an act of desperate need, even an act of love. Now it would be an act of hate with a little revenge mixed in.

"What is it you are thinking?" she said through a knowing smile.

"Nothing will go wrong."

"That's good to hear. Because, if something does go wrong, we will take what's ours then sink your ship. We'll make certain there are no survivors. I suppose it will be some consolation that your ship might one day be famous, like the *Edmund Fitsgerald*. You all will die a terrible death but...maybe they'll sing songs about you."

"I've spent years cooperating with your syndicate. If you can't trust me by now, that's your problem, not mine." Her seductive black eyes bore into his. He wanted to bend her over the table and...

"I remember our first meeting." She smiled. "I remember it fondly. You were younger, stronger...more virile than now I suspect."

"You were a good lay, nothing more."

"In all modesty, I was an *exceptional* lay. And you were, I'll admit, better than average." She took a sip from her coffee. She shifted her eyes to the TV. "Our deal was that we would use your ship to move certain materials from one place to another. We would pay you handsomely for that service. You would not interfere and you would ask no questions. You would not know or question what our cargo was or where it was hidden aboard your ship. You've profited handsomely from that arrangement."

"Yes, I have."

"And this will be the last shipment required of you."

Lattimore forced a thin smile. "Ah, that's why you're here. You're planning a retirement party for me."

"Do not take me lightly, captain. That man, the sheriff, the one your men should have killed out on the Keweenaw, he is dead. We killed him and we killed his wife. We will not hesitate to kill again."

She paused, as if a new question had occurred to her. "How is it he knew to be out that morning at that particular time and place? I've concluded that...well, we'll call her a good friend of yours, may have had something to do with that."

"I don't know what you're talking about. I had no idea that fool would be there."

"Maybe not. But I will bet *she* did."

"If I had the guts, if I really wanted to put a stop to what you and your syndicate are up to, I'd run my ship aground and go public with what I know."

Katerina crossed her legs and shook her head. A few strands of hair fell across her forehead. She brushed them aside and leaned closer. He could smell her perfume. "I know you to be a practical man and, really captain, you don't know that much about us. If you do go to the authorities, it will be you and some of your shipmates who will be going to prison, not me." She drilled her stare into his eyes. "This will be your last job. I promise you that. Once done, you can wash your hands of us and enjoy what you Americans euphemistically call your golden years." She leaned closer and, as if smitten by his dignified good looks, kissed his cheek.

She smiled. "Maybe I *will* throw a retirement party for you. We could end our relationship with a good fuck. Would that interest you?" She extended her hand, brushing her palm lightly over the side of his face. "You may have lost some of your virility, captain, but you still have your rugged good looks. I'd hate to see you lying at the bottom of the lake, ending up as nothing more than food for the fish."

"Worm food, fish food, what does it matter?"

"Getting philosophical, are we?"

Lattimore grabbed her hand, eyes on hers. He squeezed until she flinched then released it.

Katerina flexed her fingers. She used her other hand to take another sip of coffee. "Did that make you feel better, captain?"

"Yes, it did."

She checked her watch and stood, grabbing her coat. "Too bad we don't have time for more...fun."

"I agree."

"You leave port later today?"

"Yes."

"Good, you are on schedule. Please see that you remain on schedule. I will meet with you again at the mills in Detroit. Have a pleasant voyage, captain."

Lattimore watched her leave. She'd left her coffee behind. The smear of lipstick on its rim reminded him of her kiss. He ran a knuckle over his cheek. He tossed her cup out with the rest of his breakfast garbage and went up to his room. Too bad about the sheriff and his wife, he thought as he packed.

Three hours later Lattimore stood on the bridge of *Endeavor*. As the loading operation continued, he eyed the alignment of the on shore conveyor relative to the row of open cargo hatches. The steady streams of taconite rumbled aboard. Errors in alignment were rare but they were known to happen. He saw no problem today.

"Eyes on the ballast and trim, Mr. Sullivan," he ordered, trusting his XO to make sure uneven loading would not cause catastrophic stresses to the hull.

"All good, captain," responded Sullivan watching the ballast indicators. He gave a glance now and then to the bank of lights ashore that would also warn of problems.

Through a veil of yet more snow, Lattimore watched the operation as did a handful of his crew on the deck below. Each was ready to take action should anything go awry. Each wore heavy orange work coveralls making them nearly indistinguishable from one another. But yes, there was Davis holding his clipboard and Carter pacing as he always did. Lattimore knew his crew as much by the way they carried themselves as by their faces.

The loading process was nearly all automatic. The tons of taconite, destined for the blast furnaces of Detroit, would be smelted down and refined into steel eventually enjoying a brief period of usefulness as cars and appliances. Some of it would become the strong bones of buildings and bridges enjoying much longer periods of lifelike usefulness. But all of it would one day wear and rust and return to the ground perhaps to be re-mined and re-fashioned to again serve some useful purpose.

Lattimore shook his head. Katerina had been right. He found himself falling into these meaning of life, philosophical funks more often these days. But there was good reason. This was his last voyage. His useful life, if he could really call it that, would soon be at an end. How quickly it had all gone by.

The sun was nearing the horizon by the time loading was complete. The hatch covers were replaced and *Endeavor's* unloading boom was swung back into position and secured.

"Ready the engines, Mr. Sullivan," ordered Lattimore, with naval firmness.

"Aye, sir."

From below the waterline, *Endeavor*'s engines rumbled to life, gave a cough, then steadied out, idling. Lattimore could feel them through his feet. As like incense in a church, he took in the smells of oil and smoke.

The visiting pilot familiar with the harbor waters stood at the helm. This man, a new man whose name Lattimore couldn't recall, rested his hands on the controls. "Helm ready, captain," he said.

Lattimore opened the hatch and walked to the rail. The wind had picked up. He spoke into the radio mic: "Prepare to cast the lines."

Lattimore checked the harbor tower, saw the green light and stepped back inside. "Signal to cast off," he said.

"Helm ready, cast lines," said the pilot.

At the sharp sound of the deck alarm, the lines were cast, freeing the vessel from the loading dock.

With that, the pilot took over the ship. Using bow thrusters in tandem with the azimuth thrusters at the stern, *Endeavor* moved clear of the dock.

Lattimore watched the process, satisfied the pilot knew what he was doing. He took one more look at the control tower. He was surprised to see a man with binoculars standing there, staring back directly at him. Lattimore held the man's gaze then touched his cap. Here in Duluth, he had many dockside friends. Had the man been one of them, the fellow might have returned the gesture. This man did not.

The steel harbor bridge at the entrance to the harbor lifted. On passing beneath it, *Endeavor* gained speed between the breakwaters and moved past the dual lighthouses.

"The helm is yours, captain. Safe sailing to you," said the Pilot. "Looks like you'll be heading into a light chop with the wind at your stern. Mind the ice."

Lattimore thanked him and, as was customary, the two shook hands. To ignore that tradition was considered bad luck.

The pilot left the bridge and moments later, emerged on deck. Lattimore watched him make his way down the pilot's ladder then nimbly stepped off onto the pilot's boat running alongside at matched speed. The small boat veered off back into the harbor as the sun set over the Duluth skyline. At Lattimore's order, *Endeavor* kicked up to running speed, sailing east into the open waters of Lake Superior. She carried 30,000 tons of taconite ore and she carried...something else.

Later that night Lattimore stood alone in his cabin. He slid the wall photograph aside, and from the safe pulled out the cell phone. As he'd done back off the Keweenaw, he pressed the single letter *G* then hit *Send*. He waited for the *Delivered* prompt. He was about to place the phone back in the safe when he heard a beep. Probably just an acknowledgment he assumed until he checked the screen and read the terse message:

Extraction at Delta

It was the first piece of good news he'd had in a very long time.

CHAPTER 14

Jack had been half asleep for the past hour trying to ignore the conversation between Beth and Cooper. The occasional swerve over the slick road didn't help his nerves. He sat up, rubbed his eyes and watched the tall pines roll by. It was one of those cold, cloudy winter days where, like an old-time movie, there was no color, only shades of blacks and whites. "Where are we, Cooper?" he asked, catching her eyes in the rearview.

"About an hour from the bridge," she said, referring to the five-mile long Mackinaw bridge connecting Michigan's upper peninsula to the lower.

"We're going to Cadillac," said Beth.

"So, you and Cooper talked it over while I was asleep?"

"My name's Maddison. Call me Maddie."

"Okay then, Maddie. I'm stumped. Why are we going to Cadillac? Wait, is this about Mayfield?"

"Yes, while you were dozing...Jack, I got an email via a secure router from my guy in Duluth." Keeping her eyes mostly on the road, she brought it up on her phone and handed it to him.

He read silently.

Endeavor leaving Duluth this PM.
Mayfield info as follows:
Founded in 1946 by Henry Mayfield, a twenty-eight year old graduate of the University of Chicago. Wife, son, and a physics degree, had money and was well connected.
Startup was based in Cadillac, Michigan. Besides Mayfield, the company consisted of one woman and four men. Some of the startup money was supplied by the OSS but the purpose of the company and how it made its money are unclear.

Henry Mayfield later moved his business to a new facility not far from the original location. At Henry's death in 1963, his son Charles took over the business. He delegated the internal running of the company to a Professor Andrew Simeon who was said to be a close friend of Charles.

Due to unknown causes, the company burned to the ground in 1993. Charles died in the fire.

Professor Simeon is still alive and living at an elder care facility in the Cadillac area, location attached. He's a man with serious academic credentials. He may possess additional information.
End of report.

He handed the phone back. "So, that splintered wood we found at the Point, *was* from one of the crates those men were loading."

"Nothing certain, but yeah…probably," said Maddie. "Good work on your part."

"And we're going to Cadillac to find this Simeon guy."

"Yes."

"And the freighter *Endeavor* is in Duluth."

"Yes."

"How is it you know about *Endeavor*?"

"We can get into that another time, not today."

"Why not today?"

She didn't answer.

A few miles later, they pulled up to a drive through and got some fast food. They ate in the lot.

"What do we do if we find this Professor Simeon?" said Beth downing a fry.

"The guy must be in his nineties by now," said Jack, wondering the same thing. "He may not remember much."

Maddie shrugged. "Let's find the guy first. Don't ask me why, but I have a good feeling about this. Besides, it's the only lead we've got and what the hell else should we be doing right now? Our main job is making everyone believe the two of you are dead."

"What if we're being followed?" said Beth.

Jack shook his head. "If somebody was following us, they would have made their move by now, probably at our last refueling stop...or maybe right here."

"They'll probably figure it out before long," said Maddie. "It's important that we learn as much about Mayfield as quickly as we can and just hope it has a bearing on what's going on." She held up her keys. "I'm tired. Who wants to drive?"

Beth grabbed them.

With Maddie stretched out in the back seat, Jack took shotgun. As Beth merged onto the highway, he gave her knee a comforting pat.

She placed a hand on his. "You going to tell me how to drive?"

"Wouldn't think of it."

Two hours later they arrived at the elder care facility which was located a few miles outside the city of Cadillac. The afternoon had turned clear. The sun sparkled off the snow that covered the hill on which sat the *Autumn Leaves Rest Home*. Beth negotiated the winding drive and parked beside three snow covered cars.

"Terrible name for the place," said Jack getting out, eying the two story, block style institution. "*Autumn Leaves*, old, shriveled and wasting away." He noted a late model Ford F150 parked off to the side. There was no snow on it. A recent arrival then?

"What would you have called it?" asked Beth.

"Don't know. Anything but that. Maybe *Invest 'n Rest*. I hear these places cost a fortune."

Maddie led the way through the double glass doors into the spacious waiting room. Classical music played softly. The room was empty except for an attractive young woman sitting behind the front desk. She had strawberry blond hair and looked just out of high school. She wore a white lab coat with the name *Sundy* embroidered in blue. She stood as they approached then blanched and almost fell back a step when Maddie flashed her badge. "We're FBI, here to see Mr. Andrew Simeon."

Jack straightened into a lawman pose.

To her credit, Sandy recovered quickly. She queried her computer, then shook her head. "There's no one here by that name." She smiled sheepishly. "Sorry."

"We need to talk to the administrator."

"He's not normally available without an appointment," said Sandy.

"It's a matter of national security."

Sandy swallowed hard. She picked up the phone, spoke, listened, then hung up. "Dr. Lambert will be with you in a moment. Please, have a seat. There's coffee if you'd like."

They waited. Jack tried the coffee. Through the window he watched a man in a hunting jacket heading down the walk toward the parking lot. At that moment the door beside the front desk opened.

"I am Dr. Lambert. How can I help you?" His voice was soft, soothing. He was middle aged, African American, dressed in a white lab coat. He carried a clipboard in his left hand.

"We're here to see Andrew Simeon," said Maddie in her FBI voice.

"I'm terribly sorry, Mr. Simeon passed away two weeks ago. Sandy is new here. She wouldn't have known. I take it, you're not...family?"

"That's right."

"Can we see his medical records?" asked Beth, opening the front of her jacket revealing her own white lab coat.

Lambert took note but said: "Sorry, not without a warrant. All patient records are confidential."

"How 'bout we look around?" said Jack.

"Sandy said you were FBI...something about national security."

Maddie handed him her badge. "I can't get into details. But I can make this easy or I can make this very difficult."

Lambert examined the badge and handed it back. "I don't respond well to threats, Agent Cooper. And I won't be happy about it, but I can't stop you from taking a tour of the facility. I will be your guide."

"No you will not. Don't worry, we'll be discrete. But...give us a sec."

Maddie pulled Jack and Beth off to the side, out of earshot. She drew a gun from her shoulder holster. She gave it to Beth. "You're staying here with Lambert. I don't want him using a phone, I don't want him talking to anyone or going anywhere. Make sure he sees this gun but keep it in your pocket. Relax, it's just for insurance, in case he tries anything. I don't trust him. It's a little too convenient, this Simeon guy dying two weeks before we get here." She paused, eyes on Beth. "You ever fire a gun?"

"A rifle, not a handgun."

"Handgun is easier. You'll be fine."

"What about the girl at the desk? What if someone comes in...another visitor?"

"You may need to improvise. Just keep Lambert here, that's all you have to do. Dazzle him with medical talk. He's a doctor, you're a pharmacist—you'll think of something." Maddie turned to Jack. "All right, let's go."

Jack hesitated, eyes on Beth.

"Go. Don't worry, I'll be okay," she said.

Maddie turned to Lambert. "I'll take that clipboard." She pulled it from him then strode through the double doors.

Jack followed noticing Sandy shuffling casually through a few papers as if nothing out of the ordinary was going on.

"You're armed, aren't you sheriff?" said Maddie, voice low as the doors swung closed behind them.

"I left my gun in the car. I have...a pocket knife."

"Guess we should have covered that point a little earlier." Maddie picked up the pace, down the short hall through another set of double doors where they found themselves in a much longer hallway. Patient's rooms lined both sides, most with doors open. Along the hall a few gray-haired men in bathrobes stood or shuffled along. The smell of disinfectant hung in the air as did the murmur of conversations, and the occasional laugh. The classical music played on. There were no nurses or staff in sight, which Jack thought was odd.

"Don't trust the name posted on the doors," said Maddie. "Whoever you see, let them know you're looking for Andrew Simeon. Maybe somebody knows something about him. You take left, I'll take right."

Jack approached the first room on his side. It was open. He knocked and stepped in. "I'm looking for Mr. Andrew Simeon," he said to a bald man in pajamas seated upright in a recliner next to the window. The man turned a page in the book he was reading. "Not so loud, you idiot. I can hear just fine," he said, eyes on the page.

"Do you know where I can find him?"

"Find who?"

"Andrew Simeon."

"Don't know him." He lowered his book. "Say, it's about time for supper, isn't it?"

"I wouldn't know about that, sir. Thanks for your time."

Jack walked to the next room where, with minor variations, the scene repeated itself.

Autumn leaves, old and wrinkled, thought Jack, trying to think of these men as once young and active and viable. He would probably be one of them some day. He shivered at the thought.

Jack made his way, room by room to the end of the long hallway. He checked the time and wondered how Beth was doing with Lambert. Probably talking about the latest wonder drugs. Beth could talk for hours on medical matters. She might have Lambert climbing the walls by this time.

"Bingo," said Maddie, startling Jackson out of these somber thoughts. She emerged from a room on her side. "This fellow said Simeon's on the second floor, room 216."

They headed up a set of stairs at the end of the hallway, then opened a door to another hallway, identical to the first. "This is the female ward," Jack said, seeing two women, one with a walker, making their way toward them.

"We're looking for Andrew Simeon," Maddie said to them. "Do you know where we can find him?"

"Are you doctors? You don't look like doctors," said the woman with the walker, eyes wary, lips pressed tight together.

"We're friends of Mr. Simeon's," said Jack.

"Oh, well then, how nice. He'll be glad to see you. No one ever comes to visit Andrew. He was such a nice man, a writer once, you know. All the time, writing things down."

"He's not nice now?" asked Maddie.

The other woman frowned. "They shot him full of drugs and moved him up here. He hasn't been the same since. This is the women's floor. All of us love the poor man."

"Is he in room 216?"

"That's right. But all he does is sleep since…the drugs."

They left the women and found room 216. The door was locked.

"Can you break it down?" said Maddie.

Jack tried a kick, without effect. Then, leading with his good shoulder, he charged the door. A burst of pain shot through his arm with the impact. He heard and felt something give, but bounced back, the door still holding strong.

"Hit more to the hinge side. Sounds like the jam might be cracking."

Jack nodded, grimly, both shoulders throbbing. He backed up and charged again. The frame splintered, the door crashed onto the floor, Jack sailed into the room. He gained his footing, out of breath, hands on knees.

Maddie turned on the light. "Empty. They must have taken him somewhere."

"Maybe he really is dead," said Jack straightening. He looked around the room. "Except for the bed, the room looks hardly lived in. Empty hangars in the closet, there's not even a TV."

Jack opened the drapes. The late afternoon sun poured through the window that overlooked the front of the building. "The pickup that was down there is gone now."

"Lambert might know something about that. Why would he try to keep us from seeing the guy?" She put her hands on her hips.

"We should get back down. I don't like Beth being alone with that guy."

"Those women said Simeon was a writer. Always writing. Maybe..."

"Maybe what?"

"Don't know. But we're here now. Let's have a good look around."

"Not many places to hide anything," said Jack. "Maybe in the bathroom somewhere? Under the mattress?"

They checked both and found nothing. Jack walked to the closet. He ran his hand along the shelf above the hangars but found only a thick layer of dust that stuck to his hand. He winced at its smell, then went into the bathroom and washed his hands. With no towels, he dried them on his pants then noticed an air vent down near the floor. He jostled the grating with the toe of his shoe. It was loose.

Jack knelt. With his pocket knife he removed the two already loose screws. The grating fell with a clank. He reached in and ran his hand over the bottom surface of the ductwork raising more dust. He bent lower, reaching in further. "Here. There's something here," he said.

Coughing from the dust he pulled out a ragged spiral bound notebook. He handed it to Maddie who'd come over, then washed his hands again.

"This could be useful, Jack."

"Do you think it was Simeon's?"

"I just looked at a couple of pages. It's got a lot of numbers. Simeon's a professor so I'd say, yes." She closed it, blew off some of the dust and tucked it under her Jacket.

Jack replaced the grating. "Wonder how Simeon managed to get these screws out in the first place."

"Even a plastic knife could do it," said Maddie. "No sense wondering about that now. We've got to go."

They hurried down to the lobby. On seeing them, Beth stood up from the coffee table where she'd been sitting with Lambert, two empty coffee cups between them. "It's about time you got back," she whispered, angry eyes on Jack. "It's been over an hour."

"Sorry, couldn't be helped."

"Did you find the guy?"

"No."

"I told you, he died two weeks ago," said Lambert.

"Sorry to have bothered you, Doctor Lambert," said Maddie. "Thank you very much for your...cooperation." She turned to Beth. "Where's my gun?"

She fished it from her pocket and handed it to her.

Maddie pocketed the gun, took one last professional look at Lambert's clipboard and handed it back to him. "Everything appears to be in order, doctor. If we need anything further from you, we'll be in touch."

Lambert didn't say a word as they left.

CHAPTER 15

"Lambert's going to be pissed about the door I broke down," said Jack once they were outside.

"You broke down a door?" said Beth. "So, you *did* find something."

"We'll talk about that in the car," said Maddie, in a hurry, leading the way. "What happened to the girl at the desk?"

"She left for the restroom and didn't come back," said Beth. "She seems harmless."

"Hope you're right."

It was getting dark. The lights in the parking lot were coming on. Jack could hardly believe that his narrowly avoided plunge into Lake Medora had happened just that morning. Now here they were, on the run and breaking down doors at an old folks home.

Jack saw that the parking lot was empty except for their car. So at least four people had left the place since they'd arrived. Maybe one was Sandy? He wondered about the others. Inside, they'd seen no visitors and the only staff had been Sandy and Lambert. In a facility this large, there had to be others. Where were they all?

They piled into the car, Maddie at the wheel, Jack shotgun. Maddie pulled onto the main road. "We're heading for Cadillac. I'm beat and I'm hungry. We need a place to stay."

"Just what I was thinking," said Jack. He turned in his seat toward Beth. Her arms were folded, head down, face strained. She was shivering. He wished he could hold her. "It's going to be okay," he said.

"Turn up the heat. I don't know why I agreed to all this. And you're wrong. I don't think it'll ever be okay again, Jack." She raised her head.

He met her eyes and tried to think of something comforting to say. "We found a notebook hidden in Simeon's room."

"We need to go through it, ASAP," said Maddie.

Beth kept shivering.

On the edge of town, they checked into the *Bear Lake Motel*, taking the last available room. "Hunting season," explained the bearded man at the front desk. "Don't worry," he added, "There're two beds if you need them. Plenty of room for the three of you."

As she had with all their expenses, Maddie put the charge on her card. Jack hoped it had some FBI security feature to keep someone from tracking them.

They dropped their things in the room. Maddie stayed to go through the notebook while Jack and Beth took the car to get carryout. They stopped at a drugstore, bought some medicated cream and bandages for Jack's shoulder wound then decided on Chinese using the last of their cash.

"Any luck," Jack asked Maddie when they returned.

"There's a lot here," she said, straightening at the desk, the lamp lighting up her red hair.

Jack put down the sack of food. The notebook lay open in front of Maddie, her notes beside it."

"This guy Simeon was heavy into physics, high level stuff. It's way over my head."

"Do you think he's still alive?" asked Beth on the bed, sorting out the food. The aromas made Jack hungry.

"Maybe," said Maddie with a yawn and a shrug. "It was obvious he was being held there against his will. Otherwise, why would he hide this notebook?"

"He might have been paranoid," she countered.

"From all the dust over it, it had to have been lying in that vent for a long time," said Jack, starting into his orange chicken.

"We should change your bandages," Beth told him.

"I'll get to it," he said as he ate. From both walls the sounds of competing TV's filtered in from the neighboring rooms. "Wish they'd at least decide on watching the same thing." Eyes on Maddie, he took a gulp of Diet Coke. "You said the math part of the notebook was over your head. What about the rest?"

"The book definitely belonged to Simeon. He put his name on the first page over his title: *Professor of Physics, University of*

Chicago. The next pages were loosely inserted. There's no date on them but they look hurriedly written and read something like a last will and testament. He mentioned things he was proud of and he wrote about his regrets. Then he writes about Henry Mayfield. It reads much like a diary. After that, the math comes in. Some of it looks like lab data—whole pages of it." Maddie turned out the lamp and came over. "You got orange chicken for all of us?"

"Eggrolls too," said Jack. "It was on special."

She sat on the edge of the other bed and started eating.

"I might be able to help with the math," said Beth. "I had to take a lot of it in college." She carried her food to the desk and sat. She read, turning a page, taking a bite every now and then.

Jack watched her. It was good to see her occupied with something other than worries over their present predicament.

As if feeling his eyes on her, she said again: "You ought to get some of that medication on your shoulder, Jack."

"I was the one who did the stitching," said Maddie. "If it's alright with you, I can help with that." Her question seemed directed as much at Beth as Jack.

When Beth didn't reply, Maddie came over. She prepped the bandages and the cream. Her fingers felt warm on his skin. It felt weird and oddly sexual that it was she, not Beth touching him. There his wife sat, not ten feet away, wrapped up in the notebook as if totally oblivious to what he and this woman were doing. In his mind he imagined Maddie concerned with more than just his shoulder, Beth coming over, helping... He closed his eyes, shifted his weight under her touch and...

"How's your other shoulder?" said Maddie, abruptly finished.

"My other...?"

"Your other shoulder. The one you used to break down the door."

"It's okay." He began buttoning his shirt.

"It's always better to lead with the flat of your arm," she advised.

"They teach those kinds of things at Quantico?"

"Yeah, they do. How to pick locks too. Hmmm, I guess I could have tried that before you..." She shrugged. "Didn't think of it. Sorry."

Jack adjusted his shirt and turned his attention back to Beth. She was going through pages quickly now, as if at the climax of a mystery thriller. Then, at one page in particular, she stopped. She bent closer. "Find something?" he asked.

Beth held the notebook up, positioning it so the light showed through the page. Then she put it down. "Yeah, I think maybe I did. Give me your knife."

Jack flipped out a blade and handed it to her.

"What are you doing. For God's sake, don't damage it," said Maddie, coming over.

"These two pages are stuck together."

"It's probably from being in that air vent so long," said Jack. "All that dust, and moisture."

"No, it's more than that," said Beth. "They're stuck together in a uniform way as if they were intentionally glued together so they'd be mistaken for a single page" Still holding the glued pages vertical, apart from the others, she nudged them down making a small loop between them at the binding. Into that loop, she inserted the blade of the knife. She worked it carefully around the edges. "Feels like maybe rubber cement—old and brittle." Once finished, the sealed pages came apart.

Maddie bent closer, over Beth's shoulder. "What is that? Latin?"

"Yes," said Beth. "But look, it starts out with a number...not roman numerals: 2021. Must be the year? Simeon was being careful. He didn't want just anyone to read this. That must have been when he wrote this part. He sealed these two pages then hid the notebook."

"Do either of you know Latin?" said Jack.

"Not a problem. I know an app," said Maddie. She grabbed her computer. Beth stood, Maddie sat. "Do we have WIFI?"

Beth rubbed her eyes. "Yes, I saw the password when we checked in. It's…"

"Wait until I'm ready. Okay, what is it?"

"It's: *ilovetrout*. No spaces."

"Really? That's the password?"

"Yeah, all lowercase no spaces."

Maddie's fingers flew over the keyboard. "Okay, I'm ready. Now read the Latin to me, letter by letter, word by word."

Beth did so:

Hiems est, 2021
Captus sum a viris perniciosis. Foderunt me in confusionem assiduam. Haec verba scribens, effectus medicamentorum suorum quodammodo evectus sum, eorumque intentionem nunc videre possum. Sed perspicax manere conatus est, et vereor ne id multo diutius facere non possim. Hanc paginam diligenter inspice et videbis

"That's all of it," said Beth when finished.

Maddie took in a tired breath. "Okay then, let's see what we've got." She pressed a single key, then read off the screen:

"It is winter, 2021
I am held captive by dangerous men. They have drugged me into a state of constant confusion. As I write these words I have somehow risen above the effects of their drugs and can now see their intent. But it is an effort to remain clear headed and I fear I cannot do so for much longer. Inspect this page carefully and you will see

"See what?" said Jack.

"The translation ends there," said Maddie.

Jack picked up the notebook. "He wanted us to inspect this particular page carefully so…"

On it, Jack saw mostly numbers. There were mathematical formulae, and a sketch or diagram of some kind up in the header. Jack stared. He placed a finger on the diagram. "This looks familiar."

"Looks like a flux capacitor," said Maddie.

Jack felt his neck hairs prickling. "I think it's a map." He traced a finger on the straight vertical line that was centered on the diagram. "Get your phone. Pull up a roadmap of this area," he told her.

Maddie did so. Jack took her phone and held it up beside the book. "Yes, that's route 131." He traced it with his finger then, "No, that's not right. I'm wrong. I thought…"

"Let me see it, Jack," said Beth. He handed the phone to her. She stared at the drawing, then at the map on the screen, then the drawing again. "Yes, I see what you mean but…" Then she smiled, eyes brightening.

"But what?"

"You're right, Jack. It's a map. And you know, I'm beginning to like this Simeon guy. He pulled a Leonardo on us."

"What're you talking about?" said Maddie. "What's a Leonardo?"

"This drawing is a mirror image," she said, scanning the room as she talked. "DaVinci often wrote his secret notes as mirror images. This is a map, but it only reads correctly if…come on." She walked to the bathroom. Jack followed as she flicked on the light and held the notebook up to the mirror. "There's your map," she announced.

Jack saw what she meant. "Yes. There's route 55 and that's 115. And that black dot there, just north of 55…maybe that's something important."

"Something, like what?" asked Maddie behind them leaning against the doorway.

"I don't know."

"Here, let me have a look," said Maddie, nudging her way in. "Uh, excuse me, I kind of need access to the mirror."

"Hold on," said Jack, handing her the phone. "We'll clear out and let you see for yourself."

"Good idea. Thanks," said Maddie.

Jack and Beth left her alone in the bathroom.

"Wish this place had a minibar," said Beth, tossing back the last of her Diet Coke.

"That was good, you knowing about the mirror thing," said Jack, taking her in his arms. "You're even more nerdy than I thought."

She smiled. "I'll take that as a compliment. But I was just lucky." They kissed.

"No. You're a meticulous, science person. You're exactly the kind of person Simeon hoped would find those pages. Now we need to find *him*."

"He might be dead."

"Maybe not."

Jack heard the bathroom door close, then lock. He glanced at Beth. "Must have had a disagreement with her food."

Jack listened for confirming sounds then heard Cooper talking to someone. "She's on her phone."

"Who with?"

"Don't know. Don't care." He turned out the lights. The security lamp outside showed through the curtain creating dim shadows. He reached for Beth's hand and led her to the bed. They laid down. They kissed, her lips warm and sweet and...

"Jack! How could you be horny at a time like this."

"Not a good time for questions."

"I'm sorry, Jack. I...I can't, not right now. Besides, she's just in there." Beth said that last part in a whisper as she kissed him tenderly, then gently pulled away.

They were quiet for a while. Jack closed his eyes.

"Do you really think we're going to come out of all this okay?" she said.

"We take a day at a time. That's what we do. We made it through today. We're still good. And I still love you. What else matters?"

Beth reached for his hand then spoke as if through a worried smile. "I love you too, Jack."

At that moment Maddie stepped noisily out of the bathroom. "Get your stuff," she said. "We're leaving. Now!"

CHAPTER 16

Maddie drove, heading north, picking up speed,

Jack turned up the heater. "This could have waited until morning."

"No, it couldn't. If you're right about that diagram we should be within ten miles of what was once home to Professor Mayfield."

"That's the black dot?"

"I think so."

"And his house won't still be there in the morning?" said Beth from the back.

"Look, I have my reasons. That's all you need to know."

Jack rubbed his eyes. He blinked then peered through the windshield, seeing a hill up ahead. "You think someone knows we're alive."

"I think Lambert told someone about our visit. They wouldn't have to be a genius to guess we booked a room at the nearest motel. That was my bad." With a glance in the rearview, she sped up.

Jack checked the side mirror and saw nothing. "Now you think we're being followed?"

"Could be. I saw headlights back there. They're hidden now by that last curve."

"And you're going to lose them in the dark."

"I sure am, Jack." With both hands on the wheel, she hit the gas.

The car roared over the hill. The tires somehow managed to hang onto the road. Maddie flipped off the headlights. The windshield went black.

Jack braced himself with a hand on the dash.

"You could break an arm doing that," said Maddie calmly. "Sit back, don't worry. Your seatbelt and the airbag will take care of you. Do you know there are explosive pellets in the track of your shoulder belt? They go off in a collision to pull up the slack and draw the strap tight around you."

"That's...reassuring." Jack swallowed. He heard the click of a seatbelt from the back.

"I see headlights behind us," said Beth.

"Shit," said Cooper. "I was really hoping it wouldn't come to this."

Jack saw them too, still distant but coming on fast.

Maddie nudged the wheel. The car swerved, rumbling up against the berm of plowed snow like a sled on a luge track. "There's a field road somewhere along here," she shouted over the noise.

Jack hung on. "Damn-it Maddie, you're going to get us stuck in a snowbank. You don't even know for sure if that's the bad guys back there."

"It's 2AM, who the hell else would it be?" She fought the wheel, leaning close to the windshield, eyes wide.

Lit by the moon, a road sign appeared dead ahead. Jack grit his teeth. Beth screamed. Then, *thump,* the sign flew back with hardly an impact and was gone. "The turnout's just up here," yelled Maddie.

"For God's sake, we're gonna die—for real this time," shouted Beth.

"Hold on!" Maddie let up on the gas. She hit the brakes. The car fishtailed wildly. She cut the wheel, pulling them into a sharp right turn.

Jack slid sideways toward Maddie. The wheel jerked in her hands but she held strong. The car hit a bank of deep snow, skidding off the road swerving into a cornfield. Dead stalks swooshed by on both sides. The car bounced high and hit hard, Jack's head crunched against the headliner. Maddie fought the wheel over fifty more yards of rough, snow-covered ground. The engine roared but the car slowed. It made it halfway up a slope before coming to a stop.

Maddie gunned the engine. The wheels spun. The car didn't move. She shifted into park, took a breath, and fell back into her seat. "End of the line."

With the car angled up, all Jack saw through the windshield were the tops of a few cornstalks, above them, stars. "You okay back there?" he shouted to Beth. Craning his neck, he saw her doubled over, straightening then settling back into her seat. He held out a hand, trying to help her. "You okay?" he said again. She glared back but didn't answer. She was breathing hard, trying to catch her breath. Behind her, through the rear window, all he could see were cornstalks.

He turned to Maddie. "That car was probably just a couple of drunks out joy riding."

"I should have rented a Jeep."

"You're nuts," said Beth.

"Trust me, we're safer here than back at that motel."

"It's ten degrees. We're stuck in a fucking cornfield. Sorry but I'm not feeling too safe at all right now."

"Yeah, I hadn't exactly planned to have this happen but...it's not a problem."

"How can this *not* be problem?" said Jack. "We don't even have a shovel to get us unstuck."

"I've got something much better than a shovel."

"If those really were the bad guys, they'll be turning back. They'll find us," said Beth.

"It'll take them a while to track us down. By that time, we'll be gone."

"You really *are* crazy," said Jack.

Maddie checked her watch. "A chopper from Camp Grayling should be here in another ten minutes. They'll be homing in on my phone and will see that we didn't make it to the pickup spot. All we need to do now is wait." She let her head fall back against the headrest and closed her eyes.

"*You* had a National Guard chopper called in?" said Jack. "How does a low grade, FBI agent who's been suspended, pull that off?"

"I never said anything about being low grade."

It was a long fifteen minutes before they heard the sound of rotors. With more than a little disbelief, Jack saw the blinking red lights of a giant twin bladed Sikorski swooping down just as Maddie said it would.

She flipped on the headlights to help guide the chopper down to a spot about fifty yards away. "Okay, grab your stuff, time to move." She cut the engine. The three of them got out into a knee-deep drift of snow. They plodded along, thrashing through the stalks, heading for the chopper, Maddie led the way, Jack trailed behind Beth. He slipped and stumbled through the snow that caked heavily around his shoes. Up ahead, he saw the lights of the chopper. The cornstalks shook and swayed, in the wash of the rotors.

The dark body of the chopper was huge. Maddie was already crawling inside. A soldier in a heavy field jacket helped Beth up then Jack.

"This all of you?" He asked Jack.

"Yeah."

"Grab a seat and get strapped," said the soldier. "All in," he shouted to the cockpit.

Jack took the jump seat beside Beth. They strapped in.

The soldier handed each of them ear protection which they immediately put on, deadening the sound. Jack put an arm around Beth.

The chopper rose sharply and, with the cargo door still open, Jack caught sight of their SUV, sitting alone in the cornfield, headlights still on. It got smaller quickly as they ascended. With a tug from the soldier, the cargo door slid closed.

The chopper angled forward, gaining speed as it climbed. Beth's gloved hands gripped his. Only now did Jack notice the soldiers sitting on the bench opposite them. They looked like Regular Army, not National Guard as he would have expected. One of them stared back with curiosity. The others dozed; heads lolled back as if this was just another day at the office.

Jack caressed Beth's hand. Were it not for their ear protection he might have said something but he didn't know what. She said something to him that he couldn't hear then surprised him with a kiss on his cheek. She rested her head on his shoulder. Gently, he pulled her close. He could feel her warmth. Maybe everything *was* going to be okay.

Before long the chopper slowed and tilted sideways into a turn. Through the open hatch that led to the cockpit he saw Maddie. In the glow of red LED's she sat bent over an instrument panel. He realized now that the chopper was circling, searching, and she probably had her eyes glued to a night vision display of the ground below. The circling pattern kept up and the obvious became clear. They were not headed back to the safety of Camp Grayling. They were searching for Simeon's black dot.

Yeah, suspended or not, Maddie had to be much more than your average FBI agent. To have gotten this chopper and these men out here at this hour and with such short notice. Who the hell was she—some kind of Captain America?

The chopper was losing altitude. Slowly at first then faster. Through his ear protection, he heard the sound of the rotors change pitch. Like a rollercoaster on the downslope, the chopper dropped. He hated rollercoasters.

"Prepare for landing," came the pilot's calm announcement just before the craft hit the ground none too gently.

Maddie made her way from the cockpit back to where Beth and Jack sat. They took off their ear protection as she shouted over the sound of the slowing rotors. "There's a house out here, a big one. And there's no access road that I could see. This may or may not be that spot in the notebook but it seemed suspicious so we're going to have a look around."

Jack gave a nod. One of the soldiers, the one who'd helped them get into the chopper, stood and slid open the hatch. He and his four fellow soldiers, awake and alert now, piled out, rifles ready.

Maddie, Beth and Jack followed, jumping out, their landing cushioned by the snow. Up a gentle slope, a large, two-story farm house stood, dark and foreboding like something out of a B-grade horror movie. The soldiers charged quietly toward the structure in a delta formation. With the rotors coming to a stop, the night was silent except for the whistling of the wind through the tall surrounding trees.

"We're in somebody's backyard," said Jack.

"If somebody's asleep in there they're gonna be really pissed at us," said Beth.

Cooper give them the look of an irate mother tired of dealing with her two clueless kids. She waved for them to follow her. Still well behind the soldiers, Jack saw the lead man head up the steps onto the porch then try the door. It opened easily. The soldiers ran in.

"All right, so the place needs a little work," quipped Maddie moments later standing in the middle of a spacious kitchen. Lit by their roving flashlights, the place was clearly a residence. The floor groaned with every step. The windows were cracked. The glass of the one over the sink was missing altogether. Yet the room was warm.

Jack wondered if the place really might be occupied. He imagined the irate owner appearing, threatening them with a shotgun. He found a light switch and was surprised when a light over a table flickered and came on. His eyes adjusted painfully fast. Yeah, the place was a mess.

Jack heard the sound of heavy footsteps from the floor above.

"Relax, our guys are up there doing a quick check for threats," explained Maddie.

"Do you think this was Simeon's house?" asked Beth.

"Maybe."

"Or just an abandoned house owned by someone with no connection at all to Simeon," said Jack. He opened the fridge, empty but for a carton of orange juice.

"Funny the power's still on," said Maddie.

"No one here, up or down," said a soldier walking in. He held his rifle with one hand, with the other he gripped a yellowed newspaper folded over. He had master sergeant's stripes on his sleeve and the name Davis over his breast pocket. Obviously not happy, he tossed the paper to Maddie who missed the catch. Beth picked it up.

"It's been empty for a while," Davis reported, eyes on Maddie. "Maybe you'd like to tell me what's so important about the three of you and about this place that me and my men had to get up in the middle of the night, pluck you out of a cornfield, and fly out here."

"You saved our lives, sergeant."

"Next time you have car trouble, call *Triple-A*. I hear they have an FBI discount. What's the story about this place?"

"It may have something to do with a smuggling operation."

"It *may* have, huh? Smuggling what? Drugs? Weapons? What?"

"We don't know. That's what we're here to find out. Look, I'm sorry you and your men got pulled into this. We had no choice. We need to do a complete search of this house. Please carry on with that and see what you can find."

Davis held his stare, then turned. "Sure, why the hell not," he muttered, stalking off, shouting: "Hit the basement, guys. No stone unturned. If we're lucky, maybe we'll find somebody's baseball card collection." He led his men down the stairs.

"He'll get over it," said Maddie.

"It's dated June 8, 2002," said Beth, holding up the newspaper. "Could this place have been empty that long?"

"The date jibes with the expiration date on the OJ in the fridge. I didn't bother with a sniff test. Amazing the fridge still works. You'd think whoever was here last would have taken the time to unplug it."

"That's a lot of electric bills," said Maddie. "Wonder who's paying them. Then again, I didn't see any lines running into the place."

Jack saw Beth poke her head into a hallway, then walk out further. He followed her into an adjoining room where she flipped on another light. A bookcase covered the sizable length of one wall in an otherwise empty room.

She stepped closer, running her hand lightly across the books. "Look at the titles," she said. She stopped, selecting one.

Jack went to the far end. "Dickens, Tolstoy, Dostoevsky, all oldies over here."

"Same here." Beth put hers back, walked a few steps then chose another. "Here we go," she said. "This one's a technical book by...Niels Bohr."

"Who's Niels Bohr?" said Jack.

"The father of quantum mechanics," said Davis emerging from the basement.

"Right," said Beth. "And here're a few Sherlock Holmes classics plus some Agatha Christy."

"Let me know if you see any first editions," said Davis, coming over.

"Can we please get back on point," said Maddie. "We *are* conducting a search."

"Yes, ma'am," replied Davis without enthusiasm, walking off.

"Looks like Captain America has run out of friends," Jack whispered to Beth.

"I don't think she'll be calling in any more favors for a while." She paused. "You really didn't know about Niels Bohr?"

"You married a cop, not a scientist," he told her, trying to sound like it was no big deal. But it *was*. Hell, even Davis knew the guy.

"How 'bout you and I have a look upstairs," suggested Beth.

"Sure. Why not."

The stairway led up to a long single hallway lined with doors and lit by a row of ceiling lights. Each door was swung open. "It's like a hotel," said Jack. He peeked into the first room. It contained a bed frame and a bare dresser, empty drawers pulled out. A tall mirror lay shattered on the floor." He walked in, his shoes crunching over plaster debris and more than a few bug bodies. "Closet empty. Looks like Davis's men put some holes in the wall just for fun." He stepped closer to one of the damaged walls and placed a hand on the electrical conduit that fed into the light switch beside the door. "Wiring looks to be in good shape, might even pass code."

They were interrupted by Maddie yelling up the stairway. "Something in the basement you should see...you're up there, right?"

"Yeah, we're here. Be right there," answered Beth.

With no handrails on either side, a set of flimsy wooden stairs led down to the basement. They creaked with their weight. Jack counted twenty steps down to the dirt floor basement which he guessed to be about thirty-foot square. Why so large and so deep, he wondered.

It smelled of dank earth. It was the kind of smell that went with spiders and worms and scurrying mice but he saw none of these. It was warmer here. They joined Maddie near a wall where Davis's men had set up a few battery powered lights that they must have had in their packs. Yeah, always prepared.

"Now that's creepy," said Beth staring down at an earthen pit that resembled a grave in size and depth.

"Freshly dug from the look of it," said Jack.

Cooper stood at one edge next to two piles of loose dirt. She directed one of the lights down into the pit.

"We dug a few more feet before we hit a big tree root," said Davis, standing beside Maddie. "We scanned for anything metallic and checked for radioactivity but came up empty."

"Radioactivity? Why check that?" asked Jack.

"Standard procedure."

"Another point of interest is that thing over there," said Maddie, pointing to a smooth sided cube six-feet on a side, black in color. It sat in a corner on a concrete pad. From it, several pipes led up to the ceiling where they curved to follow the joists supporting the floor above. They walked over. "It's got the Mayfield logo on the side so we know we're in the right place."

Jack was both startled and relieved to see the sideways diamond logo. Yes, they were in the right place. He placed his palm on the smooth surface. "It must be the power source for the house. It's warm. And this is electrical conduit," he added, "no air ducting like you'd expect from a furnace." He shifted his hand to one of the pipes.

"Could be a battery," said Davis.

Maddie nodded. "I don't know much about batteries but if this house has been lying here dormant for a couple of decades, you'd think it would have run out of juice a long time ago. We should get some techs to check it out."

"You can get the FBI or the local authorities to help you with that," said Davis. "Me and my team are done here."

Maddie nodded, "Thanks very much for your help, sergeant." She pulled out her phone. "I'll take a couple of pics down here and around the house. Might be something interesting on the grounds outside. Then, if you don't mind, maybe you could drop us off somewhere."

"How about Gull Harbor?" said Beth.

"Sorry, ma'am, that's a little far for us," said Davis as his men started up the stairs.

"I had someplace closer in mind," said Maddie.

CHAPTER 17

An hour later, inside the descending chopper, Jack nudged Beth awake. "We're here. Time to go," he shouted, hardly hearing himself through his ear protection.

As if still asleep, Beth shoved his hand away. At the jarring thump of the wheels hitting the ground, she woke with a start, eyes wide as if surprised to find herself in her present situation.

They discarded their ear protection and got up. "You good," Jack asked her.

"Sure. Never better," said Beth.

Maddie joined them. The hatch lifted. A ramp was lowered. They hurried down the ramp then ran out beyond the wash of the rotors. Once there, Jack turned. He gave Sergeant Davis a wave as the hatch closed and the craft took off. The beat of the rotors faded quickly.

"Great, we're back in a fucking cornfield," said Beth. The sun was just coming up over the tops of the withered stalks.

"Did the sleep help?" said Jack who'd tried unsuccessfully to get some sleep himself.

"No, well yeah, maybe it did." She took a deep breath and let it out slow. "Yep, good to go," she added unconvincingly.

Maddie pointed. "The *Autumn Leaves* place should be just over that rise." She started out in that direction, Jack and Beth following.

Jack checked the time. "It's almost seven-thirty. I wonder what time Lambert comes in."

"Who knows," said Maddie. "We could be out here for a while waiting for him or he might already be there. Or it might be his day off."

"Do you really think Professor Simeon is alive and that Lambert knows where he is?" said Jack.

"Hope so. It's the only shot we've got."

They reached the top of the rise where the cornfield ended at a short wire fence. From here it was a short walk down a gentle slope to the employee parking lot which abutted the *Autumn Leaves* facility itself.

Inside the building lights were coming on. There were three cars in the parking lot.

"They're all junkers," said Beth. "I'm betting Lamber drives something more up-scale. So, he's probably not here yet."

Maddie pointed to an alcove built into the rear wall of the building. "We can wait there. At least it'll get us out of the wind. And, I see two security cameras. Try to stay away from them."

They jumped the fence and ran at an angle down the slope then across the lot. They reached the alcove just as a red Ford Flex pulled into the lot.

"That's him," said Beth.

"Well, that was lucky timing," said Maddie. She drew her gun. "Now remember, we're here to scare the shit out of him. Got it? We do not want to hurt him." She didn't wait for an answer. "Follow me. Quick now."

At a run, Jack and Beth kept up.

The car turned into a spot beside the rear entrance. In a crouch the three of them came up behind it, each on a knee at its rear bumper. Jack felt the warmth of the tailpipe.

The car idled for a moment. Then the engine shut down. The driver's side door clicked open.

Maddie dashed forward. Standing now, she jerked the door fully open nearly pulling Lamber out of his seat. "Good morning, Doctor Lambert," she said with the politeness of a hotel greeter.

Lamber recoiled. "You again!" He tried to pull the door closed.

"There's no need to struggle, doctor. We're just here to talk." Maddie aimed her gun directly at him.

Lambert froze. "What's the matter with you people? Can't you..."

"No, we can't, doctor. Now get yourself over to the passenger seat, I'll drive." He awkwardly complied, as Maddie waved for Jack and Beth to get into the car. Maddie took the driver's seat and slammed the door closed. She started the car.

Directly behind Lambert, Jack drew his gun.

Beth leaned forward close to Lambert. "We know professor Simeon is alive. You are going to take us to him."

The convincing, even sinister tone of her voice impressed Jack who, with his free hand, knocked Lambert's hat off and grabbed a fistful of his hair. He shoved the barrel of his gun hard into the back of the doctor's skull.

Maddie pulled the car around the building and out onto the highway. "Now would be a good time to start talking Doctor Lambert."

Lambert's eyes were squeezed shut. "Don't hurt me. Please, don't hurt me. They gave me no choice. God help me, I had no choice."

"You're going to be okay," said Maddie. "We don't want to hurt you. All you have to do is tell us where he is."

"They'll kill me. You...you don't know these people. They..."

"Tell us or you'll die here and now," said Jack. He cocked the gun. He pulled hard at Lambert's hair, bending his neck back. "Tell us." He shouted directly into his ear.

"Oh, God! Don't hurt me. All right, all right," the doctor screamed. "I'll tell you what I know."

He was breathing hard, his breath smelling of some kind of chalky medicine. He choked out his words: "They're holding him in an apartment in town. It's above a store."

"In Cadillac?" said Maddie.

"Yes."

"So, we're headed in the right direction."

"Yes."

"What store?" said Beth.

"*Phil's Drugs*, Second and Main. They've got him in an upstairs room. They're not hurting him. We would never hurt Andrew."

Jack let go of Lambert's hair and secured his gun.

The doctor sagged in his seat, breathing hard. "I never wanted any part of this. I'm a doctor, I never...you have to believe me." He covered his face with both hands, his body shaking. "You don't know what it's been like."

"Don't know, don't give a shit," said Beth.

Maddie drove into town and angle parked two doors down from *Phil's*. For the moment, they stayed in the car. There wasn't much traffic and only a few pedestrians dotted the sidewalks. The day was starting out sunny and cold.

Jack wondered how this was going to play out. "Been upstairs here before?" he said to Lambert.

"A few times."

"Is there a back way?"

"That'll be locked. You have to go through the store. There're stairs inside, toward the back."

"Do the store people know you," asked Maddie.

"Yes."

"Great, you'll lead the way."

They got out. From across the street a bundled-up elderly woman stared. Jack smiled. She didn't smile back.

"Tell them you're making a wellness visit," Beth suggested to Lambert as they neared *Phil's*.

Maddie prodded Lambert into the lead. They walked in. They attracted a stare from the guy behind the front counter as well as from the few customers inside. "Hey, Howard," said Lambert, forcing the words.

"Hey, Henry," said Howard at the counter, eyes on Maddie then shifting back to Lambert. "Everything okay, Henry?"

"Sure, never better."

It was a poor act but, as the four of them kept walking toward the back of the store, Howard went back to cashing out his customer.

They approached the pharmacy counter toward the back. A white coated man with a bald, bowling ball head looked up, peering over the top of his glasses. He eyed Lambert, then Beth, then Lambert again. "Hey, Henry," he said, slowly.

"Hey, Sam. We're just...we're going upstairs." He turned toward a closed door a few steps away beside the counter.

Sam took off his glasses. "They told me no visitors."

"I'm not a visitor, I'm the man's doctor. I need to make sure he's okay."

"It's a routine wellness check," added Beth.

Sam shook his head. "No need for that. My nephew's up there, you know, watching things, making sure the...well, making sure everything's all right."

This was taking too long. Jack exchanged a look with Maddie.

She stepped forward, pulling her badge. "I'm FBI, Sam. Is your nephew armed?"

Sam took a step back. His round face turned white. He shook his head. "No, why would he be armed? Look, don't hurt him. We're just making a little extra money renting the room out. That's all. I swear."

"Okay Sam, I believe you. We're not here to hurt anyone. You stay put. We may have some questions later. We're going up."

"Sure, no problem. Go on. It's not locked."

Maddie took the lead through the door and started up the dark stairway. Halfway up, she pulled her gun. "Keep quiet," she whispered to the others. She approached the door at the top. She tested it then nodded to Jack behind her.

Jack pulled his gun.

She swung the door open and ran in. "Hands up, FBI," she shouted.

Running in, Jack heard something fall onto the floor. In the far corner, a man, no, a teenage boy stood, hands in the air. On the floor at his feet lay the I-Pad he must have dropped.

"Keep your hands up," shouted Jack, stowing his gun. He walked closer and frisked the kid. Maddie kept her gun trained on him.

Lambert then Beth came into the room. Beth closed the door.

"Okay, you can sit down," said Jack to the kid. The room was a small studio apartment. There was an unmade bed in one corner and a mini kitchen diagonally opposite that.

"What's this about?" said the kid. "I'm just helping my uncle. If he's in some kind of trouble, I swear, I had nothing to do with it."

"Keep your mouth shut," ordered Maddie, lowering her gun. She held up her hand. "Hold on. I hear something."

In the quiet, Jack heard labored breathing coming from somewhere. He turned to the bed noticing the IV pole beside it. Plastic tubes ran under the rumpled covers. The blanket, he noticed, shifted ever so slowly in time with the breathing.

Beth hurried over. She pulled the sheet down just enough to expose the skeletal liver spotted body of a gray bearded man. She lifted his arm, checked his pulse, then checked the label on the bottle hanging on the IV pole. "They've got him on some pretty strong stuff."

"Can he be moved?" asked Maddie.

"His pulse is slow but steady. Yes, I think so. But he can't walk. He's barely breathing as it is. Poor guy."

"We'll have to carry him. Can you...disconnect him?"

Beth nodded. She detached the IV. "His breathing's congested but it's strong, considering. He's going to be out for a good twenty-four hours, maybe more." She gave Lambert a withering stare. "You call this man your patient? How could you let this happen?"

"I swear, we took good care of him at the home. We had no choice but to follow the decisions of his guardian."

"And you didn't think keeping him in this vegetative state was harmful?"

"You don't know the pressure I was under."

"Who is this so-called guardian?" asked Beth.

"I...I don't know exactly."

"How can you *not* know?"

"Look, all this can wait," said Maddie. "We have to get this guy out of here now. He can be moved, right?" This last directed at Beth.

"Yes, I think so. We can't leave him here."

"And we can't carry him through the store," said Jack.

"There's a back door," said Lambert.

Maddie turned to Beth, giving her the car keys. "You pull the car around back. Sheriff, you do the lifting. I'll take point."

"I'll need to grab some drugs and things downstairs...for Simeon," said Beth.

"Okay," said Maddie. "But be quick about it. And for God's sake, don't bother standing in line at the checkout to pay for it. This man's life is at stake."

"Right." Beth headed down the stairs.

Jack and Maddie wrapped Simeon in his sheet and blanket. The old man barely stirred. Jack picked him up, surprised at how light he was. He hoped he wouldn't...leak.

"You good?" said Maddie.

Jack gave a nod then said to Lambert: "You stay put, up here with the boy. Wait ten minutes then come down. The cops should be here by that time. You better have a good story to tell them. If you're smart, and if you care about this man's life, you'll keep quiet about us and about Simeon."

With the professor slung over his shoulder, Jack followed Maddie down the stairs. Halfway down, he froze at the blare of an alarm.

"Beth probably set that off with her shoplifting," said Maddie from the base of the stairs. "Come on, sheriff, keep moving. We gotta go, go, go!"

He raced down. Maddie flung the door open and charged through. Jack followed her past a few stunned customers, around the counter then past a bug-eyed Sam. Maddie reached a rear exit door labeled with a bright red *Alarm will sound* sticker. She charged through.

The second alarm blared, louder than the first raising shouts from the front of the store. Maddie held the door open for Jack. He struggled out into a snow covered alley next to a dumpster. There was no sign of Beth.

"Where is she?" said Maddie.

"She'll be here," he said, between breaths, chest heaving. With all the jostling Jack wondered if Simeon was still alive. He shifted his living burden then looked down the alley. Come on Beth. *Come on!*

An anxious moment passed.

Beneath the sound of the alarms, Jack heard a new sound, a faint roar, getting louder. A red *Ford Flex* bounded out of a turn into the alley, plowing a path directly to them. Through the windshield, he saw Beth, stone faced, gripping the wheel. The engine roared, tires spraying snow.

Jack and Maddie stepped back. The car swerved then stopped.

He pulled open the back door and tossed Simeon unceremoniously across onto the bench seat. He heard a grunt—yeah, still alive. He forced the old man's knees bent then slid in beside him and pulled the door shut.

Maddie was already inside, riding shotgun. "Go, go, go!" she shouted.

Beth hit the gas. The wheels spun. The car didn't move.

"Hold on," said Beth. "I got this." She used the accelerator, rocking the car back and forth once, then again, each time giving it more gas.

Heart pounding, Jack glanced through the rear window, the alley was still deserted.

Finally, the tires gained traction. They were moving forward, slowly gaining speed.

Beth exhaled. She kept the car moving. Faster now. Multiple sirens sounded in the distance. "Great, I'm gonna get arrested for shoplifting," she said.

"I'd worry more about kidnapping charges if I were you," said Maddie. "Take a right up here. We want to stay off the main road until we get out of town."

Beth skidded into the turn onto a plowed street. She put on more speed.

"We should turn ourselves in," said Jack leaning forward. "We're the ones who rescued Simeon. I'm a sheriff, you're the FBI for God's sake. That should give us some credibility."

"Will you *please* get it through your head? You are dead. Both of you are dead." She pointed. "Take another right here."

Beth turned, speeding up.

"No more sirens," said Maddie after another ten minutes. "We might actually make it out of this fix." She gave Beth a few more directions sounding to Jack as if she knew where she wanted to go. "How's our new friend back there?" she asked him.

"Still breathing. Where are we off to now?"

"East." She popped the glove compartment, found a map. "There's a little town called...Standish up ahead out on Lake Michigan, sorry, I'm a little turned around...Lake Huron. Either of you been there before? Any friends or relation there?"

"No."

"Good. That's where we're going. We'll stop at a store, maybe a *Goodwill* for a change of clothes and more traveling stuff. Then check into a motel—nothing fancy, the sleazier the better. I think we can all use some sleep."

"Amen, to that," said Beth, both hands white-knuckled to the wheel.

CHAPTER 18

The run to Standish proved uneventful and, as planned they were able to stop at a second-hand store for a supply of clothes. They found a cheap motel and by two in the afternoon were able to catch up on some sleep. With the curtains drawn Beth and Maddie slept in the bed closest to the window while Jack shared the other with Simeon. The adrenalin that had kept Jack awake for nearly thirty-six hours was slowly draining, replaced by his body's desperate need for sleep. He felt as if they'd been on the run for a week, but it had only been two days. Yeah, two days ago he'd gotten into his cruiser heading to Houghton then all of...*this* started happening.

Beside Jack the old man breathed heavily but otherwise did not move. He smelled of medicine with urine overtones. When they'd first gotten into the room, Beth checked his vitals. She'd been surprised to see they were nearly normal for a man his age which she guessed to be mid-eighties. Watching him in the darkness, Jack could make out his head lying inert on the pillow as if he were more a thing than a man. What secrets might that head contain? Maybe many, maybe none.

Jack rolled over. He wondered if Beth, was still awake. Their simple lives had been tossed upside down. They were on the run and there seemed to be no end to the craziness. But, whatever happened, they would get through it together. He wondered what tomorrow would bring. With that thought, he drifted off into a deep sleep.

A piercing scream shattered the silence. Jack jumped out from under the covers. He stood, staring back at Simeon whose scream had morphed into a low, monotone hum. In the faint light, he watched the old man sit up in the bed, his body swaying back and forth as if he were in some kind of psychic trance.

"He's coming out of it," said Beth, getting up, eyes on the old man.

"Scared the hell out of me."

Maddie turned on the light.

Eyes squeezed shut, Simeon seemed not to notice. He kept up his humming and swaying.

Beth took a step closer. "Mr. Simeon?"

The swaying stopped. The humming stopped. His eyes remained shut. He cocked his head.

"You're fine, Mr. Simeon. We are friends. We're taking care of you."

Simeon covered his face with his hands, holding them there as the pace of his breathing became more controlled. He opened his mouth. He hacked out a violent cough. He cleared his throat. "Am I...dead?"

Beth shared a glance with Jack. "No, Mr. Simeon, you're not dead, and don't worry, we're not going to hurt you."

Simeon lowered his hands, his eyes two narrow slits. He looked around the room taking no special interest in the three people staring down at him. "What the hell kind of shit hole is this?"

Jack almost laughed, at the unwittingly close impression of his own crotchety old grandfather.

"It's a motel room, Mr. Simeon," said Maddie. "Sorry, it's best we could do."

"You were under sedation," said Beth. "We're not sure for how long. How're you feeling?"

"I've got to take a piss. Oh, shit! You've got me in diapers."

"It wasn't us."

Awkwardly, Jack helped him into the bathroom then back to the bed where Beth re-checked his vitals. "Your breathing is labored and..."

"Hell, I could have told you that. What kind of a doctor are you?"

"We'll have to do some exercises to get your legs and arms working again. Other than that, you appear to be in decent shape considering what you've been through. Are you hungry? It'll be morning in a few hours. We'll get some breakfast."

"Where are my clothes?"

"We've got some we think will fit."

"How long have I been...?"

"We don't know exactly," said Jack. He told him the date.

"Shit, I remember...well I guess I don't remember much. It feels like a long, long time since I did anything other than sleep. And...dream. Nice dreams, some of them." His eyes opened wider, the whites a sickly yellow. "What have I done? Why did you do this to me?"

"It wasn't us, Mr. Simeon," said Beth.

"What's the last thing you remember? Do you remember anything about the people who did this to you?" said Maddie.

"You sound like a cop."

"Very perceptive, Mr. Simeon. I'm FBI. Agent Cooper at your service"

He turned to Jack. "And you?"

"I'm Jack Holiday, sheriff of Gull Harbor. This is my wife, Beth."

"I'm a pharmacist," she said. "Up in Gull Harbor."

He shook his head. "Gull Harbor...don't know it."

"We're in Standish Michigan, Mr. Simeon. Do you remember who you are?"

"I...well, I *was* a scientist. Now..." He shook his head slowly, looking as if he were about to cry. "Now, I'm just a tired old man." He was silent for a moment. "It was the Moorhouse boy. Can't say for certain, but sure as shit it was him keeping me...keeping me in that damn place. He used to be my friend. Six years it was, before they...before they..."

"He's weakening," said Beth. "It's the drugs still working on him." She helped lay him back down.

With his head on his pillow, his face crinkled into a wry expression and he managed a whisper. "They're afraid of me you know." As his eyes slowly closed, a tear escape from one of them.

"He's weak, he needs fresh air and he needs food," said Beth. "He'll probably wake up again in a few hours."

"It's 3:30 in the morning," said Jack. "We could all use a few more hours sleep." Beth and Maddie went back to their bed while Jack, deciding he'd had enough of Simeon's heavy breathing, opted for the recliner.

At seven, the three of them dressed, then gathered around the still asleep Simeon. Jack was elected to prod him awake.

He touched Simeon's shoulder, softly at first then more aggressively. He remembered his mom waking him the same way. *Time to go to school, Jacky boy,* she'd say in a sing-song voice.

"Mr. Simeon? Time to wake up, Mr. Simeon."

Simeon groaned, then sat up so abruptly that Jack jumped back. "Who the hell are you?" he said in a hoarse voice. He looked around the room. "Where the hell am I?"

As if it were a script, they repeated much of their three in the morning dialogue.

"The drugs are messing with his short-term memory," said Beth, taking Jack and Maddie aside. "We'll need to be careful not to agitate him. Pumping him for information will have to wait."

Maddie shook her head. "We don't have time. By now *Endeavor* has left Duluth; she'll be at the locks before long. We can't afford to lose her in the lower lakes."

"Is that what we're going to do now?" said Jack. "Chase freighters?"

"Yes, Jack. That is what we're going to do."

"Food will help," said Beth, eyes still on Simeon.

Jack helped the old man to his feet and with the other necessities. They checked out of the motel and drove to a nearby *Waffle House.*

At the counter they ordered food, then claimed a table in the corner. When the food came, Simeon stared at his pancakes and sausages as if not knowing what to do with them.

"You need to eat, Mr. Simeon," advised Beth. "It's the best thing for you."

"My name is Andrew. Andrew Steven Simeon. It wasn't easy growing up with that set of initials. I never forgave my mom and dad for what they insisted was a silly oversight. You can call me Andrew."

Jack knew Simeon had intended this story to be funny. It was likely one he'd told many times in his life. But now, it came out of his lips slowly, in a serious monotone. It seemed to Jack that the man was desperately trying to understand not only the things going on around him but the chaos that must be going on in his head.

"Thank you, Andrew. You can call me Beth. This is Jack and…"

"I'm Maddie."

"We're trying to help you. You understand that, don't you?"

Andrew rubbed his eyes then again looked down at his food. He picked up a sausage. "Yes...of course I understand. I'm not a child." He took a bite, then another.

They all ate quickly, Andrew finishing off the sausages and his orange juice and his coffee while leaving the pancakes untouched. No one said much until Maddie leaned forward, locking eyes with Andrew. She placed the tips of her fingers gently on his. "You are a professor, aren't you Andrew?"

At her touch, Andrew gave a start, but didn't pull his hand back. "Yes...that's right. Yes, I *am* a professor." Behind the stubble of his failed gray beard, the corner of his lips spread into a half smile. His yellow eyes glistened. His voice shook. "That was a long time ago."

"What was your field?"

"I was...Yes, it was physics. I was a professor of physics." His lips broadened further. He shook his head, his brow furrowed. "How the hell could I have forgotten that?"

"But you do remember. Is that right Andrew? You remember now? And you remember things about Mayfield Industries."

The old man took on a mystified expression, mouth open as if in awe. "You mean that was real? That all...wasn't a dream?"

"No, Andrew that was not a dream." Maddie wrapped his hand lightly in hers. "That was your *life* Andrew, and we're going to help you remember it. We're going to help you remember everything." Maddie released his hand. She took a sip of coffee, then set her cup down. "I think we can make this work."

"What do you mean? Make what work?" said Jack.

"The drugs are wearing off. The truth about Mayfield, what's on that freighter and maybe even who's behind everything that's been going on. I think Andrew knows these things."

"I do?" said Andrew.

"Yes, you do, Andrew. It'll take time, but we'll help you remember."

"And then what?" said Beth.

"I don't know yet. All I know is, with Andrew's help, we have a chance to figure this all out."

Jack shook his head. "We should take what we know and go to the police or the FBI or the CIA or Homeland Security. *That* is what we should do."

"That is not going to happen," said Maddie. "For the time being, we're going to do this my way. If that doesn't work out, then yes, we can do all those things. Believe me, the bureaucratic wheels of government move too slowly and often in unpredictable directions." She stood and put on her coat. "Remember, I'm the one who's been keeping you alive. You need to trust me to see this through."

Andrew got up. Maddie helped him with his second-hand coat. "Are you with us, professor?"

Andrew stared back. "I'm sorry but...who are you again?"

Her face softened. "I'm Maddison. You can call me Maddie. Come on Andrew, we've got to get moving."

"Moving? Where are we're going?"

"North."

CHAPTER 19

"We should at least notify the Coast Guard about that ship you're so concerned about," said Jack.

"No, we're not doing that," said Maddie as she drove. "Not yet anyway."

"Why the hell not?"

Maddie shook her head. "I...I have my reasons and...I need to tell you something." She kept her eyes on the road. Jack waited. "I'm sorry, Jack. I was going to tell you both but..."

"Just say it, damn-it."

"Harlan Lattimore, he's the captain of *Endeavor*. He's...my father."

Jack had been prepared for any number of things she might say, but not this. He gave Beth a glance then turned to Cooper. "It's like a Darth Vadar reveal. Are you serious? How..."

"I know, I know, I should have told you. I meant to but..."

"You've been protecting him," said Beth. "That's why you're trying to handle all this on your own."

Jack felt his blood rise. "Pull over. Pull over now! I'll drive. We're going back up to Houghton. You're going to tell Chief Brewster everything you know and Beth and I are going back to Gull Harbor."

"You're forgetting that somebody wants you both dead."

"I can do a much better job than you at protecting us."

"The fact that Harlan Lattimore is my father changes nothing."

"It means we can't trust you. What the hell else aren't you telling us?"

"Nothing. There's nothing else. I know I should have told you sooner. I've hated him for so long but now, he's in the middle of something really big. Maybe even 9-11 big. I don't know what it is. I'm not even sure my father knows."

"If this is all about what's aboard his ship, how could he not know?"

"My father is many things but he is not a traitor to this country."

"I remember my father," said Andrew. "He was hard on me but...fathers are important. Oh, and we need to get some food. I'm hungry."

"We just ate," said Maddie.

"Does Lattimore know you're trying to stop him?"

"Maybe. He might have put two and two together after seeing you show up that morning. He might have figured me to be the one that tipped you off."

"You should have told us."

"Excuse me, but there's a burger place up there," said Andrew pointing.

Maddie sped up. "Fuck it. All right, we'll stop." She cut the wheel hard right and pulled into the drive through lane with two cars in front. "Everyone, order something. We'll eat on the road and we're not stopping again."

"Give me your phone," Jack said to Beth.

"She's got it. She took it from me when she abducted me."

"I didn't abduct you. And you're not calling anyone Jack."

"Yes, I am. I'm..."

May I take your order?

They ordered, got the food then pulled out onto the highway.

"I'm checking in with Sharon," said Jack to Maddie. "She deserves to know we're alive and she might be able to influence the investigation into our death."

"We can't take that chance."

"She can slow things down. She can steer Chief Brewster away from the truth that we're still alive. She can conceal or even get rid of evidence. Believe me, she can be pretty persuasive."

Maddie remained silent for a moment. "So many things could go wrong Jack. But...I guess I owe you this for holding back on you. Can she keep a secret?"

"Yes. I would trust her with my life."

"That's exactly what you'll be doing. But, all right. Here, use my secure phone." Maddie balanced her burger on her knee, then fished it out of her pocket." She unlocked it and handed it to Jack. "I'm trusting you, do not screw this up."

"That's funny, coming from you. It's *you* who has to regain *our* trust, remember? I'll use her private number." He keyed it in.

"Tell her I say hi," said Beth.

"Who is Sharon?" asked Andrew through his food.

Sharon picked up with a tentative, "Hello?"

"Hi Sharon, it's me, everything okay?" He put her on speaker.

"If this is some kind of prank you can shove it up your ass buddy."

Jack smiled. It was good to hear her voice. "No, it really is me, Sharon. And I've got Beth with me. She says hi."

"Hi Sharon," said Beth.

There was silence on Sharon's end, then: "How do I know...Okay, tell me something only the sheriff would know."

"I know this is your private number."

"Pick something else."

"I have a bottle of gin in the bottom right-hand drawer of my desk."

"You do?"

"Yeah, go check."

"Well, I can't check right now. I'm in the can."

"Okay...let's see...your cat's name is Dylan. How's that? Look, I'm calling you on your private number. How many people know your private number."

"Well, lately it's gotten to be not so private."

"Okay well, I'll explain everything when I see you but for right now you've got to make sure everyone, and I mean *everyone*, thinks Beth and I are dead. Got it?"

"O...kay. That's pretty much the case already."

"Good. You need to make sure it stays that way."

"Is someone dead?" said Andrew.

"Who was that?" said Sharon. "Look, just tell me…"

"I can't tell you. It's important that everyone thinks Beth and I are dead."

"Is this a life or death thing?"

Maddie leaned over and shouted into the phone. "Yes, it's a Goddamn life or death thing for God's sake."

"Shit. Is that…"

Maddie grabbed the phone. "Yes. This is Agent Cooper FBI. Listen to me very carefully. You will tell *no one,* that you ever had this conversation with Sheriff Holiday. If you ever do, I will find out and make sure you're on the IRS audit list every year for the rest of your Goddamn life. Have you got that?"

"Okay. Okay! Holy, shit. I promise not to tell. What the hell's going on boss, has she kidnapped you?"

Jack took the phone back. "No. It's…nothing like that. Now, is everything okay there?"

"Yeah, we're good, sort of. Bob's out with the flu or something. We've got a near white out right now and the lights are flickering like the power might go out. So, Ron and I might be stuck here for the night. Except for that, we're doing fine. Everybody's really sad you're, you know…dead. I cried. They'll be having a little ceremony for…but, you're coming back, right?"

"Has Chief Brewster been by?"

"Yeah. He calls me every day. He's the one heading up the investigation into your…demise. That's what he calls it."

"He can't know we're alive, Sharon. Not yet anyway. Try to slow down his investigation."

"What? But how would I…"

"Just try, that's all. But you can't be obvious about it. We'll be in danger if the wrong people find out we're alive. I'm sorry but that's all I can tell you."

"O…kay."

"Good luck with the snow."

"Sheriff?"

"Yeah?"

"I'm glad you guys are alive."

Jack ended the call and gave the phone back to Maddie.

"I have no idea what that accomplished," she said.

"That's because nobody you care about thinks you're dead," said Jack.

Maddie drove on, staring through the windshield as if she hadn't heard. Then: "Yeah, I guess there might be some truth in that."

Jack felt better having talked to Sharon, having reconnected with the world he'd left behind. He hoped it would still be there for him when he and Beth returned.

"Sharon sounded stressed," said Beth after a few more miles. "You worried about her?"

"She'll be fine," said Jack. "The station has a backup generator."

"I meant she might be stressed about you and about managing things. Not to mention she might be snowed in alone with Ron tonight. I hear they have something of a history."

"Really?"

"Yes, really. It's amazing how you can be so good at your job and yet be so oblivious to the obvious."

"We're going to Cheboygan. I know a place," said Maddie abruptly.

"Wow, you're telling us that and we didn't even have to ask?" said Jack.

"Another motel?" said Beth.

"A cottage. It'll be empty this time of year. It's near the shore. It belongs to my dad. It'll give us time to rest and time to find out more about Professor Simeon and his journal."

"Oh, do you know Professor Simeon?" said Andrew. "I once knew him too. But now...well, I'm not quite sure."

It was dark and snowing by the time they pulled into Cheboygan. They stopped for gas and groceries, then back tracked south a few miles where Maddie pulled onto a narrow unpaved road that twisted up a gentle slope. She leaned close to the windshield peering into the darkness ahead. Their car swerved at every switch back. From both sides, dense woods leaned in. "Almost there," she said.

"I don't see a thing," said Beth. She'd unstrapped and was leaning forward, arms folded on the front seat back.

"There," said Maddie with some relief in her voice. She sped up, turned the wheel and pulled up a driveway where she parked. She kept the engine running.

In the wash of the headlights stood an A-frame cottage, tall and dark.

"Nobody home," said Beth.

"Where are we?" said Andrew.

Maddie said nothing, staring at the place.

"You've been here before," said Jack.

"A long time ago," she said, voice low. "It was a...well, yeah, a long time ago. We'd better get inside. It'll be cold. The place will have been winterized but we should be able to get the furnace up and running." She cut the engine. They got out.

Jack felt his facial skin tighten from the frigid wind. They retrieved their things from the back then headed up a gradual slope, snow crunching underfoot.

With his arms around a bag of groceries, Jack trailed the others. A gust of wind rustled the branches of the tall trees. High above them stars sparkled. His breath rose in a frosty vapor. *Beautifully dangerous*. Yeah, a man freezing to death out here might still have an appreciation for the beauty of it all.

On the porch, Maddie turned the doorknob and walked inside. "People around here leave their doors unlocked through the winter in case anyone comes along desperate to get out of the cold. It's a lot more practical than paying for repairs from a break in."

"We do the same up on the Keweenaw," said Jack, last inside. He put the groceries down onto a barely visible coffee table, then shut the door behind him. He locked it. Cooper used her cellphone flashlight and panned the room: fireplace, couch, a few recliners, a table with chairs and a kitchen

Andrew sat. "It's cold. Would someone please turn on the lights?"

It took an hour to get things settled inside. Jack found the generator, got it running then found the electrical box. One by one he flipped the breakers on. The lights came on and, to his relief, so did the furnace.

"Should be enough propane for a few days," said Maddie. "That's all we'll need. There are three bedrooms and one bathroom. There's no cell coverage out here. Nobody knows we're here. We're safer than we've been since we left Gull Harbor."

They put away the groceries and remained in their coats as the place slowly warmed.

CHAPTER 20

Lattimore focused his binoculars south through the dim afternoon haze. Well beyond the horizon lay the tip of the Keweenaw peninsula where he'd risked his ship and where, one man had drowned and another had been shot then later killed along with his wife. Three lives lost, all because of the cargo now hidden somewhere aboard his ship.

He'd seen the news reports about Sheriff Holiday getting shot, being rescued, then recovering, then finally dying along with his wife in a car accident. Of course, it hadn't been an accident.

He put down the binoculars then sat in his leather recliner that was bolted down to the deck. He eyed Sullivan at the helm.

The two of them had sailed aboard *Endeavor* for more than five years and he still didn't know much about the man. He knew he'd been married once, even had a kid somewhere that he never talked about. Just like Lattimore, Sullivan had needed some easy money and didn't seem bothered by exactly how he made it. Together one night, over a few beers, they decided all of this was worth the risk.

That was how it started. Run the ship and play dumb about whatever secret cargo was taken aboard. Get it from point A to point B. They'd both made big money under the table that sometimes tripled his above board pay.

Yeah, smuggling was easy, it was lucrative and his country owed him at least that much as payback for all the time and effort he'd wasted on his military career.

Sullivan, probably had his own way of justifying things.

Most of their crew of twenty had no idea they were involved with a smuggling syndicate. They were out here living the life of a deckhand or a galley grunt, or an oiler to pay for college or to have a story or two to tell their grandchildren. Some, like Lattimore had chosen this life as a way to forget his own tarnished past. He had gotten people killed. He had gotten kids killed. After five years on the lakes, you would think those memories would have faded. But they hadn't.

Sullivan took a gulp of coffee. "What happens after we get to Detroit?"

"We unload, we get paid and we, well I, will be done," said Lattimore. "You'll be captain once I'm out of the picture. Yes, you and Katerina will make a fine pair without me getting in your way. Or did you think I didn't know about your little get togethers. I also know about your regular transmissions to her informing her of the least little thing that happens aboard this ship."

"That has nothing to do with the performance of my duties aboard this ship or with my allegiance to you as captain…at least in nautical matters."

"But it has everything to do with your allegiance to her in all non-nautical matters." Lattimore held his outward calm. "Do you trust her? Do you love her? Do you really think she might love you? If you do, you're an even bigger fool than I am."

"I'm not ready to retire."

"You've been well paid over these years, maybe more than me. Many men retire in their forties. Why not you?"

"It's been me doing all the dirty work for her. I'm the one who knows her secrets. I'm the one who allowed you to keep your nose clean. She won't let me quit."

Lattimore shifted his weight in the recliner and laid his head back. "Do you know what it is we picked up that morning off the Keweenaw?"

"I don't ask questions."

"But you do know where it's hidden. You hid it yourself, didn't you?" Sullivan's silence answered both questions. "I think you told me you have a kid somewhere, is that right?"

"Yes, a son down in Florida. He's fifteen now. Lives with his mom. I send them money."

"Does your son know much about you?"

"He was only a few months old when my wife and I split."

"Have you found yourself wanting to look him up and see what kind of young man he was turning into? He's probably wondering who his father was and where the hell he ran off to. Or do you think your ex filled him in on that with her side of the story?"

"I didn't just run off. It was..."

"Complicated?" offered Lattimore. "Yeah, I guess things like that always are. Look at us, two relatively accomplished men, you being content with things as they are, maybe in love with Katerina or maybe not. Me desperate to get out of all of this shit. Both of us with a kid somewhere who probably doesn't know and doesn't care if we're even alive." He closed his eyes. "Sometimes it's too damn complicated to even think about."

Two days passed uneventfully until *Endeavor* approached the locks at Sault Ste. Marie. The tower guarding the entrance flashed a green light. At the helm, Lattimore throttled up to quarter speed. He gave a friendly wave to the folks in the tower as his ship entered the narrow confines of the lock then reversed engines bringing *Endeavor* to a dead stop. Down on deck his crew worked the ropes fore, aft and midship in concert with the men on shore. At the sounding of a warning alarm, the massive steel and concrete door at the entrance to the lock closed.

The water within the lock whirled and gurgled, lowering slowly, bringing *Endeavor* down to the level of the open waters of Lake Huron.

After a time, another shore alarm sounded. The doors at the exit to the lock, opened slowly. Lines were cast and Lattimore guided his ship out from the close quarters of the lock.

Once clear of the lock, Lattimore noticed one of the small tourist boats, racing off the port side having apparently shared the lock, giving their passengers a thrill at being so close to a Great Lakes Freighter. The boat was running late in the season and the few heavily garbed tourists aboard waved. It sped ahead then swerved about fifty yards off *Endeavor*'s bow as if to lead the way. He waved back then spotted a little girl standing at the stern.

Through a pair of kids' binoculars, she stared directly at him.

Lattimore stepped to the side for a better look. Light auburn hair flowing back with the wind, she stood not much taller than the waist of the woman beside her who must be her mother.

He raised a hand to his forehead, giving the girl a casual salute.

She smiled. Excited, she pulled on her mother's coat and pointed. She then adopted a rigid pose returning his salute. The mother waved her thanks.

Lattimore tipped his cap. The boat sped off.

In his mind, Lattimore replayed the determined, happy look in the girl's eyes that so reminded him of Maddie. He hadn't seen his daughter in years. Yes, he missed her. He knew she was a grown woman now and he knew much more. Yes, she had become a bright, accomplished woman. But to him, she would always be an eight-year-old little girl, excited about everything. That was how old she'd been when he turned his back on her and her mother.

As he watched the tourist boat fade in the distance, he remembered his conversation with Katerina in Duluth. She could be right that Maddie was the one who'd gotten the sheriff out there that morning. He also remembered Katerina's veiled threat.

Dry mouthed, he wondered where Maddie might be at that moment.

CHAPTER 21

Jack stepped out of the bathroom, the plumbing complaining loudly behind him. The sun gleamed bright through the windows of the A-frame, filtered by the trees yet amplified by the sparkling white snow.

Maddie already had the coffee brewed. At the table she looked up from her steaming cup. "Good morning, Jack. Sleep well?"

He poured himself a cup and took the chair across from her. "Yes, I slept very well. Nothing against Andrew but Beth is a much better bed partner. How about you?"

"Just fine. She up yet?"

"Still dozing. The place looks better in the daylight."

She pointed. "Lake Huron's right out there, only about a hundred yards. It's a fifty-foot drop to the shore so it's a good idea to watch your step if you go out there."

"You said this is your dad's place."

"We used to come out here most summers. It was fun. They fought over it during the divorce. He won."

"And your mom won you?"

"It was more like she got stuck with me. I was eight."

"That must have been hard," said Beth, walking in, heading for the coffee. "For you and for her."

"She never forgave him for what he did to our family."

"And neither did you?"

"I got over it." She said this almost in a whisper.

"Does he come here often? The place looks lived in, well kept up."

"He rents it out to locals. I don't know that he's been here much. I'm not in touch with him at all. Once...he was a good man mostly."

"And now he works as a smuggler and you never see him," said Jack.

Maddie shrugged.

"How's your mom?" said Beth.

"She died fifteen years ago. It was about the time I got out of high school. Just when I was about to stop being a boat anchor for her, she...she dies." Her lips tightened. "Yeah, hell of a family life, right? Look, I don't want to get into all this crap. It's old news. There's no changing it."

"But here you are, still caring enough about him to try and protect him."

"Yeah, I've got a streak of stupid that runs right through me. Guess I should have warned you about that." She got up and turned to the window. "Have you checked on Andrew?"

"Still asleep," said Beth.

"We need to question him. We need to find out what he knows. Right now, we're about a day, maybe two days ahead of *Endeavor* passing through here."

"So, she passes through here. What then?" said Jack. "They could deliver those crates anywhere between here and Detroit and we'd never know it. Hell, maybe they've already been off-loaded somewhere in Canada."

"Why don't you just call your dad?" said Beth.

"And say what? Pull into port? Turn yourself in? He'll go to prison."

"He *should* go to prison," said Jack.

"Maybe he'd agree with you. But I don't see it that way and neither do I."

"He broke the law. He *is* breaking the law. He's a criminal. You know he is."

"He'll do the right thing. You'll see. When things are on the line, he always does the right thing. Those Semper-Fi juices are still thick in his blood. They're so thick he..."

"He was a marine," said Jack.

"Through and through. Look, I've said all I'm going to say about my dad. We're safe here. We're comfortable. We get Professor Simeon dried out, see what he knows and we watch for *Endeavor*. Right now she's still a long way north of us. I'll use my computer to get a fix on her and we see where she goes."

"We don't have Wi-Fi," said Beth.

"It's not that far into town. I'll hit the local Starbucks, check *Endeavor*'s position twice a day. If she makes port anywhere, we can get there fast."

"That's when we get the Coast Guard involved."

"Yes," she said without as much conviction as Jack would have liked. "And once that happens, the two of you can go back home and reincarnate yourselves."

Jack gave Beth a skeptical glance. "Sounds like a plan, I guess."

On getting up at midmorning, Andrew insisted on a breakfast of eggs and bacon. Once done with that, Beth and Maddie worked with him.

"Do you recognize this?" Maddie asked, placing the journal in front of him. "We think you wrote it."

"It's not mine."

"We found it in your room at *Autumn Leaves*, the place where they kept you."

"It's not mine."

"Here, I'll read a page," said Beth.

The work at the University goes on. The work is hard and dirty. My hands are black. I don't know if they'll ever come clean again. The men in their lab coats watch, they take notes, they shout orders then lean over their desks playing with their slide rules, writing things down, scratching their heads, deep in their thoughts as if those thoughts had somehow gotten just as dirty as our hands.

She looked up from the page.

"It sounds like a good book," said Andrew with enthusiasm. "Please, keep reading."

Maddie shook her head. She packed up her computer and put on her coat. "I need to clear my head. I'm heading into town to get a fix on *Endeavor*. Anybody need anything?"

"How about a deck of cards and some popcorn," suggested Jack.

"Sure, why the hell not. It makes as much sense as anything else we might be doing right now." She left.

Through the window, Jack watched her scrape the frost from the windshield, get in and pull out.

The second day was a replay of the first, until dark. The three of them were playing three draw poker, Jack winning, the bowl of popcorn beside him almost empty. It was nearing nine when Maddie stiffened abruptly and put down her cards. She held up her hand, listening. The sounds of Andrew's snoring wafted down from the upper floor bedroom. Long seconds went by. Then, from outside, Jack heard the faint sound of a car.

"Take cover," Maddie shouted. She killed the lights.

Jack's, eyes adjusted quickly to the flickering light of the fireplace. Not smart having a fire going right now. On a knee behind the couch, he pulled his gun. "Everybody down? Beth, where are you?"

"In the kitchen, behind the counter."

"I'm beside the window," said Maddie, "Gun ready."

"Yeah, I see you," said Jack. "I'm behind the couch, gun on the door. How could anybody know we're here?"

"Maybe they're some VRBO renters," said Beth. "This could be one hell of a welcome party for them."

"You're right. Whoever's out there could be harmless, I'll do the talking. If they start firing, you know what to do." Maddie inched the curtain aside.

Except for Andrew, everything was silent.

A pair of headlights lit the curtains.

"One car. Looks like two guys. One's getting out." Maddie moved from the window to stand beside the door, gun in hand. "Everybody, stay quiet. This might still be nothing."

Jack calmed his breathing, eyes on the door.

Long seconds went by.

From outside, somebody tried the doorknob, then knocked.

Jack waited for Maddie to say something, to open the door, to do something. But she remained beside the window, perfectly still, maybe hoping whoever was out there would go away.

They knocked again.

"Who's there?" Maddie shouted as if in response to a knock knock joke. "We've got guns," she added.

"Put your guns away. We're from Captain Lattimore. I'm looking for Maddison Cooper."

Maddie shouted back: "I'm not prepared to accept visitors. Who are you?"

"Are you Cooper?"

Maddie stayed silent.

"Look, me and my buddy, he's still in the car, we're not here to harm anyone. We're unarmed. We're here for Cooper. To take her someplace safe."

"This place was pretty safe until you showed up. Go away."

"Come on, it's cold out here. We could break down this door or you could let us in. Your choice."

"How do I know you're from Lattimore?"

"His first name is Harlan. Only his friends know that. And, if you're Cooper, you're his daughter."

Maddie hesitated. She unlocked the door. "All right, come in. But put your hands where I can see them."

The door swung open. A tall man filled the doorway. Hands high, he took a step inside.

"Close the door," ordered Maddie. She turned the lights on.

The man, stocky, long bushy beard, Michigan State sweatshirt, blinked a few times, eyes adjusting. "My buddy's out there."

"He can wait in the car."

The man closed the door.

Slowly Jack stood, gun pointed at the visitor. He came around from behind the sofa.

"Shit," said the man, eyes on Jack. "We were told you'd be alone. Who's this guy?"

"A friend."

An upstairs door squeaked.

The man's eyes went up to Andrew who'd emerged completely naked from the upstairs bedroom. "And what's up with him?"

"He's old. He's harmless," said Beth, tentatively sticking her head up over the top of the counter in the kitchen.

"Shit! Are there any more of you?"

"Who are you?" said Maddie.

"We're here to…crap, I'm going to have to make a call."

The man lowered his hands. Jack stiffened, gun still raised.

"Come on. What's with all of you? I'm unarmed for God's sake."

"Well, excuse us for being a little jumpy," shouted Beth. "We've been on the run for days and someone's been trying really hard to kill us."

"You said Lattimore sent you," said Maddie.

The man gave her a shaky smile. "You're really her aren't you? You're little Maddie. He said you were a real bad ass now." He looked around the room. "Believe me, we're not here to hurt you. All I know is, we're here to…" He turned back to Maddie. "Hell, I wasn't supposed to tell you any of this but…we're here to take you to him."

"Why?"

"Hell, I don't know. We're doing your dad a favor. That's it. You don't remember me, do you. I'm Bert Finley. I'm the kid that used to take care of this place for your dad. Brought in groceries and did other stuff."

"You don't look like him."

"Well, you sure as hell don't look much like you did back then either, little honey. It's been a lot of years gone by."

Was that a blush on her face? Jack wondered.

"You got ID?" said Maddie, hand out.

The man dug a wallet out of his back pocket and tossed it to her. She inspected it and tossed it back. "Lattimore was supposed to come here. That was the plan."

"That might have been *your* plan. Guess it wasn't *his*. I'm going to lower my hands now." His eyes shifted to Jack. "That okay with you?"

At a nod from Maddie, Jack lowered his gun.

With obvious relief, Finley brought his hands down. He took a long breath. "Now, if it's okay with you, Maddie, I'm going to get my friend in here and the…six of us are going to have a friendly conversation."

CHAPTER 22

The route from the locks south into Lake Huron is circuitous and dangerous, especially in the month of November. Lattimore had made the run many times, always personally manning the helm, timing the trip with stop watch precision as if it were an Olympic event, entering the start and finish times in the logbook.

Today he had a better reason to be in a hurry.

He took another sip of coffee. He held the cup, warming his hands, and he wondered if Finley had found Maddie.

It had been a curious coincidence. First, the little girl on that boat who had reminded him so much of little Maddie, then the text he'd received a day later from the real Maddie—*his* Maddie:

Abort. Meet at basecamp.

She was trying to stop him. Doesn't she know what she's risking? Katerina would not hesitate to kill her if she viewed her as a threat. She'd told him as much in Duluth. It wasn't a stretch to think Katerina knew about his cottage on Lake Huron. And it wasn't a stretch to think she knew he used to call the place *Basecamp*.

There'd been only one solution to this problem and he'd already contacted Finley to set things in motion. Still, he worried. Timing was important.

He stood at the helm, hands on the controls with *Endeavor's* engines rumbling through the deck. Beside him, Sullivan scanned both shores where the ice stretched wide and thick. Lattimore looked to the east. It was early afternoon, the weather clear. Soon he would change course, first north then due east, guiding his ship around the north shore of Sugar Island.

He eyed the jagged ice only twenty yards out. "This will be the last run of the season. Let's make it a good one. Kick us up to twelve knots."

"Aye, that," said Sullivan without conviction.

"If you like, you can make a note in the logbook that you have concerns about our speed and I have chosen to ignore those concerns."

Sullivan made no move to do so.

Lattimore adjusted course, two points to starboard. The ship responded, centered now between tiny Cook Island to the north and Sugar Island to the south. His heart pounded. The wind howled. The snow swirled off the ice. White capped waves crashed against the hull.

Up ahead stood the Cook Island Lighthouse. Lattimore waited for *Endeavor*'s bow to come directly abreast of the it, where the channel between the ice shelves narrowed. Once there, he spoke calmly, "Log the time...now."

Sullivan called out the reading on the ship's chronometer then penned the entry in the log.

Lattimore gripped the controls, eyes on the bow and the channel ahead. He gave only an occasional glance ashore where it appeared as if the ship was gliding over ice, not water.

When *Endeavor* slipped past Drummond Island where the channel widened into the open waters of Lake Huron, Sullivan made another log entry. "You beat your best time by three minutes, captain," he said. "I hope you're happy about that."

"I am. That record should stand for a while, don't you think? Now, get Mr. Winters up here. It's time you taught him a few things about manning the helm."

Lattimore stepped off the bridge and walked to his cabin. He pulled open a drawer on his nightstand. From a half-filled bottle, he poured himself a shot of whiskey and drank it down. Not bothering to undress, he climbed into his bed.

He awoke with a start to the shaky voice of Third Mate Winters over the squawk box. Hopeful, he checked the time. It was 1:50 A.M.

So far, so good.

"We're being hailed, captain," explained Winters, Carter beside him as Lattimore stepped onto the bridge. Winters pointed over the bow to the barely discernible horizon ahead. There, like a distant star rising, Lattimore saw a flickering, pinpoint of light. "It's the mail-carrier *Charles Foster* out of Rogers City. She's still a few miles out. She's got her floodlight on. A guy named Epperson's at the wheel. Says he's got a special delivery. But I..."

"Get him on the radio," said Lattimore. He spoke into the mic. "This is Captain Lattimore of *Endeavor*. Is this Epperson I'm speaking to? You're up kind of early for a mail in the pail run aren't you?"

"You got that right, captain. And this ain't no mail run. I got four people who want permission to board your vessel. One of them is an FBI gal named Cooper. She says she knows you."

"Yeah, I know her. Good of you getting out of bed and all. Who are the others?"

"Damned if I know, and she ain't telling. Look captain, I'm out on a limb on this one. I'll let you decide if you want them aboard or not. Frankly, I'll be just as happy to turn around if you say so and take these folks back to shore. Wouldn't mind getting a few hours more sleep."

"Are any of them armed?"

"No, Finley made sure of that. Grabbed their phones too."

"Okay, we'll take 'em," said Lattimore as Sullivan stepped onto the bridge. "We'll hold course and reduce speed while you come around." He turned to Winters. "Ready the pilot's ladder on the starboard side. When our visitors are aboard you will not talk with them. You'll give them blankets. You will take them to the galley and you will tell them I will meet with them as soon as I can. Carter, you go with him."

They left. Lattimore slowed the ship.

Epperson's little boat raced closer, her bow thumping in the waves. She came along side, matching *Endeavor's* course and speed. By this time, Winters and Carter should have the rope ladder draped over the side next to the pilot's stairs that ran at an easy slant along the side of the hull up onto the deck.

Leaving Sullivan at the controls, Lattimore hurried off the bridge. Bent against the biting wind, he made his way to the starboard rail. From there, he looked down to the bounding deck of the *Charles Foster* where an orange-coated boarding party, all wearing lifejackets huddled in a tight knot. At the helm of the little boat, Epperson struggled to hold course and speed.

He had no worries about sure footed Maddie making the jump but he wondered about the others. And who the hell were they?

With Epperson's mate helping, the first man stepped to the gunwales, took the short leap and successfully grabbed onto the rope ladder. From there he leaned sideways, and made it onto the slanted metal stairs. So far so good.

Tall and ungainly, maybe older, the next man stood poised ready to jump. He held onto the steadying hand of Epperson's mate. The water rushed by only a few feet below.

"Jump you idiot," shouted Lattimore though he knew he couldn't be heard.

The mate shook his hand free. The man jumped. He made it to the netting then clung there for a moment as if content to go no further. Then, encouraged by the first man, still at the base of the stairs, he jumped. He gained his footing and started up the stairs. On the deck, Winters met him with a blanket and helped him inside.

The next person, a woman, Lattimore guessed from her stature, slipped on her jump off the gunwale but made it across and onto the stairs without difficulty. Last was the person Lattimore would recognize anywhere. Maddie stepped deftly off the little boat onto the rope ladder then, almost in the same motion, onto the stairs. Once there, she turned to catch a few duffle bags tossed to her by Epperson's crewman.

Once on deck, Maddie managed a glance up in his direction before going inside. He wasn't sure she'd seen him but he had seen her. He had seen her face. Older yes, but still his Maddie. Relief that she was here, that she was safe, overtook him. But what would he say to her? Would she be happy to see him? God, how long had it been?

By this time the *Charles Foster* had veered off into the night. Lattimore stepped back onto the bridge and pulled the hatch closed.

"Who are they?" said Sullivan. "Does Katerina know about them?"

"She'll only know what you decide to tell her. Now, bring our speed back up. I'll be down checking on them."

Lattimore left the bridge. He went to his cabin where he dried the spray from his face and changed into fresh clothes. He assessed himself in the mirror. Gaunt, pasty skin, tired eyes, unshaven face, gray hair combed but trailing over his ears. He hated for Maddie to see him like this but it couldn't be helped.

CHAPTER 23

Jack and the others sat alone at a cafeteria style table in the galley, dripping, slowly warming with blankets draped over their shoulders. The place might have been an ordinary all night diner were it not for the gentle roll of the ship and the hum of the engines. Before leaving, the crewman who'd taken them there had scrounged up a dried-up burger and a cup of coffee for each of them. "Sorry. It's all we have right now. The captain says you're supposed to stay put. He'll be down to see you…soon."

Jack tried the burger and sipped his coffee, too tired to do much else. It was nearing 3 A.M.

"I've got a bad feeling about this," said Beth.

"This is where we need to be," said Maddie.

Finley and his driver buddy Stan, both of whom seemed agreeable enough guys to Jack, had spent two days with them at the A-frame before driving them to a drafty boathouse on the shores of Lake Huron. There, they waited until well after midnight when the four of them were led along a dock to a small boat that bobbed in the waves.

"They're going to dump us overboard," cried Andrew, holding on, shivering next to Maddie on one of the two benches aft of the small pilothouse.

"No, they're not. We're going to be okay," she told him, eyes on Jack as, the engine started. It's noisy rattling prevented further discussion.

Jack and Beth sat facing them on the other bench. He watched the lights along the dock fade into the distance wondering where and when might be the next time they'd set foot on dry land.

Maddie had been the first to see the lights of the freighter. Arms folded tight, she pointed with her chin, shouting: "There she is, sheriff. There's the freighter you saw that morning."

Her rust red hull rose tall in the water. White foam boiled where the tip of the bow met the water. As their boat closed the distance a feeling of dread overtook him. The man who shot him was aboard that ship.

Now, here in the galley, he watched Maddie. Her eyes darted. Every now and then she took a long breath, letting it out slow. He had the uncomfortable feeling he might soon find himself in the middle of a high voltage, father daughter battle. Sure, small potatoes considering the fact their lives were in danger, but uncomfortable just the same. "How long has it been since you've seen your dad," he asked.

She picked up her cup and took a sip. "Long time." Her hand shook ever so slightly when she put her cup down."

"Your name is Cooper, not Lattimore," said Beth.

"Cooper's my mother's maiden name. I adopted it after...well, it was my mom's idea. It's not important." Her eyes flashed angry, or maybe fearful, only for an instant before she wiped them clear. "That first day at the cottage when I went into town, I texted him. I took a big chance. I wanted *him* to end this thing. I wanted him to come to *me*. I guess this is the next best thing. I never should have contacted him."

"Not a good time to play shoulda woulda coulda," said Jack.

A moment later, the man Jack assumed was Lattimore appeared in the doorway. He stood perfectly still. Tall, and commanding with stern brown eyes. He was neatly dressed considering the hour. His face was weathered, ruddy, creased with deep furrows. His gray hair fell long over his ears. His eyes were fixed on Maddie as hers were on his. He walked over. She lowered her eyes as if studying something interesting on the tabletop. She winced then stiffened when he placed his hand on her shoulder. "Hello, Maddie."

She had no word of greeting for him. "I told you to put a stop to what you're doing and meet me at the cottage. I never thought you'd have us kidnapped."

"More drama, eh," said Lattimore, his voice tired. "As I understand it, you came willingly and I see you brought a little entourage."

"They're under my protection. I couldn't leave them."

Lattimore took a seat on the bench opposite her next to Beth. She and Jack slid over to make room. His eyes shifted to the rest of the group. "It was my daughter I wanted here. I swear, I didn't know about the rest of you. It's long past the middle of the night so I'll keep you just long enough to make your acquaintance. I'm sure you already know that I am Captain Lattimore and this is my ship. I'm a former marine and tend to run things around here in a military manner. Whether you like it or not, whether you intended it or not, you are now involved in an illegal smuggling operation."

"Correction, captain," said Jack. "We're here to *stop* an illegal smuggling operation."

"And you are?"

"Sheriff Jack Holiday of Gull Harbor. I got shot trying…"

Lattimore smiled almost to the point of laughter. "You…are *him*? You're the fellow who almost got yourself killed on the shores of the Keweenaw? I'd heard you recovered. Then, a few days ago, you died in a car accident. a drowning, you and your wife." His eyes shifted to Beth. "I'm betting that would be you madam?"

"Yes, that would be me."

Maddie kept her eyes on her father. "As far as you're concerned and as far as your employers are concerned, they are dead."

"Yes. I can confirm, they do indeed believe the two of you are dead."

"And you're not going to tell them otherwise."

"They won't hear it from me. But they may hear of it from others onboard. You should know we have an interesting mix of allegiances aboard this ship. I promise to do my best to keep your identities secret but I can only do so much." He paused then turned to Andrew who, at that moment was staring down at his empty cup. "And you, sir? Who might you be?"

Andrew looked startled. "Excuse me? Oh, yes. The burger was quite good. Can I have another?"

"His name is Andrew," said Maddie quickly. "I think he mistook you for a waiter and this place for a restaurant. He has nothing to do with anything. We met him at the cottage. He was a squatter. He broke in to get out of the cold."

"He shouldn't be here."

"He has a touch of Alzheimer's," said Beth, following Maddie's lead. "He's harmless and we couldn't leave him there alone."

"Well, it will be up to all of you to keep him out of trouble. I can't have him, or you, getting into things." Lattimore held his stare on the old man then stood. He took Andrew's cup, refilled it and brought it back. "Sorry, we're all out of burgers."

Andrew nodded, eyes on his coffee, evidently deciding not to press his luck by asking for the cream and sugar he normally took.

"I'm sure you're all very tired from your ordeal. We can talk more in the morning. While you're aboard, you will have limited access to the ship but you will have comfortable sleeping quarters."

"We're prisoners," said Beth.

"You are guests," said Lattimore, heading for the door. "I will send someone down who'll show you to your sleeping quarters."

"At least we have some privacy," said Jack, dropping his bag on the floor, that he now supposed was more correctly called 'the deck.'

It was a square room, five paces to a side. Beside the door a chain hung from a bare bulb on the ceiling.

"It's a storage closet, Jack. We've got two fold up cots, two ratty looking blankets and a communal bathroom down the hall."

"It's not a hallway, it's a passageway well, maybe a corridor. And the bathroom is called the head." When she stared back, face reddening, obviously not appreciating his attempt at humor he quickly added, "It's better than being on the run."

"No, it's not. When we get up in the morning, we can't get in our car and drive off. We are *stuck* here Jack. We are now part of whatever the hell that crazy captain is doing." She stared at him, hands first at her side then spread in a gesture of futility. "This is a nightmare, Jack."

"I was trying..."

She took a deep breath. "I know. Oh, I know, Jack. You were trying to make me feel better. But I'm tired. I'm so tired of all of this. I want to go home. We shouldn't be here. We should be back home in our own bed. We could have done that. We could have gone back in the middle of the night, stayed upstairs in our own place, never going out, Door-Dashing our food and..."

"And hiding out in our own house?"

"Okay, maybe I haven't thought that plan through."

He wrapped her in his arms. "We're together, and right now we're safe. That's all that matters."

"I know, I know. You keep telling me that like you expect me to believe it. Well, I don't believe it Jack. Maybe I will in the morning. But not now."

They undressed. She got into her cot and pulled up the covers. Jack turned out the light and found his way to his.

Beth whispered: "I'm glad you called Sharon. It was good to hear her voice."

"We'll make it back."

"I hope you're right, Jack."

They kissed, then slept.

Maybe it was the deep drumming of the engines, or the slow rock of the ship, but Jack slept soundly that night. He awoke with a start to a double rap at the closed door. "Last call for breakfast," someone announced. Jack sat up, wondering in the dark what time it was. Beside him, her back to him, Beth breathed lightly. He gave her a nudge. Then another.

She awoke with a start and sat up. "Oh, crap! We really are on a boat."

"It's a ship, not a boat." He got up and turned on the light.

"Do not start that shit again, Jack. You are not funny."

They dressed quickly then used the head.

After finding the galley, Jack filled his plate buffet-style with a stack of pancakes and a side of bacon, then sat beside Beth and her bowl of cornflakes. Maddie sat opposite them, arms folded, an empty cup in front of her.

"Seen your...the captain?" Jack said to her, using the syrup.

Maddie shook her head. "We're getting a lot of curious looks from the crew."

Jack glanced around the half-filled galley seeing heads turn quickly, some toward him, others away. "Not much talking going on either." He managed to catch the gaze of a woman with a ponytail, dressed in grease-stained bib overalls. He gave her a nod and a smile which got no reaction. "I suppose it's just as well we mix as little as possible with them."

"Why?" said Beth. "Maybe we can learn something."

"Or we could get ourselves tossed over the side," said Maddie. "The crew might be more into this smuggling thing than you think. In these cold waters, I'd give us five minutes before hypothermia hits. Michael Phelps would have trouble making it ashore."

"Thanks, I'll keep that in mind," said Beth

"Your father doesn't seem like a criminal," said Jack. "I think he was genuinely relieved to see that Beth and I we're still alive." A few of the crew tossed their garbage and left.

Maddie got herself more coffee then sat. "My dad always loved the military more than he loved mom or I. I suppose mom should have known what she was getting into when they met in college. She was a sociology major, he was a gung ho ROTC guy. It was never a good match. I suspect it was mom being pregnant with me that brought about their marriage. I think they both resented me for it. As if it was my fault." She took a breath. "But all of that's not important right now. Just to give you a little background, it was Afghanistan that really killed him."

That got Jack's attention.

"It was all the hearts and minds crap. They wanted our soldiers to somehow become social workers. What kind of a soldier trains for that? Who even thinks it's a good idea to send in an army with orders to invade a country, figure out who the bad guys are, kill only them, then make friends with anybody who might be left over after the graves have been dug and the dust has settled? But, over there, the dust never settled. My dad always said we would have done better with a bunch of Ivy League shrinks and a shitload of comfy couches. The whole thing might have been funny were it not for the brutal way so many people died over there."

She took a sip of coffee. It was her calling Lattimore 'my dad,' as well as the bitterness that tinged her words that gave Jack the impression she still had feelings for the man. It was as if she knew that not everything that had gone wrong with his family life had been his fault. Her cup rattled as she put it down.

"My dad spent ten years there before he finally knew he'd lost too many good people. By the time he snapped, he'd made it all the way from 2nd Lieutenant to Bird Colonel. He was up for his brigadier's star when one of his units got pinned down by a barrage of fire that looked to be coming from a group of armed kids marching toward them in lockstep in the middle of a street. Can you believe it? *Armed kids*. He ordered his men to defend themselves. It was a mess. The kids were massacred. When it turned out that all the kids were carrying toy guns and the guys with the real guns were firing from covered positions behind them, my dad was court marshaled.

"Rather than risk making the incident public, the military cut him a deal. They busted him down to the rank of captain, and gave him an honorable discharge. He was forty-five years old when he left the corps. He had no experience in anything useful in the private sector, he had peanuts for a pension and he had my mother and me to support. Mom had a shit job at the time. What the hell are you supposed to do with a sociology degree and a kid to take care of?

"So, dad came back. He was lost. He didn't know what to do. He started hitting the bottle. Did drugs too. They got a divorce. Soon after, my mom and I changed our names back to Cooper."

"And your dad became a freighter captain on the Great Lakes," said Jack.

"I'm sure it wasn't as simple as that, but yes, that's what he did."

At that moment, Jack noticed a tall man standing in the doorway to the now empty galley. He wondered how long he'd been there and how much he might have heard.

The man walked closer. "My name is Sullivan," he said, addressing Maddie and Jack. "I'm the XO aboard this ship. The captain wants to see Agent Cooper and...you sir, up on the bridge."

"My wife will come too," said Jack.

"Sorry, just the two of you. But there was another fellow. There were four of you, correct?"

"He's still sleeping, I think," said Beth.

"Yes, well the captain said the fellow was acting a little strange so he thought it best one of you stay back with him. You're welcome to stay here or there's a dayroom across the passageway if you like. There's a TV and other stuff there."

"That'll be fine," said Beth.

With a curt nod, Sullivan turned to Jack and Maddie, already standing. "This way, please."

CHAPTER 24

A cargo elevator and a short corridor brought them to a door marked: *Bridge. Authorized Personnel Only.* "I'll wait for you out here," said Sullivan. He knocked once. They walked in.

Jack blinked at the bright sun. Wind whistled through the seals of the windows that spanned the room. Centered in it, stood Lattimore at the controls, his back to them. He was dressed comfortably in jeans and a dark untucked flannel shirt. A black knit cap was pulled tight covering half his ears.

For a while the captain kept his gaze fixed straight ahead out to the bow where the ship tore through the waves sending a near constant spray up and over the bow. Above the spray an American flag rippled atop its pole. Lattimore made a slight adjustment to one of the knobbed levers in front of him then turned to his daughter. They stood perfectly still, staring at one another. "What a beautiful woman you've become, Maddie," he said at last.

Maddie hesitated. "Good to see you too...dad. Your man Sullivan said you wanted to talk to us."

Jack had expected at least an attempt at an embrace, but Maddie stood stiff as a board, making it clear, there would be none of that.

Lattimore gave Jack a glance as if to say: There, you see what I have to deal with? Aloud, he said: "I've brought you here to warn you about the people I've gotten mixed up with."

With a hand on the back of the recliner Jack steadied himself against the roll of the ship. "I've been shot and run off the road and we've been on the run for a while. I think we have a pretty good idea how dangerous you and the people you work for are."

"You want us to stay the hell out of your way," said Maddie.

"That's right, I do."

"Then tell us what's going on."

"Sit down. I'll tell you what I know." Lattimore motioned them into a couple of chairs near the starboard windows. Jack took one.

Maddie took the recliner, leaned back, and looked up at her father's glare. "Oh, sorry. Did I take the captain's chair?"

Lattimore's expression softened, as if impressed at his daughter's brashness. He remained standing. "I am a delivery man. I take things from one place to another. I'm no fool, mind you. I admit I've always known I was involved in a criminal enterprise and I won't try to justify myself. But you need to understand that, while it's true I've always had command of this ship, it was always others aboard who handled the off the books pickups and deliveries. They have complete control of a secondary hold."

"Last night you mentioned the mixed allegiances among the crew," said Jack.

"Yes, and you need to be aware of them. In the parlance, the secondary hold is actually called a smuggler's hold. I don't know where it is and I've made it my business *not* to know. Hell, for all I know there might be several smuggler's holds on this ship." He shook his head then scratched his whiskered cheek, the sound like sandpaper being scraped over rough wood. "I knew the pickup on the Keweenaw that morning was different than the others. The risks we took with the ice, and a man, *you* sheriff, getting shot." He paused. "I was relieved to hear you were alive. And, as you may *not* know, there was another man lost that morning. He was the driver of the truck in the woods. One of my men pushed him off the ice into the water." He gestured. "From right out there, I saw it all happen."

Maddie stiffened. "That man was Michael Fuller. He was my inside contact. I'm as much to blame for his death as anyone. He was a good guy who fell in with the wrong crowd. He was trying to get his life together and I pushed him too hard."

"What do you know about the cargo you took aboard that morning?" said Jack, eyes on Lattimore.

"I know it's something unusual, something important, likely something dangerous."

"Where are you taking it?"

"To the steel mills south of Detroit. It will be taken ashore and it will be secured by people I trust."

"What people?" said Maddie.

Lattimore ignored the question. "We will also offload our legitimate cargo of taconite, refuel, then head back up to Duluth. This is the last run of the season. *Endeavor* will layup for the winter. I will retire. You, Maddie, will go back to the FBI and you and your wife, sheriff, will resume your normal lives."

"That's the plan?" said Maddie. "A happy ending for all of us?"

"Yes. And I'm telling you both to stay out of it."

"Just sit back and enjoy the cruise, huh?" said Maddie.

"Why not? I'm telling you, this will all be over in Detroit."

"You can't be certain of that."

"I *am* certain of that."

"Then you won't mind us searching your ship."

"What do you mean? Just the two of you and the two others you brought with you? Sure, go ahead, knock yourselves out. This ship is more than six hundred feet long. You're not going to find anything. But I won't have you interrogating any of my crew."

"You won't have a choice, captain. I'm a sheriff, she's FBI, the law is on our side, not yours."

"I see you are unfamiliar with maritime law. You will not interrogate any of my crew and you will not involve them in any way. If you agree, then sure, go ahead with your search. If you don't agree, I consider you a threat to this ship and will have you locked up. The choice is yours."

"What have you told the crew about us?" said Maddie.

"Only that you are my guests. That you're along for the ride down to Detroit. I don't think they believe it. They know you came aboard in the middle of the night. By itself, that's more than a little suspicious."

"All right, we'll be discreet with our search," said Jack with a glance at Maddie who gave him an affirming shrug. "How much time do we have before we get to Detroit?"

"Three days. But remember, I brought you aboard this ship because you're safer here than ashore. That does not mean you're out of danger. If the wrong people learn the truth about you, I will stop your little search and I'll lock you up until all this is over. It's for your own good. Understood?"

Maddie got to her feet. "Understood."

Lattimore turned to her. "Be careful, Maddie. I have control of this ship but not all of its crew."

Her lips parted but she only answered with a nod.

Jack followed her out.

After meeting briefly with Lattimore, Sullivan escorted them down to the dayroom where they found Beth nursing a cup of coffee at one of the half dozen round tables there. Across from her, Andrew dozed. Sullivan dismissed the crewman who'd been posted outside the door then left without a word.

Beth watched the man go. "No guard anymore? We're on our own now?"

"Guess so. As long as we behave," said Jack. He placed his hands on her shoulders massaging them the way he knew she liked.

"What did the captain have to say?"

Maddie sat. "He told us he doesn't know anything about the illegal cargo, what it is or even where it's hidden. He said everything's under control and that all this'll be over once we get to Detroit."

"But you don't believe that?"

Maddie shrugged. "I know *he* believes it. But it's always good to hedge our bets."

Jack sat next to Andrew. "He'll let us search the ship but he doesn't want us causing trouble. We can make pleasant conversation with the crew but we are to avoid any confrontations. Officially, we are guests of the captain."

"Well, that's good, right?" said Beth.

"Yes. I want to have a look at the aft cargo hold. That's where they brought the crates aboard that morning."

"You want to look for them now?" said Beth.

"Why not?"

"That's good with me." Maddie checked her watch. "Almost lunchtime. Most of the crew will be hitting the galley. We're less likely to run into any of them."

"Should we take him?" asked Jack, with a glance at Andrew who was beginning to stir.

"We can't leave him alone," said Beth. "Besides, we've got to get him back into the real world." She got up then shook him into alertness. Jack helped him up.

"Are we going for a walk?" said Andrew with unexpected clarity.

"Yes, we're going to be looking for something," said Maddie pointing. "Aft is that way."

CHAPTER 25

Maddie casually enlisted directional help from a few passing crewmembers as they went. She smiled and introduce herself and the group as friends of the captain. Jack was impressed by the easy way she was able to turn on the charm. Another Quantico trick?

They took the steel stairs. The drumming of the engines grew louder as they descended. Engine oil hung in the stagnant air. Leaving the stairs, they walked along a corridor that ended at a closed hatch. "This should be it," said Maddie, voice raised above the ambient din.

She worked the levered latch and pushed the hatch open. The space beyond was dark, the air cold.

"Should've brought our coats," said Beth.

Maddie stepped inside and, in the dim light thrown from the open hatch, found an electrical box. At the loud bang of an energized breaker, the lights came on and the others stepped in.

The room was cavernous. Tall metal shelves lined the fore and aft bulkheads. They were stacked full with large fiberglass containers each secured with heavy banding. Centered in the open space between the bulkheads stood a propane powered forklift. A corrugated cargo door with hydraulic cylinders attached on both sides took up most of the port side. Beside it was a locked box that obviously engaged the opening and closing mechanism. Directly below it was a bright red mushroom switch enclosed in a glass box. A sign read: *In case of emergency, break glass.*

Good to know, thought Jack thinking how close they must be to the waterline. He placed a hand on the metal surface of the door realizing there had to be a steel panel behind it that served as both a loading ramp and a watertight seal. "The crates would have come through here. They were probably loaded onto a pallet, then stacked somewhere using the forklift."

"We're looking for crates? Wooden crates?" said Andrew. "I don't see any here."

"They wouldn't have left them in the open," said Jack.

"They could be inside any one of these containers," said Beth, scanning the shelves. "There's got to be fifty of them that we can see, and more behind."

Maddie put a hand on one. "We're going to need some tools—hammer, crowbar..."

"We're not going through all of them." said Beth.

"Yes, we are," said Maddie.

"This should help." It was Andrew calling out from a darkened corner of the room.

Coming around, Jack spotted him standing beside metal tool chest. "Very good, Andrew. Yes, that'll help." He went through the tools and handed them out, choosing a long wooden handled screwdriver for Andrew.

They started on the most accessible container, the one Maddie had had her hand on, prying off its strapping.

At the squeak of the hatch, they all froze. A tall, bearded man in coveralls stepped through followed by a shorter man similarly dressed.

The two of them stared at the four of them.

"We're friends of the captain," said Jack.

"Is that right? What are you doing here?" said the taller man.

Maddie stepped forward. "We're looking for something. The captain said it was okay. Who are you?"

"We're members of the crew. We belong here. You don't." The tall man walked closer. "You said the captain knows about this?"

"Yes, he does," said Maddie, unperturbed. "We're here to open and inspect all of these containers. And frankly, gentlemen, we could use some help. You up for it?"

"What're you looking for?" This from the shorter man.

"I can't tell you. How about you open them, we'll inspect them."

The shorter man smiled and gave his buddy a glance. "I think we'll check with the captain."

"It's all right," came Sullivan's voice from the hatchway as he stepped in. "The captain has authorized it." The XO kept his eyes on the two men then turned to Maddie. "These men will assist you and they won't ask questions. Isn't that right, gentlemen?"

"Well, yeah. Whatever you say, Mr. Sullivan," said the shorter guy, his eyes resting first on Jack then darting up and down the shelves. "Shit. We're going to be here a while."

"Yep," said Cooper.

"You'd better get started," said Sullivan. "Consider it part of your maintenance duties. And be sure to use inspection tags." He pointed to the tall, bearded man. "Foster, you know where they are. We want the legal recipients to know that their containers have been legally opened, inspected and resealed." He turned to Maddie. "You will be kind enough to initial each one?"

"I'll be happy to. Thanks, Mr. Sullivan."

The XO left.

Foster stared at Maddie. "And just who are you to be legally authorized to inspect these containers?"

She smiled. "Sorry, I'm not at liberty to say."

It took five long hours to get through all the containers. They found machine tool parts, farming implements, commercial sized buckets of paint, and all sorts of hardware items but nothing in the least suspicious.

Everyone tired, Maddie initialed the last of the inspection tags then sat heavily atop the container. She ran a hand across her forehead. "Thanks for your help, gentlemen," she said Foster and to the other crewman. "Sorry it didn't pan out. We'll carry on from here."

Foster scratched his beard, eying the four of them in turn. "Whatever you're looking for, it's nothing dangerous, is it?"

"No, nothing dangerous," said Maddie.

The crewmen left.

With the four of them alone, Jack hefted himself up and sat on the workbench. "Anybody else think it was odd, Sullivan having those men help us?"

"My dad probably told him to shadow us to make sure we stayed out of trouble," said Maddie, sitting knees up, her back resting against the side of the forklift. "He probably knew we wouldn't find anything here so why *not* help us."

"So, you think your dad knows where the crates are?"

"Maybe."

Jack nodded. "We just got started with the search. It would have been a wild stroke of luck for us to find them in the first place we looked. They must have used the forklift or maybe a pallet jack to move them."

"He talked about a smuggler's hold, like it was something built into the ship," said Maddie, arms folded. "I wonder what's aft of here?" She took a long, tired breath, got up and walked in that direction heading out of sight between two closely spaced shelves. She shouted back. "There's another bulkhead. Might be something on the other side of it."

"Yeah, like Lake Huron," said Beth.

Jack heard a couple of dull thumps that he assumed was her pounding a fist on the bulkhead.

She walked back. "I suppose there could be an access panel somewhere back there," she said. "We'd have a hell of a time finding it though."

"My bet is that those crates are within a hundred feet of here," said Jack.

"That would include the engine room," said Maddie.

Andrew had been silent most of this time. Now he stirred, his back against the cargo hatch. "Our search must be conducted within the volume of a sphere of that radius." He paused. "Well, perhaps a cube of that size would be more appropriate. My point is, we should be thinking in three dimensions, not two." He added the last only after noticing everyone staring at him.

"Yes, you're right. Thanks Andrew," said Beth, sending a hopeful glance to Jack.

They headed up to the galley where the evening meal was in full swing. On entering, faces turned, the chatter of conversation faded. Jack waved awkwardly. No one waved back. He stood behind Beth in line. They filled their plates with beef stroganoff, chose a slice of pie, then looked around the room for a seat. By this time the level of conversation in the room had revived a little.

"We should sit with some of them," said Beth

"The crew you mean? Why?"

"We might learn something." She led the way to a table occupied by two women. "Mind if we sit?" Beth asked the younger of them, a slim African American somewhere in her twenties.

The woman gave her table mate a glance, then said, "Sure, have a seat."

"I'm Beth. This is my husband, Jack."

"I'm Charlotte," said the woman in a pleasant enough voice. Her black hair was pulled back and tied in a bun. "The crew calls me, Meg. Middle name's Margaret."

"I'm Beck," said the other woman, white, mid-thirties, close clipped blond hair. "And you damn well better not be calling me Beckie." She dabbed her lips with a napkin. "Tell me something, Jack, are we in some kind of trouble?"

"Not that I know of."

"Then why are you here? There are a lot of rumors floating around."

"We're with a group," said Beth. She pointed to where Cooper sat with Andrew a table over. "We're with them, just getting a lift. We..."

"We're friends of the captain. He knows we like adventure. He owed us a favor so, here we are."

"Look around you, Jack," said Beck. "Does this look like an adventure to you?"

"For us it is. We're from the Keweenaw. There's not a whole lot going on up there this time of year."

Beck met his eyes. "I heard you were looking for something."

"Who told you that?"

Beck laughed, then fingered a drop of gravy off her chin. "We're not the bunch of dumb shits you might think we are...*sheriff*. Now, maybe you're a little hard of hearing. I'll ask you again. Are we in trouble?"

"I've got no reason to think so. But you're right, I'm the sheriff of a small town. Like we said, we're just along for the ride. And, right now, I'm just trying to have a friendly conversation."

Beck pointed with her fork. "That woman over there, I hear she's FBI."

"You're well informed," conceded Jack.

So, we have a sheriff and an FBI agent aboard. And here you are, you being the sheriff, telling me you're all just along for the ride."

"That's right."

"We're carrying something dangerous, is what I hear."

"I wouldn't know."

"Maybe something that goes *boom*?"

Jack held her stare. "I don't know."

Beth cleared her throat. "What do you do aboard this ship?" She asked Beck.

"I'm Engineer's Mate," she said with a polite smile as she disengaged from Jack.

"How long have you been working on this ship?"

"Ten years off and on. Not like my buddy here."

"Only two years for me," said Meg. "I'm what you call a utility player. Do laundry, dishes, some metal work, I also fix things,"

"What kind of things," asked Jack.

"Electrical things."

"I'm a pharmacist," offered Beth.

"You all hold yourselves like you've never been on the lakes before," said Beck.

Jack shrugged. "It takes getting used to."

Beck knocked back the last of her can of Diet Coke. "Who's that old guy?"

"His name is Andrew," said Jack. "We don't know much about him. He's homeless. We met him at a cottage outside of Cheboygan."

"He owns a cottage?"

"He broke into the cottage to get out of the cold."

"So, you arrested him?"

"We've been helping him out. He's a nice guy, down on his luck," said Jack.

"That's damn nice of you, sheriff," said Beck, finished with her food. She used her napkin. "So, what you're telling me is that the four of you coming aboard is nothing to worry about. And the fact that two of you are lawmen is some kind of funny coincidence. Well, just to clarify, us crewmen don't have a say in what this ship is carrying, where she's been or where she's going."

Jack leaned closer. "But I'm sure you are aware that remaining silent when knowing a crime is being committed, is a crime in itself. Or did you miss that episode of *Law & Order*."

Beck smiled. "I like you, sheriff. And you too, being his misses, and a pharmacist and all. If I see any criminal activity, I'll be sure to let you know."

Beck got up and took care of her tray. "Complements to the chef," she said, leaving the galley with a glance at Jack, Meg following.

"So much for us keeping a low profile," said Jack, starting in on his pie.

Beth put down her coffee cup. "Really Jack, you used to be so much better at making friends."

CHAPTER 26

The search continued. Nearing the end of the second day of it, they managed to find another, smaller stash, of banded containers lined along a darkened, secondary corridor. Going through them, they found only clothing and household items.

"I feel like we're going through someone's dresser drawers," Beth said, exhausted.

"There's something down this way," said Maddie who'd gone ahead. She led them further down to a line of six corrugated, roll up doors similar to ones used in a commercial storage facility. All were locked. Fixed beside each was a numerical keypad.

"The captain will know the keycodes," said Maddie.

"I'm tired," said Andrew. "We should stop. Oh, and I'm hungry."

"I could use a break myself," said Beth to Jack. "You and Maddie can carry on here. We'll be up in the galley."

"You okay?"

"Yeah. Just tired of wasting time."

"This is important work, sheriff," said Maddie after they'd left.

"That's what I keep telling myself."

"Come on. Let's get those keycodes. This time of day, the captain will be up on the bridge."

"Those lockers contain the personal possessions of my officers," said Lattimore. "They've each got their own private code."

"You must have a master code," countered Maddie.

"I do, but I'm not giving it to you."

"Is one of those lockers yours?" said Maddie.
"Do you really think I'm the master smuggler?"
Maddie stared back.
"It's the aftmost locker. My code is six digits. It's your birthdate, Maddie."
"If you expect to get any brownie points from me for that, you're mistaken."
"You're pretty hard on him," said Jack on the way back down.
"I am not going to get into that with you, sheriff. Stay in your lane and we'll be okay."

At Lattimore's storage locker, Cooper entered the code and lifted the door. A light flickered on. Inside, strapped to the walls were a tall wooden dresser, a wood framed full length mirror, and a wheeled coatrack. Faded dry cleaning bags hung from the rack each containing a military dress uniform. Beyond these lay a stack of cardboard boxes. It was obvious to Jack that the crates were not here. "I don't see any point in..." he started. But Maddie had already walked in.

She stopped at the dresser. Plastic banding secured each of its drawers. She ran a finger across the layer of dust atop it. "I remember these things. They were from our old house, the first house I remember when I was growing up." She walked to the mirror.

She stood in front of it, adjusted its angle then took a step back. She stared at her tarnished reflection then surprised Jack by bending a knee, giving the slightest hint of a curtsey. In her tarnished reflection, her lips quivered. She touched a hand to her cheek and stood perfectly still.

"Are you okay," Jack asked.

Maddie shook her head. "Just remembering something. The captain was right. There's not much here." She walked out, her hand brushing lightly against the dry cleaning bags. She pulled the leather door strap. The door clattered down. The locking mechanism clicked.

"We'd better get up to the galley," said Jack quietly. "We need to eat and we need some rest." He led the way.

From the cook and her helper in the kitchen they scrounged some blackened hotdogs, fries and coffee. They joined Andrew and Beth at their table in the otherwise empty galley.

Andrew put down his half-finished hotdog. "Did you find anything, sheriff?"

"No, we didn't."

"Too bad. It was all young Mayfield's idea, you know."

Jack lifted his head.

Andrew tipped back the last of his coffee. He stared down at the empty cup.

"What was Mayfield's idea, Andrew?" said Beth.

The old man shook his head. With a long sigh, he placed his elbows on the table and rested his chin on his threaded fingers. "He was so proud of what he'd done. He loved to tell his story about the trains."

"Trains?" said Jack.

"What was that, sheriff?"

"You said something about trains. Someone telling a story about trains."

"Funny, I didn't realize I'd said that out loud."

"Do you want more coffee."

"That would be nice, thank you."

Jack poured. Andrew took a sip then picked up his hotdog and took another bite.

"Now what was it about trains," prompted Jack, sitting.

"Oh yes, I did say that, didn't I?" The professor wiped his napkin across his lips. "Do you like trains?"

"Yes, I do like trains. I especially like stories about trains."

"Can we hear the story, Andrew?" said Maddie.

"No one is supposed to know about it. I'm sorry. I shouldn't have said anything."

Jack tried to keep his voice casual. "If it has something to do with what we're looking for, then yes Professor Simeon, we *are* supposed to know about it."

"Oh, yes. Well, I suppose that's right." Andrew closed his eyes. He massaged them, pressing hard with his fingertips. "We *are* looking for the packages. That's what we used to call them—packages." He placed his hands on the table. "You won't tell anyone else, will you?"

"We won't tell anyone," said Maddie.

"All right then. Yes, I suppose you can be trusted. And maybe I've kept the secret long enough. Hell, after all these years it feels like it never happened. But I know it did. Well now, where to begin? It was young Mayfield's idea but his father had to have been in on it."

Jack glanced over his shoulder. Through the serving window he could see two women still working in the kitchen. He considered stopping Andrew before he began his story so they could find a place more private but was afraid the professor would fall back into his usual state of confusion. A glance at Beth told him she was thinking the same thing. Andrew went on:

"It was back in the 1940's, during the war. Of course, I wasn't alive then, but young Mayfield was. We always called him that since his father, Henry was still alive. The elder Mayfield was still somewhat active in the company by the time I came along. And he was the smart one. He was the one who worked with the other professors and scientists and the whole damn football team at the University of Chicago, hauling all those heavy blocks of graphite. That was back in 1943 if I remember right.

"Now, young Mayfield, what was his first name? Howard, I think. Yes, Howard Mayfield. Or...well, it's of no matter. We all called him...Junior. Yes, that's right, some of us called him Junior."

Maddie interrupted. "Professor Simeon, are we carrying radioactive material aboard this ship?"

"I'm getting to that, young lady," the old man snapped, hands shaking. "It isn't easy pulling these things out of the fog up here." He tapped the side of his head then pressed both hands against his temples as if squeezing out his thoughts. "It is not easy at all. Now, if you don't mind, I'll tell the story in my own way."

"Sorry," said Maddie.

Jack caught her eye. Radioactivity. The 1940's. The University of Chicago. Jack remembered the books on the shelves of the Mayfield mansion. A chill crawled up the back of his neck.

Andrew went on. "Now, this is all Junior's story. I was still in diapers when it happened so..." He popped the last of his hotdog into his mouth and chewed thoughtfully. "The OSS was running it all. Things were moving along pretty fast by the time 1945 came along. The war in Europe was finally being won. Hitler, yes, I think he was dead by that time. But there was no slowing down in the work on the project. Oh no, there was no stopping the war effort. Hell, we still had Japan to worry about. Our men were still dying by the thousands, Japs too. It had to be stopped. You do understand, don't you?" He took in each face around the table.

"Anyway, I guess I'd better get to the point, eh? Junior was still in his twenties back in '45. He had flat feet. That's what kept him out of the war. He called them his golden pair of flat feet. I guess he learned from his father about the trains. That's how they got the enriched uranium from the factory down south up through Chicago then all the way out to...was it, Arizona?"

"Los Alamos, New Mexico," said Beth, in a whisper.

"Yes, that sounds right," Andrew continued. "Trains! Can you believe it? And they weren't special trains either. Hell, it was the normal, everyday *Santa Fe Super Chief*. Two men, armed of course, carried the stuff, uranium tetrafluoride. And who do you think went along for the ride?"

"Howard Mayfield," said Jack.

"Yes, that's right! Young Mayfield was there. How he did it, I don't know. His dad must have helped, don't you think? Oh yes, his father was very wealthy. He must have paid off the guards I suppose. And so, on each of the many trips it took, he was able to collect just a few grams of the stuff. Hell, the guards didn't know any better. And the folks out in Los...Los Alamos apparently never noticed. Their lab balances should have picked up the discrepancy but apparently no one made an issue of it. Hell, maybe old Mayfield paid them off too."

Andrew beamed as if savoring the memory.

Jack tried to keep his voice casual. "These packages, the things we're looking for Andrew, are they samples of plutonium stolen from the Manhattan Project?"

"What?" said Andrew, his face suddenly transformed into an angry scowl. "I thought I made that clear. Howard Mayfield skimmed off some of the enriched uranium—U235. Of course it was a safe form of it, uranium tetrafluoride, but it was certainly *not* plutonium. They are two entirely different things."

"That's what we have aboard this ship?" said Maddie.

"Well, they're more than that. Those packages, there are three to each crate. We packed them very carefully. They are well designed mechanisms, each containing a small amount of the U235."

"They're bombs," said Jack.

Andrew's brow creased. "Well yes, they are. But it's all right. They're very small ones. Oh, and did I mention, they aren't armed." He paused. The fingers of his left hand twitched as if, by one detail at a time, he was trying to refine his memory. "At least I don't think they are…" Andrew rubbed his eyes. He stayed silent for a long while.

"Thank you, Andrew," said Beth. "It was good that you told us."

"You won't tell anyone."

"We can keep a secret."

Andrew yawned. He placed his elbows on the table, head in his hands. "It's been a very long day."

Beth stood. "How about I take you back to your room and you can turn in for the night."

"Yes, that would be nice. I would like that."

As the two of them left, Jack eyed the kitchen where only one woman was now working. "Do you think she heard?"

"I don't think so," said Maddie. "But we can't keep this secret for long. The crew will find out soon enough. Hell, they deserve to know the danger we're all in—nuclear bombs that may or may not be armed." Maddie stood. "Come on. We'll stop to pick up the professor's journal. It's time we have another talk with the captain."

The bridge was dimly lit by the red glow of the instrument panel and by the amber of the deck lights shining in through the windows. On duty they found Sullivan and the crewman Foster. Both seemed to give a start on seeing Jack and Maddie.

"We need to see the captain," said Maddie.

"He's in his cabin," said Sullivan with a glance at the journal under her arm. "He doesn't like to be disturbed but...It's down the passageway. His name's on the door."

They found it. Maddie knocked. "It's me...dad. I need to talk to you."

They heard nothing at first, then footsteps. The door opened. With his hair a tangled mess, Lattimore stood in the dark, dressed in robe and slippers. "Well?"

"We need to speak with you. It's important," said Maddie.

The captain turned on the light, let them in, then locked the door.

The cabin was smaller than Jack would have thought. Peach colored paint, peeling and scarred, covered the walls. In the center of the room, four chairs surrounded a small circular table. A bed stood against the wall, blankets rumpled. Lattimore took one of the chairs at the table. "Well, go on, sit. What the hell are you up to now?"

"Sorry to wake you but this is important," said Jack.

Lattimore waited, eyes on his daughter.

"You've got nukes aboard," she said.

Lattimore didn't flinch. "How do you know this?"

"The old man; we told you he was a homeless derelict. We lied. His name is Andrew Simeon, he's a professor of physics. He once worked for Mayfield Industries."

"He's a lunatic."

"He was drugged," said Jack.

"All right, a drugged-up lunatic then. Drugged by whom?"

"Probably by the smugglers you work for," said Maddie.

"If he was a threat, they would have killed him."

For Jack, this made sense. "He must have been drugged by whoever sold those crates—those bombs, to the smugglers. They wanted to keep him quiet so..."

"They had him in a retirement home," said Maddie. "He's starting to remember things."

"Things like..."

"Like stealing U235 from the Manhattan Project and making bombs. That's what's in those crates. Three to a crate, four crates. You've got 12 nuclear weapons abord this ship."

Lattimore showed no reaction. He queried Jack with a glance.

"Mayfield Industries did work for the government; something called the OSS," said Jack.

"Office of Strategic Services," said Lattimore, slowly as if losing some of his skepticism. "How did you find this professor?"

"The key was learning about Mayfield Industries," said Maddie. "The sheriff and his wife found pieces of one of the crates out on the..."

"...from the Keweenaw shore," interrupted Lattimore. "Yes, they did say one of the crates had come apart." He shook his head. "It's always the little things, isn't it?"

"One of the pieces had the Mayfield logo branded into it," said Jack. "From there, with your daughter's help, we found out about Professor Simeon. They almost killed him with the drugs. Whoever made the deal with your syndicate evidently drew the line at committing murder. They kept him alive, but just barely."

"We've got his journal," said Maddie. She placed it on the table in front of her father. "It's mostly a diary where he talks about his days at Mayfield. But there're also sketches and calculations which didn't make much sense to us but maybe it will to you."

Lattimore thumbed through a few pages, then closed it. He placed it on the table and leaned back in his chair, arms folded.

"This doesn't concern you?" said Maddie. "If it doesn't, I've got some friends at Langley who need to know about this."

"I am quite certain those friends of yours, and mine, already know about it."

"What do you mean, they already know? The CIA wouldn't just let a load of nukes sail the Great Lakes without..."

"Believe me, Maddison, there are many fools at the CIA. And some of those fools have the power to fuck things up in ways you can't possibly imagine. Leave this to me. You're in over your head. Both of you are."

Jack couldn't believe what he was hearing. "You knew about this all along?"

"No, I didn't know about the nukes. And, for the time being, I'm going to assume you're right about that. From what I *do* know, and from what you're telling me now, it's starting to make sense." He shook his head. "This is a high stakes gamble and we, and everyone aboard this ship, are caught in the middle of it. No, I didn't know we were carrying nukes. But I do know that the CIA has gotten themselves, and me, into the middle of something important. I also know that we're being closely watched by people at the highest levels of the CIA."

"That's why you didn't want us to interfere," said Maddie.

"That's right. Did the professor tell you how he obtained the nuclear material?"

"They skimmed off some of the enriched uranium from the Manhattan Project," said Maddie.

"It's enriched uranium? So, it's not plutonium? You're sure of that?"

"Yes."

Elbows on the table, Lattimore peaked his fingers. "Who else knows about this?"

"My wife knows," said Jack.

"Well, try and keep the professor from telling anyone else. Like I told you, this will all be over when we get to Detroit."

"The CIA to the rescue?" said Maddie.

"Yes. It's an op being run at the highest level. That is all you need to know."

"So, nothing to worry about," said Jack.

"I wouldn't go that far, but essentially yes." Lattimore stood. "Leave this to me. Do not talk about it with anyone. Get some sleep. We make Detroit tomorrow."

"But there must be something…"

"No. You both need to back off. You could easily do more harm than good." Lattimore stood, eyes on his daughter. "Did you go through my locker?"

Maddie flinched at the abruptness of the question. "It was all things from back when we were a family. I…I'm surprised you…why did you keep it?" She stood, then stopped, her eye caught by something. "And you kept that too? After all these years?" She walked to a photograph that hung on the wall.

Jack stood. The photograph was of Lattimore's A-frame cottage. On its wooden porch stood a young Lattimore, smiling, dashing in his marine officer's uniform. Beside him stood a long-haired petite woman, attempting but falling short of a smile, her face attractive but careworn. Between the two of them, stood the little girl who had to be Maddison. At seven, or maybe eight years old, she wore a white pullover top and jeans shorts. Her expression was more confusion than happiness. It was as if, even at that tender age, she knew she wasn't strong enough to keep her family together.

The room was silent. Maddie came over to her father. She kissed his cheek. "Good night, dad," she whispered.

CHAPTER 27

In a suburb north of Moscow, surrounded by quiet streets and quiet homes, sits an unremarkable two-story office building. Spartan to the extreme, the gray cinderblock structure is encircled by thirty meters of open ground which, in turn, is boxed in by a tall security fence. Brass Cyrillic letters posted beside its guarded entrance give the name of the place, loosely translated as: *X-Caliber*, then warn that entry is restricted to authorized personnel only.

Except for the occasional passerby who might wonder at the name or the need for such expansive grounds or for the elaborate fence, or for the guards, the place draws little attention.

Inside the building a staff of fifty accountants toil endlessly over the financial data of a worldwide, multi-trillion-ruble business that operates in virtual autonomy and anonymity. These accountants have been screened, handpicked, then screened again to insure against security risks. They operate with economy and rigor feeding data into a state of the art, AI-augmented supercomputer. They are well paid and they don't ask questions.

The strategic strings of this strange company are pulled or slackened by three men and one woman each of whom wield broad power and influence within the walls of the Kremlin. The lone woman in this Kremlin quartet is Katerina Sokolov.

Now, from her suite of rooms on the twentieth floor of Detroit's elite Waterside Apartments Katerina watched *Endeavor* slowly negotiate the Detroit River. This day being bright and clear, she had no trouble recognizing the freighter, but she was surprised to see a Coast Guard cutter trailing some distance behind. Adding to that, *Endeavor* was somewhat late.

Was there a problem?

Not likely. The last message she'd received from her man aboard advised that Lattimore had picked up his daughter. He was protecting her as a good father should. Well, so much the better. Ashore, the FBI woman could have caused trouble. Now, she was effectively out of the way.

Still, Katerina wondered what the Coast Guard cutter would do when the freighter approached the docks at the Stoltenberg Mill? Would she loiter close by, then move in, guns at the ready? Or would she continue south? Or would she turn north returning to her home berth in Port Huron?

Katerina reminded herself, that, when referring to ships, she'd gotten used to the customary female pronoun of the west instead of the Russian masculine. She was spending too much time in America and, though she had no family and few friends back home, she longed to return. Yes, her friends were few, but they were powerful. And soon they, and she, would become even more powerful. Yes, these were exciting times and, right now, she was at the center of it all.

Two weeks, that's all that was left of this mission. Soon it would be too late in the month for Andrei to call it his *November Surprise*. She wondered exactly what he was up to but, as with most things about the man, it was best not to know. She would do her part, then hand the ball off. She would go home, and then what? Whatever plans Andrei had, she knew she would rise with his success or fall with his failure. But the man she knew so well, had never failed. So, why should he fail now? Her heart quickened; her blood warm. Yes, it was the risk, the gamble that excited her in an almost sexual way.

She smiled. She brought her stupidly expensive *Zeiss* binoculars to her eyes. She played with the focus noting that the gap between the freighter and trailing Coast Guard cutter seemed to be closing. Should she be worried?

Katerina mused over this. She turned away from the window and walked down a short hallway to look in on Ilya. There he still sat with earphones on, his body bent close to his video gaming screen.

"I am going out," she announced in English loudly enough for him to hear. When he reacted only by the lifting of his right hand, she sighed lightly, sadly, wishing things were different for him. Though her son did not speak, he clearly understood English better than Russian.

A grown man. And all he did was play video games. No matter how Andrei's plan turned out, Ilya would remain the same. She knew she should be content with the boy, *with the man*, as he was. He seemed happy but in a very inert way. Never angry, never sad, never really alive. He slept, he ate, he played video games, that was all and that's the way it would always be.

He had passed through puberty more than a decade ago and, though his physical changes seemed normal with a few spots of acne and the sprouting of facial hair and the deepening tone of his occasional grunts, he seemed unaffected emotionally. Had he no sexual urges? By everything she could see, he did not. Or was he being secretive about them? She hoped for the latter. Yes, that would be more normal.

Current thinking in America held that a person like Ilya, or any person of his age, was already normal in their own way. She should accept him as he was, not as she felt he *should* be. It sounded simple enough, yet it was something she knew she could never do.

Katerina closed his door.

She returned to the kitchenette and took a sip from the tea she'd left on the counter. It had gone cold and bitter. She tossed the last of it into the sink and placed the cup in the dishwasher. She then picked up her phone connected by a secure satellite link to Andrei. By a prearranged signal, she texted that all was well.

Maybe she should have told him about Lattimore's daughter or about the Coast Guard cutter. But there was nothing they could do about the cutter and, and as for Lattimore's daughter well, she had her own plans.

She put on her black leather coat, boots and gloves and gave the mirror her best fashion model smile. With a flip of her bright red scarf, she walked out.

Down on the parking level, she eased herself into her bright red Lincoln and pulled south onto Jefferson Avenue. She smiled. It was both tiresome and arousing dressing like a vamp. It scared the men at the mill in a tantalizing way. They knew she carried a loaded Glock in the inside pocket of her coat. Some had seen it when, as if teasing them with a little show of leg, she'd allowed her coat to fall open. Yes, there would be no mistakes tonight. All her men knew her to be every bit as dangerous as she looked.

CHAPTER 28

"Quarter speed, Mr. Sullivan, two points to starboard," said Lattimore facing aft, his binoculars trained on the white bow of the Coast Guard cutter *Kalkaska* coming up fast on the port side. Would she hail them? Would she board them? Would they search his ship? Or would the cutter simply sail by on her routine southerly circuit down to Lake Erie? He would know her intentions soon enough.

"Is she slowing?" said Sullivan from the helm, second mate Winters behind him.

"No sign of it yet." Lattimore put down his binoculars. He turned, pleased to see the green flashing lights from the dock of the Stoltenberg Steel Mill. But wait, something was wrong. There were two lights, the closer of them red, the farther, green.

"They're directing us to the fueling dock, captain," said Sullivan. "The cargo dock is open. Why would they…?"

"I don't know. Just the same, we'll make for the fueling dock. Alert the men. I'll take the helm." Was Hanover behind this change?

At the helm, Winters silent beside him, Lattimore kept his eyes forward. The bright yellow logo of *Shell Oil* identified the fueling dock. It stood a few hundred yards past the main dock.

Ashore, the gleam of the lowering sun gave a reddish gray sheen to the piles of raw, steelmaking ore. Beyond them sat the black charred buildings of the mill, their dark stacks casting long shadows. Lattimore studied the men lined up on the loading dock. He wondered if they were as confused as he was about the change in protocol.

He was momentarily distracted by the sight of *Kalkaska*, passing them on the port side. The friendly blast of her horn caused Winters to jump.

"Answer in kind," ordered Lattimore, wondering how much his second mate knew about what would be happening tonight.

Winters gave a single blast of *Endeavor*'s horn.

Kalkaska sailed by, showing no sign of slowing.

Lattimore engaged the bow thrusters bringing *Endeavor* parallel to the fueling dock, approaching it ever so slowly. It wasn't her speed but her enormous mass that gave her a dangerous momentum equal to that of a few hundred formula one race cars charging at top speed toward a brick wall. Well, all right, a soft brick wall in this case.

Down on the deck, lines were cast and drawn tight. The hull made contact with the rubber fenders on the dock. They groaned and squealed, deforming with the impact. The pilings swayed then stabilized. It had been a long time since he, not Sullivan, had handled this tricky docking maneuver. Lattimore had enough pride in his own seamanship to not give any outward indication at the satisfaction and even relief he felt when all had gone well. Perhaps he was more on edge than he realized at what would soon be happening.

He signaled full stop. The engines went silent. Lattimore dismissed Winters.

With the sun nearing the horizon, bright lights flickered on both aboard and along the dock. Lattimore watched as Sullivan orchestrated his men. All wore heavy coats and safety vests, their vaporous breathing testifying to the cold. The fueling boom was raised out over the stern, the neoprene hose lowered onto the deck. The heavy brass fittings took two men to handle. Orders were shouted, levered connections tightened, checked, then tightened again. At a wave and a shout from Sullivan a large pump ashore started the flow of marine grade Deisel into *Endeavor*.

Lattimore turned off the lights on the bridge. He sank into his leather recliner and kicked back. Though he closed his eyes, he didn't sleep. His meeting that morning with the professor had not gone well. A relapse Maddie had called it when the man faltered at even the simplest question. Still, his journal seemed genuine and Lattimore had to concede the possibility that there may indeed be nukes aboard. Hanover was taking a tremendous risk allowing things to go this far.

Still, whatever Katerina had been planning would end tonight.

He wondered what Maddie would think when she learned the truth. He still felt her kiss on his cheek from the night before. Would he regain her as a daughter? Or would she walk away, her bitterness still forming an unbreachable wall between them? Lattimore was startled from these thoughts at Winter's return to the bridge.

"Fueling is complete," the man announced.

"Very well," said Lattimore surprised time had passed so quickly. He rubbed his eyes. He must have dozed after all. Like an old man in need of a nap, he thought reproaching himself with regret. He brought his recliner upright, then stood. "Have we been cleared for unloading?"

"Not yet," said Winters, eyes ashore. "There seems to be a hold up."

Lattimore spotted a red Lincoln idling on the dock. Beside it stood a man with a rifle. He felt a chill shoot up his spine. With a hand on Winter's shoulder, he spoke quickly. "Get below, find the four who came aboard back in Lake Huron. They should be in the dayroom or the galley. Get them all up here on the bridge. Do it, Mr. Winters. Do it right now." Winters ran out.

The car on the dock was still idling. The gunman beside it began shifting his weight from one foot to the other trying to keep warm. It was just like Katerina to keep him waiting while she sat warm and comfortable inside her luxury car.

There was a time, half a world away, when Lattimore would have mustered his men for a fight. Maybe Katerina was only being careful; being ready for anything. Or had she been warned about what was about to happen?

Moments later Maddie and her friends hurried onto the bridge.

"Is this what you were expecting? Is it happening?" said the sheriff.

"Yes, but there may be problems," said Lattimore wondering where Winters had gone. He also wondered where Sullivan was. "I don't have time to explain. Just stay here until I give the all clear. Do you understand? I'm going down on deck. There's a chance we might have some dangerous visitors coming aboard. I don't want them to see you."

"But the good guys are here somewhere, right?" said the sheriff.

"There's been no sign of them yet. Maddie, you'll be in charge up here. No matter what happens, you will all stay here. You will not leave the bridge. You will not touch any of the controls. You will keep the lights off. You will stay away from the windows. You will not make a sound. Is that clear?" He pulled his coat on and hurried to a panel built into the bulkhead. He unlocked it, and pulled out a gun. He made sure it was loaded then slipped it into his coat pocket. "If all goes well, we are about to be rescued. But we need to be ready for anything."

"We need guns," said Maddie.

"There are two more, both loaded in that same compartment. I left it open. You will use them only if you feel directly threatened. Is that understood?"

"Yes."

Lattimore saw the determined look in her eyes. Fearing she might rebuff his attempt at an embrace, he placed a firm hand on her shoulder then left the bridge.

On the way down, he pulled his phone and entered a prearranged signal. He saw that it had been sent and received but not acknowledged. What the hell? This was not a good time for a change in plans. He stowed the phone, then slowed his steps. He put a hand in his coat pocket and curled his fingers around the gun.

On reaching deck level he pushed open the hatch and stepped out into the cold. He kept one hand at his side, the other in his pocket, gripping the gun. He walked to the rail and stared at the Lincoln.

As if on cue, the driver's door opened. Looking like some over the top Disney villain, Katerina stepped out. She held his stare. Having at least had the good sense to wear work boots in place of spiked heels, she walked quickly up the pilot's stairs onto the deck, flanked by the man with the rifle.

"Good evening, captain," she said walking up to him, smiling. "I trust you've had an uneventful trip from Duluth?"

"Why is he here?" said Lattimore, eyes on the gunman.

"And why are you keeping a hand in your pocket, captain?" She didn't wait for an answer. "You are two days late and you've been trailed by that Coast Guard vessel since Alpena. Is there something I should be made aware of?"

"Considering the winds and current we made good time. As for the cutter, they're not concerned about us. They're on a routine patrol."

"That had better be the case, captain."

The wind picked up, ruffling her long hair that streamed out beneath her knit cap. The cap was the only thing unfashionable about her, well, except for the boots. She pulled the cap tighter.

"We're ready to offload," said Lattimore.

"Sorry captain, there's been a change of plans."

"My plans have not changed. We offload the taconite. You take what's yours. We settle our accounts. And we part neither as friends or enemies."

"And the CIA comes to your rescue, is that right?"

Lattimore was stunned but tried not to show it.

She shook her head. "I am sorry, but that fairytale ending was never going to happen. You aren't really *that* naïve, are you?" She folded her arms, shivering. "But I will surrender to you in your game against the cold. Please, let us go to a warmer place where we can talk."

"What about him?"

"My man will remain here. And you can keep that gun in your pocket. That's more than fair, don't you think?"

Lattimore led the way inside to a small room he knew would be empty but for a loading cart. "I would offer you coffee or tea but..."

"A shot of vodka would be better but we, well *you*, are a little pressed for time right now."

What was she up to? Where was Hanover?

She pulled a sealed manila envelope from her coat pocket. It bulged, thick. She held it for a moment toying with his curiosity. "This ship and its cargo have been sold. You are to proceed as directed according to the documents I have here."

"I will do no such thing."

"You may want to reconsider, captain." She smiled. It was a cruel smile, the kind she might take on had she been in the process of twisting a knife deep into living flesh. He hated this woman.

She handed him the envelope. When Lattimore made no move to accept it, she placed it on the cart beside him. "It is all there, captain: schedule, permits, refueling arrangements. You are to follow your instructions to the letter. At your destination, you will be paid the sum of five hundred thousand U.S. dollars. You will have another fifty thousand to keep or distribute as you see fit to your crew. Airline tickets have been arranged for flights back to destinations of your choosing. Economy for your crew, first class for you, of course."

She held his eyes and her smile for a few more seconds as if savoring the moment. "You will see when you open the envelope that time is of the essence. Should all go as planned, we will not meet again. Good luck to you, captain."

Lattimore kept his jaw rigid. He picked up the envelope. He let go of his gun and, from his pants pocket, retrieved a lighter. He produced a flame. He held the envelope over it. "This was not part of the deal," he said. "We unload tonight, you pay me what you owe me, and we are done." The corner of the envelope began to char.

Lattimore flinched at the dull sound of a gunshot from somewhere aboard the ship. The flame grew slowly. He held the envelope and the lighter steady. "What are you up to, you bitch?"

Katerina held her knife twisting smirk. "Do you think you are dealing with an amateur, captain? My man, and a few of his friends have come aboard. By now, we should have your daughter. I suggest you put out the flame."

Lattimore felt his stomach turn. "You're bluffing."

The flame grew.

Katerina moved quickly. In one motion, she knocked the envelope from his hand and pulled her Glock. She pointed it at Lattimore. At his feet lay the envelope, the flame sputtering out. "You are an old man, captain. You seem to have lost your edge." She held her gun steady. She reached into his coat pocket, pulled out his gun and tossed it aside. She then produced her phone. She thumbed a few keys. Then waited. "You will see that I am not bluffing. Ah yes, there she is now." Smiling again, this time almost pleasantly, she showed the screen to Lattimore. "Facetime is a wonderful thing, is it not?"

Lattimore stared in disbelief. The dark scene jerked sideways. There was Maddie, blood on her face. A man held her from behind, his hand over her mouth. She was already off the ship. Men surrounded her, dragging her out to Katerina's car. The scene on the phone jerked, he saw the blur of a face—it was Sullivan.

Rage overwhelmed Lattimore. He dropped the phone and ran out onto the deck. He shouted, "Maddie..." He reached the rail. She was struggling, being dragged to the car. A fist smashed her face. Blood streamed down. They shoved her into the back seat. A man forced himself in beside her and pulled the door closed.

Lattimore shouted again. He ran for the stairs but was grabbed by two men. One held him from behind in a bearhug, the other slammed the butt of his rifle into his face. He collapsed onto the deck. He struggled to get up, blood filled his eyes.

He heard Katerina shout an order.

The men pulled him up. He saw her through a red blur. "If you harm my daughter..."

"Yes, yes. You will cut out my tongue or slice up my face or kill me or something like that. Or maybe you'll hunt me down like a wild animal? I've heard it all before, Captain Lattimore, and as you see, I am still alive and well." Katerina moved closer, her face inches from his. He felt the sickening warmth of her breath. "By now I suppose you realize that your CIA has decided not to come to your rescue. Yes, I know you've been in touch with them. I'll leave it to you to figure out why they decided not to show up tonight. And, as for your daughter, I will keep her safe as long as you follow the new plan. It will be easy for you and your payment is generous."

She forced the envelope into his hands. "I warn you; we will be keeping a close watch on your ship. Any course deviations and any communications you might have with any of those powerful friends of yours will have dire consequences for your daughter. Fingers, eyes, ears and more, we have become very good at violent surgical procedures. Sad to say, we are not so good with anesthetics. In two weeks, you will have your money and your daughter and this will all be over. It is easy. All you do is follow your instructions. Do you understand?"

Lattimore fought back his rage. "You bitch!"

"You never were very good at confrontational dialog, captain. But I'll take that as a yes." She removed one of her gloves. Extending her hand, she brought the tip of her fingernail up to his bloody forehead. "Ouch," she said feigning concern. In an instant, she dug her nail deep into his wound. She tore aside a flap of skin then pulled her hand away.

Pain blazed. Hands to his face, Lattimore doubled over, eyes squeezed shut. Blood pumped from the wound, streaming over his fingers, down his face.

The man holding him from behind threw him to the deck.

"You should have that looked at, captain. Here now, you dropped your instructions again."

Lying doubled over on the deck, Lattimore felt her tuck the envelope inside his coat. He forced his eyes open, everything a chaotic blur. He caught his breath. He managed to get to his feet. He staggard to the rail. In the cold he could almost feel his blood quickly coagulate. He heard more than saw Katerina and her men head down the pilot's stairs and onto the dock. He blinked his eyes clear. He pulled himself up.

"Maddie!" he shouted once, then again. He tried to focus on the dock. He saw the Lincoln pull away. Its taillights faded fast.

His mind was a whirl of confusion. Where were they taking her? What the fuck had happened to the CIA? How did Katerina know they weren't coming? Had he been set up again?

Dread and emptiness overtook him. He had underestimated Katerina. He had overestimated his ability to deal with her. He had trusted Hanover, and it would be Maddie who'd pay the price for it all. Numb to the cold, numb to everything, he pressed both hands over his face and sank to his knees.

CHAPTER 29

Jack's head throbbed like a drum. He opened his eyes. It was quiet. He was alone, in the stairwell one deck down from the bridge—or was it two decks down? Where was Maddie? Where was anyone? He lay spreadeagle on a landing between flights of stairs. He struggled to get to his knees, then used the railing to pull himself up the rest of the way. He looked down. There was blood on the tread plate. Was he bleeding? He didn't think so. Or, was it Maddie's blood? Shit! Where was she?

Jack remembered the gunshots. He remembered her struggling with the attackers, fighting like hell. He remembered her screams. Had they taken her? He'd let her down. Was she still alive?

Jack staggered the rest of the way down the stairs to the main deck. He saw a hatch. He opened it. The frigid wind blew. It knocked him back but, at the same time cleared his head. He took a deep breath of it. He forced himself to walk out. He made it to the rail. He saw the dock. It was empty, no car, no one in sight. Then, further down the rail, he saw Lattimore slumped against the rail. Jack hurried to him. His face was covered in blood that still streamed down. "Captain! What the hell happened?"

Lattimore turned, eyes red. "*You*, damn-it. You let them take her," he roared. He tried to go after Jack but fell back. "I told you...you were supposed to protect her. They've got her. They've got Maddie. You should have..."

"There were too many of them," Jack stammered. "We couldn't fight them all off." Then he realized what Lattimore had said. "They took her? They've got her? But she's alive, right? She's still alive?"

Someone shouted from above. Jack looked up. It was Beth. He couldn't make out what she was saying but she looked all right. He turned back to Lattimore then saw an envelope on the deck. Jack picked it up then put his arm around the captain. "Come on, we need to get out of the cold."

"I'm a pharmacist, not a doctor," said Beth thirty-minutes later in what served as a clinic. "I thought you guys are supposed to have a medic aboard."

Lattimore sat on a cushioned table. "It's a damn scratch."

"You need stitches."

"Shut up and get it done."

Jack had already taken care of his own wound with a few butterfly bandages over a deep cut. He now held a rubber bag of ice over an angry red bulge on the side of his head. As Jack watched, Beth dabbed Lattimore's wound clean with a cotton ball dipped in alcohol. She then picked up the curved needle fitted with a length of surgical thread. She gave Jack what he took to be a this is all your fault glance and went to work. She pinched the bloody flap of skin on Lattimore's scalp together then poked the curved needle through. She drew the thread through then repeated the process.

Jack could see she was holding her breath. "You're doing fine, Beth," he told her as she finished the second stitch. "You seem nervous. Breathe easy."

"Would you like to take a stab at it?"

"Get it done," said Lattimore.

Ten stitches later, Beth knotted the thread, snipped off the excess and again cleaned the closed wound with alcohol.

Lattimore, who hadn't so much as flinched through the procedure, got to his feet. He took a moment to steady himself then turned to Jack, glaring. "I left you in charge, sheriff. I told you to keep everyone on the bridge. How...?"

Jack thought it best not to point out that it had been Maddie he'd put in charge. "We had no choice. They were storming the ship. Maddie and I took the guns and set up in the stairwell to hold them off. We could hear them coming up. We were ready for them. It was the right thing to do. Then, shots were fired down at us. There were a couple of men, three maybe. They surprised us. I think one of their shots hit... But the last I saw, she was still fighting. We both fired back but there were too many of them and they were coming at us in the stairwell from above and below. They charged us and knocked me out cold. When I came to, they were gone. She...was gone. "That's it. That's what happened. I'm sorry captain. I...we did all we could. Those men who fired down at us, the ones who took her. They had to have already been on board. They were part of your crew."

Lattimore rubbed his eyes. He shook his head. "It was Sullivan...and others. I should have warned you that might happen. I saw...I should have..."

"What happened to the CIA?" said Beth.

"I don't know." Lattimore stared blankly. "I'm sorry I blamed you, sheriff. If anyone's to blame, it's me. I trusted the CIA. They should have been here. They should have stopped all of this. That was the...deal."

"What was the deal?" said Beth.

Lattimore held up a dismissive hand. "They asked me to play along with the syndicate for this one last time. In return, they promised leniency for the years I'd been working with them. It had to be that asshole Hanover. He probably wanted to let this thing play out; trying to turn it to his advantage or...or catch somebody further up the food chain. They don't care about Maddie. They don't care about any of us aboard this ship. To them, we're all collateral damage."

"I found this outside on the deck," said Jack, holding up the envelope.

Lattimore took it from him. "These are my new orders. If I don't follow them by staying on course and on schedule, they'll kill my daughter."

"Where are we going?" said Beth.

"I don't know. But the two of you, and Andrew too, are not part of my crew. You do not have to come with us. I can drop you off at the next refueling port. I would suggest that you not go ashore here. I don't want you to become hostages too. We'll talk in the morning." Lattimore left.

Beth ran a sleeve across her forehead. "This could all be over for us in a few days."

Jack shook his head. "We're still safer aboard this ship than ashore."

"Come on, Jack. This is not our problem. None of it is."

"This Katerina is ruthless. She proved that tonight. We know there are nukes aboard this ship. Because of that we're a threat to whatever it is she's planning. The moment we step ashore, we'll become a target."

"She doesn't even know about us."

"I'm not so sure of that. And besides, they've got Maddie. She knows about us. They might force her to…"

"So, there's no way out of this for us."

He took a step closer, his eyes on hers. "Beth, we have a chance to put a stop something that could be another 9-11."

She held his gaze. Then she shook her head. She put her arms around him and kissed him gently on the cheek.

"I let them take Maddie. "I should've…"

"Stop it, Jack. You did all you could."

"She saved my life. I couldn't save hers."

"Don't talk like that. She's not dead yet." Her tone softened. "I care about her too, you know."

Jack took in a breath. Gently, he released himself from her loose embrace. In his mind he replayed the shootout in the stairwell. Beth was right. He'd done all he could. Still, he wished it was him they'd taken, not her. "Where is Andrew?" he said absently.

"I took him to his cabin. He'd been on the bridge asleep on Lattimore's recliner."

"Must be nice to be oblivious to all of this." Jack felt the rumble of the engines. The ship began to move.

They went back to their cabin and tried to sleep.

In the morning, an announcement drew everyone to the dayroom. "We have new orders," announced Lattimore once all were there. He had a gray, tired look about him. Understandable, thought Jack considering the little sleep he must have gotten. A dark blue knit cap covered his white hair and hid his wound. No blood. The stitches must have held. Good job, Beth.

The crew was somber. Some stood, some sat. But they were all silent. By now they all knew something had happened the night before, and some likely knew more than others.

The captain continued. "As I'm sure you all know by now, we have not unloaded our cargo. We are fully fueled and underway to a destination that some of you will learn about later." He paused. "Some of you will be leaving the ship. Today. Now, in fact."

Lattimore fended off an uproar with a raised hand. "You have no need to worry. Your pay, and this is for all of you now, your pay has been deposited as usual in your accounts. You will each see a nice kicker for what will be your last hitch aboard *Endeavor*. I will read off a list of names. If your name is called, you will go immediately to your lockers, grab all your personal belongings then meet up at the starboard side muster station."

"We're taking the lifeboats?" shouted a man.

"No. A launch has been arranged to pull alongside a couple of hours from now. It will take you to Toledo. Once there, you'll each receive money that will more than cover your travel expenses back to your homes or anywhere you choose—within reason, of course."

"How much?" someone shouted.

"Five hundred dollars," said Lattimore. "And the kicker in your pay will be three thousand."

This quieted the group, some nodding to each other.

"All of you will keep your mouths shut about your time on board. It may be that some of you think you know why all this is happening. I guarantee, you do not. I can only assure you that I have good reasons for doing what I am doing."

The room broke out into shouts. Beck raised her voice above the others. "This is all because of them, isn't it?" She turned and pointed directly at Jack who stood in the back beside Beth and Andrew.

"They are not the cause of any of this," said Lattimore.

"And where's that FBI gal?" came another shout. "I'll bet she's at the bottom of all this."

Lattimore slammed his fist down on the nearest table. "All of you. Shut the fuck up! It is not my choice that this is happening. It is happening and it is necessary because of forces outside of my control. It is happening because your welfare and the welfare of this ship requires it. That is all you need to know and that is all you are going to know.

"Now, when you hear your name, you will get your shit together and double-time it to the muster station. *Is that clear?*"

The room quieted down.

"He's getting us down to a skeleton crew," whispered Beth. "He expects more trouble."

Lattimore began reading off names from a folded up sheet of paper.

Jack kept a count of the names called as the crowd in the galley thinned out. Most went quietly. Others became belligerent when their names were called. Others became belligerent when their names weren't called. All eventually followed Lattimore's orders. "Sixteen leaving," he said quietly to Beth.

"Can the ship function with so small a crew?"

"The captain must think so."

The room, less full now, was silent. Lattimore took a drink of something, maybe water, maybe coffee, maybe something stronger. He surveyed those who were left. "You are the people I'll be counting on to do your duty to keep this ship afloat and on course."

"On course for where, Captain?" shouted Beck.

Lattimore waited for complete silence. "We're heading for the North Atlantic. I will give you more details when I can. For now, get back to your duty stations. Until further notice, you'll each be pulling one and a half times your normal work load."

"The saltwater ain't gonna do the ship any good," said someone.

"Are we in any danger, captain?" asked another.

Lattimore lowered the tone of his voice. "It is my job, my duty, to keep all of you and this ship out of harm's way. This, I intend to do. But it will be up to all of us in this room, to make that happen. Now, get back to your stations. Again, for the...challenges we'll face, you will all receive additional compensation."

"Hope we're alive to spend it," said one man.

"Guess we *are* in danger," said another.

"And one more thing," said Lattimore, pointing to a tall, lanky man wearing black framed glasses, "Mr. Carter, you have just been promoted to second mate. You will be in charge of getting the others off this ship in an orderly manner. And, for your information. Mr. Winters, has been promoted to first mate. He is presently at the helm."

"What happened to Mr. Sullivan?" said Carter.

"Mr. Sullivan is no longer aboard this ship. That is all you need to know."

The diminished crew filed out.

The captain walked over to where Jack, Beth and Andrew stood. "While Carter handles the...evacuees, I will be preoccupied on the bridge. As soon as I can, I will return here and we can talk more. Until then, you will all stay here and you will do nothing."

Andrew raised his hand timidly. "I would like to have some breakfast if..."

"Fine. You will all stay here *or* in the galley. I will be back."

CHAPTER 30

Lattimore stood on the starboard side of the bridge, his new first mate at the helm. They were well into the open waters of Lake Erie, no hazards ahead, no ice to worry about; nothing Winters couldn't handle. This was good because right now he had other things on his mind.

He stared at his cell phone, at the picture Katerina had sent. He hardly recognized Maddie. Her eyes were swollen, forehead and cheeks bruised a ghastly purple, hair ragged and streaked with blood. Above and to her right someone offscreen held a newspaper dated this same day. It was a typical proof of life photo.

He enlarged the picture until Maddie's face filled the screen. *I'm so sorry baby*, he whispered, staring. Though her eyes were nearly swollen shut, in them he could still see his Maddie. In them he could see, not fear, not desperation, but hate and anger. Lattimore smiled grimly. Yes, that was still his daughter!

There'd been no text sent with the photograph but Katerina's message was clear: If you want to see your daughter alive, you will follow your orders.

But with defiance in her eyes, Maddie had sent him a message of her own: Don't worry about me. Let's fuck this bitch!

But how exactly do we do that? Yes, that was the question.

Lattimore made a decision. "Mr. Winters, you'll have the helm a while longer. You will alert me immediately of any problems."

"Aye, captain. Can I ask..."

"No, you may not ask anything right now. I have things to attend to. I'll be back to relieve you in an hour or so."

Lattimore hurried to his cabin. He retrieved the envelope Katerina had given him then worked the combination on his safe. He pulled out the secure sat phone. As expected, its screen was blank. He secured the safe. Determined, yet worried he might change his mind, he left his cabin, made his way to the nearest hatch that led outside. He forced it open.

Ignoring the cold, he stepped quickly out to the rail and, without hesitation, threw the phone overboard. It hardly made a splash. "Fuck you, Hanover," he shouted into the wind, his grip tight on the rail. "This is *my* game now and *my* rules."

His mind clear, he headed down to the galley where he found his three visitors sitting together. They were alone. He wondered where the cook might be. He hoped he hadn't included her among the evacuees. He got himself a cup of coffee and walked over. "Coffee's better here than up on the bridge," he said, trying to sound casual.

"Any news about Maddie," asked Beth.

He couldn't bear to show them her picture. "My daughter is a strong woman. The only reason they took her is to make sure I follow my instructions. As long as I do that, she will not be hurt."

"Do you really believe that?"

"I know these people. I know Katerina."

"She's Russian?" said Andrew.

"Yes. And, as you may know, the steel mills in Detroit are owned by a Russian company. That's no secret. And there's nothing illegal about it. I have no idea who Katerina's boss might be, so she might be the top dog at the Syndicate. I also know the organization to be international in scope."

"Who is Hanover?" said Beth.

"He works for the State Department. That's all I will tell you about him. For now, he's out of the picture. My first priority is getting Maddie back. Taking down the Syndicate is a distant second."

"Taking down the Syndicate might be the only way to get her back," said Beth.

"You may be right," said Lattimore. His forehead wound began to throb. He pressed a hand to it. "Have you thought about my offer to allow you to leave this ship?"

Jack met Lattimore's eyes. "That depends. Up till now you've tolerated our attempts at searching the ship for the nukes. Will you be helping us now?"

"Yes, I will. The men I suspected of working directly for the syndicate, the ones who helped abduct Maddie, are no longer aboard. I will do whatever I can to help you."

"Then we will stay," said Beth, appearing to surprise her husband.

"Good, I'm glad to hear it. I can use all the help I can get." He turned to Andrew. "And you, Mr. Simeon, will you stay?"

"What? Oh, yes, of course I will stay. I like freighters. But tell me, captain, why are we going out into the Atlantic?"

Lattimore produced the envelope and placed it on the table. "Katerina gave me this last night."

Jack picked it up, fingering its black singed corner. He opened the envelope then pulled out the thick wad of papers inside. He unfolded them and started thumbing through them.

"It won't make much sense to you sheriff but please, keep those papers in order. I'll be needing them. Katerina informed me that this ship and its cargo has been sold. Then she made sure I knew she had Maddie."

"She sent you a picture?" said Beth.

"Yes."

"These papers look official," said Jack returning them to their envelope, handing it to Lattimore.

"I trust they are thorough, official and legal. If nothing else, the syndicate is very good at paperwork." He tapped the edge of the envelope on the tabletop. "These are our course plans and schedule, our lock and refueling permits and all the clearance papers we'll need. From here in Lake Erie, we travel east through the entire length of the St. Lawrence Seaway. Then we head out into international waters to a specific location in the North Atlantic."

"A rendezvous," said Jack. "A rendezvous with who?"

"You mean, with *whom*, I think," said Andrew.

"I don't know with...whom," said Lattimore.

"They'll take the bombs then sink this ship," said Beth.

"That, will not happen."

"What's to stop them?" said Jack.

"And what's to stop them from harming your daughter?" said Beth.

"Leave that to me. For the present, your job is to find the...bombs."

Andrew leaned in. "You still don't believe it, do you? I assure you all, if those crates the sheriff saw being loaded aboard this ship were from Mayfield Industries then you are indeed carrying nuclear weapons; twelve of them, if I remember correctly."

Lattimore leaned closer. "Excuse me Professor Simeon but, up until a short time ago, all you did was sleep. And when you weren't sleeping, you'd behaved like a feeble-minded idiot. Pardon me if I'm skeptical of everything you say."

Andrew turned white. "I...I admit, I haven't been myself lately."

Lattimore gave a shrug. "But as for the bombs, yes Professor Simeon. I do believe we have atomic weapons aboard and, after reading through that journal of yours, I do believe you to be the bomb maker. In the end, that may be worth something." Lattimore tossed back the last of his coffee, got up and poured himself another. "Coffee's better here in the galley than up on the bridge," he said, from the serving window. "Oh, I think I told you that before. Shit, I hate getting old."

"Tell me about it," muttered Andrew.

Lattimore, placed an elbow on the shelf of the serving window. "Obviously, Katerina knew about Maddie being aboard but, I don't think she knows about any of you."

"If Sullivan's with her now, he'll tell her about us," said Jack.

"Yes, he will. He knows about you and your wife, sheriff, but he still thinks Andrew's a homeless derelict. No offense, professor." Lattimore retook his seat. "I don't know exactly where the bombs are but I do have a pretty good idea as to where they might be. It'll take time but there is a chance we'll find them."

"What do we do if we find them?" said Beth.

"Let's find them first," said Lattimore. "I'll give you the mechanical drawings of the ship and you will have use of a computer."

Beth perked up. "We'll have access to the internet?"

"Yes. I have a secure *Starlink* system aboard. But there can be no interpersonal communication, phone calls, texts or whatever. We have to assume that all our conventional comms will be monitored. Stepping out of line just once could…"

"Yeah, we get the picture," said Jack.

"If you don't mind, I have a few questions," said Beth.

Lattimore took another sip of coffee, then faced her. He took in her beauty, tarnished though it was by stress and lack of sleep. For all their bickering, she and Jack were two of the most compatible people he knew. They were lucky to have each other.

"How long ago was it that you became captain of this ship?"

"I believe it was a little over seven years ago. That's public information. You can look it up."

"Back then, was this ship being used for smuggling?"

"If it was, I wasn't aware of it."

"When did you become aware of it?"

Lattimore smiled. "This is sounding more like an interrogation Ms. Holiday. Maybe your husband should read me my rights."

"You said you would help," she persisted. "And, please, call me Beth."

"Even so, I won't be treated like a common criminal. Not by any of you."

The sheriff stiffened. "You must know you will be prosecuted for aiding, maybe even leading a criminal enterprise and the charges against you could extend to attempted murder. You and your men nearly got me killed. Or did you think I'd forgotten about that? Oh, and please, call me Jack."

"That wasn't my doing, *Jack*. You were the one who almost got yourself killed."

"I was doing my job."

Beth intervened. "Look I...*we* didn't mean to threaten you. I've only got a couple more questions."

Lattimore waited, fingers drumming the table.

"Back when you became captain of this ship, how exactly did you become aware that your ship was involved with smuggling?"

"It was after our first Duluth, Detroit run."

"And how...?"

"On delivering my cargo at the end of the run I received an unmarked envelope filled with cash."

"Who gave it to you?"

"It was left for me as part of my mail pickup."

"And you had nothing to do with the loading or unloading of the smuggled goods."

"That's right."

"Do you know when this ship was last serviced for something other than routine maintenance? You know, for something major."

"Not since I've been captain." Lattimore saw her line of thinking and the reason for her question. "I can get you *Endeavor*'s IMO number so you can look up the full construction and maintenance records going all the way back to when her keel was laid."

"That'd be great. Thank you. And when can we have that computer?"

"I'll have it sent down right away." Lattimore paused. "Anything else, madam prosecutor?"

That raised an attractive smile from her. "No more questions. You may step down. Thank you, captain. Or, may I call you Harlan?"

"No, Beth. You may not. I've always disliked the name. But if I can ask, where did you pick up your interrogation skills?"

Beth held her smile, maybe a little embarrassed. "Comes from being married to a lawman, I guess. That and the fact that, back at the pharmacy, I often have to question people about their use of drugs."

CHAPTER 31

"It's the International Maritime Organization number," said Beth an hour later staring at the smudged-up screen on Lattimore's laptop.

She sat between Jack and Andrew at a table in the dayroom. Jack watched her hit a few keys which took her to a Coast Guard search site. "Apparently, it's like a VIN number for a car," she said. "From the date it's built to the day it's scrapped…or sunk, everything about the ship can be tracked with its IMO number. I'm hoping we can review the history for this ship, especially her maintenance record. We need to look for anything that might give a hint that a normal maintenance job might really have been something more."

"Like the installation of a smuggler's hold," said Jack, impressed.

"Yes." She hit a few keys, set a finger tapping at her chin, then hit a few more. "It says here *Endeavor* was last dry docked eight years ago."

"That would have been before Lattimore became her captain," said Andrew.

Jack kept his eyes on the screen. "The work took place at a shipyard not far from Saint Petersburg, Russia. So, there's another Russia connection. That's a long way to go for routine maintenance on a Great Lakes freighter. She was laid up for four months."

"Maybe she wasn't always a Great Lakes freighter. It says her keel was laid in Hamberg Germany in July of 2003." Beth scrolled slowly down. "As for the more recent work done in Saint Petersburg, it looks like there was damage to a starboard section of the hull. A bulkhead had to be replaced and some of her outer hull plates were refit. That could be where the smuggler's hold is. And see, there are pictures. Color, but low resolution." She scrolled again. "They show the repairs and a few instrumentation upgrades on the bridge none of which look suspicious." The last of the pictures showed the ship's name at the bow, freshly painted in big block white letters:

ENDEAVOR

Beth went back to the top of the page. She enlarged the screen and repositioned the computer so Jack and Andrew had a better view. "We've got to go over this closely, line by line so we don't miss anything." They leaned in.

After a while, Beth backed away from the computer, nearly bumping heads with the two of them. "Look, I'm sorry but I think I can do this better without you guys breathing down my neck."

"I like breathing down your neck," said Jack.

"You *are* wearing a delightfully fresh perfume," added Andrew.

"That's it. I'll do this better alone. I'll make notes, I'll go over it all. The two of you can take a break. Go, do whatever you want..."

"...but leave you the hell alone," said Jack.

"Yes."

"Turns out I was getting hungry anyway," said Jack standing. "How 'bout we break for some food. Want anything?"

She held out her empty coffee cup.

In the galley, he was pleased to see the cook at her post behind the serving window. He introduced himself, learned her name was Kelly, then brought a full cup back to Beth.

On returning to the galley, this time with Andrew, he found a few crewmen eating lunch. "Sorry, fellas," said Kelly from behind the window at the serving counter, "Just grilled ham and cheese with hashbrowns today. I lost my assistant you know."

On getting their food, they joined a young, clean shaven, African American man who sat alone. Jack started introductions but the man cut him short. "I know who you are. I'm Ben

Spencer." He spoke in a gravelly voice. He lifted his bloodshot eyes, meeting Jack's. "I'm a student at Michigan Tech. I took a semester off to make ends meet. I'm an oiler. See here? You can tell from my hands." He held them up, displaying the black grime that mottled his palms. "I'm told I smell like an oiler but I've been nose blind for a while now so I wouldn't know. Once I get off the lakes, it'll be a month before I'll feel clean again. *Dawn* dishwashing soap is the only thing that'll work." He shrugged. "Gets in your hair too."

"You don't like working aboard this ship?" said Jack.

Ben smiled. "You haven't been down to the engine room I guess. It's hard, hot, dirty work. But I do, or did, like the free time when I got to walk out on deck. Not much time for that now. Too cold anyway."

"What's your major?" said Andrew.

His eyes brightened. "Nautical Engineering. I want to build boats. I want to build big boats. I've got one more year to go."

"Well, good for you young man. I'm a professor of physics. Maybe I could give you a letter of recommendation once you graduate."

"You're a professor?"

"It was a long time ago so it may not do much good."

"No, I think it might. Thank you, sir. I would appreciate that." Ben turned to Jack. "Your wife said you're a sheriff or something."

"You talked with her?"

"Yesterday. I gave her a few pointers on the pinball machine in the day room. The rocking of the ship adds another degree of difficulty. If you know what you're doing, you can use it to your advantage."

"I'll have to play her sometime. You ever been to Gull Harbor? That's where she and I are from."

"Couple of times." Ben hesitated. "I guess I can't ask you why you're aboard and what you guys are up to."

"You can ask but we can't say," said Jack. "Sorry."

"We're okay, right? We're going to be okay?"

"Yes, Ben, we're going to be okay."

Ben frowned, then checked his watch. He downed the last of his food. "Well, gotta run...longer shifts and all." Standing, he gave a nod, then left.

"I hear he's a good worker, that kid," said Kelly, coming over. "You two want more hashbrowns? I'm about to throw them out to the gulls."

They both declined, then Jack said: "How's the ship doing along with the smaller crew?"

Kelly shrugged. "Too early to tell. We're all getting by on less sleep. But we're fine right now."

"If you need us to help out, let us know," said Andrew.

"Yeah, I'll be sure to do that. The captain said we're heading out into the Atlantic. Do you know why?"

"We don't know any more than you do," said Jack.

"Yeah, well I don't really believe that. Had to ask though."

"Is there any dessert?" said the professor. "A piece of apple pie would be nice right now."

"Tell me what the hell's going on and I'll make you all the pie you want."

At that moment, Beth walked in. She gave the cook a glance.

"All right, I'll leave you folks to your secrets. The pie deal still stands though." She walked back to her kitchen.

"You need to see something," Beth said to Jack, voice low.

"And *you* should have something to eat," Jack advised, but she was already headed back to the dayroom.

"I want you to take a look at that last drydock pic," said Beth, Jack and Andrew sitting opposite her. "It's the one showing the bow of the ship." She scrolled down then slid the computer over.

Jack let out a belch. He shook his head. "Sorry," he said, waiting, feeling pressure building for another, but the moment passed. To be sure, he took a breath, then looked at the computer. "You cleaned the screen."

"What do you see?" prompted Beth, getting up, standing behind them. "I mean, besides the ship itself?"

In the picture, the camera's vantage was slightly above the level of the deck as if from a work scaffold. In frame were three workers standing on the deck, each with their backs to the camera.

Beth leaned closer, her right breast brushed Jack's cheek.

"See that guy in the middle?" said Beth, backing off. "He's standing with a slouch to his left. That look familiar to you?"

Jack enlarged the photo, centering the now blurred figure. The realization was sudden. Beth was right. The way the figure stood *did* look familiar. "You think that's Sullivan."

"I think it might be, yes. And, if it *is* him, and if some secret modifications to the ship were made back then, he must have known all along where the bombs are."

"He was playing dumb this whole time," said Jack.

"When was this work done?" said Andrew.

"18 July, 2016."

The three of them were silent for a moment. Jack still had his eyes on the fuzzy image in the picture. He adjusted the picture back to its normal size so that, again, the big block letters spelling out *Endeavor* came into view. "The captain needs to see this."

"See what," asked Lattimore.

Jack turned to see the captain standing at the door. "We think we've discovered something about Mr. Sullivan that may be important."

"He's no longer aboard. He no longer matters."

"In 2016 he was in St. Petersburg Russia supervising drydock work being done on this ship," said Beth.

Lattimore walked in. "How do you know that?"

She turned her laptop in his direction. "Any of those men on deck look familiar? We think the man in the middle is Sullivan."

Lattimore brought the screen closer. "I suppose it could be..." Lattimore kept his eyes on the screen.

"Captain?"

"There seems to be only one explanation. Even back then the owners of this ship and Sullivan too, must have been imbedded with the syndicate."

Jack said, "We think the so-called repairs done in Saint Petersburg involved the installation of a smuggler's hold. We're hoping this documentation can tell us where that hold is."

"Yes, good plan."

"But why was the work done in a *Russian* ship yard?" said Jack.

"I suppose because they were the lowest bidder," said Lattimore. "Drydock work can easily run into the millions of dollars. Sailing across the Atlantic to make repairs might have simply been a good business decision."

"Or could it be that their inspection and documentation regulations aren't as well enforced," suggested Andrew.

"Or maybe it was because the Russian government was somehow involved and...may still be involved?" said Beth as if only then coming to that conclusion.

Andrew turned with a start. "Do you think the Russians are after my bombs?"

Jack winced at his choice of words: *my bombs.*

Lattimore shook his head. "Not likely, professor. The Russians already have enough nukes to blow up half the world. Some of them are tactical nukes, just like...your bombs." Lattimore dragged over a chair and sat.

"You said you didn't know *exactly* where the smuggler's hold is," said Beth. "That suggests that you at least have a good idea where it *might* be."

"I made it my business not to know. But I can make some educated guesses. I think you've got something here with this work done in Saint Petersburg. I suggest you go over the documentation carefully and see what more you can learn, then get back to me."

"What do we do if we find them—the bombs?" said Beth.

"Once we get into international waters we could toss them overboard," said Lattimore.

"No! You cannot do that," said Andrew.

"We can and we will," said the captain.

"When do we reach the Atlantic?" said Jack.

"At least a week, maybe more. We'll be nearing Port Colbourne on the eastern shore of Lake Erie soon. From there we thread our way through a series of locks. Then we take the Welland Canal down to Port Weller and Lake Ontario. After that, we've got the tricky waters of the St. Lawrence River.

"It could easily take more than a week. We'll have a busy time of it up on the bridge. So, while I and my new first mate and what's left of my crew are occupied with that, it'll be up to the three of you to find the bombs."

"You said you would get us the engineering drawings of the ship," said Jack.

Lattimore stood. "I'll have them sent down."

"Any news about Maddie?" said Beth.

"No," said the captain, walking out.

CHAPTER 32

They set up work in the dayroom, Beth with Lattimore's computer, Jack with the ship's drawings. He rolled them out over one of the tables.

Andrew looked on, excited about the entire process. "Those bombs were my life's work. And now, to be seeing them again and..."

"You heard the captain, didn't you?" said Beth. "Once we find them, we're going to toss them overboard."

"Oh, I don't think he will do that. You can't have a bunch of nuclear weapons just lying there at the bottom of the ocean."

"Why not?" said Jack. "They were buried in the basement of the Mayfield mansion for decades. It seems to me the bottom of the ocean is a better place than that. Is there something you're not telling us?"

"Well...suppose somebody finds them. Do you remember all the trouble the CIA went to out in the Pacific to try and recover a Russian nuclear sub? Oh yes, you might not have heard about that. Anyway, no, there's nothing I'm purposely not telling you but, as you know, my memory's not quite up to par yet and..."

"Let's just see if we can find them, okay?" said Beth.

"Yes, yes. You are quite right, Mrs. Holiday."

"My name is *Beth*, Andrew." She kept her eyes on the computer screen, fingers working the keys at a spirited pace.

Twenty minutes went by. Jack had long since stopped going over the drawings. He looked over not surprised to see Andrew dozing at the next table when he realized Beth's key clacking had stopped. "Find something?" he asked.

"I've gone over all the work orders, and pictures documenting the work done in Russia. The reworked, midship bulkhead is the most suspicious. They also did work on the stern which involved the dismantling of the rudder and its control mechanism. Both jobs were documented as routine maintenance but each took ten days to complete. I'm no expert but that doesn't seem routine to me. And, there are no pictures, and no additional documentation for the work."

Jack placed a hand on the drawings in front of him. "These were updated in 2018 but there's nothing suspicious in either of those areas that I can see. Maybe that, in itself, is suspicious."

"Did you find something?" said Andrew coming over.

"We think the bombs could be hidden behind a false bulkhead at midship. Around here," said Jack, a finger on the drawing. "Or somewhere here in something called the rudder trunk, at the stern.

"And what exactly is a rudder trunk, Sheriff Holiday?" said Beth, batting her eyes the way she always did when he spoke authoritatively about something he knew nothing about.

Jack plodded on: "It's the space where the stern protrudes over the rudder itself. It provides maintenance access to the steering mechanism. It's a space about ten feet on a side. Most of that is taken up by the workings of the rudder."

Beth smiled. "If you don't mind, I'll Google that." Then, a moment later, "Hey, you might be onto something, Jack. It says here the rudder trunk is often used for smuggling—even for smuggling people, up to a dozen of them at a time. While at sea, they would have been allowed limited access to the rest of the ship so it might not be as bad as you might think."

"You're defending human trafficking now?"

"I'm just saying, there're two sides to it. There are a lot of desperate people in the world who've spent their entire lives in inhumane conditions. They want something better for themselves and for their children."

Jack sighed and turned his attention back to the drawings. "Something called a maintenance well is aft of the cargo hold. The rudder trunk is a deck above that."

A blast of the ship's horn interrupted them. The engines slowed.

"We must be nearing the eastern shore of Lake Erie," said Jack. "That'll be the lock at Port Cogburn."

"It's Port Colborne," said Andrew. "I believe you're thinking about a character in a movie."

They checked in with Lattimore on the bridge who told them to search the midship bulkhead first. He offered a few suggestions then warned them: "Be careful. You'll be walking above tons of taconite. I've heard of men falling and getting buried under it. It can be like quicksand. The more you struggle, the quicker you sink until it's too late. And dress warmly. It'll be cold as hell down there."

He helped them line up the gear they'd need and gave Jack a rolled-up sheet of paper. "It's a smaller print of the ship's plans. It'll show you what the dimensions between each bulkhead *should* be. If you find any discrepancy of, say a foot or more, then you'll have found what you're looking for."

"Then we call you."

"No. Then you measure again. You confirm the discrepancy. You record the discrepancy and its exact location. Then you call me. Have you got that?"

"Yes."

"Good. Carter here will show you where to go. After that, you're on your own."

Once ready, Carter tightened his hood, pushed his glasses further up on his nose, and led the way on deck. Bent against the wind, they walked a third of the way toward the bow where he took a knee and pulled opened a maintenance hatch.

Jack looked down. He saw only darkness. Cold air, wafted up. "It's like a walk-in freezer down there."

"Yeah. I've been down there many times. It's no fun," said Carter. He reached in, flipped on a light, then stood.

Andrew was staring down at the open hatch. Even with the light on there wasn't much to see. "Are you sure you're up for this?" Jack asked him.

"Yes, I am."

Carter raised an eyebrow. "Well, good luck with whatever the hell you're up to. I'll come back in a few hours to check on you. I guess the captain already told you to be careful. Use your radio if you run into trouble."

"Will do," said Jack. He gave Beth a here goes nothing look, then stepped through the hatch onto a metal ladder that led to a steel catwalk bolted to the side of the inner hull. Once all three of them were down, he trained a flashlight forward, then aft. In both directions a long line of dim lamps lit the way. The vibration of the engines hummed all around them.

"I don't like this," said Andrew.

"I don't either," said Jack.

"Lots of iron down there," said Beth, her flashlight on the huge pile of reddish taconite lying a mere ten feet below the catwalk. The smell of it filled the air. The lamps overhead gave just enough light to manage their footing as they walked toward the bow inspecting bulkhead after bulkhead. At each they used a laser device to measure the spacing. Jack compared the measurements to the print Lattimore had given him looking for anything that might indicate the presence of a false bulkhead and a concealed space between.

Shivering and sweating at the same time, Jack worried this was yet another waste of time until a measurement seemed off. "Here," he said, staring at the readings. "I think we found something. Let's re-take that last measurement." They confirmed a six-foot discrepancy, confirmed the location, then used the radio to report back to Lattimore.

"Good work, Jack," the captain said quickly, the signal filled with static. "I'll get a cutting torch team down there as soon as I can. Now get your asses out of there."

"I'm all for that," said Beth already on her way. "This place gives me the creeps."

Endeavor had passed through the sixth lock of the Welland by the time Lattimore was able to spare a couple of crewmen. Jack went with them while Beth and Andrew stayed behind.

The men worked quickly to cut then lift out a two foot square, inch thick section of the suspicious bulkhead. Jack pulled a flashlight and inspected the space. "Looks to be a smuggler's hold all right," said one of them, a man named Tony. He got to his feet. "It's a big one too, empty though. Doesn't look like it's been used in a while. No fresh welds that I can see." The man's face was covered in grime and sweat. He ran a wrist across his forehead and met Jack's eyes. "What were you expecting to find?"

"Smuggled goods," said Jack, drawing a roll of the eyes from Tony.

Early the next day the three of them gathered outside the galley, coats loose on their shoulders. With measuring equipment and prints of the area, they started out for the rudder trunk. With Beth in the lead, then Andrew, then Jack they made their way down three decks. The resonating steel of the hull amplified the drumming of the engines. The stagnant air was thick with smells of oil and grease. They'd run into a few of the crew along the way but each of them knew better than to ask questions.

"Here it is," said Beth coming to a stop beside a hatch. She checked the directions Lattimore had given her then worked it open. Heated air and the loud noise of heavy machinery poured out. They walked in.

The space was dimly lit by way of a row of portholes spanning the stern. There was no sign of the Mayfield crates. Yeah, that would have been too easy. Jack found a switch and flipped on a light. Overhead a grease smudged bulb flickered on with little effect. Centered in the space was the rack and pinion drive that controlled the angle of the rudder. Jack marveled at the size of it. He placed a hand on the center hub. "This is the top bearing of the rudder," he shouted. "The rudder itself is down below us."

"You like this manly mechanical stuff, don't you?" said Beth.

"Yeah, I do," said Jack with a smile. On a knee, he unrolled a print of the space, creasing it lengthwise so it wouldn't roll up on itself. "We take measurements then compare them to this drawing. Remember, just like in the hold, we're only looking for large deviations, a foot or more. Don't pay attention to small inaccuracies."

They took off their coats and divided up the work. With Andrew keeping pace they used the same technique and the same measuring gear as the day before. They checked for signs of fresh welds or paint that didn't match. Jack also checked the steel treadplate underfoot figuring that, over an area this large, a smuggler's hold could easily be hidden between the supporting beams beneath them. But he found no sign of the cutting torch burns Lattimore said to look for.

Eventually, they found four suspicious areas worth a closer look. These Jack marked with yellow chalk.

"This is so much better than being down in the hold," said Beth. "Noisier, hotter, but better."

It didn't take long for them to run out of things to measure. "The maintenance well is next," said Jack, standing, eyes on the print.

"Where's that?"

He pointed down. "We're standing right above it. It's outside. We're gonna need our coats."

They descended one more deck, then followed a short corridor that ended at a steel hatch. Beside it was a keypad. Jack stepped aside as Beth entered the numerical code Lattimore had given her. This set a yellow light blinking overhead. She tried the lever to the hatch. "Little help here?" she said, straining.

Jack stepped up. Together they shoved the lever to the unlocked position. The hatch flew open with a resounding clang and the roar of wind and water.

"Oh, this should be fun," shouted Beth, gripping her coat.

Jack braced himself. He stepped out, struggling to keep his footing. His buttoned-up coat ballooned out. Beth followed. Andrew stayed back.

The wind swirled. Like walking on the wing of an aircraft in flight, Jack made it out to the steel rail that lined the edge of the six foot wide steel platform spanning the stern. Through the center of the platform a pillar of steel two feet in diameter, ran down to the rudder. Beth came up beside him.

The wind was deafening. Below them the steel blade of the rudder knifed through the water that was churned white by the massive propeller thundering beneath their feet. Two-thirds submerged, the propeller pounded the water, turning at a rate he wouldn't have thought possible for something so huge.

All his life Jack had lived around the lakes where seeing freighters like *Endeavor* was an everyday occurrence. Now, up this close, he could only gaze, transfixed by the enormity and the power of the ship. A shout from Beth brought him back to the task at hand. Yeah, they had work to do.

She pointed up to the overhanging bulge of the stern. She leaned closer, pointing. "I'll take that side, you take this side. We'll meet in the middle.

"Right, torch burns or fresh paint over fresh welds," he shouted back.

He removed a glove. He reached up and ran his bare fingers over the closest welded seam between the plates.

Frosty ice covered much of the stern plates. Jack used his gloved hand to clear it away then, with his bare hand, felt the welds beneath the paint. Lattimore had explained how a fresh weld would look and feel different than the old, but with eyes blurred by the vaporous air, and fingers numb from the cold, this was an exercise in futility. Still, he and Beth worked, checking the entire area.

Half frozen, he caught her attention, pointing to the hatch. She nodded and led the way back inside.

They pulled the hatch closed and levered it secure. The warmth and relative silence felt odd.

Jack wondered if his ears were working. He couldn't feel them or his jaw or his fingers.

"Damn, it's cold out there," Beth finally managed. She stood bent, shivering, face red, dripping wet, hair soaked.

Jack took off his cap and gloves. He shook off the loose water and ran a hand through his hair, feeling both water and ice crystals. Shaking inside and out, he kept his coat on, coughed into his fist and took a few breaths.

"Did you find anything?" asked Andrew.

"No."

"You could have easily missed seeing the spot," said Lattimore, standing further down the corridor. "We're through the Welland and out into Lake Ontario. I thought I'd stop by and check in with you. There are some very talented welders out in Duluth." He buttoned the collar of his heavy coat. "I think I'll have a look."

Lattimore walked to the hatch and entered the keycode. On his own, and seemingly without much effort, he worked the hatch open and walked out, closing it behind him.

Beth came over to Jack. "You liked it out there."

"I wouldn't go that far. But yeah, I've always had a thing about freighters. They are huge, impressive machines. But it was damn cold out there. I'm glad to be inside."

"Do you think the captain will find anything?" said Andrew.

"I doubt it." said Jack.

Minutes later, Lattimore came back inside, drenched and shivering. Saying nothing, he walked a few paces down the corridor. He barked a flurry of orders into the intercom there, then returned. "For safety reasons, I've ordered the engines to idle in about ten minutes. We need to stop the ship while they're working."

"While who is working?" said Beth.

"The cutting torch guys."

"You found the hold?"

"Maybe. Well yes, probably. I found fresh paint over new welds. Don't feel bad, sheriff. It's easy to miss. And...I could be wrong. But I don't think so."

"I don't feel bad."

"So, the bombs are out there," said Andrew, a twitch at the corner of his right eye.

Lattimore loosened his coat. "I hope so."

"What's the matter Andrew?" said Beth.

"I was...it's probably nothing..."

Jack gave the professor a long hard look wondering what was going on in that old gray head of his. In fear of a rambling reply, he decided not to ask.

The sound of the engines died to a low hum and minutes later the two-man cutting torch team rounded the corner at the far end of the corridor.

"We meet again," said Tony, eyeing Jack without enthusiasm.

"This way," said Lattimore, pulling his coat closed again. "We've got a maintenance issue at the stern. The engines are idling. I can give you an hour. I'll show you what needs to be done."

Tony and his helper followed the captain outside.

Lattimore shouted back. "The rest of you stay put. If we're lucky, we'll need help getting the...materials inside. Jack, there's a storage closet further down with a cart inside. Bring it around."

Jack found the storage room and found the steel framed cart. He rolled it back to where Beth and Andrew stood. Cold wind poured in through the propped open hatch. He could hear the buzz of the cutting torch.

Jack retreated to where Beth stood. "What's with Andrew?" he said with a glance further down the corridor where Andrew paced back and forth. "He's making me nervous."

"Yeah, me too. Could the bombs be radioactive?"

"Hope not," said Jack, who'd been wondering the same thing.

Twenty minutes later, Jack heard a shout from Lattimore, followed by a loud clank followed by the pop of the cutting torch going out.

Lattimore ushered the men back inside, helping with their equipment. "Thank you, men. That was fine, efficient work," he told them. "Get some rest. Come back down in an hour or so. That plate section you just cut out will need to be welded back in place. Nothing fancy, tack welds will do. We can't have a gaping hole in our stern for all to see, now can we?"

Lattimore waited until they'd turned the corner at the end of the corridor. "All right, let's get them inside."

"You actually found them?" said Jack, not quite believing it.

"Yes, we found them."

Andrew stayed behind while Jack, Beth and Lattimore got to work. Without the pounding of the propeller, the raging water, and the movement of the ship, it was almost pleasant outside on the stern. Jack stared at the charred cavity the men had cut into the hull. Its rough edges were blackened, still smoking. Inside were a stack of three wooden crates. Down on the deck lay the jagged edged panel of inch thick steel that had been cut out.

"The edges of the hole might still be hot," cautioned Lattimore.

"That's the Mayfield logo we saw," said Jack. He pointed to the sideways diamond brand on the crates. "You really did find them."

One end at a time, Beth lifted the empty cart up over the lower lip of the hatch. She wheeled it over as Lattimore and Jack pulled the first crate out.

"Heavy suckers," said Jack, straining. "I can see why those men had trouble that morning getting them across the ice."

With Beth helping, they managed to get the three crates onto the cart.

Once done, Jack spotted three cylindrical metal objects each about the size and shape of a bowling pin that had been wedged behind the crates. With the rocking of the ship, they rolled slowly, side to side clanking into each other within the confines of the narrow space.

"We'll come back for them," said Lattimore, hands on hips, resting. "The cart's heavy as it is. Come on, let's get it inside."

It took all three of them, Beth tugging from the front, to get the cart inside. Lattimore and Jack went back outside for the last three bombs.

"We'll pick them up one at a time. Careful now," said Lattimore.

Jack took a knee. With both hands he reached down to where the bombs lay. Straining, he lifted one out. It was heavy for its size. He guessed it to be about thirty pounds. It had a black metal shell. He got to his feet and, with both hands, carried the bomb inside. He placed it on the lower shelf of the cart.

Once all the bombs were inside and on the cart, Lattimore pulled the hatch closed. He secured it then removed one of his gloves. He bent and reached down to the lower shelf of the cart. He placed his hand on the bare surface of one of the bombs.

"Is it warm," asked Beth.

"Hard to tell. Yes, slightly." Lattimore straightened, turning to Jack and Beth. "Now, both of you, wheel the cart back into the storage closet. You'll find a tarp there. Cover it, engage the wheel brakes, then lock the door."

They did as instructed then walked back.

Lattimore took off his cap. He ran a hand through his hair. "Do not say a word to anyone about any of this. We'll talk later." He walked off, startling Andrew with a pat on the shoulder as he passed.

CHAPTER 33

Lattimore got some food then spent the next two hours alone at the helm. They had found the bombs. Now the problem was, what to do about them. And what to do about Maddie?

He expected Katerina to send him a new picture of her to let him know she was keeping up her end of the bargain. And he would keep up his end by staying on time and on course to make sure Maddie remained unharmed. Yes, she had leverage over him but, now that the bombs had been found, there should be a way for him to gain leverage over her.

He wondered what she would do if he threatened to throw them overboard. Or maybe threaten to turn them over to the Coast Guard. Or maybe turn them over to the Canadian authorities. Could he really risk Maddie's life like that?

No, he could not. It was a fait accompli—no winners, only losers. But they were still a long way from breaking out into the Atlantic. He had time.

It was late that afternoon when he met Jack, Beth and Andrew in a room one deck below the bridge. He led them inside flipped on a light and closed the door. "Grab a chair," he said, pointing to a stack of folding chairs. The room was windowless. There was no table. The setting reminded Lattimore of one of those group therapy sessions where everyone sat and shared their feelings. Well, maybe that's exactly what was needed right now.

With everyone awkwardly quiet, Lattimore began: "Our purpose here is to discuss with Professor Simeon what he knows about the bombs." He turned to the old man, as did Beth, as did Jack.

Andew visibly braced himself. His whiskered face grew rigid and strained. Was it that 'Who me?' look of a guilty man?

Lattimore spoke slowly. "Professor Simeon, what exactly did you work on at the Mayfield Lab?"

Andrew said nothing.

"Those bombs we found, you built them, didn't you Professor Simeon?"

Andrew lifted his eyes to Lattimore, his voice a hoarse whisper. "Yes, that's right. I...we built them. But nobody was interested in them. They wanted big bombs." He shook his head. "Of course, we couldn't admit we'd actually built them. We couldn't admit that we'd stolen the enriched uranium. We had to make them think that our proposal was strictly theoretical." He shook his head. "Henry tried to explain it all to the government scientists but they weren't interested. Firecrackers they called them. They didn't even think they'd work."

"They're giving off heat," said Lattimore.

"Well yes, of course. But very little. The fissionable material degrades ever so slowly over time. It's a natural process. They're atomic bombs. But they're very small ones. Much smaller than...well, that's why no one wanted them. Even the Russians weren't..." Andrew stopped short.

"Did the Russians know about these bombs of yours?"

Andrew took a breath. "They may have. All that selling crap was Henry's job. I worked in the lab. I was a scientist. I thought you knew that."

"Did the Russians know these bombs actually existed—that they weren't just theoretical."

"I don't know. But, because they'd never been tested, I suppose they might have considered them theoretical." Andrew stared at his hands tightly folded in his lap. "We were trying to miniaturize the atomic bomb. I think we succeeded, but with no way to test them none of us knew for sure. Our bombs were to be much less powerful than the bombs dropped on Japan. They were designed to destroy only a few city blocks. Back then everyone wanted bombs that could destroy entire cities."

Lattimore spoke. "So, with your help, Henry Mayfield developed what we now call a tactical nuclear weapon. And not only could he not test them, he couldn't even admit to the government that they even existed since they would have thrown him in jail for stealing the plutonium."

Andrew sighed. "It was enriched U235," he said with emphasis on each syllable. "They are two entirely different elements."

"So, Mayfield ended up hiding these prototype bombs in his basement."

"Yes. I helped bury them."

"Then, after many years, someone, not you...but maybe a colleague of yours, decided to try and sell them. They drugged you to keep you from interfering."

The old professor's eyes widened as if that thought had never occurred to him. "Why, yes. Yes, that must be what happened."

"Do you remember how the bombs worked, professor?"

"Of course. The complicated part was designing and building them. Using them is easy—child's play."

"Are these bombs armed right now, Andrew?" said Jack.

The professor coughed once, then cleared his throat. He began talking as if to himself. "It was a crude device that we used as a trigger mechanism—a stiff metal rod with a weight on the end suspended rigidly inside a split metal ring. Same as they use in a pinball machine to detect when a player cheats by tilting the table.

"But...yes, not as sensitive. It would take an intense mechanical shock in exactly the right direction to arm the bomb. Also, there was a timer. It was really all we could think of. We always planned on coming up with a better way but..." He rubbed his jaw then scratched his head. "No, we never did come up with a better way.

"The idea was that these things would be shot out of a gun of some kind. The sudden mechanical shock of being fired would cause the triggering rod to bend and contact one side of the metal ring. This would start a timer. Then, when time ran out or when the bomb hit something, such as a target..." He put the fingertips of both hands together then sprung them apart. "Boom."

"Just dropping one of them here onto the floor wouldn't set one off?" said Jack.

"No, of course not. You could drop one from a plane and it wouldn't go off. We weren't idiots, sheriff."

"But there was something different about these bombs, wasn't there?" said Lattimore. "Different from the bombs dropped on Hiroshima and Nagasaki."

Andrew stroked his chin. His lips spread forming a grim and at the same time, mischievous smile. "We had a breakthrough. It was something wonderful. Something that in theory, or at least in the context of what we knew at the time, had no business working—yet it did. Or it seemed like it should. Henry himself came up with it."

"Are you still talking about the triggering mechanism?"

Andrew went on as if not having heard Beth's question. "The original atomic bombs of World War II weighed thousands of pounds. Little Boy and Fat Man they called them. Those were the names they gave them. It might have been funny except for all the devastation they caused. But that's what it took to end the war."

"Why were they so big?" Asked Jack.

"Because that's what it took to create a critical mass. You take some U235, maybe fifty kilograms or so of it, fashion it into a sphere, then put a shaped charge of conventional explosives around it then encase the entire thing in lead, then put a metal shell around that. When the shaped charge goes off, the pressure wave causes the sphere of U235 to become smaller, therefore more dense, thus achieving critical mass. That is when the neutron-induced fission process begins and repeats on its own, over and over again each time resulting in a release of energy."

"A chain reaction," said Jack.

"Obviously" said Andrew. As a professor might do with his students, he looked at the faces around him. He waved a hand dismissively. "It's a simple process really. Get a few trillion neutrons percolating in an unstable material like U235 or Plutonium and shield it effectively with lead or Ber…"

Andrew stopped. Everyone waited.

"Or what, Andrew?" said Beth, finally.

"Or Beryllium. Beryllium! Oh, yes. *That* was Mayfield's big idea."

"You used it in place of uranium?" said Jack.

"What?" said the professor, obviously dumbfounded at the question. "No, of course not. We used it in place of lead for its neutron-reflecting properties. Ten times lighter than lead, it allowed us to miniaturize the primary explosion cavity. I believe it's in common use now, but back then it was revolutionary. Ha! We made the mistake of being late with our patent application." Pausing, he took on a wistful look. "Reduction to practice, yes, that was our big problem. We couldn't admit to actually having done it. They would have sent us all to prison. Or killed us like the…"

"Like the Rosenberg's," said Beth, quietly.

"Yes. Like them." Andrew folded his arms. He leaned back in his chair. "We also found a way to minimize the critical mass. The actual amount of enriched U235 in each of these bombs we have aboard this ship is about the size of a ping-pong ball." He rubbed his chin again, then corrected himself. "Well, maybe a golf ball."

Lattimore folded his arms. "But the fissionable material in them originated as part of the Manhattan Project during World War II."

"Yes."

"Do you think the bombs still work?"

Andrew gave a casual shrug. "They should. I don't know why they wouldn't."

CHAPTER 34

Katerina poured herself a cup of coffee, placed the cup in the microwave, and punched in thirty-three seconds. At that moment, her toast popped from the toaster. She buttered it, placed it beside the bowl of milk-soaked Cheerios on her kitchen table as the microwave dinged. She retrieved her coffee, placed it on the side of the bowl opposite the toast, then sat.

She took a spoonful of cereal then a bite of toast, then checked the time. It was exactly 8 A.M. She smiled to herself. All of her time based action indicators pointed to this being a good day. Not that she was superstitious but, as with simple things like breakfast preparations or with complex things like whatever Andrei had up his sleeve, the vagaries of fate always had a part to play.

After the night at the steel mill, she and Ilya had checked out of their comfortable, high-rise room downtown and moved into a suite of equally comfortable, but windowless rooms at the rear of an abandoned airplane hangar at the airstrip called Willow Run. Located a thousand yards north of the main airstrip, the noise of low flying cargo and charter flights sometimes rattled the dishes. Yes, that was bothersome. But the fact that her Lincoln and her private jet were both parked within the hangar more than made up for that minor annoyance. Her housekeeper, her driver, her pilot, and personal security staff all lived in separate quarters adjacent to hers inside the same hangar. Any or all of them could be called upon at a moment's notice should the need arise. And, should the situation warrant it, she could be in the air within minutes. Diplomatic immunity was a wonderful thing when it became necessary to expedite a flight plan.

Her little fortress was practical and it was secure. Still, some windows would have been nice.

She turned on CNN where some politician was being interviewed. Americans never seemed to tire of their chaotic governmental drama. She turned the sound down. She finished her cereal and toast, poured herself another cup of coffee.

Down a narrow hallway that led off the kitchen past her bedroom and past Ilya's bedroom there was a steel door secured by a digital lock. Unlike the others, the room behind this door was built with thick cinderblock walls. Its ceiling was double the height of what might be considered normal and, in each of the its four corners, was mounted a high-res surveillance camera. And her guest inside? Well, Agent Cooper was comfortable enough. She had her own kitchenette, bath, and bed. True enough, it was a confined space but it was as comfy as it could be. A few pastoral paintings on the walls completed its homey look.

Katerina opened her computer and pulled up the closed circuit screen. And there she was. Agent Cooper sat in a tastefully upholstered chair staring in a daze at nothing in particular. She might have looked more at ease were it not for the minor injuries she'd sustained during the process of getting her off the ship. Her lip had been cut in two places. The dark bruise on the side of her head had a particularly nasty look to it, and her nose had taken on the shape of an eagle's beak.

Maybe she would opt for a nose job when all this was over. Then again, she might be dead by that time.

She had put up quite a fight while the men from the mill struggled to get her off the ship, then into the car then into her room. Katerina had no remorse. It was Agent Cooper's own fault. What she did regret was that Ilya had seen her being dragged in. He'd seen her struggle trying to resist and he'd seen her take the punch to her face the result of which was the eagle's beak thing.

Blood had poured from Cooper's nose and, surprisingly, Ilya had opened his mouth as if to scream. He'd taken a step closer. But his scream remained silent and he did not intervene. Katerina vividly remembered the look of horror on his face that he'd turned in her direction as if asking his mother: *How could you let this happen?*

The moment was gone in an instant. Cooper was shoved into her room. The door was locked, Katerina's security men left and Ilya went back to his room albeit with the slamming of the door behind him. She had never seen such emotion from him.

Later that same night, Katerina had looked in on him. He was occupied as he always was, with his video games. Everything back to normal.

And now Katerina stared at Cooper's image on the screen. The agent sat perfectly still. Dried blood spotted her chin. A dish was sitting on the counter so she'd evidently eaten. As her prisoner might soon discover, there were bandages and antiseptics, towels and toiletries in the bathroom so, if she was so inclined, Cooper could take care of herself.

Katerina turned away from her computer, looking past the kitchen counter to the brownish spot where Cooper's blood had soaked the carpet. Her house keeper had tried to get it out. Well, she was just going to have to try harder.

Katerina took care of her dishes then keyed her computer. She checked her messages, then checked the position of *Endeavor*. The ship was halfway through Lake Ontario, almost right on schedule. Apparently, Captain Lattimore was behaving himself. She checked the time, pulled her cell and placed a call on a secure line.

Dmitry answered with a sneeze, a cough, and a blow of his nose. "Hello, my dear," he eventually said in Russian.

"Are you all right?"

"Allergies," he said.

"You should take something."

"I'll be fine," he sneezed again, then sniffed. "Where is the freighter?"

She gave him the coordinates and speed info.

"Any problems?"

"I've taken Lattimore's daughter. I have her here."

He replied with disapproving silence

"She's our insurance that the captain will follow his orders."

"I suppose so. Yes. But if she makes trouble, you know what you..."

"She is locked up. She will not cause trouble. Have you any news?"

"Our ships are on their way to the location as planned."

"Any word from Andrei?"

"Not yet." He stifled another sneeze.

"*Nyquil PM,*" she suggested. "It will help you sleep. American drugs are very good." She ended the call.

It was a few hours later when, after working the keypad on the door, Katerina quietly entered the guestroom. She closed the door behind her. "I brought you a fresh pair of pajamas and fresh towels," she said. "You should clean up that blood on your chin."

Cooper stood behind the counter near the fridge. She had her eyes on Katerina but said nothing.

"You are comfortable I assume? We mean you no harm. That nose of yours will need some attention. There are medical supplies in the bathroom. As you've already discovered, there is food in the fridge. We need you alive and healthy."

"So that my father will do whatever it is you want."

"Yes."

"Who is the boy?"

Katerina sucked in her breath. "He is no one to you. He has nothing to do with any of this."

"I don't think he approves of what you did to get me here."

"That was your own doing. You put up a good fight and my men did what they had to do. Believe me, you are safer here than you were aboard that freighter."

"What are you planning?"

Katerina smiled. "That is a big surprise. And I hate to spoil surprises. I will tell you this though; after it is all over, you might even approve of what we have done. Your own government is standing aside, doing nothing. They are cooperating with us." She smiled at Cooper's reaction. "Surprised? It is true. But maybe you still don't believe me? Well, all will be clear to you soon enough. You will not have long to wait."

CHAPTER 35

Lattimore stared at the latest picture of Maddie. Some of the swelling had gone down. Her face and hair were clean. And her eyes still held that fierce look of determination.

This time a message was sent along with the photograph:

"Except for a minor slowdown two days ago, I see you've been following your orders. Yes, I can see any delay and I will know immediately if your ship changes course unexpectedly. Should either of these things happen again, I promise, your daughter will pay the price. As you see, she is presently being treated well because you are behaving yourself. As long as you continue to do as you're told, I will continue to treat her well and release her to you, unharmed."

Did he believe her? Maybe. But that's not what bothered him most about this latest information.

With Winters at the helm and open water ahead, Lattimore left the bridge. He searched out Jack and Beth finding them in the dayroom playing ping-pong.

"We needed a little diversion," explained Jack. They put down their paddles.

"I've heard from Katerina," said Lattimore.

"Is Maddie...?"

"Yes, she's all right, for the time being. They sent me a picture. And a message." He brought it up on his phone and handed it to Jack as Beth came over. "It's the second picture they sent. I didn't show you the first. She looked...well, she looks better now."

The two were quiet, eyes on the phone.

Jack gave the phone back. "That slowdown was when you shut down the engines to retrieve the bombs."

"Yes, that bothered me too. Her computer must have flagged it."

"Do you really think she'll release her after all this is over?" said Beth.

"I don't know."

Jack pulled three cans of Coke from the fridge, then joined the two of them sitting at a table. "So, we just play along, sail off into the Atlantic, dump the bombs and wait for the CIA to show up and save the day like they should've done in Detroit? Is that how this all ends?"

"Dumping the bombs will be a problem," said Lattimore. "The moment we change course in the Atlantic, heading for deeper waters where we can scuttle the bombs, Katerina will know. We are a slow, commercial vessel. Whoever's waiting for us out there will easily run us down, board us, and take the bombs. And, there is another problem. Salt water is conductive. These bombs do not look water tight. From what the professor has told us about the arming mechanism, just submerging them and allowing them to leak over time could be enough to arm them."

Beth went pale. "We'd be dropping atomic time bombs."

"Yes."

"So, tossing them overboard is not an option," said Jack.

"That's right."

"There's one thing I'm not clear on," said Jack. "How much does the CIA know about what's going on? You expected them to stop this whole thing back in Detroit. What do you think happened?"

"They're playing their usual games. My guess is they want to see what Katerina and her syndicate are up to. They want things to play out a little more before making a move."

Beth shook her head. "They don't mind risking our lives and the life of your daughter."

"There are some cold, calculating people at Langley these days. You're right, they don't care about Maddie or about any of us. They feel it's their job to look at the so called, bigger picture and play for the best possible outcome. It's all a game to them. We can't count on them for help. We've got to look out for ourselves." He paused, letting that sink in before hitting them with an idea that had been percolating in his mind for some time. "We have no guns aboard with which to defend ourselves. But..."

"But we do have twelve tactical nuclear weapons," said Jack as if he'd been thinking the same thing.

"Yes, we do. And neither Katerina or the CIA have any idea that we've found them or that we have Professor Simeon aboard who knows how to use them."

"Use them?" said Beth, alarmed. "As in set them off?"

Lattimore popped the top of his Coke and took a drink. "Just one of them."

"Oh, just one atomic bomb, well that's okay then? There has got to be a better way. My God! This is just what I'd expect from a military hot head. Shit, we're all going to die." Beth turned to Jack. "And here *you* are looking all calm and cool, ready to go along with this suicidal idiot."

"What do *you* think we should do? Surrender and hand them over?"

"Yes. Let the CIA handle it."

Lattimore felt his blood rise. "No. The CIA had their chance back in Detroit to end this. Like it or not, we are on our own now." He leaned closer, lowering his voice. "The way I see it, we've got two problems. First, we have to learn more about how these bombs work. The professor gave us the basics but we need to make sure we know everything about them. In his state of mind, there might be something he's forgotten. One of us needs to go over that journal with him in detail. That will be your job, Beth. You have an aptitude for technical matters and Andrew seems to like you."

"He likes her perfume," said Jack.

"This is madness," said Beth.

"You will work with Andrew," Lattimore continued, eyes remaining on her. "By the end of this, you will know as much about the bombs as he does."

"You said there were two problems," said Jack.

"The delivery system. We can't just fling the bombs off our ship and hope they go far enough *and* in the right direction. We ourselves could be caught up in the explosion or the radiation hazard. Now *that* would be suicidal."

"At least we agree on that point," said Beth, drumming her fingers.

"We need a gun of some kind," said Jack.

"Yes. Specifically, a mortar," said Lattimore.

"And how…?"

"We build one. A mortar is a simple device; a steel tube closed at one end, open at the other. We'll have to improvise as far as the materials but we have a machine shop aboard and we happen to have a capable machinist."

"We'll need gunpowder," said Jack.

"We have flares. We pull them apart. All of them if that's what it takes. We repackage the powder into a fused charge, maybe several of them."

Beth shook her head. "You guys are chomping at the bit to blow something up."

"I don't see that we have a choice," said Lattimore. "If you have a better idea, I'd like to hear it." He was quiet for only a moment. "Get the journal. Find Andrew. We meet back here in twenty minutes."

CHAPTER 36

"This is nuts," said Beth, storming out of the dayroom.

"So, what *should* we do?" said Jack, keeping up. "If you had a better idea, you sure didn't make a strong case for it."

"What we should've done is never gotten aboard this freighter in the first place. *That's* what I think. *That* was my better idea. I'm a pharmacist, not a physicist, not a shrink, I'm a pharmacist. And you, no offense, are a smalltown sheriff. What the hell are we doing in the middle of all of this?"

"I asked what you thought we should do *now*. I didn't think I needed to clarify that."

"I'm working on it. Okay?"

"Sure, take your time. We've got three days, four tops." Once at their cabin, Jack pulled Andrew's journal out from behind a bookcase where they'd hidden it. "We should have shown this to Andrew sooner."

"We did show it to him back at the Waffle House, at the cottage too. Don't you remember? He didn't even recognize it. He thought someone else had written it."

"He wasn't himself back then. He's remembering things now. He remembered Henry Mayfield and how he got the enriched uranium. He remembered that thing about the beryllium. He'll remember the journal now."

"And we're hoping he remembers so we can try to explode one of his seventy-five-year-old bombs. Don't those things have an expiration date?" Beth paused. She shook her head. "I'm sorry, Jack. I admit, we don't have a lot of choices. And I don't want to get Maddie hurt...or killed." She sat down on the edge of the cot. "Andrew might have been a genius once but some of those drugs he was on could have permanent effects. And what if he was never anything more than a glorified lab assistant at Mayfield?"

Jack sat beside her. "Someone went to a lot of trouble and expense to keep him drugged and put up at that *Autumn Leaves* place. Andrew knows things—important things."

"Lattimore thinks Katerina doesn't know about Andrew. How could she *not* know?"

"Yeah, I've wondered that too. There could be two organizations we're dealing with. You have the Mayfield people who created these bombs decades ago. Then you have Katerina and her crowd who probably paid a lot of money for them. The Mayfield people didn't tell Katerina about Andrew because, even in his drugged condition, he represented a loose end. The Mayfield people were protecting Andrew. They didn't mind abusing Andrew with drugs but they didn't want him murdered."

"So, even if Katerina thought we'd find the bombs she wouldn't expect us to guess they might be atomic bombs."

"And they also won't be expecting us to use them to defend ourselves."

"Do you trust Lattimore?"

"He's a father who'll do just about anything to save his daughter. Yes, I trust him but it's up to us to look out for ourselves." He reached over, gently taking her hand. "We're going to get through this. We're going to be okay."

"You keep telling me that. It's not like I continually need reassurance. Well, maybe I do. But do you really believe it? Be honest."

"We're okay as long as we're together. That's what I believe." he kissed her hand. "We'd better get going. We need to find Andrew."

They found him in the galley with three members of the crew, a half-finished plate of scrambled eggs in front of him. "We need you in the dayroom, Andrew," said Jack as he and Beth walked in.

"Oh yes, of course. Give me a moment." Using his fork, he pointed out each of his table mates. "Do you know Ben? And that's Sam, and there's Becky down at the end."

"Beck," said the woman with a nod of familiarity not friendliness.

"Oh yes, sorry. We were discussing...now what was it?"

"Time to go," interrupted Jack, helping Andrew up with a hand at his elbow.

Andrew shook him off. "Let go of me, Jack. I am fully capable of getting up and walking to the...where are we going?"

"We'll have to talk later, Andrew," said Ben.

"Yes, yes. I would very much enjoy that, young man."

The three of them sat in the otherwise empty dayroom. Jack pulled the journal from under his jacket. "Do you remember this, Andrew?" He placed it on the table and slid it in front of the professor.

Wide eyed, Andrew leaned back in his chair, staring at the notebook as if it were a live snake. "It's...my book. You have my book." He reached out, gingerly gliding his fingertips over it. He pulled his chair closer. Almost lovingly, he rested the palms of both hands on it. "I hid it from them. I was hoping that...it's my life's work here, between these covers." With reverence, he opened it. He scanned the first page, then the next and the next. Line by line he ran a finger down each page, lost in the words, diagrams and numbers.

Beth gave Jack a glance, a silencing finger over her mouth. From the fridge, she brought Andrew a bottle of water.

The professor hardly looked up. "You don't happen to have something stronger, do you? Gin would be nice. Oh, and I could use some paper...and a pen."

At that moment, Lattimore walked in. Visibly straining, and using both hands, he carried one of the bombs. It was wrapped in a towel and a few work rags. Jack shared a startled glance with Beth.

Lattimore placed it on the table that tilted with its weight. He then introduced the slim African American woman who'd been trailing behind him and who, on entering the dayroom, had turned and locked the door. "This is crewman Meg Howard who, among many other things, happens to be a topnotch machinist."

"We've met," said Meg with a glance at Beth then Jack. Her business-like nod caused her hair bun to bounce a little.

The professor caught her attention as she and Lattimore both sat. "Hello, young lady. I am Andrew."

"Yes, I've seen you aboard ship. Pleased to meet you, sir."

Like the others, Jack stared at the object sitting innocently in the center of the table. The towel had dropped back exposing its dull black surface. Maybe three inches in diameter and fifteen inches long, one end was aerodynamically rounded, the other double finned. At the thought that something so small could be so powerful, Jack's mouth went dry. That thing, that bomb, was the reason he was shot that morning at the Point. Ironic that the safety of this ship and everyone aboard might now depend on it.

Jack extended his hand. With his fingertip, he touched it. He felt its roughness. And he felt the worrying warmth that betrayed its power.

"Well now, this *is* exciting," said Andrew, breaking the silence. He rubbed his hands together. "Remember, this is a prototype. We put them together rather hastily. There was no time to buff it up and give it a good coat of paint.

Lattimore spoke quietly. "I've opened one of the other crates to confirm that there are three in each. So, we do indeed have twelve of them aboard." He turned to Andrew. "Tell us about these bombs, professor."

"First of all, don't worry, sitting here like this, it can't go off."

"How do you know that?" asked Lattimore.

"These bombs have a triggering mechanism. It was my idea. I think I told you about it. We designed them to be used in a gun of some kind. The firing of the gun causes a burst of acceleration in one direction. Yes?" He went on to repeat his earlier explanation of the split ring triggering mechanism. He then took in the faces around him to be sure everyone was following along.

"All right then. Within a certain small amount of time, such as the flight time to a target, the bomb must experience an intense deceleration such as on hitting its target. This causes the rod to bend in the opposite direction and contact the opposite side of the split ring. So, it takes both the acceleration *and* the deceleration separated by a certain window of time, to trigger the bomb." He smiled and pulled back his hand. "Simple but brilliant, yes?"

"I thought you said the initial acceleration started a timer which initiated the explosion," said Lattimore.

Andrew stopped, hand on his chin. "Oh yes, that might be...We made a number of different versions. But don't worry, it's all documented in here." He gave his journal a pat.

"Is there a way to override that double shock triggering system," asked Lattimore.

"Yes," said Andrew slowly. "Oh yes, I remember now. There are two activation modes. So, after the initial burst of acceleration, an actual explosion can be triggered either by a burst of acceleration in the opposite direction or by a timer."

Lattimore persisted. "And do you remember how to switch from one activation mode to the other?"

"All the information is here in my journal." He scanned the somber faces around him. "Is someone after these bombs?"

"Yes," said Jack. "The people who were keeping you drugged and in bed all that time, sold them to some bad people."

"And what are those people planning to do with them? Well...destroy things, I suppose. That's pretty obvious. And who are these bad people again?"

"We don't know who they are," said Beth, "but they need to be stopped. They have Agent Cooper."

Andrew shook his head, confused.

Lattimore sighed. "Her name is Maddie. She is my daughter."

"Oh yes, I remember her." Andrew frowned. "And you're worried about her."

"Professor, we may need to use one of these bombs to defend ourselves," said Lattimore.

"And to save Agent Cooper," said Andrew.

"Yes. We need to know everything about these bombs. We need you to work with Beth to go through your journal. Can you do that?"

Andrew turned to her. "With you? Well yes, of course I can do that. I'll be needing a pen and paper. Didn't I already ask you for those?"

"Yes, you did, Andrew," said Beth. "You also asked for a glass of gin."

"That is not a good idea," said Jack.

"Yes, it is," growled Andrew. "You're worried about me going off the rails again. Well, I assure you, sheriff, I am back in the land of the living. And, right now, I could use a drink—maybe several."

"I'm with Andrew on this." said Meg, standing, looking for and getting a nod of approval from Lattimore. She left then came back with all the required items plus a stack of five shot glasses. She started pouring.

"Full up now. Don't spill a drop," advised the captain.

She followed orders. Each of them took a glass, Andrew hazarding a premature sip.

Lattimore held his glass. "If you're all expecting me to make a speech of some kind, you can forget it."

Beth leaned in, eyes first on Lattimore then on each face around the table. "To Maddie," she said, "and to all aboard this good ship *Endeavor*."

With the welcome warmth of the liquor, Jack knew a pact had been made. There'd be no turning back now. He placed a hand on Beth's then noticed that she'd discretely slid her still-full shot glass toward Andrew. He caught her eye as the professor quickly downed it. Could she be...?

Lattimore stood. "Well said, Beth. As I am able, I will work out the ballistics and trajectory calculations. Professor, you and Beth will go over every word of your journal. We need to get that triggering mechanism straight. When done, you will brief me. The two of you will then put together the fused charges according to the design I'll have worked out by that time.

"Crewman Howard...Meg, you will secure the rest of this gin then get down to your machine shop. Jack, you will take this bomb and go with her. Together the two of you will build us a functional, aimable mortar. She and I have already roughed out the design. I will check in on you as I am able. If any of you run into problems, you will let me know immediately. We've got three days to get this done. Let's get to it. I'll be up on the bridge."

Lattimore left.

Jack leaned closer to Beth. He whispered: "Are you...do you think?"

Beth smiled then whispered back. "I'm just being careful. Besides, I don't have a test kit."

"But you shouldn't be here. You should be resting. You should..."

"Jack, I am here now. I'm with you. And, just like you, I will do what I have to do. That's all." She kissed his cheek then moved her chair beside Andrew and opened the journal to page one.

With an effort, and with suddenly more on his mind, Jack picked up the bomb and followed Meg.

A row of bright florescent lights lit the long, narrow room that served as a machine shop. It smelled of wood, steel, and cutting fluid. Against one wall sat a lathe, a Bridgeport mill, a bending brake, a metal toolchest, and a workbench with a large vise bolted to it. Opposite these were shelves of metal stock and a drafting table at which Meg pulled up a stool and sat.

Jack placed the bomb on the workbench.

"Grab a couple of V-blocks to keep it from rolling off," said Meg pointing to a shelf where they were kept. "First thing to do is to clean it. Rags there, cleaning solvent there. Do not flood the thing with solvent. I looked over the welds. They're good but we can't have any solvent leaking into whatever's inside this thing."

As Jack got to work, Meg put on a baseball cap, carefully threading her hair bun through the opening in the back of it. She tugged it straight, sat, and started a sketch.

"Not much to a mortar," she said. "You've seen them in the movies. Long barrel, three feet long, two legs for positioning. The barrel itself will be our third leg. We'll need two adjustment screws for aiming. The main thing is not to have the thing to blow up in our faces. It would be nice if we had some tube stock just the right size but we don't. The inner diameter of the barrel will be critical. We absolutely must get that right. That means our measurements of the bomb itself must be dead-on. The professor said these bombs are rough prototypes so they're not going to be perfectly round. And, with twelve bombs in all, they're not going to be uniform in weight or anything else."

"We only need to fire one," said Jack.

"Yeah, hope he's right about that."

"This one's got some rust on it."

"I'll bet the others do too, being buried in a basement all those years. The captain filled me in on how you found them. They should have been packed in grease. We should check them all and use the one that looks best. I'll get with the captain on that. Anyway, once you get this one clean, you'll need to wire brush those weld seams and clean it again. Then we'll take some measurements."

As Jack worked, Meg finished her sketch with dimensions and tolerances to be added later. She then busied herself at the steel rack in the back corner of the shop. "Not much to work with," she mumbled to herself more than once before pulling out a sheet of stainless steel. She leaned it against the rack.

Jack finished his cleaning then the two of them handled the measurements of the bomb using a surface block and a dial indicator.

Meg shook her head. "It's nearly twenty-thousandths out of round. We'll have to identify the high spots and sand them down."

"How close do we need to be?"

"Rounder is better. That's all I know. I suppose we could put the thing on the lathe and turn it true but, even at slow speed we might somehow trigger the thing. We don't want to do that."

"And we're using that for the barrel of the mortar?" said Jack eying the sheet of stainless steel she'd set aside.

She gave a shrug. "We'll start with some rough iron piping that's close to the right inside diameter. We'll true it up. We'll bore and ream the inside diameter then press multiple tubes of progressively larger diameters around it, each made out of that sheet stock. I've got a few sheets of it. They will be what keeps the thing from blowing up in our faces."

Jack nodded. Sounded like Meg knew her stuff. "How many tubes do you think?"

"Three, maybe five." She tapped a finger to her chin, oblivious to the black char it left there. "Even with inch thick walls our three-foot long mortar tube will be crazy heavy. Zero point three pounds per cubic inch, you do the math. Once we get going on this, we'll get with the captain and see what pressures we'll be generating with the explosive charge he's designing."

"You ever build anything like this before?"

Meg flashed a smile. "Built a go-cart once."

CHAPTER 37

Québec City, Canada

Katerina hadn't wanted to leave Ilya and she hadn't wanted to leave Willow Run. But the call had come from Dmitry. Andrei needed her closer to *Endeavor* in case of problems.

"Problems like what?" Katerina had countered.

"He didn't say. Maybe he doesn't trust the captain. Maybe he doesn't trust his colleagues in the military to do their part."

"And I am supposed to somehow insure they follow his orders?"

"Arrangements have already been made," Dmitry had said, ending the call.

Clearly, Andrei was worried about something.

So, without much choice, Katerina had been flown from Willow Run to Québec city and put up here in a hotel overlooking the St. Lawrence River.

She knew it was best that Ilya stay behind. He was in good hands with her housekeeper and with the guards back in the hangar at Willow Run. She trusted them to safeguard her son.

But what of Cooper?

Ilya seemed strangely taken by her. Not only had he reacted almost violently to the rough way her men had handled her when she'd first arrived but later Katerina had found him staring at her through the hall window. She'd also caught him watching the woman on one of the monitoring screens. "She is a bad woman," Katerina had told him. But still, he stared.

And Cooper had seen him staring. She'd even raised a hand in a feeble hello through the window. Ilya hadn't waved back but in his face Katerina had seen a subtle reaction. Probably curiosity, she told herself, the same curiosity as he might show on being handed a new video game.

On leaving, Katerina had told her son: "I have to go away for a while. I have to take care of some important things. But I will be back as soon as I can."

Ilya had tensed.

"Are you worried about the woman?" she'd asked, referring to Cooper. With her hands on his shoulders, she'd held his eyes with hers. "I told you. She is a bad woman. But she is important to us. Do you understand?"

He'd lowered his head, staring at the floor as he always did.

As if giving her son a blessing, she'd placed a hand on the top of his head, leaned closer and kissed him on both cheeks. "Good bye my love."

Tired of musing about the past, Katerina walked barefoot across the plush carpet of her room to the window that overlooked the front of the hotel. It was ten at night. She expected no problems but, still, she had to be careful. She had to anticipate that, even at this late stage in the game, something could go wrong. She parted the curtains. Her view of the hotel entrance looking down from the eighth floor was blocked by an overhanging roof. A problem? Probably not.

Her gaze shifted beyond the busy street fronting the hotel, beyond the snow-covered park where the icy water seemed to shiver under the long row of ornate lamps. The dock was empty. Most of the pleasure boats had sailed south and those that remained had been raised, winterized, and stored for the winter in the large yellow sided buildings that lined the street further down.

There was no one in sight. Romantic though the scene was, it was too cold and too windy for a walk along the shore.

Katerina closed the curtains and pulled the drapes then decided that a hit of vodka sounded very good right now. She poured, took a sip, then sat. She opened her computer to her secure satellite feed showing a tiny red dot in the middle of Lake

Ontario only a little farther east than the last time she looked. Freighters! Ideal for smuggling cargo but so slow. The tiny transponder one of her men had affixed to her hull while refueling seemed to be working well. Its batteries wouldn't have to last much longer.

Lattimore was on schedule. On reaching Québec City there would be another refueling. After that things could get interesting in a good or a bad way. Would the captain follow the orders he'd been given? She and Andrei had placed a large bet that he would.

She wished she knew what Andrei was up to. Had she known, had he trusted her enough to tell her what she was smuggling out of the U.S. and why, she might have felt better. So, maybe the question she should be asking herself right now was: Did she trust Andrei? And what was he up to?

With her eyes on the computer screen, she enlarged then shifted the view to encompass the three white blips holding station a thousand kilometers out in the North Atlantic. She knew these were the old military ships Andrei had secretly procured from the Chinese. Refurbished, still fast and, if Andrei was to be believed, still lethal. They awaited the arrival of *Endeavor*. Once the cargo had been transferred, her part in this project would end and a seven-figure deposit would be made to her personal bank account. So, why did it matter to her what Andrei was up to? Yes, maybe it was better not to know.

As for Lattimore, she almost felt sorry for the old fool. Did he really expect to sail off into the sunset? He'd been surprised and so disappointed when the fools from the CIA had failed to show up. And did he really expect to get his daughter back? Too bad for them both, she thought with an almost sexual pleasure. She smiled wondering, if there was a God, how could He have given her such a passion for evil? And for what purpose?

Well, there was no point in getting philosophical or even theological at this point. She would play the hand she was dealt while bending the rules now and again. Andrei and Lattimore, and who knows, maybe even Agent Cooper would do the same.

And Fate would play its hand as well.

Two nights later Katerina aimed her binoculars through the hotel window, peering to the southwest. There she spotted a freighter approaching the refueling dock. She checked her computer. Yes, it was *Endeavor*.

She breathed a sigh of relief. The freighter would refuel then head out into the Atlantic. Soon all of this would be over. She would fly back to Willow Run the she and Ilya would fly back to Mother Russia for a long, and maybe permanent stay.

But what to do about Agent Cooper? Katerina herself was protected by diplomatic immunity so maybe she would be merciful.

Or maybe she would not.

On her last morning at the Québec hotel Katerina woke early. Her bag had been packed. She showered hurriedly giving her time to savor a gourmet breakfast downstairs. Then she boarded the pre-arranged embassy limo.

On the way out of town, she dozed, the stress of the past month draining away. It was only as the car pulled onto the grounds of the secure and private airstrip that she opened her eyes, staring out the window with concern. There on the tarmac sat, not her comfortable private jet, but a dark brown military helicopter.

She knew what that meant but sill, the sight of it came as a shock.

CHAPTER 38

It was night. Lattimore handled the controls gingerly as he guided *Endeavor* past the lights of Québec City. Through no fault of his, there had been a technical delay at the fueling dock which was not all that unusual and which Katerina would just have to put up with. He hadn't heard from her in a while and wondered if he should be more worried than he already was. He should have received another photo of Maddie, but hadn't. All he could do is hold course and speed as work on the crude gun continued.

In one day they'd be leaving the Canadian coast. It was no place for a shallow draft laker but he hoped their full load of taconite would provide enough ballast to take on the Atlantic. And if a storm should erupt? Well, he did not want to think about that.

After the open waters of Lake Ontario, the narrow confines of the St. Lawrence River had proved stressful but Lattimore had managed it so far without the normally required local pilot. In her course plan, obviously worked out by a knowledgeable underling, Katerina had somehow managed to get around that requirement as well as several others along the way.

Winters relieved him at the helm and Lattimore headed off the bridge for the machine shop. In his last conversation with Beth and Andrew, they'd gone over details about the bombs: How much acceleration at launch would be needed to arm the bomb? How great an impact would be needed to trigger an explosion? What was the expected power of the bomb? What was the expected blast radius? What was the expected radius of radioactive lethality. On all these points and more the professor had given him his best guesses.

"As you know," the old man constantly reminded him, "this is all guesswork. We took great pains to form and shape the small ball of U235 to a specific size and weight in each bomb. The uncertainty lies in the effectiveness of the conventional explosive charge surrounding the ball which, when detonated, squeezes the ball into a critical mass. I'm sure they have ways of predicting such things now. Back then, we did not."

Lattimore had put up with the bothersome habit of the man to ramble off topic. If there'd been more useful information in that old and rudely abused head of his, there was little time left to tease it out. The journal filled in some but not all of the blanks. Beth had been able to provide more clarity but there was no getting around it: guesswork and pure luck would play a large part in the success or failure of their plan.

His mind circled back to the many other considerations about the bomb itself: its specific dimensions, its weight, its expected aerodynamic resistance. Then there was windage, the roll of the ship, and more, all of which factored into the range and trajectory calculations. He'd reduced all of these to a range of numbers which he then plugged into a formula he'd found in one of his old military manuals. This gave him the maximum and minimum number of grams of gunpowder that would be needed.

To be sure, he went with the max plus ten percent. He then put Beth in charge of tearing into the dozens of flares they had aboard, collecting the gunpowder. He liked the woman and remembered fondly what she'd said when they'd all drank to the success of this risky venture. Beth now seemed glad to be doing something productive in place of the mother-henning she'd been doing with the professor.

Lattimore arrived at the door to the machine shop from which he could hear a low rumbling sound. He was almost afraid to see how little progress they might have made since he'd last been there. Their plan seemed adequate, but building a real, functioning weapon given the limited time and the tools and materials at hand, was a challenge.

He walked in.

The sheriff and Meg, both with full-face safety shields, were bent over the lathe. On it an out of shape, off centered, stainless-steel tube wobbled noisily as it turned. The two took no notice of him.

The workbench shook. With a squirt can Jack stepped closer, drenching the work piece in cutting fluid. Meg moved the cutter carriage closer. On contact, the tube let out a piecing scream that repeated with every revolution. Metal chips sprayed and, as the work progressed, the screaming and the shaking lessened and the metal of the tube began to take on a steely gleam. Meg stopped the lathe to inspect her progress only then noticing Lattimore.

"Hey, cap," she said sheepishly. "We're still working on the barrel here." She flipped up her safety shield and gave him a shaky smile, obviously exhausted. Her face was blackened and sweat drenched. Jack's the same.

Lattimore eyed the tube. "It doesn't have to look pretty. It just has to contain an explosion for 4.8 milliseconds."

"Yeah, copy that. We're trueing it up so it won't wobble too much when we tackle the inside of the tube. That'll be the real challenge: getting a smooth close fit for the bomb but not so close a fit that the bomb'll get jammed inside. I'll need to make a long boring bar for that. I don't know what I'll do for a ream but I'll think of something."

"Any chance you can cut rifling grooves inside the barrel?"

She cleared a curl of congealed hair from her forehead. "I don't know, cap. I'm not sure we can pull that off."

"The bomb will go much farther with a nice tight spiral."

"We could modify the fins on the bomb to give it a spin," said Jack.

Lattimore scratched his chin. "Maybe. But I hate doing anything with those bombs. Any way you look at it, this is going to be a Hail Mary pass. We've got to make it a good one—five hundred yards at least." He backed a step away from the lathe. "What about the support legs and aiming mechanism?"

Jack held up a piece of angle iron. "We'll have legs angling down from the firing tube to give us a fixed elevation of seventy degrees like you suggested. The whole thing will be mounted to a thick baseplate."

"That'll be a circular plate mounted to the deck at midship. The plate will swivel like a Lazy-Susan. The gun will mount to the plate. Once the target is in sight, the gun'll be turned, adjusted and locked in place."

"What's this?" said Lattimore, his hand on a u-shaped bracket welded to the baseplate.

"That'll hold the bomb while we prep the gun. Can't have the thing rolling around on the deck."

Lattimore nodded. He folded his arms, staring again at the barrel.

"It'll be heavy," said Jack as if reading his thoughts. Over two hundred pounds, give or take."

Lattimore extended a hand, giving the crude tube a light pat that coated his palm in hot, gritty and greasy cutting fluid. "Good work, so far. In two days we need to be ready to fire the damn thing."

"We'll have her done. Not sure about the rifling grooves though," said Meg.

The captain headed up to his cabin where he stretched out on his bed and closed his eyes. Trying for the sleep he desperately needed, all he could think about was Maddie.

CHAPTER 39

The two days passed quickly. The finished mortar sat heavy atop the wheeled cart that Jack pushed into the freight elevator. Meg followed him inside. Grime and soot caked her face, hands and arms, all of it covered with a sheen of sweat. Her baseball cap was ringed with it. Her stained and wrinkled work shirt with rolled up sleeves was torn. They must both look like coalminers up from the mines. Jack's watch told him it was morning, but it felt like the middle of the night.

The elevator rose with a jerk. He steadied the cart that held their two hundred fifty-pound creation. It was tall and ugly, a three-legged beast, blackened in spots, shiny in others. It was the gun that would either save them all or kill them all. Or it might do nothing at all.

At this hour he would normally be at the station in Gull Harbor going over yesterday's traffic citations. And what about Beth? She would be up, getting ready to open the store. Somewhere, life was normal, but not here aboard *Endeavor*. Instead, here he was with Meg shlepping this crude gun up to Beth where she waited with her gunpowder and detonators. How had all this happened?

Oh yeah, the phone call, followed by his stupidity, followed by his getting shot followed by...

"You still awake, Jack?"

His eyes snapped open. "Yeah, doing fine. You?"

"You looked like you were about to keel over," said Meg. "I don't know about you but I could use some coffee."

The elevator doors opened. They wheeled the cart down a corridor then turned left down another where Lattimore,

Andrew, and Beth stood beside a hatch. Beth's face was a pasty white. Her tired eyes met his. They hadn't seen each other for a day and a half. He attempted a smile, and put an arm around her. "Mmm, you smell like gunpowder. I love the smell of gunpowder in the morning."

No one laughed.

The three of them stared at the gun.

"That's it, huh?" said Beth, her face and her tone telling Jack: *There is no way in hell this thing's gonna work.*

"Should do the job," said Lattimore quickly heading off alternative opinions. If his optimism was a put on, he was doing a good job of it. He inspected the inside of the barrel.

"We put in your rifling grooves, cap," said Meg. "Oversized the bore and pressed in a two-part stainless sleeve to give us a spiral groove."

"How's the fit?"

"Twenty-thousandths all around. It'll need a little gun oil but…"

"Good work," said Lattimore. "I've got the explosive charge here." He held up what looked like an oversized, foil-wrapped hockey puck, with a coiled-up cord trailing out of it.

"How many of those you got," asked Jack.

"Just this one charge right now," said Lattimore. "The fuse is longer than necessary; we'll trim it back to time the shot. We considered an electronic detonator but, considering what we had to work with, a simple fuse was our best option."

"It's a wound cotton cord dipped in a thin mix of wax and gunpowder," Andrew explained with a degree of pride. "We refined it to burn at a consistent rate of one inch per second regardless of the ambient conditions. And it works…well, more or less."

"That's important since the roll and the pitch of the ship will affect our aim," said Lattimore. "If the bomb is launched at the wrong moment, it could end up going straight up then come back down on top of us."

"Hell of a way to commit suicide."

"Stop it, Jack," said Beth. "You are not funny."

"Is he like this all the time?" said Meg.

Lattimore intervened. "You've got four hours to rest. I can't give you any more time than that. We've prepped the mount for the gun out on deck. Right now, we're leaving the St. Lawrence and entering the Atlantic. We'll follow our charted course for another six hours then, if conditions are right, instead of turning south as our orders call for, we'll continue our heading straight out into the Atlantic."

"You're taking a chance they won't hurt Maddie," said Jack.

"It's the only way we get to choose the time and place of this meet-up," said Lattimore. "And at that point we'll be so close to the rendezvous coordinates it may not matter much to them. If there's a ship out there waiting for us, I'd expect it to turn into the wind and come at us from the south."

"That's when we fire the gun," said Andrew.

"Yes. The wind will favor the trajectory of the bomb. And it will minimize radioactive blowback."

Jack swallowed hard. The frightening thought of radioactivity shook him. By this time tomorrow, they could all be dead or dying.

"You've given up on the idea of dumping the bombs overboard," said Beth.

"Yes. We've gone over the reasons. From up on the bridge, I should have radar contact with any approaching ship and can give us anywhere from ten minutes to as much as an hour notice before visual contact. We could be facing a military vessel with some stealth capability. So, once I see trouble, we might not have much time to get a shot off. We have to be ready."

"What happens after that," asked Meg.

"Ideally, we turn around and go home and I find a way to get my daughter back."

Jack wondered if Lattimore knew how unlikely that scenario sounded.

The captain went on. "I have men working on a second package of explosives in case we have problems with the first. Now, are there any questions?" Lattimore looked from face to face. There were none. "Okay then, it's important we get some rest and some food. We meet back here at fifteen hundred to mount the gun to the deck and to go over the aiming and firing procedure. Bring your cold weather gear."

Jack showered as did Beth. They rested, too exhausted for anything else. Her easy breathing told him she'd fallen asleep quickly. But he could not. He couldn't escape the feeling that all these things were happening, not to him but to someone else. Or maybe they really were happening to him but in some alternate plane of existence. Yeah, real sci-fi stuff. What if he'd really died when he was run off the road, plummeting down into the lake? Or maybe he'd died out on the shore that morning. What if all of what seemed to be happening now was all in his head?

Then he wondered about Beth. She'd told him she didn't feel pregnant and that, with the gin thing, she was just being careful. He wondered if Lattimore had a pregnancy test kit aboard the ship. And he wondered if Beth should be going through all this stress right now. Well, there wasn't much he could do about any of that.

It was nearing fifteen hundred, otherwise known as 3 P.M. He sat up on the edge of the bed. The roll of the ship was more pronounced here in the Atlantic. He abandoned all thoughts of an alternate reality and became convinced that, for better or worse, he was alive and all of this was really happening. He stroked Beth's arm then shook her awake.

They met the others at the hatch all in bright orange thermal jump suits, gloves and heavy parkas. They raised then tightened their hoods. Lattimore gave them each a glance then opened the hatch and stepped out. The wind rippled his coat in the shifting gusts. He held the hatch open for the others. Jack gripped one side of the gun tightly, Meg the other, Beth helping from the rear. Together they lifted the thing off the cart, out through the hatch, then onto a forklift parked on deck.

With Beth and Andrew staying back, Jack climbed up, arm crooked around the rollbar. Meg did the same on the other side. Lattimore started the motor.

"Pretty calm right now," shouted Lattimore, as they pulled out with a jerk.

Off the starboard rail and as far as Jack could see, the ocean churned deep blues and brilliant whites under the sun. The wind knifed into his skin.

It wasn't until Lattimore turned then stopped the forklift at midship that Jack saw the mounting spot. They jumped down onto the deck.

Three threaded studs had been welded onto the metal plating of the deck. Their arrangement matched the hole pattern in the mounting plate of the gun. It was clear what needed to be done.

The three of them lifted the gun, positioned it over the studs then lowered it slowly. A slight mismatch in alignment caused the mounting plate to jam momentarily but a little manhandling to one side seated the gun properly. Lattimore dug into his pocket and produced three heavy hex nuts. With a wrench, they secured the gun to the deck.

On his knees, Lattimore tested the Lazy Susan swiveling plate, its locking mechanism, and the elevation adjustment screw. He stood, looked aft, then up toward the bridge. He pulled Jack and Meg close so they could hear him. "Once I get a radar fix on a target, I'll radio the direction and distance readings. You will load the explosive charge. You'll route the fuse, then gently lower the bomb into the barrel using the string harness we made. Once the gun is armed and loaded, you will wait until the target is in sight and clear of the horizon. If the target is closer, the fuse may need to be trimmed. Jack, you will have a knife. You will handle that. You will also judge the timing of the waves. Meg, you remember the..."

"Yep, got it. According to the timing of the roll."

"Yes, good. At that point sheriff, you cut the fuse and prepare to light it. I will signal you with the radio when they're at two thousand yards."

"Then we light the fuse and run," said Jack.

"Yes." Red faced from the cold, Lattimore surveyed the area as if worried there might be something important that he hadn't considered. He took a breath, then went back to the forklift and pulled off a tarp. The three of them draped it over the gun and tied it tightly in place.

Using the forklift, they motored back to the hatch.

That night Jack lay with Beth in the dark of their cabin. He stared at the ceiling he couldn't see. He listened to her uneven breathing. She turned toward him and move closer. He found her hand and held it, her fingers soft, compliant. "How are you feeling?" he said.

"I don't feel pregnant, if that's what you mean."

"You shouldn't be going through all this stress."

"Neither should you, Jack. None of this should be happening. But it is, and we'll get through it." She placed her hand on his cheek. "You're the one who's supposed to be upbeat and confident. Just say, things'll work out. Even if you don't think they will, say it anyway." She waited. "I mean it Jack, say it."

Jack forced a smile. "Of course, things will work out. They always do."

She kissed him lightly. "That's better," she whispered.

CHAPTER 40

Lattimore squinted into the sun as it rose a few degrees off the bow. The weather looked good. There were no ships in sight. He stood alone at the helm, his hand resting lightly on the controls. Down on deck at midship the sand-colored tarp that covered the gun shifted in the wind not as a fabric but as a rigid thing, frozen by the cold. He wondered if what he was now calling the gun crew, would have a difficult time removing it. Would they have trouble lighting the fuse? Maybe they should have gone with an electric detonator. He worried about these things and the dozen others that might go wrong.

It had been five hours since he'd gone off the prescribed course, sailing now with the wind.

The radar was set at max range with an alarm that would sound off on spotting anything larger than a dinghy. Like the ticking of an old alarm clock, its steady beep kept his tension up like an overwound mainspring.

He checked the wind speed and direction, made a minor course adjustment, then switched on the autopilot.

He took a long breath and backed away from the controls. The radar alarm went off.

Lattimore checked the screen. It showed a blip to the northeast, at a range of seven thousand yards. It was coming on fast—too fast for a commercial vessel. He hit the ship-wide intercom. "Lone threat advancing fifteen degrees off port," he shouted. "Repeat, fifteen degrees off port, range, seven thousand yards, coming on fast. Everyone to their stations. Now!"

He picked up his binoculars and scanned the horizon. He saw nothing. He jumped at a second radar alarm. Three blips now, in a cluster. They were coming in force and as he knew would be the case, there was no way *Endeavor* was going to outrun them. He switched off the autopilot. He adjusted, then set the course putting the wind directly astern. They were committed now. He signaled all ahead full. "Bring it on you bitch," he said under his breath.

He checked the horizon again—still nothing.

Heart pounding, he opened the hatch and hurried out to the rail. He was relieved to see the gun crew already out on deck. By their gait Meg was first then Beth. Slowed by the bomb he carried, Jack was last. They headed for the gun, coats flying. "Faster, damn-it," shouted Lattimore though he knew he couldn't be heard.

Jack put the bomb down on the baseplate bracket.

They untied the tarp. One of them pulled hard falling back onto the deck just as the tarp caught the wind and flew off unveiling their weapon.

From this distance the gun looked fragile and harmless.

Jack looked up at him, holding his radio.

Lattimore keyed his radio and shouted, "Three ships dead ahead now. Coming fast. Figure five thousand yards now. We should see them anytime now."

Jack acknowledged. The three bent into their work. Heart drumming, Lattimore watched the fuse being threaded down into the barrel then run out the base of the gun. The explosive charge was placed into the barrel and the fuse strung out. Jack lowered the bomb into the barrel.

"Lube the barrel," Lattimore shouted into the radio. "Lube the damn barrel!"

Down on deck Jack stood, the wind ripping his coat.

"Fuck it. I forgot to lube it," shouted Meg, pulling the squeeze bottle out of her jacket.

"Do it now," shouted Jack.

Meg squeezed the liquid out into the barrel. She tossed the bottle aside, then used the rod and cloth she'd fashioned to coat the inside of the barrel. "Best I can do."

Jack glanced out to the horizon, still seeing nothing.

Meg stood. She doublechecked Beth's adjustments, gave her a nod then pulled her stopwatch. "Get ready to cut the fuse. Let me know, the second you see anything," she shouted, eyes on her watch checking the timing in the pitch and roll of the ship.

"There," shouted Beth a moment later. She held onto a hatch cover. She pointed straight off the bow. "Shit, there're three of them."

Jack saw them, three dim dots clustered at the horizon, their movement hardly discernable.

Meg put her watch back in her pocket. "We've got a steady eight and a half second pitch; not severe. The roll is negligible. Cut the fuse to thirty-two inches, ready the lighter, then wait for my signal."

On a knee, Jack made the measurement and cut the fuse. He handed the end of the fuse to Beth, then pulled a lighter. He cupped his hand over it against the wind, but stopped short of raising a flame.

Beth held the fuse. Braced against the wind, they waited.

"They're coming on fast. They look like military ships," shouted Meg, using her binoculars.

"What if they're friendlies?" said Jack.

"If they were friendly, cap would have heard from them by now and would have let us know. Coming on like that, they don't look friendly to me. Get ready, sheriff."

Jack looked up to the rail off bridge. There was no sign of Lattimore. "Ready here," he shouted, turning back, holding his breath, disbelief setting in. *Yes, this was really happening!* He swallowed hard, still on a knee, trying to keep his balance while bracing himself against the wind.

The radio sputtered. "Range, approaching two thousand yards..."

"Ready to fire," shouted Meg.

Jack flicked the lighter, producing a flame that wavered in the wind. He held it steady in one hand. Beth held the end of the fuse, an inch away.

Over the radio, Lattimore shouted. On my mark, two thousand yards...Now!"

Meg waited for the next pitch of the deck. "Fire!" she shouted. "Light it up."

Just as Jack brought the fuse to the flame, the flame went out. Shit! Heart in his mouth, he fumbled with the lighter.

"Hold on! Hold on!" Shouted Jack. He grabbed the knife. With Beth still holding the fuse, he strung out the fuse then cut off five inches."

"Okay, damn it. Hold on now," shouted Meg.

Jack gave his lighter a shake. Would they have enough time to clear the area before the gun went off?

Meg's eyes back on her watch, she shouted again, her voice amazingly calm: "Okay, just get me a flame."

Jack raised a spark, then a flame that he shielded again with his cupped hand. He held his breath.

Meg shouted. "On my mark: Four, three, two, one...Now! Light it!

Beth shoved the end of the fuse into the flame. It sparked and sputtered to life.

Jack couldn't take his eyes off it. Fear quickly replaced relief. He stood. As if in slow motion he turned seeing the three targets, discernable as warships now, speeding toward them. They're too close, he thought, just as Beth yelled something, pulling his arm. Yep, gotta run. The three of them raced for the hatch where he could see Andrew waving frantically to them, holding it open.

From behind, Jack heard a roar. Was it the sound of their gun? He felt a vibration ring through the deck as he kept up his run. This was good, he thought. Yes, their gun must have gone off, the bomb had been launched—or the gun exploded. Or they were taking fire from the advancing ships. Or...

Ahead of him, Meg and Beth kept up their run. Nearly there.

"Hurry," shouted Andrew from the hatch, braced against the wind.

Meg dove inside, then Beth, Jack last. He hit the deck hard. He heard the clank of Andrew pulling the hatch closed. Jack's eyes adjusted to the near darkness. Out of breath, he crawled to Beth. She pulled him close, her body and his both shaking from the cold and from what they had just done.

"Brace yourselves," shouted Meg.

Lattimore watched from the bridge. Seeing Meg take a knee the second time, he'd known something was wrong. Light the fuse, goddamn-it! He'd shouted, gripping the controls, ready to take *Endeavor* into a wild turn to starboard as soon as the bomb was in the air.

He waited. The warships sped closer, spewing smoke and waves of heat from their stacks. He'd ignored the orders they'd radioed for him to turn back, to resume his original course. He knew they didn't consider him a threat. Hell, their guns probably weren't even loaded. They were planning to board his tired old freighter, toss its belligerent crew overboard and take over the ship. The last thing they'd expect *Endeavor* to do was take a shot at them. He kept his eyes on the mortar down on deck.

His heart was hammering, racing wildly. "No, you're not failing me now," he shouted, a hand at his chest. Arrhythmia. He'd had bouts of it before. He took a breath, then another. Like a yoga master, he forced himself calm. His heart steadied then slowed and strengthened. He straightened. Eyes clearing, he saw a puff of white smoke taken sideways. The fuse had been lit. He watched Beth, Meg and Jack running, racing for the hatch still a hundred feet away. "Run, damn-it, run," he shouted, a hand still at his chest until he lost sight of them.

"I hope to God we're doing the right thing, Maddie," Lattimore said under his breath, turning his attention back to the gun where the fuse still burned. An ill-timed wave could spray the deck and put it out. Or the ship might roll unexpectedly, affecting the aim of the mortar. Or the gun might blow up.

He raised his binoculars. There was no more smoke. Had the fuse gone out? Lattimore's stomach churned. Time seemed to stand still. Then...

A bright flash, and a cloud of whitish orange smoke engulfed the gun. A loud boom rattled the windows. Though he couldn't tell if the bomb had been launched, Lattimore grabbed the controls. He cut their heading hard to starboard. *Endeavor* responded with a sharp list. He kept his eyes on the gun. It sat there as if nothing had happened. But the deck around it was charred black. Had the bomb launched? He looked at the oncoming ships. They looked exactly as they had before the explosion—except closer.

Another radio message from them, same as the ones before, blared from the speaker. "Attention American vessel. You will stop your engines. You will prepare to be boarded."

"Fuck no! We will not stand down, you assholes," he shouted back.

Then, he saw it. No more than a tiny black dot against the hazy sky. It might have been a bird. But no, this bird was streaking straight down from a high altitude as no bird would have. It could only be the bomb. Hell, the thing had gone farther than he'd thought. Too far? He watched the tiny dot, gaining speed. He tracked it all the way down, he saw it splash harmlessly into the water at least two hundred yards beyond the warships.

Lattimore's body went slack. They'd overshot. He waited, eyes on the onrushing ships. Nothing to do now but wait to be boarded. He'd known the bomb had been a gamble but...

Without warning, the water in the distance behind the warships turned a brilliant white. A blinding flash lit the bridge. *My God, had the thing exploded?*

He fought the urge to look. In his gut, he knew that was about the stupidest thing he could do. He dropped to the floor, on his knees still managing to hold onto the base of the controls console. He braced himself against it. A wall of fiery hot air hit hard. He fell back. *Endeavor* shuddered. The hull rang. The ship listed, hard over. Lattimore held on, able to keep himself from sliding. Shit, were they going to capsize? The ship remained at that crazy angle for what felt like minutes, then began to right itself; slowly at first, then with gathering speed. Lattimore held on tight. The ship moved in a distinctly odd way. Sideways? Upward? The ship should still be turning hard to starboard but...no. It was settling out. They were still afloat. The deck was...yes, the deck was level.

Without knowing what exactly was happening, a surge of surprise and exhilaration coursed through him. That little bomb, no larger than a bowling pin, had caused all this. And what about the warships? They were so much closer to the explosion? Did he dare hope they'd been destroyed?

With the ship stabilizing and his ears still ringing, Lattimore staggered to his knees, then to his feet. He surveyed the bridge. The coffee pot lay rolling in a pool of coffee grounds. Beside it lay the overturned hotplate which, owing to its short cord, had the decency to unplug itself. Shattered cups littered the deck.

The forward windows were riddled with cracks but they were still in place. Through them he saw that his ship remained intact all the way out to the bow. Even the hoses and lines remained hung and coiled in place. He scanned the sea for any sign of the three military ships but saw nothing. Had they sunk? Or...maybe *Endeavor*'s turn had put them astern? Yes, that was more likely.

He cupped his ears and took in a deep breath to get them working again. There, that was better. He could hear the hum of the engines now. Then he heard the steady beep of an alarm. *That* was not good. He checked the readings on the console. He spotted a light blinking red in time with the alarm. Something was wrong with the rudder. A serious problem but, could that be the only damage? They were still afloat. He checked the ballast readings. They were not taking on water. The hull was intact and he was more than happy to take this as a win.

At that moment a phone went off; *his* phone. He pulled it from his coat pocket and eyed the number. It was not one he recognized. Not a good time for a spam call. Still, he brought the phone to his ear. "This is Lattimore, who is this?"

CHAPTER 41

Jack's ears rang painfully. Everything was dark. He tried to turn his head, to move any part of his body but found himself pinned at the bottom of what felt like a football scrum. He pulled a hand free. He felt hot breath on his face. He tried to focus his eyes, barely able to see Beth's eyes only two inches away looking back at him in the darkness. He moved his hand again. "Is that your leg?" he asked.

"It's *my* leg," said Meg from somewhere.

"Oh, sorry. Can you...can you get off me?"

"Yeah, trying." Meg shifted her weight, then lifted herself off.

"You okay," Jack asked Beth.

"Yeah. I think so. Should I be offended that you couldn't tell her leg from mine?"

"We're still afloat," said Meg, on her feet. "And we're still underway."

"My God, the bomb did all that! We nearly capsized."

Together Beth and Jack struggled to get up. Unsteady, Jack leaned against the bulkhead next to the hatch. He scanned the darkness spotting Andrew nearly at his feet, lying prone, not moving. He bent over the professor. "Oh, crap, there's blood on the floor. Andrew, Andrew! He's breathing. Got a nasty gash on the side of his head, though."

Jack tried tearing a strip of fabric from the hem of his shirt, but couldn't. He removed his coat and took his shirt off. He folded it over and pressed it to the side of Andrew's head just as the lights flickered on.

"There, he's got his eyes open," said Jack. "You're okay, professor. You're okay. That bomb of yours packed a wallop."

Andrew blinked through a blank expression.

Meg grabbed a first aid kit from somewhere and prepared a bandage.

"Hold on." From the kit Beth pulled an antiseptic wipe. She dabbed the spot clean. "Okay, now the bandage," she said. "It's a little deep but not bad. He doesn't need stitches."

"He's just...staring," said Jack.

"Might be in shock." She lifted Andrew's wrist. "Pulse is good, breathing strong."

"I'm all right," said Andrew, raising himself to a sitting position.

"Our gun and your bomb seemed to have worked, Andrew," said Beth. "I'm not sure that's a good thing but..."

"Well, something big exploded out there," said Meg. "For all we know, those ships fired on us and have us under their guns right now."

"Can you stand?" Jack asked Andrew.

With help, the professor stood. He put both hands on the hand rail, leaning heavily against it, face pale. "I...I...yes, I'm okay. Little dizzy but..."

Jack jumped at a loud clank that rang through the ship. "What the hell was that?"

No one spoke. The engines died. The lights dimmed. Jack looked around, half expecting the ship's hull to crack open, water storming in. Yeah, he'd seen one too many disaster-at-sea movies.

"It came from the stern," said Meg. "We're not listing but that didn't sound good." She worked the hatch open. Sunlight poured in along with the cold wind.

"Here, put your shirt on big boy," said Beth, handing it to Jack. "You look great but..."

Jack put it on, then his coat.

Meg stepped through the hatch. "Shit!"

Beth and Jack followed, joining her at the rail.

A few hundred yards out two warships floated, dead in the water. One listed heavily, the other was pitched down at the stern. The water around both was dotted with what Jack knew were the heads of crewmen struggling to stay afloat. Rising and falling in the rolling water, they reminded him of kids in a waterpark pool, all waiting for the next big wave to take them up then down. It was a comically morbid thought.

"Most might be dead already," said Meg staring. "There's going to be radiation out there."

Lattimore's shout came down from the bridge. "We're lowering the lifeboat. Get your asses to the stern. Do it now. I'm coming down."

Jack looked up, quick enough to see Lattimore go back inside the bridge. He turned to Meg. "Are we sinking?"

"I don't think so," said Meg. Her face took on a stony look of urgency. "But, come with me, all of you. I know the way. Quickly!"

They met up with Lattimore and the rest of the crew at the stern. There were two lifeboats, one on the port side, the other on the starboard side, both of the old, open style. He spotted the college kid Ben, in one of them.

Climb aboard, quickly, Jack," shouted Lattimore, getting in. "Just the three of us. You others stay here."

"Are we sinking?" shouted Beth. "What about the crew?"

"We're okay," said Lattimore, waving for Jack to hurry. "There's trouble with the rudder but I think that's all. We're okay."

Jack climbed up and into the lifeboat. He took a seat and held on.

"We're going to try and rescue some of those people out there," said Lattimore, loud enough for them all to hear. At his nod, the motorized lowering mechanism started.

"What about the radiation?" said Jack.

"That shouldn't be a problem."

"An atomic bomb goes off and radiation is not a problem?"

Lattimore glared. "If you don't want to be part of this, sheriff, get off now."

"Get off, Jack. Stay here," Beth shouted as the lifeboat descended.

Jack stared up at her, a bad feeling in the hollow of his chest. The lifeboat was already halfway down. Not much choice now. "It's okay. We'll be fine," he shouted back.

Once in the water, the little boat rocked like a bull ride in a Texas bar. Jack detached the line from the bow while Lattimore handled the line at the stern. Ben started the motor and handled the tiller guiding the little craft over the roll of the waves, heading for the doomed ships. Both were hulled over now. What Jack couldn't see from his low vantage, were the heads of the survivors bobbing in the water. But he knew they were there. He wondered how many of them were still alive and how many they could fit aboard their small lifeboat.

And he wondered about the radiation.

CHAPTER 42

Fate! It was fate that brought her to this time, this place, this desperate moment. Fate that had aborted the original plan to fly her from Montreal back to Detroit aboard a comfortable private jet. Instead, she'd taken that rattle trap of a chopper far out to sea to land on what she knew was once named the *Xi-An*, an old ship built as a prototype for the Luyang III-Class destroyer of the People's Republic of China. This ship, along with her two sister ships had been scheduled for scrapping. Instead, Andrei had bought them on the cheap. They were what he called his Dark Fleet.

Katerina suspected, but couldn't be sure, that Andrei had wanted her aboard to tie up any loose ends with Lattimore. Or maybe he wanted to impress her with the magnitude of his grand November surprise.

Then, fate intervened.

How was it that Lattimore was able to fire some kind of weapon at them from his tired old freighter? She knew the man still had friends in the American military but what was it that could have sunk all three of Andrei's ships?

Only twenty minutes ago she'd been standing on the bridge of the lead ship as their three ship squadron raced to intercept the harmless Great Lakes freighter. It was exhilarating. Yes, right up until the moment Katerina had seen through her binoculars, a tiny puff of smoke rise from the deck of Lattimore's ship. Almost imperceptible, the smoke had been taken by the wind leaving her to wonder if she'd really seen it.

"Gun fired, captain," came the call over the intercom. "It will overshoot. Should we return fire?"

"No. Hold course and speed," the captain had said. She remembered the smirk on the captain's face as he turned to her. "Your foolish captain sends a mosquito to defend himself against three dragons."

Katerina had returned his look with a smile. She'd calculated the odds of the mission failing at this late stage as being nearly nonexistent. So, the warships raced on, the captain, Katerina and all aboard, ignoring the non-zero chance of everything turning to shit. The secrecy of the mission had kept all of them in the dark as to the nature and purpose of this rendezvous with the freighter.

At the critical moment, she'd turned to the aft windows on the bridge and, from there saw a tiny splash in the water several hundred meters behind the ship, well past her wake.

And nothing happened.

Then, the ship vibrated. The water behind them began to churn. In an instant, it turned from blue to a brilliant white, then blossomed into a terrible gold. The ocean swelled up as if to make room for something rising from the deep. It would have looked beautiful under the bright sun had it not been accompanied by the intense shaking of the vessel. Katerina's blood went cold. She grabbed the rail. At a sickening roll of thunder, the bow of the ship rose.

Like a surfboard, the ship accelerated on a gigantic wave of churning water. With violence, it tore through the water, pitching side to side. The rest was a blur.

She lost her grip. Still on the bridge, she tumbled across the deck. In the roar of wind and water, pain stabbed her ears. As if in a terrible dream, she pulled her knees up to her chin, wrapping her arms around her legs. She squeezed her eyes shut. She felt a scream leave her throat but heard nothing. The world jerked and rolled. The deck pitched one way then the other and she with it, pounding into bodies and bulkheads before finally settling into a corner of the bridge. She opened her eyes. The deck was tilted at a terrifying angle. Men beside her were struggling to stand.

And, there was smoke.

God almighty! What just happened?

She gasped. She coughed hard, and took in a desperate breath of acrid air. Her dulled hearing came back. Sirens were going off. She tasted blood and felt the warmth and wet of it all along the side of her face. She looked around.

Bodies lay everywhere, some moving, others not. Supported by a bulkhead that had once been vertical, she got to her feet. The lights had gone out but she saw sun and sky through the port side windows. She glanced to starboard and saw the waves alarmingly close, still foaming white from the explosion.

But what had exploded? What could possibly have done all of...this?

She stepped over broken glass and over bodies. She made her way across the tilted deck to the starboard windows now angled down to the waves. Water ran wild in one spot near midship. It had to be rushing in through a gash in the hull. Men worked the rope pullies, trying to get the lifeboats launched. But something was wrong. The lines were tangled. Yeah, this was an old ship. Men jumped into the water. They had life jackets.

The ship was sinking. She brought her hands to her face. She had to think clearly. Her life hung in the balance. She looked off into the distance and saw Lattimore's freighter. Undamaged?

At that terrible moment she realized she had one last card to play. She felt in her pocket for her sat phone. She struggled to pull it out.

Head throbbing, she blinked the blood from her eyes. She worked her phone. Miraculously, she heard a voice: "Lattimore here. Who is this?"

"I...I can save your daughter, captain. But..."

"Katerina? Are you...?"

"I am alive. Others are too. I am on the largest ship..." She felt a rumble run through the vessel. She screamed. The ship jerked over a few more degrees. She caught her breath. She spoke fast. "...I can save your daughter. But...Captain Lattimore, you must save me. Please I..."

The phone slipped from her hand. It clattered across the deck. The ship reverberated with a piercing metal-on-metal scream. It pitched back toward the stern. Men were scrambling for life jackets. She grabbed one. They were going down. She had to move fast.

She pulled the life jacket on, cinching it tight. She fought her way to the hatch that led outside. There was no time to think. She climbed over the rail, and took a running leap.

Her head was only briefly under the water before the life jacket brought her bobbing up. The water was warmer than the cold air. It felt oddly comforting. The doomed hulk of the ship towered above her, blocking the sun, listing at an impossible angle. With the others in the water, she swam madly, trying to gain distance from the doomed warship before it sank, sucking her down with it.

She moved her arms frantically making slow headway. Tall waves fought against every stroke as did the drag of her life jacket. Then, completely out of breath, she gasped for air. She looked back. Others were just now jumping off the deck, everyone shouting and screaming. With all her panicked efforts she'd gained precious little distance from the ship. But it would have to do. She was exhausted. She rolled with the waves, bobbing with the other heads in the water as like so many apples in a barrel. For all the power and prestige she'd possessed only moments earlier, like the others, she was totally helpless.

Would Lattimore come? Would he save her?

She rested.

Her body grew numb. From time to time, she wiped the seawater from her eyes. She lifted her eyes, somehow the sky was still blue and serene even after all this terror. Ha! A real Tolstoy moment. Guess I haven't lost my Russian roots after all. Maybe it was time, to start believing there was a God? She almost laughed bitterly, recalling the lyric to a Canadian song that sang of Jesus: *Only drowning men could see Him.*

Her thoughts shifted to Ilya. How would he get along without her? He'd probably spend the rest of his life in an institution, maybe in America but probably in Russia. He'd be better off without her. How could she have sunk so low as to admonish him when he'd tried to protect Lattimore's daughter? Over his entire life she'd worried about his…condition, hoping he'd somehow become transformed into a normal man. Could it be that, all along it was she, his mother, who was the least normal of the two? Could it be that it was *he* who had spent his whole life hoping *she* would one day change?

Maybe all she'd needed to do was to abandon this crazy and dangerous life of hers and take care of him like a real mother would have.

Time passed. Her thoughts drifted again, this time to a story she'd heard about an American warship, sunk at sea in the final days of World War II. Yes, the *Indianapolis*. There'd been many survivors but most of those, with their heads bobbing in the water as hers was now, waiting to be rescued, had been eaten alive by sharks. Katerina's stomach churned. She bent her knees, drawing her legs up closer to the rest of her body.

CHAPTER 43

With hands gripping both sides of the center bench, Jack steadied himself in the lifeboat as it sped toward the sinking ships. From fifty yards away, he could make out faces in the water. Most were alive, wide eyed, shouting, waving to be saved. Behind them the gray hulls of two ships lay rolled over on their side, rocking gently. Survivors dotted the hulls of both. "There must be a hundred men out here," shouted Jack over the noise of the motor. "We should have taken both lifeboats."

"We can take fifteen at a time," said Lattimore from the bow. "They'll all get rescued in due time, but not by us.

Jack looked around but saw no other ships in the area. He got the feeling Lattimore knew something he didn't.

Lattimore knifed a hand toward the larger of the two vessels. "Take us there, Mr. Spencer."

Jack saw no flags or markings on either of the stricken vessels. "What happened to the third ship?"

"She's already down," said Lattimore. "She must have been the one trailing the formation. She was closest to the explosion. That small bomb did all this. And it wasn't anywhere near a direct hit. The wave must have been huge."

Ben slowed the motor. "Another hour, maybe two, these ships'll be down."

"Do you know about the bomb?" Jack asked him.

"Yeah, cap told me. Hope you did the right thing."

"If we hadn't, we'd all be prisoners now."

"Or dead," added Lattimore.

Jack heard the sound of rushing water. He could see the open hole in the hull of the ship they were heading for.

Lattimore shifted to his knees on the forward bench, a hand on both gunnels. "Katerina is out here somewhere," he said.

How do you know that?" said Jack.

"She called me. It must have been just before she jumped into the water. Said she'd tell me where Maddie was if I'd come out and save her."

"So, this is all about saving your daughter," said Ben. "That's why we're out here risking radiation exposure."

"I have no way to measure the radiation, but considering how far the bomb overshot, and considering the windage, the radiation should be minimal." Lattimore, kept his attention directed out at the faces in the waters ahead. "Would you have stayed back and let all these men die?"

"You said they're going to be rescued anyway," said Jack. "But I don't know by who. There're no other ships around."

Lattimore said nothing.

One of the floundering men grabbed onto the side of the boat. With Lattimore's help, Jack pulled him up into the lifeboat and gave him a blanket. Panting and spitting up water, the man gathered it around him but kept his head lowered and did not speak.

They approached a second man. Ben cut the motor as Lattimore tossed him a line. They pulled him up and into the boat.

The two rescued men wore the same work clothes but neither had markings showing a military rank. Ten men were saved in this way before Lattimore stood, pointing. "She's over there, Mr. Spencer. The only head in the water without a military brush cut." Ben started the motor

To get to her, they had to pass a group of floundering men, one of whom was able to grab the side of the lifeboat and pull himself aboard without help. Jack averted his eyes from the other men they had to pass by to get to the Russian woman. "Wait," he told them. "We'll be coming back." The lifeboat was already sitting low in the water.

Over the sounds of the motor Jack heard a low howl coming from somewhere. He looked to the horizon and saw a pair of black dots.

"F-35's," shouted Lattimore. "About fucking time they show up."

Even as the sound grew to a rumbling thunder, Lattimore kept his eyes on the woman who must be Katerina. She took a couple of strokes closing the gap.

"I've got her," said Jack, pulling her aboard just as the jets screamed overhead.

Jack ducked, feeling the heat of their exhaust. The water went white in their wake. The lifeboat rocked. Everyone held on as the thunder died and the water calmed.

"Couple of goddamn hot doggers," said Lattimore. "Take us back to *Endeavor*, Mr. Spencer."

Bent, pale and shaking, the woman sat shoulder to shoulder with her fellow survivors. Jack gave her the last blanket.

"Do that again and they'll sink us," said Ben, staring at the jets, already no more than black dots closing on the horizon.

"You've been expecting them," said Jack to Lattimore.

"A nuclear explosion's bound to attract some attention. Besides, I'm sure they've been watching us for a while."

"You fired a nuclear weapon at us?" said Katerina, staring.

"It was *your* nuclear weapon. *That* was your secret cargo and there're eleven more just like it aboard my ship. Don't act like you didn't know," said Lattimore.

Katerina pulled her blanket around her. "I swear to you, captain, I did not know. I..." She went silent."

Once clear of the bobbing heads, Ben gunned the motor, and turned the lifeboat into the wind.

As soon as they'd tied up next to *Endeavor*, Lattimore pulled Katerina up, leaving her blanket behind. She grabbed onto the rope ladder. She faltered, then found her footing stepping onto the pilot's stairs. Lattimore joined her there then turned and shouted back. "Mr. Spencer. Get the rest of those survivors aboard. Make sure they're not armed. Ask Carter and Winters to help. Take them to the galley, dry clothes, water and food. Treat them as guests until they show they are otherwise. Jack, you're coming with me and our friend here."

"What about the other men in the water?" asked Ben.

"They'll be picked up in due time by the U.S. Navy. Those were carrier jets doing the fly by. I expect we'll be seeing the lead ships of the carrier group off to the west soon enough."

With Jack following, Lattimore took Katerina, still dripping wet, up to the bridge. The place was a mess. Cracks ran across every window. The deck was a clutter of papers and spilled coffee. A book lay covered with coffee grounds. Lattimore's recliner, having been screwed to the deck was the only thing still in place. Lattimore shoved Katerina into it. She was shivering. Her hair, wet and knotted fell across her shoulders.

"Where is my daughter?" Lattimore demanded.

Katerina spoke quickly. "Your daughter is safe, captain. I promise you she is safe."

"Where?"

"Near Detroit. It's a secure facility."

"Secured by who?"

"There are men guarding her. They do not answer to me."

"KGB?"

"Unofficially, yes."

"You're telling me we have to rescue her by force?"

"They will not give her up willingly."

"I save you; you save my daughter. That was our deal."

"I will do all I can to save your daughter. My son is there as well." Her eyes were tired but alert, even…calculating. Except for the shivering, her face was calm and unstrained.

Lattimore's eyes blazed. He placed both hands on the armrests of the recliner and cleaned closer, his face inches from hers. "You will contact those men. You will instruct them to free her now."

"If I do that, those men will kill her and destroy all evidence that she was ever there. I'm sorry, captain, I will help you get her back, but I can only do so much."

Lattimore backed off.

"She needs a blanket," said Jack.

"She needs a good kick in the teeth, sheriff."

Katerina flinched. "You are Sheriff Holiday?"

"Yes. And you're the woman who's been trying to kill me."

"Your wife is alive too?" At his nod, she shook her head. "You are a lucky man, sheriff."

At that moment, two jets streaked across the bow. The damaged windows rattled. "Damn fools are acting like they're at an air show," muttered Lattimore. He stepped to the radar console. "Looks like fleet-week out here," he said, eyes on the screen where Jack could see multiple blips converging on their position.

Lattimore picked up the radio, keyed it and spoke clearly: "This is Captain Lattimore of the United States freighter *Endeavor*, requesting immediate assistance. Over."

A clear, firm voice replied: "You will stand down, *Endeavor*. You will stand down immediately and prepare to be boarded. You will slow your engines now or you will be fired upon. Is that understood."

"Understood," said Lattimore, complying as he continued speaking. "Be informed that we have a rudder problem. Also, there are people in the water due east of us. Request your assistance to rescue."

"Understood, captain. We will assist."

Lattimore flipped a switch on the console. "Damage report." he said twice.

Seconds passed, then Jack recognized Beck's voice. "We're in decent shape, captain, considering. We're not taking on water and the engines are working fine..."

"Something's wrong with our rudder," Lattimore interrupted.

"Yeah, I was getting to that. Pinion's cracked. We got it unjammed but there's no getting around it, we'll need a new one. The rack looks to be in good shape."

"Can you mill up another one?"

"Not anytime soon. Meg might have some ideas on that."

"All right. Stand down then. We're about to be boarded by the good guys. Make sure the crew cooperates." He put down the mic and turned to Katerina. "Who are you working for? What were they going to do with those bombs?"

"I told you before, captain, I don't know anything about the bombs. As for who I was working for, he is not someone you would know."

"Try me."

"I will help you get your daughter back. That is our deal. That is all I will do."

Lattimore turned to Jack. "Take her down to the galley. Find her a blanket or a coat. Get her some food, then lock her up, I don't care where. She will not mix with the crew and she will receive no visitors without my say-so. Is that understood?"

The last thing Jack wanted to do was to babysit Katerina. He wondered where Beth was. "I don't have a key to..."

"Here's a master key. You figure it out." He tossed it to Jack. "Until you have her locked up you will not let her out of your sight. I don't care if she needs to take a shit, you will stand by her side. Have you got that?"

"Got it."

When Katerina made an effort to stand, Lattimore grabbed her arm and yanked her up the rest of the way. He pulled her close. "If those men harm my daughter in any way, I swear I will kill you."

"You have kept your word, captain. I will keep mine."

CHAPTER 44

Jack ate with Katerina in the galley, filled now with survivors none of whom gave her so much as a glance. Neither she or Jack said a word. With a blanket draped around her, her hair dry but rumpled, she looked nothing like the Russian vamp he'd seen on the docks back in Detroit. Done with her food, she used the head, again not speaking, Jack standing nearby. He then took her to an empty storage room. "Lattimore or I will be back to check on you," he told her as he locked the door, glad to be done with her.

He met up with Beth in the dayroom where she sat with Andrew, both nursing half-filled cups of coffee. Beautiful as ever, she sprang to her feet, ran to him and pulled him close. He put his arms around her, feeling the energizing warmth of her lips against his, the warmth of her body against his. A profound sense of relief overtook him. "It's all over," he said once they parted.

"Yes, thank God it's all over. Are you all right? What was it like out there? The radiation..."

"I don't think it was bad. I didn't feel a thing. Like the captain said, the wind must have taken most of the radiation away."

"Have you had anything to eat? Can I get..."

"I'm good. I ate with Katerina in the galley."

"You had lunch with...Katerina? The Russian bitch?"

He filled her in. "Don't worry, she's locked up." He nodded in the direction of the galley. "Those sailors we fished out of the water seem to think they're prisoners of war."

"They may be right, sheriff," said Andrew soberly. "We *are* an American vessel and we *did* just fire a nuclear weapon at them."

"We were defending ourselves. Hell, we didn't even know for sure that bomb of yours would work."

"I wasn't so sure of that myself. I'm excited, pleased and shocked, all at the same time." The professor took in a long breath, staring down at his coffee. "I wonder how many men we killed today."

"We saved ourselves and we pulled a lot of survivors out of the water. The Navy's picking up the rest."

"And Katerina was out there," said Beth. "Did you learn anything about Maddie?"

"Katerina says she's in good shape. She promised to help get her back. I'm not sure Lattimore believes that."

"Those men in there," said Andrew, "they sound like Russians. I heard a few of them talking. They aren't wearing naval uniforms but I'm betting the color of their clothing has to do with their rank. There're a lot more blues than reds and only one or two in black clothing I've seen. They're hiding the fact that they're a military group. Then again, I might be looking for a pattern where there is none."

"You seem to be feeling better today, professor," said Jack.

"Nothing like a big explosion to clear the head, I suppose."

"Go get yourself some coffee, Jack," said Beth, tossing back the last of hers then holding out her empty cup. "Mind getting me a fill up?"

"Oh, yes, I'll have another too," said Andrew.

By the time their fresh cups had again been emptied, Jack heard a commotion from the deck below. He stiffened, eyes on Beth. Neither said a word as the sound of thumping boots drew closer.

A marine armed with an M-16 appeared at the dayroom door. Beside him stood a sailor with a handheld tablet. "You will stay in your seats," shouted the marine. "Now, one at a time, you will tell me who you are and what your function is aboard this ship." He pointed to Beth. "You first ma'am."

She put on her best smile, gave her name, then added: "I'm a pharmacist."

"Jack Holiday, Sheriff of Gull Harbor Michigan."

Andrew looked surprised when the marine turned to him. "Oh, yes. Me too, eh? I am Professor Andrew Simeon, Professor of Physics. And there's no need to shout, young man. There're only the three of us in here."

The marine ignored the thumping of helicopter blades coming from outside. He ordered them to stand. The tablet guy checked them for weapons.

"I will escort you back to your cabins. You will stay there until ordered to do otherwise. If you try to leave without being specifically told to do so, you will be considered hostile and you will be physically restrained. Is that understood?"

"I assure you, soldier, there is nothing hostile about the three of us," protested Andrew as they were marched off. "We're harmless...well, except for that explosion we just..."

"Understood, corporal," said Jack quickly.

Once back in their cabin, Jack sat, then stretched out on his cot, Beth beside him on hers. "We're still alive," he said.

"Yeah, locked in a cabin with an armed guard at the door, aboard a disabled freighter somewhere out in the Atlantic surrounded by the U.S. Navy."

He kissed her. "We're alive and we're together. The rest will take care of itself."

"You're such a hopeless romantic, Jack."

It wasn't long before they, along with Andrew, were led back to the dayroom. The marine closed the door behind him.

The room was crowded with *Endeavor*'s crew, along with a number of stern-faced naval officers each in navy blues. As they took a seat near the pinball machine, Jack noticed another man, middle aged with wire rimmed glasses. He wore jeans and a sweatshirt and was having a quiet discussion with a square-jawed gray-haired man who wore a single star on each shoulder—a rear admiral. The two of them glanced in his direction then resumed their discussion.

"They're talking about you, Jack" Beth whispered. "What do you think..."

She was cut short by the admiral breaking off his conversation and taking center stage. The setting had the look of a mission briefing room from an old war movie. Bomber pilots about to go out on a mission fraught with danger. All that was missing was the big map on the wall. The room went quiet.

"I am Rear Admiral James Lawrence. I'm here to tell you that, as of this moment, you are all under suspicion, and liable for prosecution for the part you played in the unlawful smuggling of illicit materials out of the United States with the expressed intention of rendering aid to a foreign power."

"You've got to be kidding me," shouted Beck, jumping to her feet. "That'll never stand up in a courtroom."

"I'm sorry sailor, that's not for me to say." Apparently well versed in leadership techniques, the admiral let that sentence hang dramatically in the air as he stared her down. Hands on hips, his voice shifted almost comically into a light Texas drawl. "I promise you all that you will be treated fairly and according to the letter of the law."

Jack felt blood rush to his head. Before he knew it, he found himself standing up. "You showed up awfully fast today, admiral. We could have used your help a week ago back in Detroit."

"You are Jack Holiday, *Sheriff* Jack Holiday."

"Yes."

The Admiral lowered his hand to his side. "Please, the two of you, take your seats." Beck, more reluctantly than Jack did so as the admiral continued. "Those were three warships you sank. They once belonged to the PRC. That's the Peoples Republic of China. We've had our eyes on those ships for the last five days. Over that time, we were surprised to see them holding station, staying put as if waiting for something to happen. This obviously had us a little worried.

"Then, we were surprised to see them suddenly move out at high-speed heading directly for the U.S. coastline. We scrambled a couple of F35's. That's when we saw you guys. And we wondered, what the hell a Great Lakes freighter was doing out in the Atlantic well outside normal shipping lanes. *And* you were sailing directly toward those oncoming warships. Fortunately, we already had a carrier group on the way to this general area."

"You should have warned us," said Beck.

"What's your name, sailor?"

"Beck Foley."

"Well, Seaman Foley, you might be right about that. We should have at least spotted you earlier than we did and figured there might be a connection between you and the warships." He scratched the side of his head. "Yet that didn't really make much sense to any of us. In any event, right or wrong, we decided to watch things play out." He paused taking in each face in the room. "I've got to say, we were ready for any number of possible things to happen, all of them bad, but a laker launching a tactical nuke and sinking those three ships; well now, *that* was something we hadn't anticipated."

"You said those ships were Chinese," said Ben. "The men we pulled out of the water didn't look Chinese."

Lawrence glanced at the wire rimmed glasses guy who gave a slight nod.

"I am not at liberty to say anything more about those ships or about their crew. But, this ship, *Endeavor*, is an American flagged commercial vessel. It was used earlier today to launch a nuclear weapon in a hostile manner causing the loss of lives and property. So, that makes this freighter and her crew, that's you folks here, part of the highest level international incident to occur since the end of World War II." Another pause. "This incident was tantamount to an unprovoked unilateral first nuclear strike by the United States in international waters against a foreign power. What I'm telling you all is that, depending on what the Russians do right now, you folks right here on this freighter might have just started a nuclear war."

Andrew shouted: "There, I told you this would happen."

"And who might you be sir?"

"I am Professor Andrew Simeon."

"Professor?" said the Admiral. "What's your field, professor?"

"Nuclear physics," said Andrew. "And, if you don't mind, I would like to know where the rest of my bombs are."

"They are not *your* bombs. And they are no longer aboard this vessel." Admiral Lawrence took a step back and looked around the room. "This is a serious situation. Men died out there today. Our diplomats are trying to smooth things over. We should all hope and pray they are successful."

"What are you doing with the survivors we picked up," asked Jack.

"They're being transferred to one of our destroyer escorts. And we are picking up more as we speak. We are also picking up a few dozen bodies. The survivors are being treated well and are being questioned now. It seems your bomb fell well beyond those ships and exploded underwater. The resulting swell and shock wave is what hulled-over those ships. Your ship too would have capsized if she hadn't been far enough away from the explosion."

"The full load of iron ore we had as ballast helped with that," added Meg.

"Good point, sailor." The admiral scanned the room. "This is a State Department problem now. It's their feeling that the foreign powers involved *might* be content to keep this whole thing quiet and avoid the embarrassment of having partnered with a criminal enterprise to smuggle nuclear weapons out of the United States. We'd all better hope they're right about that."

"Where is Captain Lattimore?" someone asked.

"Let's just say, he's preoccupied elsewhere."

CHAPTER 45

Lattimore wore a heavy orange jacket, hood down. He stood arms folded just off the stern helipad, between two armed marines. In the distance the carrier group loitered, lining the horizon the carrier itself only about two miles out. The combined crew likely numbered in excess of seven thousand men.

Hell, a dozen men would have done the job back in Detroit. But no, someone had decided it wasn't important enough to arrest Katerina and her men and keep Maddie from being taken.

He shaded his eyes and lifted his gaze, knowing that the man responsible for that non decision was probably snuggly seated in the chopper hovering only a hundred feet up.

Lattimore ignored the wash of the rotors, as the craft descended. Even through the chill of it, he felt the heat of his blood rising, his fingers curling into fists. The chopper touched down, the wheels cushioned the impact, the rotors slowed, and the hatch opened.

And there, right there, stood Under Secretary of State Brian Hanover. He wore a naval jump suit, baseball cap and aviator sunglasses. Yeah, a real action hero look.

Hanover jumped down onto the deck, eyes on Lattimore.

Even before he knew he was doing it, Lattimore strode out toward him, arms stiff at his side, fists like hammers, ready to pound some nails. He heard the marines running from behind, trying to stop him.

Hanover walked closer, a stupid, angry scowl on his face. Yeah, no doubt ready to tell him how he'd really fucked up this time. To hell with that.

Lattimore's right fist caught him on the left side of his jaw. The glasses went flying. The diplomat, if he could be called that, fell in a satisfying way like a sack of potatoes. He struggled to get back up.

Lattimore leaned over him and would have struck again had the marine guards not grabbed him pulling him back. "Where the fuck were you?" Lattimore shouted. "Damn it, where the fuck were you?" He hoped to see blood on the man's face. There was none. He struggled, trying to hit him again but the marines had his arms pinned back.

Hanover got to his feet. He pressed a hand to the side of his face, then moved his jaw as if to see if it were still working. He spit out some blood, "You and I need to talk *now*—in private."

Lattimore shook off the marines and led the way inside to a storage room. With the heat of the moment still simmering, he switched on a light. Hanover waved off the guards and closed the door.

Lattimore spoke first, his emotions on a hair trigger. "They have my daughter. Katerina took her off my ship and threatened to kill her if I didn't do what she wanted. You should have been there, you idiot. This all should have ended in Detroit. Not here. Not now. That was the plan."

"Plans change. You know that," said Hanover. "Look, I'm sorry about your daughter. I didn't know about that. What the hell was she doing aboard your ship?"

"She was meddling in things and I was trying to keep her safe. I was trying to keep her from fucking up your plan of catching Katerina and her men red handed. *In Detroit.*"

"Yeah, well sorry, that didn't work out."

"And why the fuck was that?"

"The stakes of this thing had gotten too high. We were trying to...adjust. We were trying to contain and control information."

"And I didn't have a need to know."

"That's right, you did not have a need to know. It was only thanks to the work of your daughter and a sheriff from somewhere up on the Keweenaw who somehow got mixed up in all of this that we found out about the nukes. That changed everything. We didn't want those nukes in Detroit or anywhere else in the United States, while they were under the control of some Russian oligarchs."

Lattimore paused. "That's what you think those people are? Russian oligarchs?"

"That's what we *know* they are. They're being led by Andrei Bulanov. Maybe you know the name. He's a west-leaning capitalist. Your friend Katerina works for him." He lowered his voice. "We think they were planning a new Russian Revolution."

Lattimore was stunned. He didn't say a word.

"We think they were planning to blow up the Kremlin."

"Shit! And you wanted to help them do it. You *wanted* them to have the nukes."

"We wanted to see how it would play out. We thought we could control the situation. Then you came along."

Lattimore straightened, his mind ratcheting through all the possible implications of what he'd just heard. "The old enemy of my enemy is my friend strategy."

"Yes...broadly speaking. It would have led to a regime change in Russia. And all we had to do was to sit on the sidelines and watch."

"And that became your new plan."

"Yes, that was plan B. And now, because you fired off one of those damn nukes and sank those three ships, we are on to plan C."

"And what does that look like?"

"We're working on it." Hanover paused. "I see now that you learned about the nukes from your daughter. You got lucky in finding out where they were hidden, but how did you figure out how to set one of them off?"

Lattimore realized Hanover must not know about the professor—not yet anyway. On general principal, he decided to keep the diplomat in the dark. "I have a rudimentary knowledge of nuclear weapons," he said. "It wasn't difficult."

Hanover checked his watch. "We have to get going. Like it or not Captain Lattimore, you'll be in the loop this time. So will Katerina. I'm told she's aboard."

"My cooperation is entirely contingent on the rescue of my daughter."

Hanover nodded. "I'll try to make that happen."

"You *will* make that happen."

"All right, captain, you have my word, I *will* make that happen. Now, where is Katerina?"

"Follow me. Sheriff Holiday has her locked up somewhere."

"Sheriff Holiday? I thought he was dead."

"The sheriff is very much alive. Sorry, you didn't have a need to know," said Lattimore.

The helicopter carrying Lattimore, Under Secretary of State Hanover and a disheveled Katerina touched down aboard the U.S. Carrier Dwight D. Eisenhower. Four armed marines conducted them two levels below the flight deck and through a corridor. In a low voice that visibly allowed him to favor the left side of his jaw, Hanover explained: "They've got a SCIF on board. That's a Sensitive Compartmented Information Facility. The President and the Russian Premier have been waiting for us. My boss too."

"I will not speak," said Katerina.

Ignoring her, Hanover stopped at a desk where a marine officer checked his credentials and handed them back saying: "If any of you need to use the head, now is the time."

None did.

With a loud clank, as if it were a jail cell, a metal door behind the desk opened. The three walked in. Lattimore felt his ears adjust to a different source of ventilation. The small room contained a bare wooden desk fronted by two chairs. A framed American flag hung on the side wall. The marine brought in a third chair. He positioned it beside the others, then gave Hanover a questioning look.

"Thank you, Lieutenant. We'll be fine."

The hatch closed. The lock clicked.

In the unnatural quiet Lattimore felt his ears adjust again. He'd been in SCIF's before but it had been a while.

Hanover took the center seat. "No slouching," he said, picking up what looked like a standard TV remote. "We'll all be on camera. You will speak only if asked to speak. Understood?"

"Yes," said Lattimore.

"I will not speak," said Katerina.

Hanover entered a code into the remote. The middle third of the wall in front of them transformed itself into a black flat-screen. The lights in the room automatically dimmed. The first image to appear was the seal of the President of the United States, next was the seal of the Russian Federation. After a fade to black, the screen split and re-lit.

On the left side of the screen Lattimore recognized the oval office where the president sat stern and stiff, not happy, at his desk. Behind him, the Secretary of State stood in a solemn pose. On the right half of the screen the Premier of the Russian Federation sat alone at his desk, hands cupped in front of him. Creases lined his facial skin making him appear older than the mid-sixties Lattimore knew him to be. He looked…sleepy? Lattimore wondered what time it was in Moscow but didn't feel like working the math.

From above the screen, a new light came on directed at the three of them sitting there in the SCIF. Lattimore blinked. They were on camera. He composed himself, eyes straight ahead. From somewhere inside his head, his mother's voice said: *Sit up straight, Harlan.*

The Secretary of State spoke from behind the President's chair. "We are here to gain clarity regarding an incident in the North Atlantic that occurred at 15:23 hours GMT." He went on describing the incident. A Russian translator could be heard in the background.

He was not yet finished when the Russian Premier held up his hand. "I will interrupt you here," he said through the translator. "Yes, of course we know about the nuclear explosion. As to why it happened and who was behind it, please understand that I am in a hurry to know these things. I see Katerina Sokolov is present. Please, I must hear from her without delay."

"Very well," said the Secretary of State. "Ms. Sokolov, will you please enlighten us all."

Katerina sat mute; eyes locked straight ahead as if focused on nothing.

The Premier stared coldly at her through the screen.

Lattimore gave her a glance. She sat rigid. Both hands gripped the armrests. Whether she realized it or not, she was holding her breath. She blinked once. The only other movement he saw was the slightest quiver in her lower lip.

A faint smile appeared on the Premier's face. "By international law you will honor her diplomatic immunity and deliver her to our embassy in Washington. Under no circumstances will you grant her asylum. Is that understood, Mr. President?"

"We have no intention of doing so. Yes, that is understood," said the President.

The Premier's eyes shifted again. His face broadened into a passive smile. He leaned closer and spoke in halting English: "My dear, Katyusha, I am very much looking forward to seeing you here, on the sweet soil of Mother Russia."

Lattimore gathered his intent and was certain Katerina did as well. A stark white, she took a breath and swallowed hard but remained silent.

Hanover spoke. "As you see, Mr. Premier, we also have Captain Harlan Lattimore of the United States freighter *Endeavor*. He has a request of you."

The Premier turned, appearing to look directly into Lattimore's eyes. "Please, you may speak, captain," he said in English.

Lattimore leaned in. To keep himself from fidgeting, he cupped his hands tightly in front of him realizing too late he'd assumed a posture strikingly similar to that of the Russian Premier. He wondered what that might mean to those body language experts on both sides who'd no doubt be analyzing the video of this meeting.

"Mr. Premier," he began. "Ms. Sokolov kidnapped my only daughter and was threatening to kill her if I didn't follow her instructions. As you may know, even at this moment, she still holds my daughter and..."

"We will be helping to get her back," said Hanover beside him.

"And I have agreed to cooperate in this," said Katerina, finally breaking her silence.

Lattimore went on, "This will result in a small delay in delivering Ms. Sokolov to your embassy. No more than a day or two."

The Premier gave a shrug. "Yes, that is all right. Two days, no more. But please, try not to get Ms. Sokolov killed. She is important to me."

"Thank you, Mr. Premier," said Lattimore. "While she is with me, Ms. Sokolov will be under my personal protection. Let me also add, I regret the loss of life that resulted from the explosion. It was the only way I knew, to protect my crew and my ship from what I perceived to be a clear and present danger."

"Ah, a term made famous by an American novel," said the Premier in an admonishing tone mimicked by the translator. "Sorry, but that book is not very popular here. As for the men on those ships today, they deserved to die. You did me no favors by saving the ones you did." He turned. "I trust they will be returned here as well, Mr. President?"

"Yes. They will receive medical attention and will be transported to your embassy without delay," said the President.

The Premier shifted in his chair. "Now please, I believe that we are done. I have other matters to attend to. He stood to go then stopped, his eyes back on Lattimore. In English, he said: "Daughters are a true blessing. I hope you get yours back, captain." He walked off camera. His side of the screen went dark.

"I do as well," said the President to Lattimore.

The screen went fully dark. The bright camera lights went dark, the room lights came up.

Hanover spoke to Lattimore. "You realize captain, this does not exonerate you or your crew of any guilt in the matter of your smuggling operation. Others will be deciding that."

The words were expected but they stung just the same. "Yes, I realize that," he said standing. He turned to Katerina. Still in her seat, she was trembling.

CHAPTER 46

The night was moonless and clear with a steady wind bearing from the west. Running lights off, the chopper circled the northern quadrant of the Willow Run complex at a low altitude.

On receiving radio clearance to land from the friendlies on the ground, the pilot tore off his night vision goggles and threw them aside. "I hate these damn things," Lattimore heard him say. The pilot skillfully worked the controls, lowering his craft onto the snow covered concrete. The hatch beside Lattimore rolled open. Cold air and the roar of the slowing twin rotors poured in.

He jumped out first. His boots hit hard, stinging his feet. His legs were stiff from having sat in the chopper for so long. They'd refueled multiple times on the trip from the carrier to Willow Run. The team of marines already on the ground formed a ring around the aircraft, rifles at the ready.

Lattimore turned the collar of his coat up against the bitter wind, then limbered his legs with a couple of shallow knee bends. He felt his joints creak. Behind him, more combat ready marines jumped out, Katerina with them. She stumbled then straightened, roughly shaking off help from one of the soldiers. Except for a few directional instructions she'd given the pilot, she hadn't said a word over the entire flight.

She looked around as if getting her bearings, then pointed across an open field to a large white building a hundred yards out. "That way," she said. "It's a small hangar with living quarters and a storage and maintenance area for my jet."

"You mean for what was once your jet, I think," said the major in charge of the marine group. He ordered his men into a double-time trot across the field, skirting drifts of snow as they went.

Two men from the chopper stayed with Lattimore and Katerina as they lagged behind.

"Maddison had better be there and she'd better be alive," said Lattimore at a fast walk.

"Or, what will you do, captain? You're unarmed. You're a prisoner here just like I am. But, unlike you, I will be free in a few days."

"Do you really think you will live that long?"

"I have powerful friends," said Katerina.

"I don't think the premier is one of them."

He hated her, but at this moment, he was counting on her help to rescue Maddie. It was not a good time to be pushing her hot buttons. He kept pace with her, regulating his breathing not wanting her to hear him huffing and puffing. They slowed, as they approached the building where the marines were already in place at its tall cargo door. Walking closer, Lattimore placed a hand on one of the door panels. "Steel armor," he said wondering if that might present a problem.

"Were you expecting a welcome mat and a doorbell?"

The major turned to Katerina. "How many men are inside? How are they armed?"

"Four of my men plus four more from the freighter."

"Sullivan's in there?" said Lattimore.

"I think so, yes. They'll have semi-automatics."

"At your order they'll surrender."

Katerina shook her head. "You are a smart man, captain, but you will never understand we Russians. For these men here, surrender makes no sense. They'll die here quick and easy, maybe even heroically. If they surrender, they'll die hard in Russia as traitors. Their choice is obvious. They will stay and fight and they will die. I myself would step in front of a bullet this very night, were it not for my son."

"Sullivan is not a Russian."

"Still, if he makes it through this alive, his outlook is rather...bleak, wouldn't you say?" She turned back to the major.

"Remember, my son is in there. He is harmless; dysfunctional you call it? You will not hurt him."

"I've been ordered to take good care of you and him, *in that order*. You, and you too, Captain Lattimore, will keep to the side, behind my men, out of the line of fire."

"And just how do you plan to get through this steel door?" said Katerina.

The major adjusted his helmet. "Sorry to disappoint you, ma'am, but this door will not present a problem." He keyed his radio twice. "You might not want to stand right there," he added.

From down the slope, behind a cluster of trees, an engine sputtered to life; in seconds it became a powerful roar.

"Everyone, stand back," the major shouted. "Guns ready. Remember, there's a female hostage inside. Our mission is to save her and capture, not kill but *capture*, the men holding her."

Eyes on the trees, Lattimore saw a pair of headlights blink on. A vehicle began to move. It threw aside the snow, noisily picking up speed, already only fifty yards out. Lattimore recognized it as an armored, track driven SWAT vehicle. A soldier in the turret mounted above the cab held a machine gun aimed dead ahead.

The ground shook.

The line of marines drew back, Lattimore and Katerina with them. The vehicle roared, accelerating.

Lattimore braced for the impact.

Its steel ram hit with a resounding bang and a crunch. Bolts and rivets holding the door together blew apart sounding like gunfire. Metal crumpled and bent. The vehicle slowed then stopped and pulled back ten feet.

The major held up his hand. "Hold your position," he shouted to the vehicle and to his men. He then spoke into a bullhorn. "You are surrounded. Surrender now. I repeat, surrender now."

For a moment there was silence. Then guns erupted from inside the building.

With a resigned shrug, the major knifed his hand toward the door.

The SWAT vehicle revved its engine. It charged forward. With a jarring crash it pushed aside what was left of the armored door. The vehicle gained speed, rolling over everything in its path until it was fully inside the building. Then it stopped. Its headlights lit the way as, at a shout from the major, he and his men poured into the building, guns blazing.

Lattimore broke away from his guards and charged in close behind.

Gunfire flashed. Smoke filled the air. The marines fanned out. Lattimore shifted to the right side where a cinderblock wall ran deeper into the building. From the corner of his eye he saw the marines, with riot shields, still charging, some shouting, some taking cover behind the darkened shape of a sleek private jet.

The chaos of battle. It all looked so familiar. And yet the stakes for him had never been this high. Somewhere past the smoke and confusion Maddie was guarded and probably tied up. Her life could depend on what he did in the next few seconds.

He kept up his run, eyes straight ahead into the smoke. He spotted an inner wall. There was a door. He headed for it. Bullets pinged and sparked, none close. He felt naked without a gun but firing back would have drawn return fire. He guessed there might be more than the eight defenders Katerina knew about. Had they been tipped off?

The marines had their hands full.

He raced for the door. He tried to speed up but felt himself faltering. He pushed himself harder, forcing his legs into a sprint. He turned his shoulder to the door. He leaped. He met it straight on. The wooden jam gave way with a loud crack and in a hail of splinters. He tumbled through.

He fell, then gained his footing. Body bent, chest heaving, he coughed, drawing in the smokey air. He spit it out. He peered through the darkness and saw... a kitchen counter on which sat a toaster and a microwave. *He was standing in someone's kitchen.* The sounds of the fighting lessened. He heard a scream—a woman's scream.

He shouted frantically. "Maddie? Where are you, baby?" He listened but heard nothing over the din of the fight.

There was a hallway. He swallowed hard then ran down it. "Maddie? Maddie I'm here."

He found an open door, the room empty. Further down the hallway was another door, this one locked. He tried to kick it in, and failed. He tried again. The door gave a little. His heart stuttered. *Shit! Not now you bastard!* At his third kick the door gave way, but still hung on by the top hinge and by a dead bolt. He leaned heavily against it, forcing it aside, forcing his way in.

He fell to the floor. Out of breath, chest heaving he opened his eyes.

Inside the room stood a dark hulk of a man. The man stared back at him as if not knowing what to do.

Lattimore struggled to his feet. Then, he saw her. She stood beside a bed staring back at him, eyes wide. *She was alive.* She was shouting something that he couldn't hear. But none of that mattered. *She was alive!*

As if an electric charge had gone off somewhere inside his body, Lattimore ran at the man who stood between him and his daughter. Did he have a gun? Did he have a knife? He didn't care. With both hands, he grabbed the man's throat. He squeezed hard. They toppled to the floor, the man on top of him. Lattimore struggled under his weight, all the while squeezing the man's throat.

The man gagged, gasping, trying to break Lattimore's grip.

Lattimore tried to shout, to scream to let loose a barrage of obscenities. But he had no breath left. He had no strength left.

A hand pulled at his grip. "Dad! Dad! Let him go. He didn't mean it. Let him go. He was protecting me. Let him go."

Lattimore held his grip. He stared at Maddie, her face bruised, her eyes desperate, her hands on his trying to pry them off the man's throat. It made no sense, but he trusted her. He let go.

The man sagged off Lattimore, rolling onto the floor. Lattimore's lungs burned. He tried to get up but could not. He rolled onto his side, bent, coughing, unable to breathe.

Then he felt hands, *her hands*, lift his head, cradling it. He wanted to speak her name but could not.

His lungs began to work. He took in one enormous breath, then another. He looked up at her.

"Yeah. It's me dad," she said, with as much of a smile as the cuts on her lips could manage. She kissed the side of his face. He felt the wet of her tears against the stubble of his cheek. "Oh, Maddie, dear Maddie, you...you're okay?"

"Yeah, dad. I'm okay."

"Thank God. Oh, baby, thank God."

"Nice of you to call in the marines."

"Who is...?"

"He's a friend. He took care of me. He...he doesn't talk."

The realization came slowly to Lattimore. "He's Katerina's son."

"Yes."

The gunfire had stopped. Lattimore struggled to sit upright. She helped him up, they walked to the edge of the bed.

"My father," Maddie explained to Katerina's son who was just now getting to his feet.

But the man, more boy than man, seemed to have forgotten all about him. He had his eyes on Maddie. He reached over and tried to smooth her matted hair.

"My father," Maddie told him again, a hand on Lattimore's shoulder.

This time the boy looked at him.

"You put up a good fight, young man," Lattimore told him.

The boy stood, perfectly still. There was the brief hint of a nod, then a smile. He opened his mouth. He gave Maddie a glance, then turned back to Lattimore. With his hand he thumped his chest proudly. "I-lee-ahh," he shouted. "I-lee-ahh!"

It was only then that Lattimore saw Katerina standing beside what was left of the door. Her eyes were on her son, mouth agape. A single tear ran down her face.

She ran to Ilya and held him in her arms.

CHAPTER 47

It took two days for the Navy to jury-rig a fix for *Endeavor's* rudder. By that time the navy squadron had departed leaving only a destroyer escort vessel to make sure the freighter and her crew behaved themselves on their way back to port.

The crew had been interviewed at length about the incident. Professor Simeon was excited about all the attention given him and seemed to relish the prospect of being transferred to the escort vessel for further questioning. Everyone else had been provisionally cleared of any wrong doing.

Marine Lieutenant Benjamin Evans along with a small contingent of navy personnel, assumed overall control of *Endeavor*. With a deep throated rumble and a stream of black smoke, *Endeavor* turned west, heading back to the shores of North America.

It was at the end of that same day that Jack and Beth stood together out on deck bundled up, getting some air.

Evans came up behind them. "We have news from the shore team," he said.

They turned, Beth blurting out: "Is Maddie..."

"Agent Cooper has been rescued. She's got a few injuries, nothing major."

"Good to hear," said Jack, relief flooding over him.

"Several men among the rescue party were wounded, none serious, but Captain Lattimore appears to have had a mild heart attack. He's okay, but his sailing days are probably over."

"As for Katerina's men, four were killed. I understand one of them was Mr. Sullivan, the former XO of this ship. Evidently, he was caught in the crossfire. The others were captured and are being interrogated now by the CIA. Some might end up being handed over to the Russians but you didn't hear that from me."

"And, Katerina is still alive?"

"Katerina? A woman you mean? The only woman I know about is Agent Cooper."

"That's okay," said Jack, realizing that info on her and the fate of Katerina's men must be above Evan's pay grade. "I must have been mistaken. Was there anything else?"

Evans shook his head. "That's all the information I have. There was tight security around the whole operation. We're on the QT just getting you back to port. I think you've been warned about..."

"Yes, if we tell anybody anything about any of this, they'll lock us up for the rest of our lives," said Beth, adjusting her cap against a gust of wind.

The three were silent for a while. Then, Evans said: "How well do you know Captain Lattimore?"

"Not well," said Jack. "We met him a few weeks ago aboard this ship. Seems longer though. A lot has happened."

"Within the Marine Corps, Captain Lattimore is something of a legend. Yeah, he had a tough time in Afghanistan. It was a terrible thing. But his men loved him. He was a fine officer."

"Did you serve under him?"

"Not me. My dad did, in Iraq. He talked about him often." Evans gave a thoughtful shrug and went back inside.

With an arm around Beth, Jack watched the whitecapped waves, feeling the throb of the engines through his feet. The wind was picking up. It was getting colder. Still, he couldn't bring himself to suggest they go back inside. Gently, he pulled Beth closer. "Bet you can't wait to get back to the pharmacy."

"How did you know that's what I was thinking?"

"Just a guess."

"Do you really want things to go back to the way they were?"

He turned to her. "Yeah, I do...mostly."

"What would you change?"

"I think I'd have a greater appreciation for little things. You know, the routine of coffee and donuts in the morning, going into the station, going over the previous day's reports and traffic citations from Bob and Ron. Coming back home to you for lunch at noon, supper at six."

"So, you wouldn't change anything?"

Of course, he knew what she was getting at. "Well, we did talk about starting a family."

"If you remember, we did a little more than talk about it." She turned to him. "I'm pregnant, Jack."

Jack was stunned. "What? I mean, I knew you thought you might be, but…"

"Meg had a test kit."

"And how…"

"They're 99 percent accurate when used as directed."

He smiled. He pulled her close. "Oh, Beth…I'm so happy for us"

"You realize, that will change everything."

"It'll be like sweetener in our coffee."

She looked up at him. "Did you practice that line?"

"Nope. It just popped into my head." They kissed long and tenderly. On parting slightly, he took in a deep breath. Fatherhood. He wondered what that was going to be like. They were both silent for a while. "'What about all the stress you've been under?" he asked. "And the radiation could…affect things. I'm so sorry, Beth. I didn't think…"

"We talked about that Jack. We made our decision together. We did what we had to do. We'll be home in a few days," she said. "I'll see Doc Ambrose."

"But you're feeling okay?"

"I'm feeling fine. Well, I'm freezing, but let's not go in just yet. I like being out here just the two of us."

"Me too."

The were quiet again, both looking out to sea.

"I'm glad Maddie made it out of this whole thing all right," said Beth.

"She must have gone through hell. And now with her dad facing prison time…" He paused. "You like her, don't you."

"Yeah, I do. It'd be nice to see her again sometime under better circumstances." She raised her head. "It's going to be strange getting back. I wonder if the town still thinks we're dead."

Jack shook his head. "There's no way Sharon can keep a secret that long. I'm worried that she'll have a problem turning command of the station back to me. All that power of being a small-town sheriff, it can go to your head you know."

She rested her head on his shoulder. "It bothered you, didn't it? Me calling you that."

"Maybe a little. But hey, you're a small-town pharmacist. I guess we were made for each other."

She smiled. "Yes, I believe we were."

With his arm around her, Jack looked out over the length of the ship, out beyond the rippling flag at the bow, out to the glowing western horizon where the sun had just set. A few rays still lit the clouds in golds and blues. It would be a clear, cold night. Overhead a few gulls circled and a few stars were starting to twinkle.

Funny, how many things had changed for him and for this good woman he held close, while so many others remained the same. Through the layers of her coat and his, he could feel her shiver.

"Jack?"

"Yeah?"

"I can't feel my toes."

"I'm cold too. Let's get inside."

EPILOGUE

In January a secret hearing was held. In it, retired Marine Captain Harlan Lattimore, Captain of the Great Lakes freighter *Endeavor* was found guilty of conspiracy to smuggle illegal goods into the United States. Due to certain considerations, he was given a suspended sentence. He now serves at the Pentagon as a civilian consultant. His duties are classified.

****

Maddison Cooper was reinstated with back-pay, given a commendation then promoted to Senior Special Agent at the FBI office in Duluth.

****

As a member of the Russian diplomatic corps, Katerina Sokolov faced no criminal charges in the United States for her role in the events related here. As was agreed, she and her son were delivered to the Russian embassy in Washington D.C. then returned to Russia. Her condition and her whereabouts are unknown.

****

With his family, relatives, friends and colleagues all long passed, Professor Andrew Simeon accepted the offer of Honorary Chair of the physics department at Michigan Technological University in Houghton, Michigan. Once there, he quickly took up the habit of smoking a pipe, wearing suspenders along with thick woolen sweaters. He is known to roam the university's Fisher Hall freely sharing his opinions on everything from the climate crisis to what he considers to be the bleak future of electric vehicles.

****

It was the opinion of all involved that Sharon had done a fine job as the interim sheriff. True to her word, and to Jack's surprise, she'd kept quiet about both he and Beth still being alive. At his return, she'd given him a smile and an awkward hug then handed his badge back to him. 'Glad you're back, sheriff,' she'd said. 'Those two deputies of yours have been a real pain in my butt.'

There'd been a big write-up in the Gull Harbor paper about Jack and Beth and their return from the dead. As to how everyone had gotten the idea that they were dead in the first place, the paper laid the blame for that squarely on the interim sheriff.

Everyone, excepting Pastor John, who'd presided over the double funeral and had publicly shed a few tears, got a big laugh over what had happened. Any speculation as to how the sheriff and his wife had made it out of their car alive, then disappeared for nearly the entire month of November, was discouraged. And everyone seems content to allow that mystery to remain a mystery.

****

In the new year, spring came late to Gull Harbor. Even now, in mid-May, snowdrifts still survive in the deep woods and cakes of ice still dot the Lake Superior shoreline.

Today is a Sunday. In their home above *Holiday Drugs*, Sheriff Jackson Holiday reads his national edition of the Sunday paper and Beth sits finishing a crossword. She appears confident that good old Dave is keeping things running down in the store. Their lives have gotten pretty much back to normal but both know that is about to change yet again.

From their regular visits to Doc Ambrose, all indications are that they will become the parents of a healthy baby boy sometime in July.

AUTHOR'S NOTE

I hope you enjoyed *The November Plot*.
I have always admired and often envied those men and women who brave the lakes and the oceans as a way of life.
In the writing of this book, care was taken to ensure the accuracy of historical references, technical information and nautical terminology. I am sure some readers, especially those with direct experience on the lakes, will spot certain inaccuracies. To those readers, I proactively apologize and invite you to give me an admonishing shout at www.tomulicny.com
As with all my books I very much look forward to hearing from all my readers. Your comments and reviews are always greatly appreciated.

ABOUT THE AUTHOR

A longtime resident of Rochester Hills, Michigan, Tom is dad to three wonderful daughters and granddad to four beautiful grandchildren. A retired engineer, he is the award-winning author of six full length novels. His genres include, Historical Fiction, Mystery/Romance, Psychological Suspense, and Literary Adventure. He's earned scores of five-star reviews on Amazon and Goodreads. When he's not writing, Tom enjoys woodworking, playing guitar and travel.

Made in the USA
Columbia, SC
18 January 2025